# COWBOY'S
## *Christmas*
# FAMILY

MIX
Paper | Supporting
responsible forestry
FSC® C001695

Published by
Mills & Boon
An imprint of Harlequin Enterprises (Australia) Pty Limited (ABN 47 001 180 918), a subsidiary of HarperCollins Publishers Australia Pty Limited (ABN 36 009 913 517)
Level 19, 201 Elizabeth Street
SYDNEY NSW 2000
AUSTRALIA

® and ™ (apart from those relating to FSC ®) are trademarks of Harlequin Enterprises (Australia) Pty Limited or its corporate affiliates. Trademarks indicated with ® are registered in Australia, New Zealand and in other countries.
Contact admin_legal@Harlequin.ca for details.

Printed and bound in Australia by McPherson's Printing Group

# COWBOY'S
## *Christmas*
## FAMILY

**CATHY GILLEN**    **ALLISON**
**THACKER**      **LEIGH**

MILLS & BOON

# CONTENTS

# CONTENTS

# A Texas Cowboy's Christmas
*Cathy Gillen Thacker*

**Cathy Gillen Thacker** is married and a mother of three. She and her husband spent eighteen years in Texas and now reside in North Carolina. Her mysteries, romantic comedies and heartwarming family stories have made numerous appearances on bestseller lists, but her best reward, she says, is knowing one of her books made someone's day a little brighter. A popular Harlequin author for many years, she loves telling passionate stories with happy endings and thinks nothing beats a good romance and a hot cup of tea! You can visit Cathy's website, cathygillenthacker.com, for more information on her upcoming and previously published books, recipes, and a list of her favorite things.

## Books by Cathy Gillen Thacker

## Harlequin Special Edition

### Texas Legends: The McCabes

*The Texas Cowboy's Quadruplets*
*His Baby Bargain*

## Harlequin Western Romance

### Texas Legends: The McCabes

*The Texas Cowboy's Triplets*
*The Texas Cowboy's Baby Rescue*

### Texas Legacies: The Lockharts

*A Texas Soldier's Family*
*A Texas Cowboy's Christmas*
*The Texas Valentine Twins*
*Wanted: Texas Daddy*
*A Texas Soldier's Christmas*

Visit the Author Profile page at Harlequin.com for more titles.

# *Chapter 1*

"I blame *you* for this, Chance Lockhart!" Molly Griffith fumed the moment she came toe-to-toe with him just inside the open-air bucking-bull training facility of Bullhaven Ranch.

Chance set down the saddle and blanket he'd been carrying. With a wicked grin, he pushed the brim of his hat back and paused to take her in. No doubt about it—the twenty-seven-year-old general contractor/interior designer was never lovelier than when she was in a temper. With her amber eyes blazing, her pretty face flushed with indignant color and her auburn curls wildly out of place, she looked as if she were ripe for taming.

Luckily for both of them, he was too smart to succumb to the challenge.

His gaze drifted over her, taking in her designer jeans and peacock-blue boots, before moving upward to the white silk shirt and soft suede blazer that cloaked her curvy frame.

Damn, she was sexy, though. From the half-moon pendant that nestled in the hollow of her breasts to the voluptuous bounty of her bow-shaped lips.

Exhaling slowly, he tamped down his desire and prompted in a lazy drawl, "Blame me for what?"

Molly propped her hands on her hips. "For telling my son, Braden, he can have a live bull for Christmas!"

Somehow Chance managed not to wince at the huffy accusation. He set down the saddle and narrowed his eyes instead. "That's not *exactly* what I said."

Molly moved close enough he could inhale her flowery perfume, her breasts rising and falling with every deep, agitated breath. "Did you or did you not tell him that Santa could bring him a bull?"

Chance shrugged, glad for the brisk November breeze blowing over them. Still holding Molly's eyes, he rocked back on the heels of his worn leather work boots. "I said he could *ask* Santa for a bull."

Molly harrumphed and folded her arms beneath her breasts, the action plumping them up all the more. "Exactly!"

Working to slow his rising pulse, Chance lowered his face to hers and explained tautly, "That doesn't mean Santa is going to *bring* it."

Chance picked up the gear, slung it over one shoulder and stalked toward the ten-by-ten metal holding pen, where a two-year-old Black Angus bull named Peppermint was waiting.

One of the heirs to his retired national championship bucking bull, Mistletoe, he bore the same steady temperament, lively personality and exceptional athletic ability of his daddy.

After easing open the gate, Chance stepped inside.

Aware Molly was still watching his every move, he proceeded to pet the young bull in training. Once gentled, he set the saddle on Peppermint's back.

Swallowing nervously at the thousand-pound bull, Molly stepped back. With an indignant toss of her head, she continued her emotional tirade. "You really don't have a clue how all this works, do you?"

Chance sighed as he tightened the cinch and led Peppermint into the practice chute, closing the gate behind him. "I have a feeling you're about to tell me."

Molly watched him climb the side rails and secure a dummy on the saddle via electronically controlled buckles.

Feeling the unwelcome extra weight, Peppermint began to snort and paw the ground within the confines of the chute.

Even though she was in no danger, Molly retreated even farther. "A child writes a letter to Santa, asking for his most precious gift. Then Santa brings it."

Chance plucked the remote control out of his pocket. "That wasn't how it worked in my home." He signaled to his hired hand Billy to take his position at the exit gate on the other side of the practice ring. "I remember asking Santa for a rodeo for my backyard in Dallas. Guess what?" He shot her a provoking look that started at her face and moved languidly over her voluptuous body before returning to her eyes. "It didn't happen."

Molly rolled her eyes, still staying clear of the snorting, increasingly impatient Peppermint. Digging her boots into the ground, she fired back, "I cannot help it if your mother and father did not appropriately censure your wishes in advance."

Chance hit the control. Immediately, the sound of a rodeo crowd filled the practice arena. He released the gate, and Peppermint, tired of confinement, went barreling into the ring.

For the next few seconds, he bucked hard to the right and came down. Went up and down in the middle, then bucked to the left.

And still the crowd sounds filled the air.

Adding to the excitement, as Peppermint bucked higher and higher…and seeing the kind of athletic movement he wanted, Chance rewarded the bull with the release of the dummy.

It went flying. And landed facedown in the dirt.

Billy whistled.

Peppermint turned and followed the waving Billy out the exit gate and into another pen, where he would receive a treat for his performance.

Chance cut the crowd sounds on the intercom system. Silence fell in the arena once again, and Chance lifted a hand. "Thanks, Billy!"

"No problem, boss!" he replied before going off to see to the bucking bull.

Molly said, looking impressed despite herself, "Is that how you train them?"

"Yep."

"Too bad no one can train you."

"Really? That's juvenile, even for you, Molly."

He knew where it came from, though. She brought out the irascible teenager in him, too.

Chance went back into the barn, checking on his thirty bucking bulls, safely ensconced in their individual ten-by-ten metal pens, then took a visual of those in the pastures. Finished, he strode across the barnyard to a smaller facility, where his national champion was kept.

Mistletoe's private quarters, his ranch office, veterinary exam, lab and breeding chute, and equipment facility were all there. All were state-of-the-art and a testament to what he had built.

"Look, I'm sorry," Molly said, dogging his every step. "But I'm trying to help my son be realistic here."

Chance paused to pet Mistletoe. The big bucking bull had a little gray on his face these days, but he was still pleasant as ever to be around. "Is that what you're doing for Braden?" He gave his beloved Black Angus one last rub before turning back to Molly. "Helping him temper his expectations? Or censuring all his dreams?"

Molly muttered something he was just as glad not to be able to understand, then threw up her hands in exasperation.

"I want my little boy to grow up being practical!"

Chance spun around, and she followed him back down the center aisle. "Unlike certain idiot cowboys who shall remain nameless."

There she went with the insults again, but it was better than dealing with the smoldering attraction they felt whenever they were together.

Chance paused at the sink in the tack room to wash and dry his hands, then walked out to join her. Saw her shiver in the brisk, wintry air.

Aware the day looked a lot warmer than it actually was, he turned away from the evidence of her chill and drawled, "I think I *might* know who you're talking about." Rubbing his jaw in a parody of thoughtfulness, he stepped purposefully into her personal space.

Watching her amber eyes widen, he continued, "That rancher brother of mine, Wyatt, down the road. None too bright, is he?"

Molly made a strangled sound deep in her throat. Rather than step away, she put her hand on the center of his chest and gave him a small, equally purposeful shove. "I'm talking about you, you big lug."

Delighted by her unwillingness to give any ground to him, he captured her hand before she could snatch it away and held it over his heart. "Ah. Endearments." He sighed with comically exaggerated dreaminess.

Temper spiking even more, she tried, unsuccessfully, to extricate her fingers from his. "You're playing with fire here, cowboy."

So he was. But then he had to do something with all the aggravation she caused him. And had been causing, if truth be known, for quite some time.

He let his grin widen, surveying her indignant expression. Dropping his head, he taunted softly, "The kind of fire that leads to a kiss?"

"The kind that leads to me hauling off and kicking you right in the shin!"

It was good to know he could get to her this much. Because she sure got to him. The pressure building at the front of his jeans told him that.

He lowered his lips to hers. "Didn't your parents ever tell you that you can catch more flies with sugar than spite?"

Abruptly Molly's face paled.

Too late, he realized he should have bothered to find out what kind of life she'd had as a kid before hurling that particular insult.

She drew a deep breath. Serious now. Subdued.

Aware he'd hurt her—without meaning to—he let her hand go.

She stepped back. Regaining her composure, she lifted her chin and said in a solemn tone, "I want you to talk to Braden. Tell him you were wrong. Santa doesn't bring little boys live bulls."

At that particular moment, he thought he would do just about anything for her. Probably would have, if she hadn't been so socially and monetarily ambitious and so out of touch regarding what really mattered in life, same as his ex.

But Molly was. So...

Exploring their attraction would lead only to misery.

For all their sakes, Chance put up the usual barbed wire around his heart. "Why can't you tell him?" he asked with an indifferent shrug. "You're Braden's momma, after all." And, from all he'd seen, misguided goals aside, a damn good one.

Molly's lower lip trembled, and she threw up her hands in frustration. "I have told him! He won't believe me. Braden says that you're the cowboy, and you know everything, and you said it was okay. And that's what he wants me to write in his letter to Santa, and I cannot let him ask Saint Nick for that, only to have his little heart broken."

She had a point about that, Chance realized guiltily. He'd hate to see the little tyke, who also happened to be the spitting image of his mother, disappointed.

Sobering, he asked, "What *do* you want Braden to have?"

Molly's features softened in relief. "The Leo and Lizzie World Adventure wooden train set." She pulled a magazine article out of her back pocket that listed the toy as the most wanted preschool-age present for the holiday that year. Featuring train characters from a popular animated kids' television show, the starter set was extremely elaborate. Which was no surprise. Since Molly Griffith was known for her big ambitions and even more expensive tastes.

It made sense she would want the same for her only child.

Even if Braden would be happier playing with a plastic toy bull. Or horse…

Sensing she wanted his approval, Chance shrugged. Wary of hurting her feelings—again—he mumbled, "Looks nice."

As if sensing his attitude was not quite genuine, she frowned. "It will bring Braden hours of fun."

*Enough to justify the cost?* he wondered, noting the small wooden pieces were ridiculously overpriced—even if they were in high demand. He squinted at her. "Are you sure you don't work for the toy company?"

She scowled at his joke but came persuasively closer, even more serious now. "Please, Chance. I'm begging you."

*This is new*, Chance thought, surprised.

He actually kind of liked her coming to him for help.

She spread her hands wide, turning on the full wattage of maternal charm. "Braden just turned three years old. It's the first Christmas holiday he's likely to ever remember. I really want it to be special." She paused and took a deep breath that lifted the lush softness of her breasts. "You have to help me talk sense into my son."

For a brief moment, Molly thought she had finally gotten through to the impossibly handsome cowboy.

Then he folded his brawny arms across his broad chest and let out a sigh that reverberated through his six-foot-three-inch frame. Intuitive hazel eyes lassoed hers. "I want to help you."

Pulse racing, Molly watched as he swept off his black Stetson and shoved a hand through the rumpled strands of his thick chestnut-colored hair. "But?"

Frowning, he settled his hat squarely on his head. "I can't do to your son what my parents did to me."

"And what was that?" she asked curiously.

"Try and censor and mold his dreams—to suit your wishes instead of Braden's."

Had Lucille and the late Frank Lockhart done that to Chance? The grim set of his lips seemed to say so. But that had nothing to do with her or Braden.

Molly stepped closer, invading his space. With a huff, she planted both hands on her waist and accused, "You just started this calamity to get under my skin."

His sexy grin widened. "I was already under your skin," he reminded her, tilting his head to one side.

*True, unfortunately.* Molly did her best to stifle a sigh while still stubbornly holding her ground. She wished he didn't radiate such endless masculine energy or look so ruggedly fit in his gray plaid flannel shirt and jeans. Never mind have such a sexy smile and firm, sensual lips…

She could barely look at him and not wonder what it would be like to kiss him.

Just as an experiment, of course.

"So you're really not going to help me?"

Chance's brow lifted. "Convince him he doesn't want to be a cowboy when he grows up? And have a ranch like mine that has all bulls on it? Or get a head start on it by getting his first livestock now?" His provoking grin widened. "No. I'm not going to do any of that. I will, however, try to talk him into getting a baby calf. Since females are a lot more docile than males."

"Ha-ha."

"I wasn't talking about you," he claimed with choirboy innocence.

*Yeah…right.* When they were together like this, *everything* was about the two of them.

Molly shut her eyes briefly and rubbed at the tension in her temples. With effort, she forced her attention back to her child's fervent wish to be a rancher, just like "Cowboy Chance." Who was, admittedly, the most heroic-looking figure her son had ever had occasion to meet.

Trying not to think about what a dashing figure he cut, Molly turned her glance toward the storm clouds building on the horizon. It wasn't supposed to rain for another day or two, but it looked like it now. "I live in town, remember? I don't have any place to keep a baby calf."

Chance shrugged. "So ask my mother to pasture it at the Circle H Ranch. You're there enough anyway."

Molly wheeled around and headed back to the driveway next to the log-cabin-style Bullhaven ranch house, where she had parked her sporty red SUV. "Even if that were a plausible solution, which it's not, Braden and I aren't going to be here past the first week of January."

Squinting curiously, he matched his strides to hers. "How come?"

Trying not to notice how he towered over her, or how much she liked it, Molly fished her keys out of her jacket pocket. "Not that it's any of your business, but we're moving to Dallas."

Chance paused next to her vehicle. "To be closer to Braden's daddy?"

Her heart panged in her chest. If only her little boy had a father who wanted his child in his life. But he didn't, so...

There was no way she was talking to Chance Lockhart about the most humiliating mistake she'd ever made. Or the fact that her ill-conceived liaison had unexpectedly led to the best thing in her life, a family of her very own. Molly hit the button on the keypad and heard the click of the driver-side lock releasing. "No."

"No, that's not why you're moving?"

He came close enough she could smell the soap and sun and man fragrance of his skin.

Awareness shimmered inside her.

He watched her open the door. "Or no, that's not what you want—to be closer to your ex?"

Heavens, the man was annoying!

Figuring this was the time to go on record with her goals— and hence vanquish his mistaken notions about her once and for all—Molly lifted her gaze to his. "What I want is for my son to grow up with all the advantages I never had." Braden, unlike her, would want for nothing.

Except maybe a daddy in his life.

Not that she could fix that.

Chance's lip curled in contempt. "Ah, yes, back to social climbing."

He wasn't the only one who misinterpreted the reason behind her quest to get an in with every mover and shaker in the area. And beyond…

But for some reason, Chance Lockhart's contempt rankled.

Which was another reason to set him—and everyone else in Laramie County who misread her—straight. "Look, I don't expect you to understand. You having grown up with a silver spur in your mouth and all."

He grinned.

"But not all of us have had those advantages."

His hazel eyes sparkled, the way they always did when he got under her skin. "Like?"

"Private school, for one."

Chance remained implacable. "They have private schools in Laramie County."

"Not like the ones in Dallas."

He squinted in disapproval. "Which is where you want him to go."

Stubbornly, Molly held her ground. "If Braden attends the right preschool, he can get into the right elementary, then middle, then prep. From there, go on to an elite college."

Chance poked the brim of his hat up with one finger. "I'm guessing you aren't talking about anything in the University of Texas system."

Molly studied the frayed collar on Chance's flannel shirt, the snug worn jeans and run-of-the-mill leather belt. It was clear he didn't care about appearances. Coming from his background, he did not have to. "If Braden goes to an Ivy League school, the world is his oyster."

Chance rested his brawny forearm on the roof of her SUV. "I can see you've got it all mapped out."

Molly tried not to notice how well he filled out his ranching clothes. "Yes, unlike you, Braden is going to take advantage of all the opportunities I plan to see come his way."

"How does Braden feel about all this?" Chance asked, not bothering to hide his frustration with her.

Had Molly not known better, she would have thought that the irascible cowboy did not want her to leave Laramie County. But that was ridiculous. The two of them couldn't get gas at the same filling station at the same time without getting into a heated argument. More likely, Chance would be delighted to see her depart. "My son is *three*."

"Meaning you haven't told him."

"He has no concept of time."

"So, in other words, no."

"I will, once Christmas is over," Molly maintained. She moved as if to get in her vehicle, but Chance remained where he was, his big, imposing body blocking the way.

"Has it occurred to you that you're getting ahead of yourself with all your plans to better educate and monetarily and socially provide for your son?"

Chance wasn't the first to tell her so.

She hadn't listened to anyone else.

And she wasn't about to listen to him, either.

Ducking beneath his outstretched arm, she slid behind the steering wheel. Bending her head, she put the key in the ignition. "What I think is that one day, my son will be very grateful to me for doing all that I can to ensure his dreams come true," she retorted defensively.

Chance leaned down so they were face-to-face. "Except, of course, ones that have to do with livestock."

*What is it about this man?* Molly fumed inwardly. He not only provoked her constantly—he had the potential to derail her at every turn, just by existing!

Pretending his attempts to delay her so they could continue their argument were not bothering her in the least, Molly flashed a confident smile. "You're right," she admitted with a sugary-sweet attitude even he would have to find laudable. "I have gotten way, way off track."

He chuckled. "Back to train analogies?"

She gave him a quelling look.

He lifted an exaggeratedly apologetic hand. "I know. Even some of us big, dumb cowpokes who passed on Ivy League educations know a few big words."

She'd heard Chance had been just as much of a problem to his wealthy parents growing up as he was to her now. "How about 'aggravate'?" She looked him square in the eye. "Do you know what that means?"

He grinned. "I think that's what I do to you, on a daily, hourly, basis?"

*So true.* Molly drew a calming breath. She started the ignition, then motioned for him to step away. When he did, she put her window down. "I'm going to be at the Circle H this afternoon, meeting with your mother about the proposed kitchen renovation."

"Well, what do you know," he rumbled with a maddeningly affable shrug. "I will be, too."

She ignored the fact that their two contracting companies were competing for the renovation job. "Braden will be with me. It's your chance to make things right with my son. Please, Chance." She paused to let her words sink in. "Don't let us down."

If Molly hadn't framed it quite like that, maybe he could have bailed. But she had, so at five past three Chance found himself driving up the lane to the Circle H ranch house.

Molly's SUV was already on-site. She and her son, Braden,

were by the pasture, where a one-week-old Black Angus was pastured with his momma. Little arms on the middle rung of the fence, Braden was staring, mesmerized, at the sight of the nursing bull.

"Can I pet him?" Braden asked as Chance strolled up to join them.

Her pretty face pinched with tension, Molly shook her head.

Chance hunkered down beside Braden. The little tyke had the same curly red hair, cute-as-a-button features and amber eyes as his mother. "Petting the bull would scare it, buddy, and we don't want that, do we?"

Balking, Braden bartered, "I know gentle. Mommy showed me." Realizing Chance didn't quite understand what he was saying, Braden continued with a demonstration of easy petting. "Kitty cat—gentle. Puppy—gentle. Babies—gentle."

"Ah. You're very gentle with all of those things," Chance concluded.

Braden nodded importantly. "Mommy showed me."

"Well, listen, buckaroo," Chance continued, still hunkered down so he and Braden were eye to eye. "It's always good to be gentle," he said kindly. "And it's great to be able to see a real baby bull."

Braden beamed. "I like bulls!"

"The thing is, Santa doesn't really have any bulls to bring to little boys," Chance told him, quashing the kid's dreams against his better judgment.

"Uh-huh! At the North Pole," Braden said. "Santa has everything!"

"No." Chance shook his head sadly but firmly. He looked the little boy in the eye. "There aren't any bulls at the North Pole."

Mutinously, Braden folded his little arms across his chest. "Santa bring me one," he reiterated stubbornly.

Out of the corner of Chance's eye, he saw Molly's stricken expression. Yeah. She pretty much wanted to let him have it. Given the unforeseen way things were developing, he could hardly blame her.

"For Christmas," Braden added for good measure, in case either Molly or Chance didn't understand him. He pointed to the pasture. "Want mommy bull. And baby bull."

Okay, this was not going according to plan, Chance thought uncomfortably.

"Baby needs mommy," Braden added plaintively, just in case they still weren't getting it.

Molly lifted a brow and sent Chance an even more withering glare.

Fortunately, at that moment, his mother walked out of the recently renovated Circle H bunkhouse, where she was currently living, her part-time cook and housekeeper, Maria Gonzales, at her side. The young woman often brought her own three-year-old daughter, Tessie, to work with her. The little lass peeked at Braden from behind her mother's skirt.

"Braden, Maria and Tessie were just about to make some Thanksgiving tarts. Would you like to help them?" Lucille asked.

He looked at his mother for permission.

Molly gave it with a nod, then pointed to the ranch house on the other side of the barns. "Miss Lucille, Chance and I are going to walk over there and have a meeting. Then I'll come back to get you. Okay?"

Braden took Maria's outstretched hand. "'Kay, Mommy."

Maria and her two young charges set off.

In the past, the sixty-eight-year-old Lucille had ignored interpersonal tensions for the sake of peace. However, a recent series of life-changing events had caused Chance's mother to rethink the idea of sugarcoating anything. And now, to everyone's surprise, it turned out she could be as blunt as Chance's older brother, Garrett.

"What's going on between you two?" Lucille demanded as she looked from Molly to Chance and back again. "And don't tell me nothing, because I can feel the mutual aggravation simmering between you a mile away!"

Chance would have preferred to keep their tiff private. Unfortunately, Molly had other ideas. "Chance told Braden that he could ask Santa to bring him a real live baby bull for Christmas!" she sputtered.

Lucille turned to him, formidable as always in an ultrasuede sheath, cashmere cardigan and heels.

"I was trying not to quash his dreams," Chance insisted hotly.

"So, instead, you lit fire to impossible ones, and now he wants not just a baby bull but a bovine mama to go with it, too," Molly accused him, looking furious enough to burst into tears.

"Look, I—" Even as the words came out of his mouth, Chance had to wonder how Molly had managed to put him on the defensive.

She stomped closer and waved a finger beneath his nose. "If you hadn't brought that baby bull over with his momma to pasture at the Circle H—"

"If you hadn't brought your son with you to discuss making a bid," he volleyed right back.

Molly planted both her hands on her slender hips. "I had no choice!"

He mocked her by doing the same. "Well, neither did I!"

Completely exasperated, Lucille stopped worrying the pearls around her neck and stepped in between them.

"Enough, you two!" she chastised. "You are acting like ornery children. It's five weeks until Christmas…we will figure out a way to work this out."

Chance and Molly separated once again.

Satisfied things were calmer, at least for the moment, Lucille walked up the steps to the rambling, homestead-style ranch house and across the spacious front porch. "In the meantime, I have a job big enough for the two of you," she said over her shoulder, leading the way into the house.

Chance and his crew had spent the fall getting the two bedrooms and bathroom upstairs remodeled, the staircase rebuilt and all new energy-efficient windows installed. A new roof and fiber-cement siding had been put on, and the exterior had been painted a dazzling white with pine-green shutters. They'd also followed the plans of the structural engineer and gutted the downstairs into an open living-kitchen-dining area, a laundry room and mudroom, and what would one day be a spacious master suite with luxury bath for Lucille.

For the moment, however, only the framework of the redesigned first-floor rooms and the original wood floors—which were in need of refinishing—stood.

In the center of the space, in front of the original limestone fireplace, were two big easels. One held Molly's proposed design, the other Chance's.

Lucille turned to her son. "Although I love the rustic nature of your plans, honey, I am going to go with Molly's vision for the first floor."

There wasn't a lot of difference in the plan for the master suite, since Lucille had been very specific in what kind of fixtures and the size closet she wanted. As for the rest…

"You know that's going to cost you twice what mine would," Chance pointed out.

Lucille nodded. "True. But your vision for the space is so...utilitarian."

*Exactly!* It was what made it so great.

Chance pointed to the samples of his proposed maple cabinets and black granite countertops, the top-of-the-line stainless steel appliances and plentiful pantry shelving. "It'll get the job done, Mom."

Where he had been trying to be economical, his competition had gone all out. Dual dishwashers, two prep areas, double ovens and countless other features. Everywhere you looked there was some sort of up-charge.

Lucille smiled. "Molly captured what I was looking for. Unfortunately, I don't think she and her crew can manage to finish the entire downstairs in the next five weeks."

Molly's triumph faded. "Did you say five...weeks?"

Lucille nodded. "I want to reserve December 19 for delivery of the furniture from my previous house in Dallas that's currently in storage, the twentieth and the twenty-first for decorating and the twenty-second for my planned fundraiser for the Lockhart Foundation and West Texas Warrior Assistance program. And of course Christmas Eve and Day for my family celebration."

Chance frowned. "Which means all the wiring, plumbing, drywall and paint, as well as kitchen and master suite bath, will have to go in by then."

His mother remained undaunted. "You have six people on your crew, Chance. Molly has seven. If you have all thirteen people working, it's easily feasible. I'll pay overtime if necessary."

All business, Molly nodded. "How are we going to divide the work?"

Matter-of-factly, Lucille explained, "Molly will be in charge of the design and the materials, and Chance will supervise the construction and installation. Then, of course, Molly, I'd like you to do the yuletide decorating." She flashed a smile her way. "I'll give you a free hand with that since part of the reason for the rush is to help you showcase your skills during the fund-raising open house, and make the connections with my Dallas friends that will help you drum up business there."

Chance turned to his mother and gave her a warning look. He would have expected Lucille, who, better than anyone, knew the downside of leaving the warm, supportive utopia of Laramie County behind, to be urging caution. Not cheerleading. "You're really supporting Molly in this lunacy?" he blurted before he could stop himself.

Molly had a growing business. A home. Dozens of people who looked out for her. A young son who was thriving in the small-town environment. Why she would want to leave all that for the coldness of the big city he had grown up in was beyond him.

"I wouldn't call it that." Lucille regarded him sternly. "And, yes, I fully understand Molly's desire to be all that she can be."

Resolved to inject a little common sense into the conversation, Chance scoffed, "In terms of what? Money? Social position?"

Molly glared at him. "Don't forget dazzling professional success! And all the accoutrements that come with it."

Chance looked heavenward. "I don't expect you to understand," Molly said stiffly, her emotions suddenly as fired up as his.

"Good," Chance snapped back, running his hand through his hair in exasperation. Then, pinning her with a glare of his own, he said exactly what was on his mind. "Because I don't."

# Chapter 2

"Avoiding me?" a husky voice taunted.

Molly thought work had wrapped up for the day. Which was, as it turned out, the only reason she was at the Circle H ranch house this late.

Turning in the direction of the familiar baritone, Molly took in the sight of the indomitable cowboy. Clad in a knit thermal tee, plaid flannel shirt and jeans, a tool belt circling his waist, Chance Lockhart strode toward her purposefully.

Working to still her racing heart, Molly held her clipboard and pen close to her chest. She lifted her chin. "Why would you think that?"

Chance stopped just short of her and gave her a slow, thorough once-over. "We've both had crews working here ten days straight, and you and I haven't run into each other once."

*Thank God.*

Aware the last thing she wanted was to give Chance another opportunity to tell her what he thought of her plan to improve her and her son's lives, Molly shrugged. "I guess we have different schedules."

His, she had deduced, kept him at his ranch, taking care

of his bucking bulls early mornings and evenings. Hence, it was usually safe to arrive at the remodeling site during those hours.

Except today, he'd varied his routine. Why? To try to catch her in person, rather than communicate through endless emails and texts?

What she knew for certain was that it would be dark in another fifteen minutes, and all she had for light was a 220-volt camping lantern.

As seemingly unaffected by their quiet, intimate surroundings as the cell phone that kept going off with a sound that usually signaled an incoming text message—checked, then unanswered—in the holster at his waist, he glanced around. "What do you think thus far?"

*That even with rumpled hair and a couple of days' growth of beard on your face, you are without a doubt the sexiest man I've ever seen.* Which was too bad. Molly sighed inwardly, since Chance wasn't at all her type. But if he were…she could definitely lose herself in those gorgeous hazel eyes, big hunky body and wickedly sensual lips. Luckily he didn't know that.

With effort, she switched on her camping lantern, set it on the floor and got out her tape measure. She measured the front windows and door for window treatments and wreaths. The fireplace and staircase for garlands. Jotting down the numbers in her leather notebook, she said, "I think our combined crews have made amazing progress."

Under Chance's direction, new rooms had been framed out and a first-floor powder room for guests added last minute. Plumbing and electrical wiring had been installed, new drywall put up and taped, crown molding and trim work done.

Chance moved to the fireplace. He ran his big, calloused hand along the new wooden mantel. It was cut out of the same rustic oak as the support beams overhead. "The floors will be repaired where needed and sanded tomorrow."

Which took them all the way up to Thanksgiving, she knew. The one day every one of them would have a break from the demanding schedule.

"You got the tile for the kitchen and the bathrooms, and the paint colors picked out?"

Trying not to think what he would be doing for the holidays, Molly replied, "Still waiting on final approval from your mom. She wants to see samples in the light here before she decides. But we've narrowed it down to a couple of shades for each space."

Chance ambled over and switched on several of the portable construction lamps. "The new appliances and light fixtures?"

Instantly the downstairs became much brighter. "On order."

He walked around, inspecting some of the work that had been done. Finding a tiny flaw, he stuck a piece of blue painter's tape on it. "Kitchen and bath cabinets and countertops?"

"Will all be delivered in time to meet our schedule."

He nodded, as aware as she that one major glitch could throw everything off. Fortunately, thus far anyway, luck had been completely on their side.

He came toward her.

Her heartbeat picked up for no reason she could figure. Molly cleared her throat. "Speaking of the holiday... I wanted to talk to you about Thanksgiving." She moved around restlessly. "I've given my crew the day off."

Joining her at the hearth, Chance took a foil-wrapped candy from his shirt pocket. "Same here."

There was no way, she thought, he could know that was her very favorite. Trying not to salivate over the treat, Molly continued, "But they've all agreed to work on Friday."

He nodded, ripping open one end. Immediately the smell of dark chocolate and peppermint filled the small space between them.

"Mine, too."

Chance's cell phone buzzed again, this time with the ringtone "I Saw Mommy Kissing Santa Claus."

Telling herself that particular choice in no way involved her, either, Molly watched as, once again, he checked the screen and ignored it.

He held out the partially unwrapped confection. "Want one?" he asked.

Now she knew he was flirting.

"I've got another..." he teased.

Hell, yes, she wanted some of his dark chocolate peppermint. But if she started taking candy from him on a whim, who knew what might be next?

She returned his assessing look and said as innocently as possible, "Thanks, but no."

His eyes gleamed.

"I don't really like those."

His sexy grin widened all the more.

Then his phone buzzed yet again. With the maddeningly suggestive holiday song...

Thinking maybe he really should answer that, and would if she weren't standing right there, Molly picked up her lantern before she ended up doing something really stupid—like kissing the smug look off his face—and headed for the staircase.

Able to feel the heat of his masculine gaze drifting over her, she tossed the words over her shoulder. "I've got to measure the upstairs windows before I go."

"Want help?"

"No!"

He chuckled, as she had known he would.

Molly fought back a flush. This was exactly why she had been avoiding him. Luckily she had work to keep her busy. Chance might even be gone before she left.

She had just finished measuring the first window when she heard a door open, then close. Lucille Lockhart's lyrical voice echoed through the first floor. "Chance? Why aren't you picking up? I just got another call from Babs Holcombe. She said she's been trying to reach you for days!"

*Who the heck is Babs?* Not that she should be listening…

"Been a little busy, Mom," Chance growled.

Lucille's high heels tapped across the wood floors. "You owe her the courtesy of a return call. Or at the very least an email!"

"After the way things ended with Delia?" Chance scoffed.

*Delia?* Molly perked up, edging a little closer despite herself.

"I admit that wasn't one of their finer moments," Lucille conceded reluctantly, "but they've both done a lot to support the Lockhart Foundation in the three years since."

"Okay," Chance countered gruffly.

"Okay you'll call her," Lucille pressed, sounding beside herself with irritation, "or okay you won't?"

Silence reigned once again.

Molly could imagine the bullheaded look on Chance's face. The disapproving moue of his mother. There was a brief murmur of disgruntled talk she couldn't decipher, then the sound of Lucille leaving. The front door shut. Chance's heavy footsteps crossed to the center of the house. "You can come down now!" he called cheerfully up the stairs.

Aghast that he knew she had been eavesdropping, heat flooded her cheeks. Measurements taken, she walked back down, pocketing her pen. "Sorry. Didn't mean to intrude."

He gave her a look that said, "I'll bet."

Falling into step beside her, he accompanied her out onto the front porch. The air had the distinct damp chill of late November. Dark clouds gathered along the horizon, where the sun was setting in streaks of purple and gray.

"How is Braden doing? Were you able to steer him toward the Leo and Lizzie World Adventure train set?"

Surprised that Chance recalled the name of the toy, Molly grimaced. "Ah, no. Not yet."

Concern etched his ruggedly handsome face. "Meaning you haven't really tried yet?"

Molly only wished that were the case. Taking her first real break of the day, she perched on the railing edging the front porch. "Meaning, like with most men, subtlety doesn't work on Braden. Nor does direct conversation."

Chance took a seat opposite her, mesmerizing her with the blatant interest in his eyes. "So he still wants a live baby bull and a momma."

"As well as a daddy bull."

"Wow."

She sighed, relieved to be able to talk about what had been bothering her all day. "Wow is right."

His expression grew thoughtful. "What are you going to do?"

With effort, she forced herself to meet his probing gaze. "Honestly? I don't have a clue."

"I had a few ideas."

Molly pushed to her feet. Feeling her pulse skitter, she turned her head to the side. "I think you've done enough," she quipped, using sarcasm to hide her worry.

He accompanied her down the steps to her SUV. "Seriously. I think I might be able to dissuade him, given another opportunity. And since you have Thanksgiving Day off and so do I, and my mother is hosting her annual dinner at the bunkhouse, I was thinking you and Braden might want to come as my plus two."

Aware the mood between them was quickly becoming highly charged and way too intimate, Molly unlocked her vehicle. "You're asking me for a date?"

To her consternation, he didn't exactly deny it.

"There will be a lot of people there. Three of my siblings and their significant others and or friends. And a few other family friends."

Molly tossed her bag into the front passenger seat. "First of all, your mother and I get along so well because I know my place."

His brow lifted.

"Furthermore, Braden and I have our own holiday tradition."

He rested a muscular forearm on the open driver-side door. "You cook?"

Molly lifted her chin. "I take him to the buffet at the cafeteria in San Angelo."

Sympathy lit his gaze. "Sounds…lonely."

Lonely, Molly thought, was being a fifth wheel at the big family gatherings of friends. Knowing, you'd never enjoy the same.

She shrugged. "Crowded is more like it. But it's not too bad if we get there at eleven, when it opens, and then Braden and I have the rest of the day to do whatever we want." Which usually involved a family activity of their own.

Chance stepped back. "Well, if you change your mind, the invitation stands."

Molly slid behind the wheel. "Thanks, but I won't." She looked up at him.

Whether Chance admitted it or not, she was out of his league socially, too. "And don't worry about Braden. I'll figure out a way to handle his misconceptions about what is possible for Christmas. And what is not."

Except she wasn't handling it, Molly thought the following day when they entered the popular San Angelo cafeteria. At least not as well as she or her son would like.

"I'm hungry, Mommy," Braden complained as the line of customers inched forward.

Although she had been hoping to make this Thanksgiving really special for him, he'd been grumpy since waking that morning. "I know." Molly inched up slightly, clear of the entrance. "It will be our turn soon. See?" She pointed to the lighted display cases up ahead.

Braden stamped his cowboy boot. "Don't want to wait," he fumed.

"I know." Thinking he might be overheated, Molly knelt down in front of him and unzipped his fleece hoodie. She figured he would be fine once they sat down. Avoiding a meltdown before that concerned her.

"Can we go home now?" Braden persisted.

"Oh, you don't want to do that," a familiar low voice said from behind them. "I hear the holiday buffet here is not to be missed."

Braden lit up like a Christmas tree. "Cowboy Chance!"

"Hi, buddy!" Chance held out his palm. Braden high-fived him.

Slowly, Molly straightened to her full height. To her dismay, she was ridiculously glad to see him. Especially looking so fine.

Like her, he had upped his game a notch. Slacks, a starched shirt, tie and tweed Western-cut blazer, instead of his usual flannel shirt and jeans. "Aren't you supposed to be at your mom's today?"

"Already made my appearance."

Which accounted for his neatly combed chestnut hair and freshly shaven jaw.

"I'm tired," Braden complained.

Molly inhaled the sandalwood and leather fragrance of Chance's cologne, mixing with the usual soap and fresh air scent of his skin.

"Probably a little bored, too." Chance winked. He reached into his jacket pockets. "Which is why I brought you these." He pulled out a toy reindeer with a big red nose and a coordinating winter sleigh.

Braden beamed. "Rudolph!"

Molly gave Chance a look her delighted son could not see. "What are you doing?" she demanded sweetly.

Grooves deepened on either side of his mouth. "Working on that solution."

Aware how easy it would be to fall for this sexy cowboy's charms, Molly stiffened. "I fail to see how—"

He clapped a hand on her shoulder. "All in good time, my darlin'. All in good time. And—" he nodded at the space behind her "—you're going to want to move on up."

The line was indeed pushing forward.

Molly inched ahead. "I don't remember inviting you," she murmured so only he could hear, while her son energetically played with the reindeer and sleigh.

Chance leaned down to whisper in her ear. "That's the good thing about having Thanksgiving here. You don't need an invite." He looked around, impressed. "Although given how crowded the establishment is quickly getting, it would probably be considerate of the three of us to share a table, rather than unnecessarily take up more chairs than we need."

"You're impossible." Despite herself, she was glad to see him.

Braden tugged on Chance's blazer. He tilted his head back so he could see his idol's face. "Thank you for toys."

Chance ruffled her son's hair. "You're welcome, buddy. It was my pleasure."

To Molly's surprise, it was hers, too.

"So what next?" Chance asked as the three of them finished their turkey dinners.

Molly looked out the cafeteria windows. The rain that had been threatening since the previous evening had started mid-meal. It was now coming down in sheets. She sighed. "No playground, unfortunately…"

Braden stopped playing with the toys Chance had brought him long enough to scowl. "Promised!"

Molly used a napkin to wipe some cranberry sauce off her son's chin. "I know, honey, but everything will be all wet, so we'll have to do something indoors."

"Bouncy house?"

"Afraid not. It's closed because today is a holiday."

"Cowboy Chance play. My house."

She did have activities planned there, two they had already started, in fact, in addition to Braden's usual time set aside to do whatever he wanted. "I'm sure Mr. Chance has other things to do, honey."

He met her eyes. "Not really." Chance turned back to Braden, his cordial tone as reassuring as his presence. "What kind of toys do you have?"

"Trucks and cars."

"Trains?"

Braden shook his head.

Abruptly Molly saw where Chance was going with this.

If he did have an idea how to convince her son to yearn for the holiday gift she had chosen for Braden…could she afford to turn Chance down? Especially if the end result was Braden's happiness?

Braden tugged on her sleeve. "Go now, Mommy!" He stood on his chair and held out his arms to their lunch companion. "Cowboy Chance, too!"

Chance caught Braden in his big arms.

Trying not to think how natural the two looked together, Molly said, "We won't expect you to stay long."

Chance stood, Braden still in his arms. "I won't wear out my welcome. On the other hand..." He winked and shrugged in a way that opened up a ton of possibilities. A shiver of awareness swept through her. He probably would be a good time, Molly thought despite herself. Too good a time.

She shook off the awareness. Stacking their dishes and trays, she asked, "You know where I live?"

He nodded, looking as unexpectedly content in that moment as she felt. "Spring Street in Laramie."

Molly led the way. The drive back to Laramie took thirty-five minutes. It was still raining when Chance parked behind Molly's SUV and got out of his pickup truck.

Her home, a former carriage house, sported a three-foot-high white picket fence and was sandwiched between two large Victorians. The one-story abode, while much smaller and set back a ways from the sidewalk, was just as attractive—if not more so—than every other home on the prestigious street. A front porch with white wicker furniture spanned the width of the thousand-square-foot house, which featured gray clapboard sides, white trim and black shutters.

The scent of fresh-cut pine hit Chance the moment he walked in the door.

A Christmas tree stood in the corner of the comfortably outfitted living area, boxes of lights and decorations beside it.

The state-of-the-art kitchen, situated at the back of the main living area, was banked by a wall of floor-to-ceiling windows that flooded the small, cozy space with light. Plentiful cabinets, painted a dark slate, and an island that also served as a dining area were a nice counterpoint to the white quartz countertops, bleached wood floors and stainless steel appliances.

Standing there, noting how beautiful her home was, he couldn't imagine why she would ever want to leave it.

Her son, however, had other things on his mind.

Barely standing still long enough for his mother to wrestle him out of his damp rain jacket, he set his Rudolph and sleigh on the coffee table, next to a soft blue blanket, then headed importantly for the kitchen, where a delicious fresh dough and orange smell emanated. "Come on, Mr. Chance. We cook!"

Braden grabbed a tyke-size navy chef's apron off the hook, and then handed Chance one, as well—frilly and floral. "Put on!" he demanded.

Molly's amused expression dared Chance to do so.

Clearly, he noted, she did not think he would. Which just showed how much she knew. "Sure thing, buddy," Chance agreed drily, pulling the garment over his head. The cloth barely covered his broad chest, and the waist hit him at mid-sternum. Tying it seemed impossible, given the fact he couldn't find the strings.

Grinning, Molly stepped behind him. "Allow me."

Her hands brushed his spine as she secured it in place. His body reacted as if they'd kissed. Fortunately, she was too on task to notice. She opened a drawer and pulled out a plain white chef's apron, that was, as it happened, much more his size.

She tilted her head, her gaze moving over him humorously. "Want to trade?"

Aware this was the first time he'd seen her eyes sparkle

so mischievously, he motioned for her to turn so he could tie her apron strings, too. She needed to goof around like this more often. Not be so serious all the time. "Nah, I'm good."

The three of them took turns washing their hands; then Braden climbed onto the step stool next to the island. "Ready, Mommy?" the tyke asked eagerly.

"Let's see." Molly pulled a linen towel away from the top of a large bowl. Inside was a billowy cloud of dough. "I think so."

She positioned the bowl in front of her son. "Ready to punch it down?"

With a gleeful shout, Braden went to town, pummeling the buttery dough until all the air was released. "What are we making?" Chance asked. It sure smelled good, even at this early stage.

Molly moved close enough he could catch a whiff of her perfume. It was every bit as feminine and enticing and delectable as she was.

"Christmas *stollen*." She tilted her head curiously. "Ever had it?"

"I don't think so."

"Well, you're in for a treat." She turned the dough onto a floured wooden board and divided it into three sections—which she quickly rolled out into long loaves. Wordlessly, she retrieved a bowl of dried cherries, cranberries and almonds, soaking in what appeared to be orange juice, and drained the excess. "Time to sprinkle on the extras."

Braden—no novice at baking—positioned his fruit and nuts very seriously, dropping them one by one onto the dough. "You, too, Cowboy Chance."

"Yes, sir," Chance said, soberly following Braden's lead. Molly joined in.

When they'd finished, Braden clapped his hands. "I done now, Mommy?"

"Yes. You did a very good job." She wiped his hands with a clean cloth. "You can go play while I get this ready for the second rise."

He hurried off to retrieve his Rudolph and sleigh. Then he brought out his toy dump truck to give them a ride.

With Braden playing happily, Chance settled on a stool at the island. "Where did you learn to do this?"

"My mother taught me." Molly showed him how to knead the dough until it was soft and elastic, and then shape it into loaves. Carefully, he followed her lead. "Her grandparents emigrated here from Germany. Baking was an important part of their holiday tradition, and she passed it on to me, as her mother had to her."

Remembering his earlier faux pas, he trod carefully. "Where is your mom now?"

Sorrow pinched Molly's face. "She died of meningitis when I was fourteen. My dad never really got over the loss, and he died in a car accident just before I graduated from high school."

He wished he had been around to comfort her, but that had been years before he'd moved to Laramie. "That must have been rough."

"It was." Molly carefully transferred the loaves onto baking sheets and covered them with linen cloths, the actions of her hands delicate and sure. "But I had a lot of help from the people in the community. The local bank gave me a second mortgage on this house, so I'd have somewhere to live, and enough funds to get by on while I studied construction and interior design at the local community college and did what was necessary to obtain my general contractor's license."

His gaze drifted over her. She wore a long-sleeved emerald

dress that made the most of her stunning curves, black tights and flats. Her auburn hair was curlier than usual—he supposed it was the rain. "What made you want to pursue that?"

Molly lounged against the counter, her hands braced on either side of her. "Tradition, I guess. My mom taught classes in nutrition and cooking at Laramie High, and she did interior design work on the side, and my dad was a general contractor who did mostly handyman work."

She paused to rub a spot of flour from her hip. "Following in their footsteps made me feel closer to them. Plus, both my parents had substantial client lists that I initially utilized to get work. So I was able to get on my feet financially a lot faster than I would have otherwise."

Braden walked into the kitchen. He stepped between them merrily. "Puddles, Mommy?"

Grinning, Molly looked out the window. The rain that had been landing in torrents was now coming down gently. "You want to go outside?"

Braden nodded.

"Then let's get you suited up." Molly walked into the mudroom off the garage, then returned with a pair of yellow rain boots, matching slicker and wide-brimmed hat. Braden brimmed with anticipation. "You come, too, Cowboy Chance?"

"We'll both watch you from the front porch," Molly promised. "Unless…" She paused to look at Chance. "You have somewhere else you need to be?"

# Chapter 3

This was Chance's opportunity to make a graceful exit.

To his surprise, he wasn't in a hurry to leave. In fact, he was sort of lamenting the fact that the time would eventually come. "Actually," Chance admitted good-naturedly, "I was hoping I'd be able to see what the Christmas *stollen* looks like when it's finished."

"Yummy!" Braden declared, rubbing his tummy.

Chance chuckled. The little buckaroo's enthusiasm was infectious. "You think so?"

Braden nodded magnanimously. "We share. Mommy. Me. You."

Chance turned to Molly. "Is that okay?" he asked casually, wanting to give her the option of throwing him out—if that was what she wanted.

"You probably should see what you've been missing," she said drily.

He had an inkling. And he wasn't just thinking about baked goods.

"Outside?" Braden asked again, impatiently.

"Let's go." She grabbed a rain jacket for herself, then

opened the door. A blast of unexpectedly warm air hit them. No doubt brought in by the front. "I was going to offer you a cup of coffee," Molly said, looping the jacket over a wicker chair, "but maybe it should be iced tea."

"Coffee's fine." Chance smiled. "Thanks."

Molly watched her son march down the front steps and out into the light rain. They both grinned as Braden lifted his face to the sky and stuck out his tongue to catch a few raindrops. Fondly, Molly shook her head, then turned back to Chance. "Can you keep an eye on Braden for a minute? He knows not to go outside of the picket fence."

"No problem." Chance took the seat she indicated on the front porch. For the next few minutes, he watched Braden investigate everything from the water running out of the gutters to the drops pearling on the leafy green shrubs.

He'd forgotten what it felt like to look at the world with such unvarnished appreciation.

Maybe it was time he remembered...

"Sure you wouldn't rather be at your mom's watching football with your brothers?" Molly teased, returning with a tray containing a carafe, two mugs, sugar and cream. She set it on the table between them.

Chance grinned at her son, who was now hopscotching his way through a series of puddles on the front walk.

He turned his attention back to Molly. Her cheeks flushed with happiness, her auburn hair slightly mussed, a smudge of flour across one cheek, she had never looked more beautiful. Or content.

He liked seeing her this way.

"Oh, there's no football at my mom's on Thanksgiving." Her delicate brow pleated. "Seriously?"

As she neared, he caught the fragrance of her lavender hand soap mingling with the sweet, sexy scent of her hair and skin. Pushing the electric awareness away, Chance sat back in his chair. "She says that's why DVRs were invented. Social events require socializing properly with each other, not tuning everyone out watching TV."

Molly handed him a mug of steaming coffee. She wrinkled her nose at him. "Sounds like Lucille."

Chance watched as she settled in the chair beside his. The hem of her knit dress rode up a little. She crossed her legs at the knee and tugged it down discreetly, but not before he had seen enough of her long slender thighs to make his heart race.

Chance worked to keep his mind on the conversation. "No doubt about it. My mother's big on etiquette, always has been."

Molly waved at her son, who was now marching around the perimeter of the inside of the fence. Braden stopped to lift his arms high and turn his face to the slowly clearing sky overhead. "Still, the menu would probably have been better..."

Chance couldn't recall when he had enjoyed a holiday meal more. "I thought we had a fine meal at the cafeteria. Turkey. All the trimmings. Not to mention choice of dessert."

She chuckled, holding her mug against the softness of her full lips. "You did have two pieces of pie."

He watched her blow lightly on her coffee, then take a dainty sip. Shrugged. "Couldn't make up my mind."

He was certain about one thing, though.

He wanted to ravish Molly Griffith.

And would...

"Look, Mommy!" Braden shouted. "Rainbow!"

They both turned in the direction he was pointing. Sure enough, there was one arcing across the sky.

"Come here, Mommy! Come see!"

"Just when I wish I had my camera out," she murmured with a rueful grin, rising to join her son.

Not wanting to intrude, Chance stayed behind to make her wish come true.

Chance Lockhart was full of surprises, Molly thought minutes later, looking at the series of action photos he had taken on his cell phone while she and Braden had admired the burst of colors streaking across the late afternoon sky.

"Thank you for capturing that moment," Molly said softly when they walked back inside a few minutes later to put the *stollen* in the oven. Chance had not only gotten several nice shots of her and Braden together—something that rarely happened on the spur of the moment since she had no other family member to do the honor—but he'd also managed to capture a close-up of the wonder on her little boy's face.

Priceless.

"I thought you would want to remember it. Not every day you see a rainbow on Thanksgiving."

Not every day she spent a holiday with such a sweet, handsome man. Not that this was a date. Even if it had started to feel like a date.

Molly finished getting Braden out of his rain gear, then showed her little boy the photos Chance had taken on his phone and emailed to her.

"That's me," Braden said gleefully. "And Mommy!" He pushed the phone away. "Can we dec'rate tree?"

That had been her original plan.

Chance shrugged his broad shoulders affably. "I'm up for it if you are," he said.

"You're really into Christmas, aren't you?" She hadn't met many single guys who were.

Or were this kind to her son.

"Hey." Chance aimed a thumb at the center of his chest. "When the opportunity to be chivalrous presents itself…"

He was on board, Molly thought. Which just went to show how badly she had misjudged the gorgeous cowboy.

By the time the oven timer went off half an hour later, they had the lights strung and on. Half a dozen ornaments later, the fruit-and-nut-studded pastry was cool enough to finish.

Aprons went back on. Although this time Molly made sure that Chance had the larger garment. Together, they all brushed on melted butter, then sprinkled the tops of their masterpieces with granulated sugar.

"And now for the pièce de résistance!" Molly declared triumphantly, showing her son how to use the sifter to cover the pastry with a final snowy-white cover of confectioner's sugar. She handed the sifter to Chance, watched as he did the same to his and then followed suit.

The three pastries made a lovely, Christmassy sight.

"Eat now?" Braden asked.

Molly grinned. "Let's taste it." She cut off a two-inch slice for Braden, a larger one for Chance and a slightly smaller one for herself.

They all bit down on the soft, citrus-flavored nut-and-fruit bread with the sweet and slightly crunchy exterior. "Wow." Chance's hazel eyes lit up. "That's...amazing."

"Yummy," Braden agreed.

Molly had to admit, between the three of them they had done a good job. Before she could think, she offered, "Want to take a loaf home with you?"

Luckily he didn't read any extra meaning into her impulsive gesture. An affable grin deepened the crinkles around his eyes. "Sure you don't mind?"

Remembering what her late mother had told her—that the way to a man's heart was through his stomach—Molly shrugged off the importance. "I'll be baking all month long."

His gaze skimmed her appreciatively. "In that case—" he winked "—I'll have to remember to come around more often."

Molly caught her breath at the implication.

Was he truly interested in her?

She knew she desired him. Always had. Even though they were clearly all wrong for each other. Still...

"All done, Mommy!"

Switching quickly back to parenting mode, Molly gently wiped the sugar from her son's hands and face. Braden reclaimed the Rudolph and sleigh, along with his favorite blue blankie. Yawning, he snuggled on the sofa.

Chance arched an inquisitive brow. "Nap time?"

"Two hours ago," Molly confirmed softly, watching Braden struggle to keep his eyes open.

"Oh." A wealth of emotion—and understanding—in a single word.

"Yeah. I was hoping—" Molly moved closer to Chance, whispering even more quietly "—he'd be able to get through the day without one. Especially since it's so late."

Chance shook his head fondly. Putting an easy hand on Molly's shoulder, he nodded in the direction of the couch. "Looks like he's already asleep."

Molly took in the sight of her child, blissfully cuddled up, auburn lashes fanning across his cheek. She sighed. "Indeed, he is."

Chance caressed her shoulder lightly. "That's a problem?"

Molly's heart raced at the casual contact. "He'll be grouchy when I do wake him up before dinner and may have trouble falling asleep tonight."

"Anything I can do?"

*If you were here, sure. You won't be.* Molly looked up at Chance. Time seemed to suspend. Suddenly there was just the two of them. "Cross your fingers for me?"

His eyes darkened. He brushed his thumb across her lower lip and continued to regard her steadily. "How about something even better?" he said huskily, lifting her hand to his lips. He pressed a kiss across her knuckles. She caught her breath. And then she was in his arms. Wrapping both his hands around her small waist, he caught her against him, so they were length to length.

Molly's breath hitched again.

"Chance," she whispered.

His head lowered. Slowly. Purposefully. "Just one, darlin'..." He tunneled his hands through her hair and his eyes shuttered. "That's all I'm asking."

Molly saw the kiss coming, and she knew she should do something to stop it. She was attracted to Chance enough already. If his lips were to actually touch hers...

With a small, sharp intake of breath, she lifted both hands and spread them across the muscular warmth of his broad chest. His heart was beating, strong and steady. His head lowered even more. And then there was no stopping it. Their lips connected, and a shiver of pure delight went through her. Her usual caution gone, she opened her mouth to the seductive pressure of his. He tasted like rich black coffee and freshly baked *stollen*. And man. And she could no more deny him than she could deny herself. It was Thanksgiving, after all. A day to count blessings. Be happy. Thankful. At ease. And she'd never felt more at ease than she did at that very moment.

Chance knew he was taking advantage, that Molly deserved a lot better than the overture he was making. He also knew opportunities like this did not come along all that often.

Molly had a wall around her heart, strong enough to keep the entire male species at bay. She was driven by fierce ambition. And a robust little chaperone that kept her on the straight and narrow.

Had he spent time with her before now, he would have realized what a beautiful, complicated and magnificent woman she was.

He would have known there was a lot more to her than her need for tremendous financial security, and the social status that came with it. But he hadn't, so he had squandered the two years he had resided in Laramie County. Two years in which he could have pursued her like she was meant to be pursued.

Fortunately, he still had a month left.

He wasn't going to waste it.

Or make any more mistakes.

So he kissed her passionately until she kissed him back and curled against him. And it was only then, when they started to make the kind of connection that rocked both their worlds, that she suddenly gasped and wrenched her lips from his.

"Is this the point where you haul off and slap me across the face?" Chance joked.

It was definitely the point where she gave herself a good hard shake, Molly thought. What in all Texas had gotten into her? She couldn't start getting involved with someone! Or even have a fling. Not when she was getting ready to leave rural Laramie County and build a life in the city.

Reluctantly, she stepped out of the warm cocoon of Chance's strong arms. She went to a drawer on the opposite side of the kitchen and pulled out a roll of plastic wrap.

Her lips and body still throbbing from the thrilling contact, she lifted a staying hand and admitted softly, "That was my fault every bit as much as it was yours."

"Fault?" With displeasure, he zeroed in on her low, censoring tone.

"Holidays can be really lonely."

He gave her a considering look. "They don't have to be."

Irritated he saw so much of her feelings when she wanted him to see so little, Molly admitted, "It's easy to find yourself reaching out in ways you normally wouldn't."

His eyes filled with a mixture of curiosity and compassion. "Is that what happened with Braden's daddy?"

"No," Molly said, trying hard not to succumb to the unexpected tenderness in Chance's expression.

He leaned against the counter, arms folded in front of him, and continued to study her. "Then?"

Maybe if Chance knew the worst about her, he would forget the sizzling physical attraction between them and realize their backgrounds were too diverse for them to ever be more than casual friends.

Molly drew a deep breath. "I don't want to go down the wrong path again."

"With me."

It upset her to bring this up, but she knew for both their sakes, it had to be said. Chance had to start facing the fact they were and always would be all wrong for each other. "With anyone who was born outside my social standing."

His brow furrowed. "You really think I'm that much of a snob?"

She flushed and dropped her gaze to his muscular chest. "I think, in this respect, you might be as naive as I once was."

"I'm listening," he said.

Molly grabbed the spray cleaner and paper towels, then began scrubbing down the counters. "I never really dated much after my dad died. I was too busy trying to put myself through school and get my business going."

He moved so she could reach behind him. But not quite enough. As she reached, her shoulder lightly brushed his bicep. "Sounds like you had to grow up pretty fast."

Molly straightened. "All that changed when Aaron Powell

III came to Laramie to look for lakeside property that could be flipped." She grimaced at the memory. "I was asked to give a bid. I did and won the work on several houses that he and his family purchased." She removed her apron and hung it back on the hook. Recalling her first taste of unfettered luxury, she admitted reluctantly, "I'd never been friends with anyone that ostentatiously wealthy, and Aaron swept me off my feet."

Chance's expression relaxed in understanding. "How long were you together?"

"About three months."

Taking her by the hand, he guided her onto the stool. Sat down beside her. "You didn't expect it to end?"

Molly shrugged, still wishing she hadn't been quite so naive. Shifting so the two of them faced each other, she said, "I knew Aaron's life was in Houston, that his shuttling back and forth continuously would stop when my work was done and the lake properties were listed. But I was okay with that. I was perfectly willing to move where he was."

Chance's expression darkened. "He didn't want that."

Humiliation clogged Molly's throat. "He didn't think that would go over so well with his fiancée."

An awkward silence fell.

"You had no idea," Chance guessed in a low, even tone.

"None," Molly was forced to admit. Restless, she got up and began to pace the confines of the kitchen. "Unfortunately, I was pregnant by then. And I'd already told him."

Giving Chance no more opportunity to ask questions, Molly rushed on. "The next thing I know the Powell family lawyer is at my door with a contract for me to sign. All I have to do is agree—in writing—not to ever publicly acknowledge paternity and a nice six-figure check is mine."

Jaw taut, Chance stood. "I'm pretty sure that's not legal."

Molly nodded as he circled the counter and strode closer.

"I could have forced the issue in court. I also knew if I did that, Aaron and his attorneys would use my modest financial circumstances to allege I was a gold digger and make our lives a living hell. My only priority was to protect my child from hurt."

The compassion in Chance's hazel eyes spurred her to go on.

"So I hired a lawyer and countered with an offer of my own. I would never pursue any claims of paternity, or child support, if Aaron would promise to do the same and allow me to raise Braden completely on my own." She drew a breath. "Aaron was more than happy with that, since he didn't really want children, never mind a bastard son from a woman from a lower social echelon." Molly wrung her hands and lifted her chin defiantly. "So we signed an agreement...and that was that."

Chance searched her face. "Did you ever regret it?"

Wasn't that the million-dollar question!

Molly shrugged, the barriers coming up to protect her heart once again. Steadily, she held Chance's gaze. "I regret mistaking big, expensive romantic gestures for love. And the fact that Braden doesn't have the devoted daddy he deserves."

His gaze drifted over her, igniting wildfires wherever it landed. "The latter could be fixed," he pointed out matter-of-factly.

*Maybe someday.* For the first time, she was beginning to see that.

In the meantime, she had the next phase of her life plan to execute. Molly handed Chance the wrapped, freshly baked *stollen* and escorted him to the door. Wary of her still-sleeping son, she eased it open, then stepped with him all the way out onto the porch. It was unseasonably warm, and the sun sparkled down on them.

"The point is, even if fate works against us and Braden never gets the loving daddy he deserves, I still have to support my son to the very best of my ability."

"Which means?" Chance prodded, suddenly looking a lot less pleased.

Molly said determinedly, "I've got to move to a place where I can make a lot more money than I am now. And give Braden the kind of boundless future that he deserves."

And that meant no more getting too friendly with Chance. And definitely no more kissing him!

# Chapter 4

"How was your Thanksgiving?" Chance asked the two newest members of the Bullhaven family, now temporarily quartered in a private pasture at the Circle H.

"Mine was the best I've ever had." He set out premium feed. "You think I'm exaggerating, but I'm not."

Even though Molly had sort of kicked him out at the end, he'd left with a warm feeling in his chest that had continued through the night and had still lingered there when he woke up, maybe because he was going to see her again soon.

"Yeah, yeah, you're right. I've got it bad..." But there were worse things than knowing what you wanted. And what he wanted right now was a Christmas holiday spent with Molly. And her adorable son.

The momma Black Angus came toward the bucket, her bull calf, Mistletoe Jr., at her side. While she ate, the calf searched for a teat. Momma mooed gently in approval and then licked at her calf as it started to nurse.

Satisfied all was well, Chance went to his pickup truck. The morning was slightly cool, and rain had left the air smelling clean and brisk. He got out the rest of his breakfast—a thick wedge of Christmas bread—and a thermos of hot black coffee.

Leaning against the fender, he enjoyed the early morning quiet. Until his brother Wyatt drove up and parked beside him. An ornery look on his face, he nodded at the confection in Chance's hand. "What's that?"

Chance savored another bite. *"Stollen."*

Wyatt blinked. "A—what?"

Chance let the citrus-flavored bread melt on his tongue. "It's a German Christmas bread made with fruit and nuts."

Wyatt nodded, practically salivating now. "Looks good," he said.

It was more than simply good, Chance thought. It was the most amazing thing he had ever eaten. Better yet was the fact he had helped Molly and Braden make it.

"Can I have some?" Ready to help himself, Wyatt ambled closer.

Chance held it out of reach. "Sorry."

Wyatt blinked in surprise. It wasn't like his brother to be greedy. "What do you mean no?" he demanded.

Chance moved farther away. "I'm not sharing."

His brother stared at him as if he'd grown two heads. "Why the devil not?"

Chance shrugged as Molly's car turned into the lane and parked in front of the Circle H ranch house, too. "Just not."

She emerged from the driver's side, looking as stunning as usual in a pair of faded jeans, a long-sleeved white T-shirt and a cropped denim jacket. She had a pair of fancy burgundy engineer boots on, a tape measure attached to her belt and a pen stuck behind one ear. Clearly she was ready to work.

Wyatt angled a thumb at him as she approached. "Can you believe this?" Wyatt grumbled. "Chance is eating *stollen* and refusing to share."

Mischief lit her pretty amber eyes when her gaze fell to the treat in his hand. Chance gave her a look, imploring her not to give his brother information to dissect. What he and Molly had experienced was too special, too fragile, to risk or share.

The corners of her lips turning up all the more, she sipped coffee from the travel mug in hand. Then shrugging, she gave Chance a barely tolerant look before turning back to Wyatt. "Can't say I'm surprised." She sighed loudly. Exactly the way she would have before they'd started working together on this job. "Your brother has never had particularly *good* manners."

That had been true, up to now, when it came to Molly. That was going to change. Because now they'd stopped quarreling long enough to kiss, he couldn't imagine being anything but a complete Texas gentleman around her.

Wyatt exhaled in frustration. "Fine." He swung back around to Chance, growling as Chance popped what was left of his breakfast into his mouth. "Where did you get it then? 'Cause I don't remember Sage making German bread at her coffee shop in town."

Quickly, Chance shut down that line of inquiry. His only sister was worse than his mother when it came to interfering in his love life.

"Wasn't there," he confirmed.

"Then where was it?" Wyatt persisted hungrily.

Molly stepped between the two brothers. She interjected, "Maybe he made it?"

Wyatt shook his head. "Nah. I don't think so." He squinted, about to deliver another round of questions.

Figuring Molly'd had enough amusement at his expense for one morning, Chance lifted a hand. "If you must know, it was a holiday gift from someone I do business with. Okay? Happy now?" Ignoring Wyatt, he turned to Molly. "You ready to go over the project financials…make sure we're still on budget?"

Her reply was cut off by the loud *thump-thump-thump-thump* of a helicopter approaching overhead.

This wasn't an uncommon sight. A lot of wealthy people had homes in or around Laramie. They often flew in and out of the local airstrip either via private jet or chopper. The hospital used air ambulances, too. But this chopper was flying incredibly low. And coming right toward the Circle H.

While the momma cow and her baby bull hurried for cover in a strand of faraway trees, the chopper hovered over a large pasture, currently empty of livestock, and slowly, noisily set down. The motor slowed, then cut, the gusts of air fading.

"What the...?" Chance and Wyatt murmured in unison. The door to the chopper opened. And just like that, Chance was taken back to a time and place he had never wanted to revisit.

Feeling every bit as stunned as the two men beside her, Molly watched as a fiftysomething woman in a long white fur coat and ostrich boots stepped out. The silvery blonde was followed by a tall, lanky man in chinos, a sweater, a black leather biker jacket and sneakers. He had a decidedly unathletic air and appeared to be in his early forties. Last out was a thin, sophisticated blonde about Molly's age who looked like a younger version of the first woman. She had chic sunglasses over her eyes that matched her all-black clothing and body language that screamed indifference.

"Do you know them?" Molly asked, aware that the normally unflappable Chance seemed more perturbed than the unexpected landing should have made him.

Nodding at the approaching trio, Wyatt leaned over and quipped in Molly's ear, "The lady in fur is Babs Holcombe, Chance's would-have-been-mother-in-law-from-hell."

*Oh, dear.*

"And his ex, Delia Holcombe."

Who was, Molly noted, quite beautiful in that dissolutely wealthy way.

"No clue who the other dude is," Wyatt continued helpfully.

An unwelcoming look on his handsome face, Chance looked past them to where Mistletoe Jr. was cowering next to his momma. Sharing the concern, Wyatt touched his brother's arm. "I'll see to them. You take care of this."

Stopping just short of them, Babs looked at Molly. "You can leave, too."

Before Molly could react, Chance had an arm around her shoulders. "She stays," he said gruffly.

Molly hadn't been planning to. But…okay…if Chance felt in need of some kind of backup, she would provide it.

Watching as Chance dropped his arm, Babs said drolly, "Hello, Chance."

His scowl deepened. "Did you have permission to land that chopper here?"

Babs waved off any difficulty. "I'm sure your mother won't mind."

"What do you want?" he demanded.

Molly hitched in a surprised breath. In all their time together, she had never heard Chance be that rude.

"To introduce you to Mr. X—the founder of the X search engine."

No wonder the tall, sort of geeky guy looked familiar, Molly thought. She'd seen him being interviewed on TV. He'd also starred in commercials featuring the product that was on par with Google and Yahoo. One of the most famous new faces on the tech front, he stood to make much more than the billions he already had.

"Mr. X would like to purchase your bucking-bull business and Bullhaven Ranch."

Chance snorted as if that were the most ridiculous thing he had ever heard. And with good reason. Molly couldn't imagine the tech mogul running a rodeo enterprise. Even through proxy.

Chance's ex, who was lingering in the foreground, still appeared as if she wanted to be anywhere but there. Molly could hardly blame Delia. Coming here unannounced was a bad idea all around.

But Mr. X did not appear to know it. Grinning enthusiastically, he told Chance, "I've already purchased an alligator farm in Louisiana, a minor league hockey team in Minnesota and a salmon fishery in Washington State."

Babs explained, "He's aggressively adding to and diversifying his business portfolio. And he's willing to pay top dollar."

Chance folded his arms, biceps bulging beneath his denim work jacket. "How nice for him."

Molly winced at Chance's biting sarcasm. Glaring, he continued flatly, "My bucking-bull enterprise is not for sale."

Undaunted, Babs handed over a piece of paper. "You haven't seen his offer yet."

Not surprisingly, Chance refused to accept or even look at it.

"At any price," he reiterated flatly.

Delia took off her sunglasses and rubbed at her temples as if she had a migraine. She gave her mother a sanctioning look, then stepped forward slightly. "Just look at it, Chance. Please."

"You'll be pleasantly surprised," Mr. X predicted happily.

Chance turned to his ex. Something painfully intimate passed between them. Exhaling, he took the paper. Read the number, shook his head. "Not for a thousand times that."

Before anything else could be offered, a powder-blue Cadillac drove up behind them and parked in the drive. Chance's mother emerged, looking coiffed and pulled together, as always. "Isn't this a surprise!" Lucille Lockhart said.

More introductions of Mr. X followed. Babs explained why they were there. Lucille Lockhart nodded agreeably. "Let's all go down to the bunkhouse, where I'm living now," she said.

Mr. X consulted his watch. "Actually, I'm not sure we have time. I have to get back to Silicon Valley for a board meeting this evening, and I really want to tour Bullhaven Ranch before I go." The billionaire frowned, impatient. "We could only see so much from the air."

Delia gauged Chance with the wisdom of an old friend. "I don't think it's going to happen."

Her mother sent Delia a swift, censoring glance, which seemed to deflate the young woman's spirit, before flashing a triumphant smile Chance's way. "Never say never!" Babs murmured, linking arms with Lucille. "But you're right. We do have some catching up to do first…"

Or in other words, Molly thought, Babs was planning to use Lucille to pressure her son into cooperating.

At Lucille's cheerful urging, the trio climbed into her Cadillac while the chopper pilot appeared to get comfortable in the aircraft. In the distance, Wyatt could be seen herding the momma cow and her calf toward the safety of the barn.

Chance was already bolting for his pickup, which made Molly wonder if he and Delia were really over or not. Every feminine instinct she had told her there was definitely some fragile connection remaining. What, precisely, she didn't know. Nor did she understand why it mattered so much to her what that connection was based on. Anger? Lust? Regret? It wasn't as if she were jealous or anything…

"I have to go check on Bullhaven," Chance called to her. "Make sure their flyover inspection didn't cause any ruckus there."

Molly hurried to catch up with him. "What about going over the financials on the project as we planned?"

He made an offhand gesture. "I'm not doing it here with Babs and crew still in the vicinity."

She could hardly blame him for that. She resisted the urge to compassionately squeeze his arm. Stepping away, she asked, "Where then?"

His gaze skimmed her face. "My place. Unless you want to wait until later today or tomorrow?"

"No. It really needs to be done ASAP." She headed for her vehicle. "I'll follow you over."

By the time Molly got out of her SUV, Chance was already talking to his hired hands.

"Everything okay?" she asked when he joined her in the parking area adjacent to the garage.

"Yeah. Luckily, none of the bulls had been put out to pasture yet. So they were all in the barns when the helicopter flew over."

"That's good."

"No kidding." Chance compressed his lips and ran a hand through his thick chestnut hair. "If any of them had been spooked…"

Molly wouldn't want to be around to see the fallout from that. "So where did you want to go over the project statistics to date?" she asked. She'd seen a small office in the barn.

"Ranch house."

Molly nodded. That was her choice, too. It'd be more comfortable, and they were less likely to have interruptions from his hired hands.

Although she had viewed his home the day she'd driven over to talk to him about Braden, she had never been inside the sprawling log-cabin ranch house.

It was just as she would have expected. Big, open living area with a cathedral ceiling and massive fieldstone fireplace. Finished interior walls that were light enough to soak in the sun pouring in from the plentiful windows. Dark trim and wide-plank floors that matched the arching beams overhead. Leather furniture.

Chance strode to the kitchen, which bore a remarkable resemblance to the one he'd wanted to install for his mother in the Circle H.

He shrugged off his denim jacket and went to the sink. Rolled up his sleeves and lathered up to his elbows with gusto. "Can I get you something?" He rinsed his powerful forearms one at a time. "Coffee? *Stollen?*"

*How about you?* she thought, then pushed the forbidden notion away. Just because they'd spent a pleasurable afternoon together and kissed did not mean they needed to pursue the attraction.

A little flirtatious banter, however, wouldn't harm anything. "Really?" she teased, splaying a hand playfully across her chest. "You'd share with me?" 'Cause he sure hadn't been willing to share with his rancher brother.

He gave her an audacious wink. "You're cuter than Wyatt. Have better manners, too."

Her heartbeat picking up, Molly circled around to the other side of the island. Maybe banter wasn't such a good idea.

"Good to know."

He opened the well-stocked fridge, peered inside. "Juice?"

Since he was already pouring some for himself, she said, "Sure." Her throat was feeling a little dry. Their fingers brushed as he handed her the drink. Molly ignored the tingling sensation. "So..." She cleared her throat. "About you and Delia."

He cocked a brow. Turned, let his glance drift over her

lazily. "I was wondering how long it would take you to get around to that."

Promising herself that her interest was purely that of a friend, and in no way meant to protect her heart, Molly savored the sweet-tart apple juice. She tilted her head, and their glances clashed once again. He hadn't shaved that morning, and the stubble lining his jaw gave him a ruggedly handsome look. "How long ago were the two of you an item?"

*More to the point, is there any chance the two of you will ever reunite?* Because if there was one thing Molly did not want, it was to be involved in a love triangle again. He quaffed his juice in a single gulp, then poured some more.

"We ended our relationship three and a half years ago."

*Molly took her laptop computer out of her bag and set in on the counter.* "Delia's mother seems bitter about it."

Chance sent her a bemused look, retrieved his laptop and set it on the counter. Then he sat down next to her. "Babs is all about accruing more money."

"So?"

"She didn't like the fact that my parents decided too much money would be the ruin of their children, and instead bequeathed us each property in Laramie County, where my parents had both grown up."

Trying not to think how cozy it felt, being with him like this, Molly forced herself to recollect the facts she knew about the Lockharts. "Sage got a bakery and an apartment in town. Garrett was gifted a Victorian and an office building in Laramie that now houses the Lockhart Foundation headquarters and West Texas Warrior Assistance. You and your other two brothers received ranches. And your parents bought the Circle H, your mom's childhood home, for the two of them."

"Right. The rest of the wealth my parents had amassed over the years—and there was a lot of it since my dad started and ran a very successful hedge fund—went into the Lockhart Foundation."

"Which originally operated out of Dallas."

Proudly, Chance said, "The charity helped over one hundred nonprofits until roughly half of the funds were embezzled."

Molly let out a slow breath. "I remember that," she said sympathetically. "It was all over the news last summer."

The family had been trashed for weeks before eventually being vindicated by the embezzler's daughter, Adelaide Smythe.

Chance shifted in his seat, the hardness of his knee briefly brushing hers in the process. "Since then, it's become a much smaller organization, with my brother Garrett as CEO. Although my mother is building it up again with constant fundraising, the upcoming Open House being her largest effort yet."

Molly nodded. The two of them got up simultaneously to move their stools a little farther apart, so crowding wouldn't be an issue. She climbed back on her stool. "That's all very meaningful and noble. Why didn't Babs understand that?" Weren't the truly wealthy supposed to be into philanthropy, too?

For a moment, she thought Chance wouldn't answer. Then something shifted in his expression. As if there was a chink in his armor. Exhaling roughly, he finally explained, "Delia and I grew up together. We dated on and off for over ten years."

That was a very long time, Molly thought with a pang.

"And were about ready to get engaged when my parents made their decision and it became clear that I was not going to be the multimillionaire son-in-law Babs had expected."

"Still, it was Frank and Lucille's decision to make."

"Not in Babs Holcombe's view. She wanted me to convince

my parents they were making a mistake. And if I couldn't do that, then fight the terms of my father's will in court."

"You refused."

His jaw tautened. "Damn straight."

"Why?"

His broad shoulders flexing beneath the soft cotton chamois of his shirt, Chance sighed. "Because my dad was right. Too much money is more of a burden than a blessing."

*Not in my book*, Molly thought uncomfortably. *There could never be enough in the bank to make me feel safe.*

"And I wanted to be my own man and make my own fortune," Chance continued. "However much it turned out to be."

Their eyes met and held.

Noting the charcoal color of his shirt made his hazel eyes look more gray than green, Molly nodded. She valued her independence, too. Unable to help herself, she touched his arm gently. "I can understand and respect that."

Chance caught her hand before she could draw it away and turned it over. Tracing the lines on her palm with his fingertip, he exhaled, admitting, "Initially, Delia did, too. Until her mother convinced her that she would never be able to be happy with a struggling cowboy on what was then a broken-down ranch." He dropped her hand and sat back. "So Delia ended it, and that was that."

Molly felt bereft from the absence of his touch. She kept her eyes on Chance. "Except now Delia and Babs are back."

He got to his feet and walked over to the coffeemaker. "Only because Delia is part of the business sales and acquisitions company her mom owns. And Mr. X is a pretty big fish."

And recently single, if the gossip mags were correct about him getting dumped by a famous Hollywood actress who wanted a "less nerdy" beau.

Molly watched Chance put a paper liner in the filter. "Do

you think Babs is trying to matchmake Mr. X and Delia?" Otherwise, what reason could there have been to have the recalcitrant Delia along? She certainly hadn't been actively trying to sell anything.

"A billionaire and her only child?" Chance opened a bag of dark roast coffee. "Oh yeah."

Restless, Molly got up and walked over to the windows overlooking his backyard. Neatly fenced pastures as far as the eye could see. "Then why bring Mr. X here, if that was Babs's goal? Surely there are other ranches they could have shown Mr. X." *Without running into you*, Molly thought a little jealously.

"True. But…" Chance added cold water to the machine. "Bullhaven is the best bucking-bull outfit in Texas."

Molly folded her arms in front of her, recalling the way Chance and Delia had looked at each other at the end of the meeting. There'd been a lot of residual emotion between them. Not attraction, but something she couldn't quite put her finger on. "It seems like there's more to it than that," she insisted stubbornly. Wishing, once again, that he would be more forthcoming.

Chance squinted. "Like what?"

Molly shrugged as the tantalizing fragrance of fresh-brewed coffee filled the room. "Maybe Babs wants to use your studly presence."

The rich sound of Chance's laughter filled the room. "Studly?"

Molly flushed. "You know what I mean."

"Yeah." He waggled his brows suggestively, ambling closer. Cupping her shoulders lightly, he gazed down at her. "And I'd like to know more."

The last thing Molly wanted was to find herself in the midst of a resurrected love affair. She'd made enough of a mess of things falling for Braden's daddy without first making damn certain Aaron wasn't romantically entangled with anyone else. No way was she doing that again.

She drew a breath. "Is it possible that Babs is trying to use your past relationship with Delia to make Mr. X jealous and realize if he doesn't act—and soon—in pursuing her gorgeous single daughter that someone else, like you, will?" And if that were the case, was it possible something could be reignited between Chance and Delia? Even if only for a short time?

Chance cut off her speculating with a resolute shake of his head. "Not going to happen."

Molly propped her hands on her hips, trying not to notice how masculine and undeniably sexy Chance looked in the sunlight pouring in through the abundant windows.

Unexpected emotion simmering inside her, she pressed the issue. "You're saying there is no reason for Mr. X to be worried about you and Delia? You don't feel anything for her?"

Chance's gaze sifted leisurely over her face, lingering on her lips, before returning slowly to her eyes. "I feel pity."

Now they were getting somewhere, Molly thought, still feeling as if she were pulling oil out of shale. Tingling all over, for no reason she could figure, she demanded, "Why?"

"She's never been able to stand up to her overbearing mother."

And there it was, the trademark chivalry of the Lockhart men. The same chivalry that had brought Chance to her and Braden's rescue at the cafeteria on Thanksgiving Day.

"You wanted to help Delia do that when you were together?" she guessed.

"Initially, yes." Looking as if he wouldn't want to be anywhere else, he lounged against the kitchen island, watching as Molly went back to their "temporary work area" and pow-

ered up her computer. "But eventually I realized Delia had
to do that on her own."

Too restless to sit down again just yet, Molly curved her
hands around the back of the counter stool, and asked, "What
does Delia feel for you?"

Lifting one broad shoulder in an indolent shrug, he came
toward her. "No clue."

"You don't want to know?"

She caught her breath as he neared. He shook his head,
serious now; whatever initial irritation he'd had at seeing his
ex again had faded completely. Now he was focused solely
on Molly. And that focus was causing all sorts of chaos deep
inside her. "What Delia and I had is over," he informed her,
his voice a sexy rumble.

Molly wanted to believe that, just like she wanted to be
rich. In money and family and love. "But if…"

"Molly." His impatience mounting, Chance gave her a look
of pure masculine need. "There's only one woman I'm interested in," he told her, taking her in his arms and pulling her
flush against him. "And that woman is you."

# Chapter 5

Chance could see Molly didn't believe him. So he did the only thing he could to convince her. He lowered his head and, ignoring her soft gasp, covered her lips with his.

She resisted at first, splaying her hands across his chest, but his instinct was to deepen the kiss.

Claim her as his. The need to protect her triumphed. He lifted his head enough to look into her eyes. The mixture of desire and need told him all he wanted to know.

The two of them had been destined for this moment, from the first time they'd laid eyes on each other two years before. All the quarrelling and mistrust had been nothing but a prelude to what was turning out to be a magical Christmas season.

"Let me love you," he whispered, kissing her cheek, her temple, the sensitive spot just beneath her ear. His body hardened as he felt her quiver.

She lifted her face to his, then looked at him with all the yearning he had imagined she felt and knew he experienced. Then kissed him back with a sensuality that further rocked his world. Her hands slid around his waist, and she pressed

intimately against him. Her moan of compliance was as blissful as her touch. "Only if you promise it'll be a no-strings-
attached kind of thing."

Was she that kind of woman? He didn't think so, even as
her soft, pliant body surrendered against his. But if she needed
to believe so… "Whatever you want, darlin'," he promised,
heartbeat quickening. "Starting now."

He swept her up into his arms and carried her down the
hall to his bedroom. He laid her gently on the rumpled sheets,
then followed her down. The kissing resumed, deep and evoc-
ative, every fantasy he'd had fulfilled. Molly moaned low in
her throat. His body hardened all the more.

He pushed the edges of her sweater up, drew it over her
head and reached behind her to unfasten her bra. Her nipples
peaked into rosy buds of arousal. Cupping the silky globes
with both hands, he drew first one, then the other into his
mouth. She put her hands in his hair, holding him close, and
arched against him as if she never wanted to let him go.

Loving her response, he lifted his head. Unbuttoned the
clasp of her belt. Feeling intoxicated by her nearness, by
the fact she was finally…*finally*…about to be his, he asked,
"More?"

Cheeks and eyes flushed with excitement, she smiled.
"Even better, cowboy. Free rein."

"Exactly what I wanted to hear." Pure male satisfaction
pouring through him, he paused to tug off her boots, then
drew the zipper down and eased her jeans down her long,
lissome legs.

Her bikini panties were made of silk. "Nice…" He slid his
fingers beneath, finding the soft, damp nest. "But not as nice
as this," he said, kissing her through the cloth until her back
arched off the bed.

"Nice doesn't begin to cover this." Molly whimpered, uttering a strangled sigh that drove him wild.

The truth was, she thought, tangling her hands in his hair and hauling him close, she had never felt so cherished and adored. So completely overpowered by what was happening between them. And they had barely gotten started.

"But we're getting ahead of ourselves here," she warned, wiggling free. If they were doing this, it was as equals. "I haven't done my part yet." Sitting up, clad only in her panties, she swung one leg over him. Once fully astride him, she shimmied down the hard, masculine length of him, kissing everywhere she passed, admiring his broad shoulders and muscular chest.

He was so strong and virile. And willing to let her take them wherever she wanted, however she wanted. Grinning, she paused to kiss the burgeoning arousal beneath his jeans, through the cloth, then moved lower still. Taking off his boots. Moving back up to unbutton his shirt. He lay quietly, a complicit smile on his handsome face. Catching her hand, he kissed the back of it. "I could get used to this."

So could she.

Not sure she should tell him that—at least not yet anyway—she opened the buttons on his shirt, drew it, and the T-shirt beneath, off. His chest was as sleek and powerfully muscled as she had imagined, with a sexy mat of chestnut hair that spread across his nipples before arrowing down past his navel to the waistband of his jeans. Her fingers followed the path, eliciting a few groans from him and a bigger thrill for her. Wow, did she ever desire him. Every inch of her was throbbing, pounding with the need to be touched, loved, held. But first...

"I've got to see where this leads." Sating her curiosity, she unbuttoned his belt. Undid his fly.

"Trouble," he muttered.

"Then it's my kind of trouble," she purred, slipping her hands inside his pants and finding the hot, hard length of him.

Their reaction was simultaneous. He groaned. She trembled with pleasure.

Eager to explore him more fully, she divested him of his jeans and boxer briefs. Her hands moved across his abdomen. Down his thighs. Upward. Caught up in something too primal to fight, she cupped him again, with both hands, and then bent to kiss the hot, satiny length of him.

He groaned again, on the verge of losing control.

"I think it's time you found a little trouble of your own," he murmured, shifting her onto her back. The next thing she knew, he had taken complete control and whisked her panties off. Hands spreading her thighs wide, he found her with lips and mouth and hands. Exploring. Adoring. Sensation spiraled through her, unlike anything she had ever known. She gripped his shoulders, urging him upward. "Now," she gasped. "Before I…"

"Patience…" he said roughly, sweeping past the last of her barriers. She arched again as he found the most sensitive part of her and brought her to the very edge. She quivered as his hands took on an even more intimate quest. She was close. Too close. Fisting her hands in his hair, she panted. "I want you inside me when…" *Oh heavens!* "…we…"

"You'll have that, too," he promised as a wave of sensation started deep inside her. With a growl of satisfaction, he pulled her toward him. And just that suddenly, her release came, her entire body melting in boneless pleasure.

He kissed her navel, still stroking the insides of her thighs. "Worth it?"

No fibbing about that when she was still shuddering with the aftershocks of a 6.0 quake. "Yes." She gasped as he palmed her breasts and took her taut, aching nipple into her mouth. "Heck, yes..."

Grinning, he slid upward and once again captured her mouth with his. "I aim to please."

*No kidding*, she thought, opening her mouth to the commanding pressure of his.

They kissed as he stretched out over top of her and brought his whole body into contact with hers. She could feel his erection pressing against her, hot and urgent. Desire welled inside her. "Now?" he rasped, pausing only long enough to roll on a condom, then kissing her in a way that was so wild and reckless it stole her heart.

"Now," she gasped, knowing she would hold on to this moment forever.

Hands beneath her hips, he spread her thighs and slid inside, penetrating deep. She couldn't get enough of the taste and feel of him, the confident and soulful way he merged his body with hers, the seductive, indomitable manner in which he possessed her.

To her delight, he seemed just as hungry for her. Intent on taking his time. Drawing out the unimaginable pleasure. He kissed her with the same insistent, tantalizing rhythm, letting her know how much she deserved, how much he wanted her to have. And then she was wrapping her legs around his waist, drawing him deeper, exploding with emotion, awash in sensation. With a low groan of pleasure, he followed. And together, at last, they found blissful release.

Chance rolled onto his back, taking Molly with him. A mixture of fierce physical satisfaction and raw emotion washed over him as he savored their closeness. He pressed his face into her hair, drawing in her scent, her softness, while Molly snuggled closer. Still wrapped in his arms, Molly tucked her face against his neck, her eyes closed, body still shuddering, her breath slowing.

Finally, she drew a deep breath, her body still pliant and molded tentatively against his. Lifting her head, she smiled and opened her eyes. "Well. Christmas sure came early," she drawled.

He laughed, relieved that the regret he had half feared he would see was nowhere in sight. "It sure did," he returned softly. He couldn't wait for the next round.

The picture of sated elegance, Molly rose, wrapping the sheet around her midriff. She ran a hand through the mussed layers of her hair, then bent to gather up her clothes, giving him a fine view of her curvaceous backside in the process. "It's too bad it can't happen again."

Whoa. He had definitely missed something here. "What do you mean?"

Looking as if she suddenly found his bedroom too intimate for comfort, she disappeared into the adjacent bath to dress. When she walked back out, she had a too-serene-to-be-believed expression on her face. "Once is a fling." She sat down on the edge of the bed to put on her socks and boots. "Any more than that is complicated." She paused to give him a meaningful glance as he got dressed, too. "And my life is complicated enough right now."

He could see that she wanted him to argue with her.

Persuade her otherwise.

Only she wasn't about to let him convince her. At least not in this moment. "You're right," he fibbed, putting on his boots, too.

She stood. "I am?" Skepticism rang in her sweetly pitched voice.

Aware two could play at this game—and that's all it was,

a game—he shrugged. "You're moving to Dallas." *Unless I can work a holiday miracle.*

She brushed by him in a drift of the lavender perfume she favored. "Exactly."

He fell into step behind her. "It's a phenomenally busy time of year."

She shot him a look over her shoulder as she glided down the hall with womanly ease. "And the holidays are always ridiculously sentimental."

*Which makes Christmastime all the more perfect for finding someone*, he thought. Aware she likely did not want to hear that, either, he watched her rummage through her shoulder bag. "And you have a son to care for."

Molly plucked out a lip balm and smoothed some over her kiss-swollen lips. Finished, she pressed her lips together to set the soft gloss. Dropping it back into her purse, she brought out a brush and began running it through her soft auburn curls. Although she looked much neater now, she still glowed from the inside out. Anyone who knew her, seeing her, would know she had just made love.

With him.

And though Chance liked his privacy, he wouldn't mind anyone knowing that Molly was spoken for.

"Not to mention," Molly continued, oblivious to the serious nature of his thoughts, "a problem regarding Santa and a trio of bulls to solve."

He studied the color in her high, sculpted cheeks. Had she ever looked more beautiful than she did at this moment? "I have that covered."

"You think you do," she said skeptically.

Grinning, he closed the distance between them. It was all he could do not to take her in his arms again. "I know I do," he corrected her arrogantly.

Molly danced away. "We'll see about that."

Determined to make this the best Christmas she and Braden had ever had, he chuckled. "You bet we will."

Molly took a calculator out of her bag. "In the meantime, we still have to reconcile the projected numbers on the Circle H renovation project with the actual costs thus far."

Another thing they had in common. They both took the success of their businesses very seriously.

Chance nodded. "Let's get to it."

An hour and a few cups of coffee later, Molly sat back in her chair and looked at Chance with amazement. "We've not only managed to stay exactly on schedule, we're fifteen percent under where we figured we would be in terms of projected labor costs."

He shared her pride in a well-managed project. Something that only happened when everyone came together as a team. "We work well together."

They did, indeed.

But apparently wary of reading too much into it, she said, "If this holds through the rest of the project, how would you feel about passing the extra revenue on to members of the crew in terms of an additional year-end bonus?"

Once again, the two of them were completely in synch. A miracle in itself, considering how much they had argued about literally everything a few short weeks before.

Chance smiled his approval. "I think it would make for a merry Christmas for everyone. And let's face it—as diligently as our crews have worked, they deserve it."

Molly smiled back and continued surveying him curiously. She moved her counter stool ninety degrees so she faced him. "Can I ask you something?"

He pivoted his seat, too. "Sure."

"How come you're still wearing two hats professionally?"

He nudged her knee with his. "You do the same thing."

She wrinkled her nose and took another sip of coffee. "Interior design and general contracting sort of go hand in hand. Bucking bulls and remodeling do not."

He reached for the thermal carafe. She covered the top of her mug, signaling she'd had enough caffeine, so he emptied what little was left into his. "Actually, they do. If I hadn't had the skills, I wouldn't have been able to remodel my ranch house or build the barns at anywhere near the cost I paid."

Molly powered off her laptop. Seeming as reluctant to leave as he was to see her go, she raked her teeth over her lush lower lip. "How did you get into both businesses anyway?"

"Construction was my first job out of high school," he replied, shutting down the accounting program on his computer.

Molly smiled at his screen saver—a photo of the retired Mistletoe being inducted into the Bucking Bull Hall of Fame. Their gazes met. "You didn't go to college at all?"

"My parents made me apply, and I was accepted, but I knew it wasn't going to work. I'm just not the kind of guy who's happy sitting at a desk."

Her eyes softened with compassion. "I'm guessing Lucille wasn't happy about that."

*Talk about an understatement.* "She and my dad both went through the roof. They also cut off my allowance and took away my car, thinking that would shake some sense into me."

"It didn't."

"I got a construction job and learned the trade that way for a couple of years. When I tired of doing that in the Texas heat, I went to Wyoming for a while. Lived in the high country and got a job on a ranch as a hired hand."

Her intense interest made it easy to confide in her. "That's where I learned cattle management and the rodeo stock business. And started saving up for my own ranch. But I also knew—" he stood and carried his coffee mug to the sink "—that goal wasn't going to be achieved in this lifetime unless I upped my income."

She grinned and joined him at the dishwasher. "Sounds familiar." She slid her cup in next to his.

They straightened, bumping shoulders in the process.

Aware all over again just how much he had enjoyed holding her in his arms, he let his gaze rove her face. "We do have ambitious natures in common."

"Sorry. I derailed you."

He tugged on an errant lock of her silky auburn hair. "You constantly derail me." *In a good way.*

It was her turn to laugh. "Go on."

He suspected he had better if they didn't want to end up in bed again.

"I want to hear how you came to be so good at ranching and building."

With effort, he turned his attention back to the conversation at hand. "Mostly by working both jobs simultaneously. I worked out a deal with my employer to help him with some home renovations, in addition to my usual duties as hired hand. I started saving every penny I could, took some business courses online and got my general contracting license." He cleared his throat. "I was about to buy a place in Wyoming and open my own general contracting firm when my dad got sick. So I came back to Texas, and my parents gifted me with Bullhaven. Then I moved to Laramie, and the rest, as they say, is history."

"Are you ever going to give up being a general contractor?"

"No. I like doing both. Plus, it gives me the cash flow to keep expanding my bucking-bull business without going into debt or taking on partners there."

He paused, happy to see she didn't think it odd—or unnecessary—to want to keep honing both skills. "What about you? Would you ever give up being your own general contractor on jobs just to concentrate on design?"

Her lips twisted thoughtfully. "In a perfect world, maybe. But I probably won't because having my own crew ensures the quality I want on every project."

"And control is important to you," Chance guessed.

Molly nodded. Returning to the island, she packed up her computer and then grabbed her shoulder bag. "Very."

"Cowboy Chance coming? See me?" Braden asked hours later.

Seeing her son's excitement, Molly couldn't help but wonder if she was doing the right thing. He had no father in his life; Chance could easily fill the bill. If things were different...but they weren't.

She was moving.

Chance was staying here.

Hence, it was best to keep them in the strictly friends category, even if Braden—and the most womanly part of her—clamored for more.

"Doorbell, Mommy!" her son shouted, racing toward the door. Molly expected her heart to give a little leap when she saw the man on the other side of the portal. It seemed to do that a lot these days regarding Chance. However, she didn't expect the sexy cowboy to be carrying a rectangular folding table and three chairs. "Are we playing bridge?"

"Cute. Want to hold the door for me?"

"Whatcha doing, Cowboy Chance?" Braden planted both hands on his little hips.

Chance sidled past, being careful not to bump his cargo into anything or anyone. "I'm bringing in a present for you and your mommy."

"I like presents!" Braden declared.

Chance winked. "I thought that might be the case, buddy."

Unsure how this was related to their baby bull problem, Molly gave their guest a quizzical look.

"Patience," Chance said, setting up the table in a corner of the living room, well away from the tree.

He'd said the same thing when making love to her earlier that day. She flushed at the memory, all her girlie parts tingling.

His gaze raked her lazily from head to toe. With a tip of his hat, he said, "I'll be right back."

Molly and Braden stood at the door, watching, while he went to his truck. He returned, this time with a piece of plywood covered in sturdy white fabric, with cotton balls glued along the edges, and a shopping bag.

"Now I'm really curious," Molly admitted.

"Me, too!" Braden jumped up and down.

Carefully, Chance set the piece of cardboard onto the portable table. Molly wasn't surprised to see it fit precisely. He reached into the bag and pulled out a small colorful building. "Guess what this is," he asked Braden.

Molly read the letters on the front. "Santa's Workshop?"

"Right!"

"And some elves." Chance handed her son several figurines.

Braden set them down on the "snow"-covered board next to the building. Then ran off. "I get Rudolph and sleigh!"

The rest of the bag was empty.

Molly blinked in surprise. "No Santa?"

"Patience..."

Her body reacted. Again.

Flushing, she whispered, "You have to stop saying that."

"How come?"

She admonished him with a lift of her brow. "You know why," she breathed.

Mischief radiated from every fiber of his being.

Braden returned, the two toys Chance had already given him clutched in his hands. He climbed on the chair and set the sleigh and Rudolph next to Santa's Workshop. "I like this!"

Chance patted her son on the shoulder. "I'm glad you do, buckaroo."

Molly propped her hands on her hips while her son began to play with the four toys on the snow board. "I take it there is a method to this madness?"

Chance folded his arms across his chest. "There is. But for the next phase, it will require the two of you coming out to Bullhaven tomorrow morning."

Being alone with him, even with a small chaperone along, always seemed like a dangerous proposition to her way too vulnerable heart. She cleared her throat and lifted her chin. "Really?"

The corners of his eyes crinkled. "Really," he said just as firmly.

She stared into the hazel depths. "To do what?"

"See where and how real bulls live."

But was that all, Molly wondered, studying the sparkling invitation in Chance's smile, that he wanted her to see?

# *Chapter 6*

Chance wasn't sure Molly would take him up on his invitation, even before she gave him a halfhearted, "We'll have to see how things go tomorrow morning… Braden can be pretty tired by the end of the week."

He knew that they'd made love too soon. And because of that she was every bit as determined to keep him at arm's length as he was to get her back in his arms. He also knew that she and her son were a package deal.

Convincing her that condition was more than okay with him, however, was going to be tough. Fortunately, he knew, even if Molly didn't yet, that he was more than up to the task. And he was ready to prove to her they could have something more than dissension between them. She'd finally accepted his offer. Late Saturday morning, she drove up the lane.

He walked out to greet them. "Glad you both could make it."

"Braden really wanted to come and see all of your bulls." She emerged from the SUV and sent him a meaningful glance as she opened the rear passenger door. "And I got to thinking, maybe you're right, that it's a good idea for Braden to learn where and how real live bulls live."

He was glad she understood at least this much of his plan. "That they're only babies, pastured with their momma for a very short time."

She nodded.

"Hey there, pardner," Chance said, after Molly got Braden out of his safety seat. He held up his palm for a high five.

Grinning, Braden fit his small palm to Chance's.

"You're just in time to see some bucking bulls get loaded onto a truck."

Behind them, an 18-wheeler headed up the lane.

Molly lifted her son into her arms.

The three of them watched as the truck parked just outside the barn. The driver—a husky, dark-haired cowboy in his early fifties—got out. "Three of our bulls are going to compete in a rodeo in Arizona next weekend," Chance explained.

Molly blinked. "They're leaving now?"

Noticing Braden was a little heavy for Molly, Chance put out his hands. Grinning, Braden slid into his grip. Amazed at how right it felt to hold the little tyke in his arms, Chance explained, "Bucking bulls can only travel ten hours in one day before needing to be pastured at night at one of the rest ranches along the way. And then they need an equivalent time to recover from the rigors of travel once they do arrive at the rodeo site."

Chance's hired hand Billy walked the first bull out of the barn. The sleek Black Angus had a name tag on his ear and, as always, was perfectly content to be led into the divided compartment readied just for him on the truck. "That's Kringle," Chance explained.

A second bull was walked out by Pete with equal calm.

"And Saint Nick," Chance said, grinning as the third bull was walked out.

"And last but not least, Dasher," Chance concluded as Braden waved merrily at the bulls.

Amused, Billy and Pete both waved back at Molly's son.

She turned toward him in a drift of orchid perfume. Was that new? If it was, he had to admit he really liked it.

"Are all your bulls named in response to the Christmas holiday?" Molly asked wryly.

His gaze trailed over the hollow of her throat, past her lips, to her pretty amber eyes. "You might say we have a theme going."

She shook her head, clearly not sure what to make of that.

Before she could say anything more, a ruckus sounded in the pasture. Noticing what was going on at the semitrailer, Mistletoe had crossed the grassy terrain and come to the fence. Looking straight at the truck, he lifted his head and let out another loud bellow.

Molly moved in closer to Chance and put a hand up to protect her son. "What's going on?" she whispered nervously.

Chance laughed. Holding Braden in one arm, he wrapped his other around Molly's shoulders. "Mistletoe may be retired, but he's still a prime athlete and he still wants to compete. He understands getting on a semitruck means riding to a rodeo, and he wants to go, too."

Braden looked at Chance, listened to Mistletoe and then let out a loud bellow of his own. "Mist'toe," the little boy repeated, then again imitated the loud bellowing sound.

Chance and Molly both laughed.

Mistletoe looked in their direction and bellowed again.

Chance shook his head. "What can I say?" he joked as Molly, understanding they were in no danger, relaxed beside him. "Once a competitor, always a competitor."

The driver came over. Last-minute instructions were given. Papers signed. They all waved as the truck headed back down the lane. Mistletoe remained against the fence in disappointment.

"You want to know what might make Mistletoe Jr.'s daddy feel better?" Chance murmured.

"What?" Braden asked eagerly.

"A bath."

Molly stared at Chance. This morning was turning out to be quite a surprise. She had worried a little he had just invited them out to try to hit on her. However, she could see, given how much was going on at the ranch, she needn't have worried.

There was a lot more to him than an ability to make mind-blowing love and seduce her into tearing down boundaries and spending time with him. He was good with kids. Especially Braden. Kind. And fun to be around.

Had she not been moving 150 miles away, he might have been the perfect man.

If he hadn't also grown up wealthy, that was.

Aware Chance was grinning at her, as if wondering where her thoughts had drifted, she blinked herself back to ranching activity. "Bulls take baths?"

"Well, more like a shower, but yeah, they do."

Braden clapped his hands in excitement. "Hurrah!"

"This we've got to see," Molly agreed.

While she took charge of her son again, Chance grabbed a halter from the barn and went to get Mistletoe. As he brought his prize bucking bull back across the yard, he pointed toward a building on the other side of the complex of barns and training facilities.

At the end of the big bull barn was a cement-floored paddock that was the size of a drive-through car wash. The sides were open, but there was a stop gate along the back. The big black bull stepped calmly up to it. Whistling merrily, Chance tied Mistletoe to the steel gate, then went to get two folding chairs for Molly and Braden and a box full of grooming gear.

He got them situated on the other side of the stop gate, far enough away so there appeared to be no risk of them getting wet, then walked around to grab the long hose hanging on the wall.

"Do all bulls get washed?" Molly asked.

Chance put down the hose long enough to remove his denim jacket. He tossed it on the grass next to Molly, then pushed up the sleeves on his light gray thermal-knit T-shirt. "All of mine do."

Molly's mouth went dry as she watched the powerful muscles of his arms and back flex beneath the clinging cloth. Remembering how all that satiny skin and sinew had felt the day before, beneath her eagerly questing hands, she asked, "How often?"

"Once or twice a month."

"Do you always do it yourself?" she asked.

"Pete and Billy help out." He turned on the water. "But I usually wash Mistletoe myself," he admitted.

It was clear, Molly thought, from the way Chance looked at the bucking bull that Mistletoe was as much a beloved family pet as impressive revenue source. Which went to show yet again how loving and gentle a man Chance was, deep down.

He wet the bull from end to end, then turned a dial on the handle of the hose and directed a sudsy stream into the hide. It seemed to work on the massive animal like a massage.

"Mis'toe likes it!" Braden exclaimed, clapping his hands again.

Chance chuckled and followed the soaping with a thorough rinse. "You're right. He does."

Molly leaned back in her chair as the fragrant smell of the soap filled the air. "When and where did you get him?"

Smiling fondly, Chance turned off the water and plucked a big brush from the bag of grooming tools. "My first Christmas in Wyoming. I was working at a cattle ranch, and one of the pregnant cows went missing. She'd gone off to give birth, got caught in a blizzard that killed her." Chance stopped brushing long enough to pat Mistletoe's head. "This fella was barely breathing when I found him."

Molly could only imagine how horrifying that had to have been. "But you revived him."

Chance sobered. His low tone took on a sentimental rasp. "Against all odds. Even the vet said he'd never make it, but if he did, my boss said, I could have him."

And Chance loved a challenge.

"So..." He got out the clippers and trimmed some of the stray hairs around the bull's face and tail. "I spent the next few months bottle-feeding Mistletoe in the barn, seeing he stayed warm and healthy, and the rest, as they say, is history."

Finished, Chance dried off his hands with a towel. Pride radiating in his handsome face, he retrieved his phone and showed them more photos of the two of them in the barn. Apparently, Mistletoe wasn't the only one who'd been young and cute, Molly noted with an appreciative smile.

Chance turned on a blower to move the air through Mistletoe's sleek black coat.

"So now," Molly gathered, holding on to Chance's phone for him, "Mistletoe is the oldest of your bucking bulls."

"As well as a national champion and the sire to every other bucking bull I own." Chance patted Mistletoe fondly. The bull let out a low sound that seemed like the cattle version of a purr of pleasure.

Molly flushed, recalling when she had done the same beneath the caress of those large, talented hands.

"Mis'toe likes baths!" Braden noted yet again.

"Do you think he would fit in the bathtub at your house?" Chance asked Braden with exaggerated curiosity.

Molly saw where the handsome cowboy was going with this. It was all she could do not to applaud his subtlety.

Braden shook his head defiantly. "Mis'toe too big!" he declared.

"I guess you're right." Chance pretended to consider the matter. "I guess he'll have to continue taking his baths here with all the other bulls."

Braden spread his arms wide as inspiration hit. "Mommy build big tub!" He aimed a thumb at his small chest. "My house."

Molly had to hand it to her son. He had a talent for solving problems.

Chance squinted at Molly. "The perks of having a contractor for a parent?"

"Or a too-bright-and-imaginative-for-his-own-good offspring?"

In any case, they had yet to solve the quandary of how to convince Braden he couldn't possibly have a real live bull for Christmas.

Pete suddenly appeared. "Boss? There's someone here who wants a word with you."

Chance responded to the interruption with a lift of his palm. "Tell them I'll call them back later."

The hired hand winced. "Ah. I don't think she's going to…"

*She?* Molly wondered.

*Please tell me I haven't made the same dumb mistake I*

*made with Aaron, that Chance is not involved with some-one else, too.*

"Chance?" Delia rounded the side of the bull wash. She whipped off her sunglasses. "We have to talk!"

Of all the people Molly had expected to see that morning, Chance's ex was not one of them. She started to rise.

Chance waved Molly back down. Then he informed Delia curtly, "Tell Babs the answer is no."

Delia put her sunglasses on top of her long silvery-blond hair. Once again, she was dressed all in black. "You don't even know what my mother said."

He nodded at the folder in her hand. "Is that an offer?"

Delia straightened, indignant. "Yes."

He handed the grooming box off to Pete. "Then we've got nothing to discuss."

The hired hand exited quickly.

Ignoring Molly and Braden, Delia moved imploringly to-ward Chance. She looked her former lover right in the eye. "Look, I'm not into chasing lost causes any more than you are, Chance. You know that better than anyone! But Mr. X authorized our firm to purchase your bucking-bull business for *well over* the assessed value."

Her words fell on deaf ears.

Chance unhooked the lead and began steering Mistletoe out of the washing area. "Maybe you and Babs should try show-ing him some ranches and rodeo operations that *are* for sale?"

Delia stomped closer to Chance, staying well clear of the bull. "He wants *yours*."

His jaw set. "Then Mr. X is going to be disappointed," he predicted grimly.

"At least think it over." Delia pushed the folder at him. When he refused to take it, she shoved it into Molly's hands before turning and sauntering back to the waiting limo.

"What do you want me to do with this?" Molly asked Chance when the newly tranquil Mistletoe had been put back out to pasture and they'd retreated to the house for the casual lunch Chance had promised.

She couldn't help but notice that although there had been no yuletide decorations of any sort the day before, now he had a tree up and a wreath on the front door.

Had he done all that for her and Braden?

Or just simply because it was time?

There was no clue in the impassive set of his features.

Chance looked at the sleek black-and-white Holcombe Business Sales & Acquisitions folder and nodded in the direction of his desk. "There's a shredder over there."

Molly's jaw dropped. "Seriously?"

Nodding, Chance brought out what looked to be a brand-new box of plastic building blocks for Braden and set them in the middle of the living room floor. Together, they opened it and dumped them out. He patted her son's shoulder. "Have at it, buddy."

Braden settled in the midst of the toys, beaming up at their host. "Thanks, Cowboy Chance!"

"No problem." He rose to his feet.

Folder still in hand, Molly followed him over to his workstation. Keeping her voice low and tranquil, she looked him in the eye. "You're not even going to look at it?"

"No need." Handsome jaw set, he took it from her, walked over and fed it to the shredder, cover and all. He closed the distance between them and took her hands in his. "Why does this surprise you?"

Her pulse raced. "I don't know. I figured you'd at least be curious." She would have been in his place.

He dropped his grip on her and walked into the kitchen. "I know what Bullhaven means to me."

As always, his ultramasculine presence made her feel intensely aware of him. "There's no price for it?" she guessed, wishing he hadn't been quite so quick to let her go.

"No." He went to the fridge and brought out a package of hot dogs, buns and all the fixings. "I gather you don't feel the same way about your own home and business?"

Molly sat at the island, watching as he turned the flame on under the stove-top grill. "I love the home I grew up in. I'm going to do everything I can to keep it as a retreat. My work will go with me."

Something flickered in his expression, then disappeared. "Any of your employees planning to move to Dallas with you?" he asked her casually.

Molly cast a look at her son, who was now happily stacking blocks. "No. But I've made calls on everyone's behalf. They'll all have jobs in the area after I leave."

He turned, his expression deliberately closed and uncommunicative. "You didn't call me."

She flushed under his continued scrutiny. "We weren't on friendly terms last fall."

"Ah." He moved toward her, throwing her off guard once again. He stopped just short of her. "Are we now?"

"More so…"

The wicked gleam in his eyes said if they were alone, he would have kissed her. And she would have let him. Luckily for them both, a faint chime sounded. Averting her gaze from his, she pulled out her phone.

"Expecting something?"

Molly drew a deep breath, glad to have someone to confide in about this. "A couple of things, actually. You know that special T-R-A-I-N set I had my eye on? It's all sold out. I can't find it anywhere online. And I've set up alerts."

He picked up a pair of tongs. "A knockoff maybe?"

"The reviews on those aren't nearly as good." Molly sighed.

The hot dogs sizzled as they hit the grill, quickly filling the room with the delicious smell of roasting meat.

He wrapped the buns in foil and set them in the oven to warm. "What else?"

This was a little harder to talk about. But she did need to vent. Molly rested her hand on her chin. "I was supposed to hear from Elspeth Pyle, the headmistress at Worthington Academy regarding an appointment for Braden. They're interviewing and testing prospective students and their parents next week. But so far there's nothing on my phone, or email, although something could still come via the postman this afternoon."

"You thought he was going to get one?" Chance asked sympathetically.

Molly sighed again. She knew she was reaching for the stars on her son's behalf, but she had really hoped. "Alumni recommendations are supposed to carry weight in the admission process, so the letter Sage wrote on his behalf should have helped."

His gaze narrowed. "Is that really what you want for him?"

Why wouldn't she? Molly ignored his clear disapproval. "The school is one of the very best in Dallas."

"Mommy?" Braden joined them and tugged on the hem of her fleece. "Hungry."

"Well, that's a good thing." Chance winked. "Because lunch is ready!"

Half an hour later, replete with hot dogs, chips, clementine slices and ice cream, Braden could not stop yawning. "I better get him home for an N-A-P," Molly said, leery of wearing out their welcome. Though, to his credit, Chance had been a very good sport about keeping up a nonstop conversation with her loquacious three-year-old son.

"No. Nap." Braden yawned again.

Molly figured he'd last maybe five minutes on the drive home before conking out. "You can look out the window then and wave at all the cows and horses."

Braden cheered. "'Kay!"

Molly found her son's jacket. "Can you say thank you to Cowboy Chance?"

Braden hugged Chance's knees. "Thank you."

Chance ruffled the auburn hair on the top of his head. Then he picked him up in his arms for a face-to-face goodbye. "You're welcome, buddy."

Molly accepted Chance's offer to carry her son out to her SUV. Though she knew it was past time, she really hated to leave.

She paused, her hand on the driver-side door. Then she said, "Seeing the bulls was fun, even if it didn't yet have the desired effect."

He looked down at her, his chestnut hair glinting in the sunshine. "It's early," he told her with his usual confidence. "Speaking of which," his eyes softened even more, "would it be too much for me to bring by another installment of the 'solution' this evening?"

Molly's heart leapt at the thought of seeing Chance again so soon. She also knew the faster they were able to adjust her son's expectations regarding the bulls, the better. Besides, it was Saturday. "Not at all. But come ready to work," she cautioned with a smile, soaking in his charismatic presence.

As long as they kept it casual and had a little chaperone, their relationship would stay safely in the just-friends zone. Wouldn't it?

Molly smiled. "We're baking Christmas cookies this evening, too."

# Chapter 7

Braden answered the door at seven that evening, Molly by his side. Chance looked at the smiling penguin wearing a Santa hat on the front of Braden's knit shirt and the red-and-white stripes on his pants. "Nice pajamas."

Braden took in the second plywood board, covered in white, and folding table Chance carried in his right hand, the shopping bag of goodies in his left. His eyes widened in delight. "Mommy, look!" he shouted happily.

Molly wrinkled her brow. "You're going to spoil us," she said.

Chance winked. "Then mission accomplished. And by the way—" he let his glance drift over her cream-colored V-neck sweater and formfitting black yoga pants "—you're looking mighty fine, too."

"Then that makes three of us," she said, nodding at his green corduroy shirt and jeans. Grinning, she opened the door wide. A front had blown in since they had seen each other earlier, bringing gusting winds and taking the temperature down to freezing. Worse, it was the kind of damp cold that went right through your clothes. Molly reached past him to hold the door. "Come in out of the cold."

With a nod of his head, Chance obliged.

"What's that?" Braden asked as Molly shut the door behind them, once again sealing them into the cozy warmth of her home.

Chance winked at the little boy. "Let's see." After handing Molly the bag, he took the folding table over and set it up flush against the matching one he'd brought over the previous night. The white fabric-covered board went on top.

"We've got a North Pole over here, with Rudolph and the sleigh, and what is going to be a Christmas ranch over on this side."

"I like ranches!" Braden jumped up and down.

"Then let's build one, shall we?"

Together, the three of them set up a corral, a barn and a snow-covered ranch house decorated for the holidays. Three horses, a dog and a cat completed the menagerie. Last but not least were a number of snow-covered trees that could be placed on either side of the increasingly elaborate Christmas village.

Yet there was plenty of room for more.

"I play?" Braden asked.

"What do you say first?" Molly prompted.

Braden encompassed Chance in the biggest hug he could manage. "Love you, Chance!"

A lump the size of a walnut formed in Chance's throat at the unexpected declaration.

There was no doubt the earnest little boy meant it.

Chance knelt down, aware this was a first. "Love you, too, buddy," he said thickly, accepting Braden's joyous hug. In the foreground, he saw Molly, tears shining in her eyes. She needed a moment as much as he did.

Braden went back to playing.

Molly returned to the kitchen. She plucked an apron off the hook. When she had a little trouble tying it, he stepped behind her and did it for her.

He caught the scent of orchids before he stepped away. She was wearing that perfume again.

But then maybe she wore it a lot.

Maybe he had just never noticed.

"I guess this is what they mean when they say Christmas is for kids."

She nodded, her head bent over the handwritten cookie recipe on the counter. "Thank you for helping us with our dilemma, although I'm still not sure I see how that's going to convince him that it's not likely he will get a L-I-V-E trio of B-U-L-L-S."

"Patience," he teased. He saw her blush, just the way she had when they'd made love.

His body reacted in kind.

Aware this was no time to be going down that path, however, not with her son in the next room, he took an apron off the hook for himself and put it on. "We'll work it out."

Brightening, Molly put six eggs into the mixing bowl of her stand mixer and turned it on high speed. "Speaking of things working out unexpectedly...guess what I got shortly before you arrived?"

Chance watched her pour milk and baking powder into another bowl.

"A call from Elspeth Pyle, the headmistress at Worthington Academy! Braden has an interview on Monday afternoon. They'll give us a tour of the school at that time and also talk to me privately. Which means I need to take another adult along."

Maybe more than she knew if things went the way they

usually did at the Academy. Casually, he volunteered, "I wouldn't mind going." For starters, it would give him more time with both of them. There were other things in Dallas that could be accomplished, as well.

As Molly zested the skin of a lemon, the bright flavor of citrus filled the room. She paused to look up at him. "I didn't think you were gung ho about this."

He shrugged, not about to enter that particular minefield and chance spoiling the evening.

A furrow formed along the bridge of her nose. She added softened butter to the whirring mixer, then sugar. "Not going to confirm or deny?"

He fought the urge to take her in his arms. "If you need someone, I'll be there. It'll give us a chance to take care of another matter while we're in the city."

She peered at him through a fringe of thick auburn lashes. "Like what?"

"I got a call from our tile guys this afternoon. They said some of the tile for the kitchen backsplash was damaged or is not as perfect as you want it to be."

She frowned, already taking the matter in stride. "That's a special-order material."

"I know. I found some at a warehouse in Dallas, but I think we should probably take a look at it before we buy it, make sure the same flaws don't exist in that batch."

Molly nodded. "Absolutely." She paused, thinking. Then ran a hand across her brow. "This is going to put us behind, isn't it?"

He stepped closer. "A little bit."

Their eyes met, and he felt the connection between them deepen. "How come no one called me?"

"I told them I'd talk to you about it. Just in case you wanted to—" conscious of her little boy playing a short distance away, he mimed an arrow to the heart "—the messenger."

"Smart-ass." They all knew neither of them ever took any of their frustrations out on the crew. Mix-ups and snafus were par for the course of any building project. Molly took them in stride, just as he did.

The customer was not always as understanding. "Did you tell your mom?" Molly added lemon zest, anise extract and salt to the mixer.

Chance shook his head. He really enjoyed watching her move about the kitchen and work her magic. "I thought you might want to do that."

"I do, since it really falls on the design side. I'll see if I can get her to pick out something else as backup, just in case we don't have time to get her first choice and still make the Open House deadline."

"Sounds good."

She turned the speed down on the machine and handed him a bowl of flour. "Can you put this in, a cup at a time, while the mixer is still going?"

"Without making a mess?"

Her amber eyes glittering jovially, she patted his biceps. "I have faith in you."

He was glad someone did. He was competent in the kitchen but not a pro like her.

Still, it was nice to be included, he thought, carefully adding the first of what looked like half a dozen or so cups of flour.

He watched her retreating backside as she went off to get out the baking sheets. She looked good in jeans and skirts, but this was the first time he had seen her in something as formfitting as the black yoga pants. They hugged her slender but curvy frame with disturbing accuracy.

Whirling back around, she came toward him once again. Standing next to him, she watched him add the last of flour. As soon as it was mixed, she turned.

He cleared his throat. "So what are we making here?" he asked. When all he wanted to make with her was love…hot, wild love.

She smiled, oblivious to the effect she had on his libido. "*Springerle*. It's a German shortbread cookie with a design stamped on top."

Feeling the pressure building at the front of his jeans, he noted with mock gravity, "Fancy."

She laughed, bending forward to remove the latch holding the mixing bowl in place. The V of her sweater gaped slightly as she moved, giving him an unexpected view of the delectable uppermost curves of her breasts and the satin edge of her bra.

His body hardening, he resisted the urge to take her in his arms, and instead, contented himself, watching her move gracefully about her task.

"It's one of those things that looks harder than it actually is." She picked up a wooden rolling pin with pictures carved into it. "Thanks to this."

"*Really* fancy."

She laughed again. Nodded at the other room. "Want to tell Braden that it's time for him to come and help?"

Chance gestured toward the sofa. "Ah, I think it might be too late for that." Braden was curled up, his favorite blanket beneath his cheek, the Rudolph Chance had brought him in one hand, a horse from his Christmas village in the other. "Long day?"

"Very." Molly unlooped the apron from around her neck, then set it aside. "I'm going to have to carry him to bed."

Aware he had flour all over the front of his apron, Chance took his off. "Want me to do the honors?"

Suddenly looking as if it had been a very long day for her, too, Molly sighed. "If you think you can without waking him."

"What's that saying?" He tilted his head. "Anything you can do I can do better?"

She elbowed him in the ribs, taking the joke in the spirit it was intended. "Just don't disappoint me, okay, cowboy?"

It was a casual request.

Yet one he wanted to take seriously.

"Never." He leaned down and lightly kissed the top of her head. Then after carefully picking her son up in his arms, blankie, toys and all, Chance followed Molly up the stairs.

Molly tried not to react to the sight of Chance gently laying Braden in his toddler bed. But it was impossible. The sight of the big, strong man tenderly cradling her son, and setting him down on the pillows, created an ache in her heart that was so fierce it nearly brought tears to her eyes.

Up until now, she had convinced herself that Braden was better off with one parent who loved him with all her being. Now, with Chance in their lives, even temporarily, she could no longer deny the truth. Her son needed a daddy.

He deserved one.

Had circumstances been different, had she and Chance been more compatible in all the ways that really counted when it came to long-term relationships, their future might have been different.

But they weren't the same.

He was the kind of man who could reject financial offers without even looking at them.

She was a woman who would upend her entire life to better financially provide for her son.

And money, she knew, was on the top three list of things couples fought about.

"Tell me you're going to let me stay around long enough to at least taste the *springerle*," he said when they were back downstairs again.

What harm could there be in a little more time with him? Molly wondered. Especially when the two of them were becoming such good friends. "Sure." Molly drew a bolstering breath and handed him his apron. "But be warned," she said with a playful look. "I plan to put you to work."

And work they did.

After rolling out the dough and then using the special pin to leave an imprint, they carefully cut and transferred the stamped cookie dough onto parchment-lined cookies sheets. Finally, it was time to put the first two pans in the preheated oven. "What about the rest of the dough?" Chance asked.

Molly smiled at the way he was really getting into the holiday baking. "I'm going to save that for Braden to do, first thing tomorrow morning." She covered the bowl and set it in the fridge.

"So now we wait," he said.

"We wait," she confirmed, her stomach suddenly clenching with excitement for no reason she could figure.

She liked cookies.

But she wouldn't empty the bank for them.

On the other hand, to be held in his arms again and or have another one of his kisses...

Hazel eyes glittering with a wealth of emotions she wasn't so sure she should decipher, he brushed aside a lock of her hair. "Have I told you how much I appreciate you having me here, with you and Braden?"

She laughed off the significance of her actions and tried to harden her heart. "No choice really, given the ongoing live-bull situation."

Looking confident they would solve that dilemma, Chance wrapped his arms around her, pulled her close. "Oh, there's always a choice, Molly," he murmured huskily.

And the first one she had to make was whether she was going to let him kiss her again.

Chance saw the indecision in her eyes. Luckily for both of them, there was no indecision in him. He knew exactly where he wanted this liaison of theirs to go. Giving her no room to protest, he lowered his mouth over hers. She smelled like an intoxicating mix of orchid, cookies and delectable woman. And she tasted just as sweet, her lips as heavenly soft and supple as he recalled. Her body just as warm and although not quite yielding, not pulling away, either.

He slid a hand down her spine and back up again. Worked to erotically deepen and further the kiss. The move was rewarded with a soft, sultry moan and a surge against his body that had him hard as granite, and hungering for more. "Chance..."

Sensing she was a woman who had never been valued the way she should be, he wove his hands through her hair. "Just a kiss or two, Molly," he rasped, kissing his way up the nape of her neck, the sensitive place behind her ear. "That's all I'm asking."

And all, he was certain, she meant to give. She uttered another soft sigh. Wrapped her arms around his neck, rose on tiptoe and pressed her breasts to his chest. "Two kisses, then," she whispered, her eyes a dreamy amber as she looked up at him. "That's all."

Two kisses that would mean everything, Chance determined, savoring the way her heart pounded against his.

Resolving to make her realize how much they could have if she just gave them the opportunity, Chance resumed kissing her. Soft and sweet, slow and deep, and all the ways in between. He let her know with every stroke of his lips and tongue how much he wanted to be there for her, to let her know he cared. Enough to be as patient and gentle as she required, while cherishing and honoring her as she never had been before.

He kissed her until she was as caught up in the all-consuming passion as he was. And it was only then that he realized the kitchen smelled of burning sugar.

Molly noticed at the same time he did.

She broke away. Stared in dismay at the smoke coming out of her oven vents. Then jumped into action, as did he. She swiftly hit the power-off button on her oven and covered the vents with two oven mitts, stilling the smoke and cutting off the flow of oxygen before anything could burst into flames. Chance grabbed a chair, stepped up and undid the plastic covering on the smoke alarm just as the first earsplitting warning screech sounded for half a second, then abruptly stopped when he managed to disconnect it.

Chance and Molly tensed, waiting to hear if Braden cried out. Thankfully, only silence reigned.

Her face pale, she opened the oven door. The cookies inside were indeed burned black, but not on fire. With a grimace, she pulled out both sheets, carried the horribly smelling cookies outside and set the pans on the concrete patio behind the house.

He went in the opposite direction and opened a couple of windows at the front of the house for cross ventilation. Almost instantly bitter-cold air swept into the living area and wafted through the kitchen, easing the smoky smell.

Molly jerked in another breath, still distressed. "I'm going upstairs to check on Braden." She dashed off while he stayed behind. And as soon as the residual smoke was cleared out by the winter wind now gusting through the downstairs, he reassembled the alarm.

Eventually Molly returned. She still looked a little shaken but was composing herself quickly.

Aware how quickly the temperature had dropped inside her home, as well as between the two of them, he moved to shut the windows. "'Everything okay up there?"

She nodded, her face flushed blotchy pink with embarrassment. "Braden's still asleep. No smoke made it up there."

He gave her the physical space she seemed to need. "Sorry about the cookies."

She scoffed and ran a hand through her hair. "I'm not."

How was that possible, he wondered, given how much work they'd put in?

Molly retrieved her baking pans and shut the door behind her. Back stiff, she carried the remains to the sink and dumped the contents. Whirling to face him, she lifted her chin. "I needed a reminder to stay focused. And not get distracted by this...attraction between us." She swallowed, amending half-apologetically, "Nice as it is."

At least she admitted that.

As for the rest...

She held up a hand before he could interrupt. "I'm not going to lie to you, Chance. I enjoyed making love with you." She squared her shoulders defiantly. "But I meant what I said. It's not going to happen again. And this disaster here—" she indicated the burned-black cookies now filling her kitchen sink "—is evidence why."

Chance could have argued the culinary disaster was not a harbinger of events to come, but the look on Molly's face told him their relationship—and it *was* a relationship whether she wanted to admit it or not—would be better served by giving her some time alone to sort out her feelings. So he called on every bit of gentlemanly reserve he had, bid her good-night and left.

On Sunday, Molly was "too busy" to see him.

He had a lot to do before he left Laramie, too. Including making hotel reservations for the three of them Monday night and an appointment with the tile vendor first thing Tuesday morning. He also arranged a surprise for Molly and Braden that he hoped would go a long way toward solving their "live bull" problem.

Unfortunately, when he went to pick them up first thing Monday morning, Molly looked more stressed out than he had ever seen her. Her son was in a foul mood, too.

"Something wrong, buddy?" Chance asked gently, figuring it would be best to talk to the little fella first. He and Molly could discuss whatever was on her mind while he was driving.

Braden crossed his arms over his chest, looking every inch as stubborn as his mommy. "Want my friends," he said.

Chance looked at Molly. She compressed her lips. "He knows today is Monday, and that's a school day."

Braden stomped his foot. "Go school *now*!"

Molly sighed. "I've explained we're going to visit another school this morning, one that's a little far away."

Braden dug in further. "No 'nother school."

Molly turned her glance skyward. "Let's just say he is not in a cooperative frame of mind," she said under her breath. "On this of all days."

*No kidding*, Chance thought. He turned back to Braden. "Some people like playing hooky."

Braden made a recalcitrant face at Chance.

"He doesn't know what that is," she explained, wringing her hands.

And there was obviously no time to go into it.

"Right." Realizing that Molly was probably nervous enough about how things were going to go at Worthington Academy for all of them, and further delaying their departure would not help that, he glanced at his watch. "Maybe we should just hit the road."

Molly relaxed enough to send him a grateful glance that made him glad he had decided to tag along and provide the much-needed moral support. "We really don't want to be late," she agreed.

At her request, they took her SUV. He drove.

Braden fell asleep in his car seat soon after they started out. And they arrived in the city with just enough time to eat a quick lunch. Molly changed Braden—who'd gotten ketchup on his clothes—in her vehicle. A wash of his face and hands and a quick brush of his hair and they were ready to head for the Worthington Academy campus.

As they approached the glitzy private school, Chance shot Molly a reassuring glance, even as he wondered whether she would feel instantly at home there or completely out of her depth. And what either of those options would mean for Braden, or for the two of them.

Given how much research she had done on private schools in the upper echelon of Dallas society, Molly thought she would be prepared for her first glimpse of Worthington Academy. She wasn't even close. And hence, she could only stare as Chance drove through the manicured grounds at the Colonial-style ivy-covered brick buildings and numerous athletic fields, all with individual bleachers.

With the familiarity of an alumni, Chance pointed out the PE building that housed the indoor swimming pool and basketball and volleyball courts. Braden gaped at the students in uniform, walking in orderly lines across the quad. "It's even lovelier than the brochure photos," Molly murmured, impressed.

Chance nodded, his face an inscrutable mask.

"And you and all your siblings went here?"

Chance nodded as he stopped and waited for the cross-country team to run en masse across the street in front of them.

"Did you like it?"

Chance drove on. "Wyatt and I had a tough time with all the rules."

*Not exactly a ringing endorsement.*

"Zane, Garrett and Sage thrived." He parked in the visitor lot, outside the administration building. Paused long enough to put on his tie and jacket, and then they were off.

Elspeth Pyle, the headmistress, greeted them cordially. The slender fortysomething brunette was as elegant as Molly had imagined she would be.

She introduced them to the sophisticated silver-haired woman at her side. "This is Dr. Mitchard. She's our school psychologist for the pre-K division. She'll be administering the cognitive evaluation for Braden while you tour the facilities and observe an actual classroom environment. And this is Julianne." She pointed to a young woman who looked fresh out of college herself. "One of our tour guides."

"Mommy. You stay," Braden said when Dr. Mitchard attempted to usher him into the testing center.

Molly knelt down. "Chance and I'll be right back, honey. You just go with Dr. Mitchard and answer her questions. Okay?"

Braden's lower lip trembled.

For a second, Molly thought her little boy was going to have a complete meltdown.

But something in the confident, encouraging way Chance was looking at her son bucked him up. Braden squared his little shoulders and took Dr. Mitchard's hand. They disappeared into a room filled with toys and puzzles. Moments later, Molly could hear him chatting happily.

The testing under way, Molly and Chance were led down a hall, to the wing that held the pre-K classes. The doors had glass insets. A press of the intercom button next to the door, and they could hear what was going on inside.

In one, A. A. Milne was being read and animatedly discussed.

In another, the teacher was holding up large prints. The children were confidently and correctly calling out the name of the artists—Monet, Rembrandt, Picasso.

Molly was unable to help but be enthralled. Her son would thrive here. She was certain of it. And she would be able to rest easy, knowing she had made sure he started out life with every advantage.

To her relief, Braden certainly looked happy when she had finished her own interview with the admission counselor and headmistress.

She joined him and Chance in the preschool lobby, where they were seated in armchairs, side by side, engaged in some sort of nonsensical game that had her son quietly giggling.

Unable to recall when he had enjoyed another adult's company so very much, Molly smiled at them.

Chance smiled back.

Braden, Molly noted, wasn't the only guy really enjoying himself here.

"We go, Mommy?" Braden ran over and embraced her fiercely.

Hugging him back, Molly nodded.

Braden moved between them, taking her hand and Chance's.

Together, they followed the brick path through the elegantly landscaped quad to the visitor parking lot.

"Good meeting, I guess?" Chance said.

Molly nodded. All her questions had been answered. "The staff was surprisingly thorough."

"When will you find out whether he's admitted or not?"

Molly jerked in a breath, suddenly feeling anxious again. Aware Chance was waiting for her answer, she replied, "The decisions will be made by the end of next week, and all mid-year applicants will receive a letter via regular mail the week after that."

Which meant she would know before Christmas. Would her wish for her son be granted? Molly could only hope. Meantime, they had what was left of the afternoon ahead of them. Work on the Circle H ranch house that still needed to be completed. And to do that, they needed all the supplies.

"Do you think it's too late to go to the tile warehouse?" Molly asked after getting into her SUV.

Chance glanced at his watch. "They close at six. With traffic, probably. But there's a place nearby that I'd like to show you."

Braden piped up from his safety seat in the back. "Want to play!"

Chance shot him an affectionate look in the rearview mirror. "I think that can be arranged."

"Wow," Braden breathed when they walked into the Highland Village Toy Emporium.

Wow was right, Molly thought, taking her son by the hand. The exclusive store was decorated for Christmas and filled to the brim with all the latest playthings.

A well-heeled older woman approached them, a huge smile on her face. "Mr. Lockhart!" she said, introducing herself to

Molly and Braden as the store owner, Rochelle Lewis. "A little early."

Chance flashed a winning grin. "Not too early, I hope?"

"Definitely not!" Rochelle beamed. "We can take you upstairs now, if you like."

"What's upstairs?" Molly asked curiously.

Chance reached out and took her and Braden's hands. "You'll see."

They followed Rochelle through an employees-only door, up a set of cement stairs, through another big door.

Inside, the large area had been divided into three sections. Elaborate dollhouses with thousand-dollar price tags and play kitchen sets on the left, very fancy riding toys in the middle. On the left was the elaborate Leo and Lizzie World Adventure train set and all the accoutrements, which was sold out everywhere.

Braden, who couldn't have been less interested when Molly showed him the brochure, had an entirely different view when confronted with the reality of the fancy wooden tracks, windmills, stations, bridges and locomotive engines and sidecars. "Wow," he said again.

In addition to the basic components—which could have been located anywhere—there was a mini-set featuring the Golden Gate Bridge in San Francisco. Another that traveled through the Grand Canyon. One with Big Ben and Buckingham Palace and the Thames in London. The Eiffel Tower in France. The pyramids in Egypt. Even one with the River Walk and the Alamo in San Antonio, Texas—a place where Braden had actually visited. Twenty in all, thus far. With new adventure sets coming out twice yearly.

"Take as long as you like," Rochelle said.

"I'm not sure showing him this is a good idea," Molly whispered to Chance while Braden moved a train along the wooden track, looking thoroughly entranced. "Given that we—I mean I—can no longer get even the basic components."

Chance shrugged with the ease of a man who had grown up with an unlimited bank account. "True, but the emporium has two remaining deluxe collector's sets left that include every item made to date. One of which is yours, if you want to buy the whole thing."

"They won't break it up?"

"Manufacturer won't allow it. Already asked."

Rochelle was back, price list in hand.

Molly took it.

And when confronted with the total, nearly fainted.

She had barely recovered when her son turned to her plaintively. "Want Leo and Lizzie trains, Mommy."

"I know, honey." She forced herself to smile, as the store owner trailed off to give them some privacy. "Aren't they wonderful?" And when the basic set did come back in stock, probably at some point after the holidays…

"Santa bring?" Braden inquired hopefully.

"Santa Claus has all kinds of trains," Chance soothed him. He was obviously more prepared to handle the situation than she was.

Braden got the mutinous look back on his face. "Want these," he stated, then turned and again began to play.

Chance stepped back. When she joined him, he whispered in her ear, "They have locomotive sets at the superstores, in a much less costly version."

But it wasn't the one she had wanted and now Braden yearned to have, Molly thought in disappointment.

"I checked. The other brands are in stock, too, so if you want me to go out tonight, while you know who is asleep, and take care of it for you…" Chance continued.

Molly drew a deep breath.

The store owner returned "I hate to rush you, Mr. Lockhart. Especially given how much your family has patronized our emporium over the years, but there are two other customers, standing by, ready to…"

Molly looked at the train set again.

Then the price.

With the kind of tuition she was going to have to pay at Worthington Academy, she just couldn't do it. "I'm sorry," she said reluctantly. "The deluxe collector's set is a little much for him right now."

Oblivious to the whispered negotiations going on behind him, Braden continued moving the train along the tracks.

"I understand."

Rochelle looked at Chance.

"I'd still like the stuffed giraffe we talked about for my nephew, Max," he said.

"Certainly."

Chance turned to Molly. "Mind if I go down and take care of it?"

Molly forced a smile. "No, of course not."

It would give Braden a little more time to play.

Which sadly, as it happened, was going to be as close as he got to owning a Leo and Lizzie World Adventure train set this holiday season.

"Sorry. I didn't mean to upset you," Chance said when they were leaving the upscale toy emporium.

She knew his heart had been in the right place. It always was where she and her son were concerned. She reached over and squeezed his hand. "It's good to have reminders why I need to work harder, bring in more salary, so that next year at this time, cash reserves won't be an issue." *A few of those jobs for Lucille's über-wealthy friends*, she encouraged herself silently, *and*...""I'll be able to do whatever I want, whenever I want.""

Chance studied her, his emotions as veiled as his eyes. Once again, they seemed at odds.

Finally he said, "You really think Braden would know the difference between the high-priced versus the low-priced locomotive sets?"

"Before he'd actually seen and played with them? Probably not, but I would," Molly admitted honestly.

She could see she had disappointed Chance with her frankness. She couldn't help that, either, she thought on a troubled sigh.

He'd always had money. She'd never had enough. And like it or not, that created a divide between them that was not liable to go away.

# Chapter 8

Noting it had been quiet for a good twenty minutes now, Chance crossed the hall. Rapped quietly on Molly's hotel room door. There was a pause; then she opened it just enough so they could talk, without inviting him in.

"Everything okay?" he asked her quietly.

"You heard the meltdown?" she whispered back.

Chance doubted anyone on their end of the hall hadn't heard it. But figuring she didn't need to be reminded of that, he complimented facetiously instead. "Your son's got quite a set of lungs on him."

She cracked a faint smile at the joke. "Tell me about it."

"But he's asleep now?"

Nodding, she moved so she was no longer blocking his view, and Chance could see inside the room. Braden was curled up in the middle of the king-size bed, his favorite blue blankie tucked beneath his chin. His cherubic face still bore the evidence of his earlier tears, but he seemed to be resting peacefully now. Molly shook her head. "He finally exhausted himself."

Chance commiserated with the little tyke. "And no wonder. Given the trip from Laramie to Dallas this morning, the afternoon spent being tested at the Worthington Academy—"

"Followed by the trip to the emporium to see the toy trains, and the dinner out he really did not want to sit through."

Even though they had tried to make it simple and fast.

Molly leaned against the door frame, still keeping her voice low as she confided, almost as one parent to another, "Usually his bubble bath relaxes him, but tonight not even that did the trick. He just went into full temper tantrum. It was all I could do to get him into his jammies, never mind read him his usual bedtime story."

Chance wished she had called on him to help. "Tomorrow will be better," he soothed.

She looked doubtful.

Wishing he could take her in his arms and make love to her until her tension eased, he said, "Can I get you anything? Bucket of ice? I don't mind hitting the gift shop if you want juice or milk."

"That's really sweet of you."

Sweet was not exactly the way he wanted to be perceived.

"But I think I'm going to take a cue from my son and try to get as much sleep as I can tonight."

"Okay. Just so you know, though. My room may be a few doors down, but I'm just a text away."

"Thank you. For everything today." Without warning, Molly rose on tiptoe and pressed her lips to his cheek. She drew back and looked him in the eye. He caught her against him and kissed her back. At first on the cheek, gently, reverently, and then as she turned her face to his, on the mouth. Not in the way he had when the cookies were burning, but in a way that encouraged her to give him—them—a second chance.

Again, Molly drew back.

The yearning was in her amber eyes, even if she remained conflicted.

Yearning, Chance thought, was good.

Down the hall, the elevator dinged. Heavy metal doors could be heard opening. Voices, as other guests stepped off.

Aware he really did not want to push it, Chance reluctantly let Molly go. "Tomorrow then?"

"Bright and early," she promised.

To Molly's relief, by midmorning the next day, Braden's mood was much improved. He handled their visit to the tile warehouse with his usual good cheer, and was still smiling and chattering exuberantly, as they all headed home.

"I like trains!" He lifted his hands high in the air, despite the constraints of his car seat safety harness.

Glad her son was so excited about Christmas, even if she had yet to exactly work out a solution regarding his gift, Molly countered cheerfully, "I know you do."

Braden kicked his feet energetically. "I like bulls!" he shouted.

As usual, Chance showed no worry over that issue. Which made Molly wonder what he knew that she didn't. "Mistletoe and Mistletoe Jr. like you, too," Chance reassured him.

Braden let out a joyous whoop. "Santa bring me trains *and* bulls!"

Again, Chance seemed confident it would all work out.

Again, Molly was not sure how.

Deciding, however, not to worry about it at this moment, when she had so much else on her agenda, she clapped her hands together and shifted toward her son, as much as her seat belt would allow. "Who wants to sing Christmas carols?"

Braden grinned. "Me do! Me school!"

Chance sent Molly a glance. "You're going to have to translate…"

Trying not to notice how handsome he was in profile, or how closely he had shaved that morning, she explained, "He's talking about the Christmas program his preschool is having. They've been working on the music for weeks now."

Chance looked interested. "When is it?"

Molly's heartbeat picked up. "December 18th, "

"What time?"

"Seven p.m."

"Can anyone go?"

*Meaning you?* "Yes," Molly said cautiously, her excitement rising.

"But?" he prodded, when she said nothing more.

She took a deep breath. Aware her son never missed a beat in a situation like this, she parsed her words carefully. "I'm just not sure."

He flashed her a sexy sidelong grin. "I'd be interested?"

Clearly he was.

In lots and lots of things.

Her.

Braden.

Kissing her again.

Maybe more than kissing…if the strength of his arousal during the cookie-burning incident was any indication.

Heavens, Molly brought herself up short when she realized the silence had gone on too long and Chance was clearly wondering why. What was wrong with her? Why was she such a welter of feeling and desire whenever he was around? She'd certainly never reacted like this before!

Not with Braden's daddy.

Not with anyone!

Except Chance.

"Because," the object of all her wildest fantasies continued persuasively, "I am interested, Molly. Very much so."

Swallowing around the knot of emotion in her throat, she tried again. "I know. I can see that."

"Then?"

She gestured inanely, wishing she were driving because then she'd have something else to concentrate on other than how ruggedly masculine Chance looked, even in a navy flannel shirt and jeans, or how good he smelled, like soap and sandalwood and man.

With effort, she babbled on. "Those programs are a lot to handle. Overeager parents. Way too excited kids." *And me, making a sentimental fool of myself, getting all misty over the slightest thing.*

Did she really want Chance to see her like that?

"Chance watch me sing!" Braden called from the backseat.

Chance smiled as if the matter was settled. "Sounds good, buddy!"

Braden clapped his hands. "Hurrah! Chance see me!"

They really had to get out of this loop before Braden invited Chance to anything else.

"Speaking of singing," Molly said brightly. "Here we go, now! 'We wish you a merry Christmas...'"

Chance joined in, along with Braden, their voices blending in if not perfect harmony, at least perfect good cheer. The sound of that and the other holiday tunes that followed was enough to warm her heart. For the first time, she wished she could stay in Laramie, and see where this was all going with Chance and still give her son everything he should have. But she couldn't. The visit to Worthington Academy had shown her that.

To do that, she was going to have to be all in—in Dallas. Not leaving her heart behind with Chance.

* * *

"Does Braden always fall asleep like that?" Chance asked twenty minutes later. The child had dropped off midsong. A check in the rearview mirror had showed him snoozing away.

Molly shot him the kind of affectionately rueful look he imagined mothers gave their babies' daddies. The one that said, "We're in this together."

And they were...

"Pretty much. Especially in the car. It's good though." As their eyes briefly met, he felt warmed through and through. "We have to drop him at preschool when we get to Laramie."

*We.* He liked the sound of that.

Molly thumbed through the calendar on her smartphone. "And he has a playdate with his best friends, Will and Justin, right after school, so I can meet your mother at the ranch house to look at the new tile we picked out this morning. Make sure she likes the way it looks in the light there before we take what's already up of the current backsplash down."

"I'm sure she will."

"I hope so," she said, her soft lips tightening anxiously. "A lot is riding on this job."

A lot was riding on a lot of things, Chance thought. He continued driving while Molly got on the phone with the crew working at the remodeling site.

He'd never considered himself that much of a family guy.

But then he'd never traveled with anyone like Molly, or anyone as cute as Braden, either.

He'd been cast in the daddy role and found he liked it. A lot. But then this holiday season was full of surprises, he realized, as he hit the town limits and parked in front of Braden's preschool.

Molly woke her son and walked him in, then Chance drove Molly home, so she could change clothes before driving out to the ranch to meet him and his mother and the rest of their work crews.

He walked her as far as her front door.

She rummaged for her key. "You don't have to stay."

"Don't want me to come in?"

She paused and looked at him in a way that said she did. "We're already running late."

And he knew if he did go in, they might very well be even later.

Putting his disappointment aside—this was something that could be picked up later—when they weren't rushed— he turned and headed for his own truck, which had been left parked at the curb. "I'll see you at the Circle H."

Smiling, she waved goodbye. "I won't be long."

He grinned back, aware he was counting on that. And much more.

"You look happy," Lucille observed, when he walked in to the renovation in progress, at the Circle H ranch house.

He felt happy. Not wanting to discuss his feelings, he shrugged, and turned his glance to the work that had been done in their absence. "Time of year, I guess."

"Mmm-hmm."

"Don't read more into this, Mom," Chance warned.

"Hey." Lucille lifted her well-manicured hands in surrender. "I'm just happy you're happy."

"Who's happy?" Molly asked cheerfully, strolling in, too.

"Everyone, it seems." Lucille smiled.

*Especially Molly*, Chance thought. She had never looked better in a pair of designer jeans, cranberry cashmere turtleneck and a black down field jacket. Sexy. Competent. Warm. Kind. Feisty. Pretty much everything that was on his list for the perfect woman.

Oblivious to the direction of his thoughts, Molly asked his

mom, "What do you think of the substitute tile we picked out, now that you can see it in person?"

Lucille viewed it from all angles. "I actually like it better than the original."

"Good." Molly's body relaxed in relief. "Then we'll get started on taking down what we put up, so we can go forward."

"Wonderful!" Lucille said.

Tank, one of the construction guys on Chance's crew, entered. "Express delivery service van from Dallas out here for you. Somebody want to sign?"

Chance bit down on an oath. *Not good.*

"I'll get it," Molly volunteered.

"That's okay." He moved around her, motioning for her to stay put. "I'll get the tile."

Molly shot him an odd look and dug in. "I want to check it out before he leaves." They'd taken the samples in her SUV. The rest had needed to be delivered via courier. "You can do that in here," Chance said gallantly. "The guys and I will carry the boxes in."

Molly gave him another odd look. "I can carry some."

"You really don't need to do this," Chance dissented.

Molly looked mutinous, but then Lucille stepped in. "Goodness, let's all go then."

They'd barely made it through the door when the delivery driver said from the back of the van, "Are the boxes from the Toy Emporium going here, too?"

Molly looked at Chance. He wasn't about to get into this here and now. "Those should go to the bunkhouse," he decreed quickly. "Mom, would you mind showing the driver?"

An old pro at social maneuvering, Lucille covered her confusion. "Not at all."

Molly peeked into the back of the van. "Are *all* those for here?"

The uniformed driver nodded. "Somebody's going to have a *very good* Christmas from the looks of it."

Except it wasn't a good surprise for Molly, Chance noted, judging by the aggrieved look on her lovely face as she turned around, got in her car and left the ranch. It was more like her worst nightmare.

Lucille patted him on the arm. "Looks like you have some explaining to do, son."

*And then some*, Chance thought, wincing.

It would be better done without an audience.

Molly had no sooner gotten home than her doorbell rang. Chance stood on her porch. "We need to talk."

She glared at him, not sure when she had felt so hurt and simultaneously left out. "Do we?" She didn't think so.

He brushed past anyway. Waited for her to shut the door behind them. Then shrugged out of his coat, his tall body seeming to fill up the space of her foyer the way the rest of him filled up her heart. Grimly, he surmised, "You're mad at me because I bought a train set for Braden."

Knowing she had to do something with her hands or she would probably throw something at his handsome head, Molly went back to what she had neglected to do earlier—unpack her overnight bag.

Grabbing the handful of dirty clothing from the day before, she carried it to the back of the house to the laundry room.

"It's not just any train set, Chance. It's the deluxe collector's edition. The one with every Leo and Lizzie component ever made thus far. The one that costs more than some small cars!"

Brawny arms folded in front of him, he watched as she sprayed the ketchup stains on Braden's clothing with prewash, then tossed them into the washing machine. "As you once pointed out to me, it's quality stuff that will last for years. And could even be passed down to the *next* generation."

She threw up her hands in exasperation. "Please don't tell me you actually believe that!"

"Okay, how about this?" he countered, reaching for several pieces of laundry she had dropped.

Unfortunately, it was her red satin bra and bikini set.

He crumpled them in his hand, much as he had the first time he'd undressed her. "I wanted him to have it."

Snatching the lingerie from his fingers, Molly tossed them in the wicker basket she kept for unmentionables. Trying not to put momentary pleasure ahead of long-range goals, she tried again to talk sense into Chance. "I'd *like* Braden to have a lot of things, but this is way too much."

He lounged in the portal, gaze moving over her lingeringly, as if he were already mentally ending this argument by making love to her. "So let me give him some of it now, and then some more on his birthday and so on. Kind of like I've been doing with the Christmas villages, which, by the way, aren't finished yet."

Molly put two shirts in the washer, then realized they were navy and black and everything in the tub was white. She plucked them back out again, lest she get further sidetracked, start the darn machine and then have everything she washed turn an ugly blue-grey.

Deciding to leave starting the machine for later, she marched past him. "This is different, Chance."

He followed. "How?"

She removed Braden's blanket and Rudolph from the suitcase and set them on the sofa for him to find when he returned home.

Aware Chance was truly trying to understand now, she drew a deep breath. "It was one thing for you to buy a brand-new set of building blocks for Braden to play with at your place when you invited us to lunch. It made sense for you to have something for him to do," she told him kindly. "And you can use those for your nephew Max when he comes over to play." So it wasn't all for Braden.

"But?"

Molly could tell from the sardonic curve of his lip he still thought she was in the wrong. "This excess on your part just highlights the difference between us when it comes to money. To you, this is nothing. To me, it's a year of mortgage payments!"

He came closer. "If you are so concerned about excess, then why apply to Worthington Academy, where the tuition is more than some colleges?"

"A place like that will bring him boundless life opportunities."

"It will still cost an arm and a leg."

Ducking her head, she zipped the suitcase and reluctantly admitted, "He's applying as a scholarship student." Embarrassed to have to say that, because it made her feel like a failure, as a parent, to have to rely on charity to meet her son's needs, she rushed on, "The stipend Worthington Academy offers doesn't pay everything, of course. But it's *enough* that, if Braden does get in, I could afford it and then, hopefully, after a couple of years at a much higher income for me, he wouldn't even need that financial assistance to go there."

Chance spread his hands wide. "Look, if he gets in, I can help you with that—if it's what you really want for him. You don't *have* to rely on scholarship."

Molly carried the suitcase to the garage and stuck it on a shelf. She spun back around and marched into the house. Once again, he was using money—his money—to solve everything. "You're missing the point, Chance," she said angrily.

"No. You're missing the point!" Chance returned gruffly. "I did what I did because I care enough about you and your son to want to see you *happy*."

Tears of frustration blurred her vision. With trembling fingers, Molly wiped them away. "Buying us extravagant stuff won't achieve that!"

"Then what will?" he demanded, taking her by the shoulders.

*Love*, Molly thought.

Shocked by the notion, she shook her head. Too late, he had seen the raw need reflected in her eyes. He caught her hand and pulled her to him. The next thing she knew he was sliding his fingers through her hair, kissing her lips, her cheek, her hair and then, ever so wantonly, her lips again. It was almost as if he were on a mission, not just to make her his but to give her every Christmas wish she had ever wanted.

A man in her life who would give her everything.

A man who adored her son as much as she did.

A hot affair.

Someone to share life's up and downs with.

He cradled her cheek in his hand. "Tell me you forgive me for overstepping," he whispered, kissing her hotly, thoroughly again. "Tell me you'll give me a second chance."

"To be friends?"

"To be a hell of a lot more than just friends." He slid a hand beneath her knees. Lifting her into his arms, he carried her up the stairs, down the hall to her bedroom. He had never been in there before. And she wouldn't have wanted him to see it now, with clothes draped everywhere. "Burglary?" he joked.

"Wardrobe crisis," she murmured in a strangled voice. *For the trip to Dallas. Because I wanted to look good for you.* Somehow she managed not to hide her eyes. "Don't ask."

"Okay if we clear a space?" He set her down gently on the floor.

"I'll help." Her sense of humor returning as quickly as her smile, Molly picked up an armload of garments and tossed them onto a nearby reading chair. He laughed and carried the rest over and set it on top.

The sheets were already rumpled. She hadn't had time the previous morning to make her bed.

"Now, where were we?" he asked her, easing his hands beneath the hem of her sweater.

"Kissing and making up?" At least that was where she wanted them to be. She hated fighting with him. Hated the thought that they might go back to what they had been, irritants who did nothing more than get each other's goat.

He grinned. "I think I can pick up there..." He gathered her close and lifted her face to his. Their mouths met, and she savored the feeling of his lips moving over hers. He kissed her like there was nothing standing between them, nothing but this moment in time. And it wasn't hard to stay in the moment, not when his hands were sifting through her hair, his tongue was playing with hers, even as the powerful muscles of his chest abraded the softness of her breasts and, lower still, his hardness pressed against her belly.

Something was happening between them, something that thus far had surpassed her wildest expectations. And she could no more deny it than the desire welling up inside her. Her knees weakening, her whole body swaying, she threw herself into the kiss. She ran her hands over his chest, unbuttoning his shirt, tugging the thermal tee from the waistband of his jeans. She smoothed her hands over the warm, satiny muscles of his pecs, finding out his nipples were as hard as hers. She kissed his neck, savoring the salty taste of his skin.

He did the same, easing his palms beneath her sweater, unfastening her bra, then smoothing his palms over her breasts. Quivering as he found the taut, aching buds, Molly lifted her mouth to his. And still they kissed. Caresses pouring out of them, one after another. Feelings built and desire exploded in liquid, melting heat. Unable to stand it any longer, they undressed. Quickly. Then joined each other in the mussed sheets of her bed.

He found protection, and she strained against him. Wanting. Needing. Pleasing. She lifted her hips. The hard length of him pressed into her. She had time to draw one breath and then they were kissing again, as if the world, their world, was going to end. Her inhibitions fled, and she arched against him, drawing him in.

He held her arms above her head. Timing his movements, increasing her pleasure, then his. Building, probing, taking her to the very depths. Until she was clenched around him, gasping his name, and he was saying hers. They were racing toward the edge, spinning over, drifting ever so slowly back to consciousness. Then holding each other, kissing ravenously, they started all over again.

"I'm going to work late tonight. Want to join me?" Chance asked an hour later.

Molly shook her head. "I have to pick up Braden from his playdate."

"I could come by later. We could all have dinner together."

Silence.

"Or not," he said.

Molly swallowed. Clad only in her bra and panties, she sat on the edge of her bed. Now that the lovemaking was over, and it was back to the normal routine, whatever that was, she seemed confused and on edge. And that gave rise to an unexpected insecurity in him, as well.

Molly paid an inordinate amount of attention to the act of putting on her wild purple socks. "Even with the nap he had in the car this morning, en route back from Dallas, it's been a really long day for him."

Chance resisted the urge to take her in his arms and make love to her all over again. Until she finally believed, as did he, everything was eventually going to be okay. "You want to put the little tyke to bed early?" he presumed.

Turning, Molly nodded.

"You want to put yourself to bed early, too?"

She trembled with exhaustion and something else. "I think so, yes." She flashed a weak grin.

He wished he were invited, but he could see it wasn't going to happen. Not tonight anyway. He rose and began to dress, aware there was one thing they hadn't finished. "About the Leo and Lizzie toys..."

Her eyes lifted to his. The turbulent sheen was back. "I know you went to a lot of trouble, but I'm going to have to think about that. Let you know."

Another harbinger of trouble to come? Or just a necessary time-out? Chance couldn't tell. And he still didn't know when he got back to the Circle H. The guys were preparing to work late to finish the removal of the last of the backsplash tile that had already gone up. Chance told them to go on. "I'll finish it," he said.

"Sure, boss?"

He nodded. Truth was, he needed some time alone. Needed to be busy. Needed not to think about what would happen if Molly did what she was promising all along, and left for Dallas in January.

"Things went badly with Molly, hmm?" Sage observed, walking in, covered dinner plate in hand.

Chance looked up from his hammer and chisel.

The lovemaking between he and Molly had been spectacular. To the point he was still replaying it in his mind, and would be, he figured, all night. Molly's reaction afterward, the way she had pulled away emotionally yet again, had not been so great. But none of this was something he wanted to discuss with his sister, even if he could see she was trying to help.

"What makes you think that?" he asked casually.

"Duh. Mom told me how upset she was about the Toy Emporium boxes." Sage set his dinner plate down. "Sounds like you really blew it."

Chance kept right on chiseling off tile. "You wouldn't think that if you could have seen Braden's face when he was playing with those trains, the way he lit up. Plus, it'd be a great way to get him off the subject of expecting Santa to bring him a live bull for Christmas, if he had to make a choice." In fact, Chance was pretty sure it would solve the problem entirely. And hadn't that been the goal from the outset?

Sage settled on the sawhorse. "Look, there's no denying your heart was in the right place, even if it was your stubborn attitude that got you into this mess in the first place. But you have to understand. To do all that on top of what you did to get Molly and Braden interviewed at Worthington Academy—"

A piece of tile fell out of his hand and shattered as it hit the floor.

Grimacing, Chance hunkered down to sweep up the shards. "Molly doesn't know I had anything to do with that. She thinks it was your alumni letter of recommendation that opened the door."

Sage paled. "If she finds out."

"She won't. I talked to Elspeth Pyle, the headmistress."

Sage paused. "Is Braden's acceptance a sure thing?"

Chance shook his head. "No. The decision, whatever it is, will be merit based. I made sure of that."

Another heavy silence fell. Finally, his sister got up to hold the dustpan for him. "What I don't understand is why you got involved with any of this elite private school stuff at all, Chance. Given the way you felt about your education there."

He took the pan and emptied it into the trash barrel with the rest of the broken tile.

Aware Sage was still waiting, he explained, "I did it because it was what Molly wanted." And he wanted her to have everything she wanted and more.

Sage settled on the sawhorse once again.

Figuring if he ever wanted his little sister to vamoose, he was going to have to eat, Chance picked up the plate and removed the foil. "And because up to now it's been more idealistic than real for Molly." He shoveled up a bite of tamale pie that was, he admitted, as delicious as everything else his chef sister made.

"In what sense?" Sage asked.

"Molly's a small-town girl from a protected environment. She hasn't had a clue what she would really be getting into, moving among those kind of people." He paused to eat a little more and let his words sink in. "I wanted her and Braden to see and experience it firsthand."

Sage went to the cooler they kept for the workers and fished out bottles of flavored water for them both. She uncapped and handed him his. "Did the tour of the academy discourage Molly the way you hoped?"

That was the hell of it. "No."

"So she may still be leaving Laramie County after all," Sage surmised, as unhappy for him as he felt.

"She's still got time to reconsider," Chance said.

Sage studied him, empathy in her eyes. "But you want them here with you."

He did. More than he wanted to admit. Even to himself.

# Chapter 9

"You've got company," Billy said.

Chance turned in the direction his hired hand indicated. Sure enough, a red SUV had parked in the drive beside the ranch house. His pulse picked up as he saw the driver-side door open. Molly stepped out.

It had been nearly seventy-two hours since they'd spoken. Although it had been hard as hell, he'd given her the space she requested. Hoping that once she thought more about it, she would see that his heart had been in the right place, even if his actions regarding Braden's gift had been—in her view, anyway—completely misguided.

"Want me to take over for you?"

"Yeah." Chance opened up one last gate. Jingle All the Way lifted his head and eagerly moved out of his stall into the bull exerciser. With all four slots filled, Chance turned toward his visitor.

Molly came toward him, a vision in a red wool coat, snowy white blouse, jeans and boots. That quickly his heartbeat sped up.

She inclined her head toward the circular slow-moving

metal fence that connected to a long chute from the barn. "That looks like an open-air revolving door."

Chance closed the distance between them. Just as he had hoped, she was wearing that orchid perfume he liked. "Bucking bulls are athletes. They need to stay in shape." He pointed out the four individual sections that kept the animals apart. "The competition of following the bull in front of them keeps them interested."

Molly smiled and stepped even closer to Chance. "Pretty cool way to keep them in shape." She tilted her face up to his. "How long do they stay in there?"

"Thirty minutes daily."

"Impressive."

He quirked a brow. "That why you're here?"

"Nope. I need to talk to you. In private, if possible."

He wanted to be alone with her, too. As they headed away from the bull barns, and the attention of his hired hands, her soft lips twisted ruefully.

"I want to apologize for not being more appreciative the last time we saw each other." She paused to get a pretty glass container with a ribbon wrapped around the top from her vehicle. She had to lean across the driver seat to reach it. The hem of her coat rode up, revealing her nicely rounded derriere and slender, shapely thighs.

She inhaled deeply, as she straightened and faced him once again. Solemnly, she continued, "In retrospect, I see you were trying to help me achieve my goal of gifting Braden the Leo and Lizzie toys in a way that was impossible for me. So, if you will accept my peace offering of *Vanillekipferl*, or almond crescent cookies, I'd like to make a deal with you."

He accompanied her up the steps to the ranch house. Aware he was happier than he'd been in three days, he paused to hold the door for her. "I'm listening."

She scooted past. Allowing him to take her coat, she waited for him to remove his, then handed him the cookie jar. "I'd like to purchase the Leo and Lizzie World Adventure train table from you. The basic starter track set. And one of the destination kits from you. Preferably the San Antonio River Walk setup, since Braden's actually been there."

Tenderness spiraled through him. "The rest?"

"You can do whatever you like."

Then that was easy, Chance thought. He'd keep them for the future, to give to Braden, one at a time, on the holidays and birthdays to come.

Oblivious to his thoughts, Molly suggested, "You can sell the other components to parents who are still looking for them or gift them to your nephew Max."

Chance worked the lid off the jar and ate one of the cookies. *Delicious.* "He just took his first steps so he's a little young yet for the train."

Molly paused. "Right. Well, anyway, does that sound good to you?"

What was right was having her here again, in his home, meeting him halfway on an issue that was very important to both of them. He couldn't help but think that was a sign of more good things to come.

"I took all the boxes and put them in the spare room I use for storage. They're still in the shipping cartons, so you may want to open them so you can get a better look at what you'd be buying." There were colorful pictures on every box.

Molly's amber eyes gleamed. "Sounds good."

He went into the kitchen and got a pair of scissors for her.

Figuring he'd give her more of the space she had requested, then join her when she was ready for his company, he pointed down the hall that led to the bedrooms. "First room on your left."

"Thanks." With another grateful look, Molly disappeared down the hall.

Outside, a purring car engine halted. Doors slammed.

Chance went to the window and swore at what he saw.

Molly had just cut open the first box when she heard the feminine voice coming from the living area. "Stop being so stubborn, Chance Lockhart!" Babs's distinctive drawl echoed through the home. "This is a fantastic offer!"

"I told you," Chance growled back. "I'm not selling to Mr. X, and I'm certainly not going to become partners with him!"

"Think of the capital he's ready to infuse!"

"Rather not, Babs."

Silence.

"If you do things Mr. X's way, you'd finally be able to make it up to Delia—"

"Mom! Our commission on this deal is not Chance's responsibility!"

*No kidding*, Molly thought.

"Wouldn't it be nice to finally be able to give Delia what she deserves?" Babs persisted. "Since you wasted nearly ten years of her eligibility, stringing her along, *pretending* to be interested in something long term, like marriage?"

*Ouch*, Molly thought. Although she could hardly imagine Chance pretending anything. He was usually as straightforward as possible.

"First of all, *Mom*," Delia cut in again. "Those weren't wasted years! Chance and I learned a lot from each other."

Chance's heavy footsteps moved across the wood floor. "Ladies, thanks for stopping by. Next time—" the front door opened "—save yourself the trip."

Molly surreptitiously looked out the window blinds into the yard. A miserable-looking Delia was already getting into the sleek black limo. Her fur-clad mother was unable to resist one last insult lobbed Chance's way.

"And here I was hoping you would have gotten at least a little wiser when it comes to what is important in life." Babs sniffed, glaring at Chance. "Apparently not!"

Molly moved away from the window as the limo drove off.

She walked back to the main living area in time to see Chance feeding another set of papers to the shredder.

"You heard."

"Impossible not to. You okay?"

"Just frustrated."

"Why do they keep coming back when you've already told them no?" Molly thought about the lingering emotional connection she'd heard briefly in Delia's voice. Babs had to be aware of it, too. "Is Babs trying to reunite you and Delia via reverse psychology?"

Chance laughed mirthlessly. "I would hardly think so."

But there was something devious going on with the older woman. Molly felt it in her bones.

"The last thing Babs wants is her daughter on a ranch in the middle of nowhere. Even if the proposal she just hammered out would likely quadruple my income in the next year."

She did a double take. Unable to suppress her shock, she echoed, "Quadruple it? *Really*?"

He lifted his broad shoulders in a derisive shrug. "Sure, if I wanted to sell half interest in all thirty of my bulls and start aggressively marketing bull semen."

They were standing so close she could feel the heat emanating from his powerful body. "Why don't you want to do that?"

He walked over to plug in the Christmas tree. The lights added a cheerful glow to the glittering silver-and-gold ornaments. Noticing the star at the top was listing slightly to one side, he reached up to straighten it, then turned back to her.

"If you partner with someone on a rodeo bull, the partner gets an equal say in how often, when and where, you let the bull compete."

"And that's a problem because...?"

He opened up a tin of the dark chocolate peppermint patties he favored and offered her one. This time she took it.

"Partners can get greedy and think more about the bottom line than the health and welfare of the animal."

Eyes still on his, she ripped open the foil covering. "What about stud services?"

"Again, I prefer to pick and choose. Keeping the offspring genetically admirable keeps the price high."

He opened the fireplace screen. "Letting just anyone breed off your bulls can affect the quality of calves, and that in turn can affect reputation. And lowered reputations mean lowered prices." He added a few more logs to the grate, adjusting them just so. "Plus, I like the size of the ranch and stable I have now." He added tinder and lit a match. "I don't want any more."

Molly moved close enough to admire the leaping flames. "I can understand that. Sometimes independence is more important than more money in the bank." She stepped back as he closed the screen again and stood, too. "What I don't understand is why Babs is so fixated on arranging the sale of Bullhaven to Mr. X. I mean, I know that Mistletoe is a national champion, and you have an incredible reputation within the business, but it's not like she couldn't find another bull operation in Texas for Mr. X to invest in." She furrowed her brow in confusion. "And since he wants to add venture capital, too, and become a half-interest partner, he could easily find people with the skills to vastly improve whatever bucking-bull operation he does end up purchasing."

The brooding expression on Chance's face indicated this was bothering him, too.

Molly paused. "Is she trying to wreak some sort of revenge on you for not giving her daughter the kind of pampered life-style Babs feels Delia deserves? By either taking away or disrupting what she knows means the most to you? Your ranch?"

He grinned, his ardent gaze roving her upturned face. "You sound protective."

Molly flushed. She *felt* protective. Even though, technically, she really had no right to be that involved in his life. Given that they were simply friends—and temporary lovers— Molly squared her shoulders and drew a bolstering breath. "I just don't want to see you used by someone who definitely does not seem to have your best interests at heart. No matter what Babs tells her daughter. It's not right."

"Right or not, that's the way Delia's mother operates."

Molly squinted, her need to protect Chance and everything he held near and dear increasing tenfold. "What do you mean?"

"Babs always has an agenda. Right now, my guess is that it has more to do with Mr. X than me, since it's his billions she wants for her daughter."

Molly took a moment to think about what he was saying. "So Babs is using you and your past with Delia—" *and Delia's residual feelings for you, whatever they are* "—to make Mr. X jealous."

"Maybe." Chance shrugged, not seeming to care either way. He walked toward her and took her in his arms. Molly gasped as he ran a hand down her spine, flattening her against him.

"What are you doing?"

He scored his thumb across her lip before continuing in a voice that melted her resistance, "Giving you that make-up kiss I owe you."

\* \* \*

Chance wasn't sure that Molly was going to let him make love to her. At least not then. It was, after all, the middle of the workday.

Yet the moment he took her in his arms, he felt her cuddle against him. As if she had been waiting for and wanting this moment, too.

Grinning, he reached into his pocket. Found the little branch of leaves and berries he had been carrying around in his pocket. "I also want to get at least one kiss in under the mistletoe this holiday season," he teased, holding it above her head.

She rose up on tiptoe, the scent of her inundating his senses. "I think," she whispered, her yearning for him clear as day, "this is the place where I get a kiss in under the mistletoe, too." Her mouth opened beneath his, and their tongues mated in an erotic dance. Pleasure swept through him as he stepped between her legs. Anchoring an arm beneath her softly curving derriere, he lifted her up and situated her so her weight was against his middle. She wrapped her legs snugly around his waist, and his blood heated even more.

He carried her down the hall to his bedroom, loving the way she felt against him, so warm and womanly. Their eyes locked as he set her down next to the bed. Undressing her felt extraordinarily intimate, pleasurable.

She eased off his shirt, kissing him, her lips softening beneath his. She clung to him, her fingers dipping into his shoulders, back and hips. Savoring everything about this moment, he delighted in the sweet taste of her. Of the way she continued undressing him, just as he had unwrapped her.

They drank in the sight of each other. She moaned as he rained kisses across her cheek, behind her ear, down the slope of her neck, before zeroing in on her mouth again.

She surged up against him, wrapping her arms around him, then tumbled him onto the bed.

He laughed in surprise. Tempestuous need glittered in her eyes as she followed him down and playfully straddled his middle. She threaded her fingers through his hair and stretched her body out languidly over the length of his, her heat cradling his pulsing hardness. He knew she thought this was just about sex. But it wasn't, he thought, as he let her deepen their kisses and rock against him. It was so much more.

Determined to make this lovemaking more memorable than either of them had ever had, he rolled so she was beneath him. He parted her knees and lay between her thighs. She came up off the bed as his lips lowered, suckling gently. Her thighs fell even farther apart as Chance kissed and stroked. And still it wasn't enough for either of them.

Molly teetered on the edge as he found a way to touch her that made her feel pleasured and desired, wanted and protected. Although she had promised herself she would wait for him, there was no delaying. She shuddered and fell apart in his arms. He held her tenderly until the aftershocks passed, then took her mouth again in a long, hot, tempestuous kiss. She shivered as the hardness of his chest teased the sensitive buds of her breasts, and lower still, the velvety hardness of his arousal nestled against her sex. She was so wet and so ready. And still he kissed her, until she throbbed and whimpered low in her throat. And only then, when she could stand it no longer, did he slide inside in one smooth, languid stroke. She clenched around him as he filled her completely. Taking her and making her his. Letting her possess him in response. Until her wildest Christmas wish was every dream fulfilled.

Afterward, Molly snuggled against him. He stroked a hand

through her hair. Then she asked, "Would you ever consider moving to Dallas?"

His hand stilled. He continued to study her as if trying to figure something out. "I grew up there, Molly."

She focused on the unmistakable warning in his voice. "And never want to go back?"

His eyes darkened. "I don't mind visiting."

*You'll never get what you want if you don't try.* She drew on all the courage she possessed. "Would you ever consider visiting Braden and me, when we move there next month?"

He sat up against the headboard, the sheet draped low across his hips. "As...?"

Molly drew her gaze away from the flat plane of his abdomen. A distracting shiver tore through her. "What we are now. Friends."

He ran a hand down her arm. "Lovers?"

She wished he didn't look so damn good, even in his disheveled state. "If we can work it out." It would mean babysitters. Rendezvousing. Arranging things in a way that wouldn't leave Braden—or her—confused.

Molly understood that Chance wanted more than that. Yet he also had to know what a big step this was for her.

He watched her tug the sheet a little more snugly beneath her arms. "Does this mean we're exclusive?"

Heat gathered in her chest, and spread, from the tops of her breasts into her face. She worried her bottom teeth with her lip. "Does it?"

"I already feel that way about you, darlin'."

Molly relaxed. Her body nestled against his. "I don't want you seeing anyone else, either," she admitted softly.

"Then that settles it." He pulled her against him for a long, thorough kiss that quickly had her tingling from head to toe. "We're officially a couple."

She splayed a hand over his broad chest, aware they still had a few hurdles left. "We will be," she stipulated firmly. "After the Open House your mother is hosting."

He paused. "What are you talking about?"

Molly swallowed and sat up against the headboard. She had to be completely honest with him or this would never work. "Lucille has invited me to attend as her protégé. She wants to give my design business a big boost."

"I knew that."

She wet her lips. "If it were known that I was also seeing you romantically, it might look like I was only with you to get ahead, or she was just helping me as a favor to you."

He sobered understandingly. "You'd be called a gold digger."

She nodded. Embarrassed, but determined. "I don't want to complicate my business future like that." She jerked in a breath, rushed on. "Because if Braden does get accepted at Worthington Academy, I'm really going to need more than just the two small jobs I already have lined up to make a real go of it."

She studied him, a wry smile tugging at the corners of her lips. "So, can you keep our relationship under the covers for just a little while longer?"

It was Chance's turn to look pained. "Are we talking weeks?"

"I'd rather not say anything until much later in the spring."

So months, he realized unhappily. He pushed a little higher against the headboard, too. "You don't think people are going to catch on to us spending so much time together?"

Molly took his hand. "If I were still living in Laramie, yes, of course. If I'm in Dallas…it's a lot easier to keep things on the down low there if we stay out of the high-profile places." She squeezed his hand lightly. "What are you thinking?"

Chance frowned. "I've never been asked to stay in the shadows before. Usually people are all too eager to claim a relationship with me, whether one really exists or not."

"Exactly." Molly laid her head on his shoulder. "You're the son of Lucille and Frank Lockhart. You come from one of the most socially prominent families in the state. People want to make use of that connection." She lifted his hand to her lips, kissed the back of it.

"Only you don't," he said, threading his fingers through her hair, lifting her face to his. He slanted his mouth over hers, kissed her again, softly, appreciatively.

Her worry, that they wouldn't be able to make this work long-term, fading, Molly swung her body lithely over top of his. Her heart swelling with all she felt for him, she confided, "I don't want anything from you. Except friendship." She nipped playfully at his lips. "And this..." To show him how deeply she cared, she made love with him all over again.

# Chapter 10

"What you got me, Cowboy Chance?" Braden asked early one evening, a week and a half later when Chance came through the door, another yuletide shopping bag in hand.

"Whoa now. You don't know that's for you," Molly told her son. Although for most of the last ten nights, Chance had been there with her and her little boy, baking cookies, and working on their Christmas village in progress.

But prior to this, he had shown up with only one new item at a time.

Molly had appreciated his restraint.

Tonight, however, appeared to be different, Molly noticed as she and Chance exchanged looks.

"That's true." Chance backed up her efforts to instill manners in her little boy. He hung his jacket up and walked over to the sofa. "But as it happens—" he winked at Braden as they drew all three folding chairs up to the folding tables "—what's in here is for you and your mommy."

"Can I see?" Braden asked eagerly. "Please?"

Chance motioned for Molly to sit down on the other side

of her son. He opened up the bag and lifted out a rectangular figurine. "Let's start with this."

Braden's eyes widened in appreciation. "That looks like our house," Molly said of the bungalow with the white picket fence.

Her son set them up carefully between the ranch and the North Pole.

Chance opened the bag. Braden pulled out more. "Mrs. Santa Claus!" her son exclaimed. "And more reindeer!"

"To go with Rudolph and the sleigh."

Braden hopped up and down and put them in the North Pole section of their Christmas village.

"Maybe we should let Mommy open the next one," Chance said.

Braden clapped. "Yes. Mommy do it!"

Not sure what this was all about since Chance wouldn't tell her much except that he had decided he needed to vastly accelerate his "plan," to allow for more focus on the Leo and Lizzie train set as they got closer to Christmas, Molly opened it up. Inside were two figurines to add to the ones Chance had already brought. One of a modern Western woman with auburn hair similar to Molly's, and one of a redheaded little boy—also in Western gear. Beneath the figurines, Chance had written the identifying information.

"Gosh," he said, leading the conversation. "That sure looks like you, Mommy. And this one looks like you, Braden."

"I think it is us!" Touched, Molly laid her hand across her heart.

Braden admired both, then reverently put them by the bungalow with the white picket fence. He studied the scene for a long, thoughtful moment.

To Molly and Chance's mutual dismay, his happiness turned to confusion. Plaintively, he walked over to Chance and looped his arms around their visitor's neck. "Where you, Cowboy Chance?"

"Sorry about that," Molly said after Braden had finally gone to sleep. She moved around the kitchen, baking that evening's batch of cookies—*hausfreunde*. "When Braden gets stuck on a question, sometimes he can't get off of it."

Chance understood the little boy's need to make them a family. He felt it, too. He sampled the buttery almond-apricot sandwich cookie dipped in bittersweet chocolate that Molly handed him. "Do you want me to get a likeness of myself?"

Molly dipped another cookie, then set it on waxed paper to dry. "I don't know. I mean…you might not even be with us next year." She paused to send him a hesitant glance— the kind that only came up when they were discussing their relationship.

She swallowed, her soft lips compressing, and turned her glance away. "If the long-distance thing doesn't work…"

He caught her around the waist and tugged her close. Bending his head, he kissed her lips lightly. Tasting chocolate. "It'll work, Molly. And I'll be here."

He studied her as they drew apart. "So what else is going on?"

Molly bent her head over her baking, a clear sign she was evading. "What do you mean?"

He gave her the room she seemed to need. "I could tell something was bothering you the minute I walked in the door."

This time, Molly did look up. Her eyes glittered with disappointment. "I received a letter in the mail today. Braden was wait-listed at Worthington Academy."

Chance didn't know whether to celebrate the fact that Molly's reasons for leaving Laramie in January had just diminished or share in her deep disappointment. "I'm sorry, darlin'."

He took a seat on the other side of the island. *Tread cautiously.* "Did they say why?"

"No." Molly's lips twisted into a troubled line. "But I was offered a Skype conference with the headmistress and admissions counselor, so I plan to see what kept him from getting in, and what his chances are of getting off the wait list. And if they aren't good, if there is a chance he will be admitted in the fall semester."

Chance couldn't help but be disappointed that Molly had yet to change her mind about enrolling Braden there. He sent her a brief commiserating glance. Then, speaking from his own heart, he encouraged firmly, "Braden's a great kid, Molly. He will thrive no matter where he is."

"I know." Her eyes still glimmered with tears, but she shook off the rising emotion. "I just really wanted him to have this opportunity. But if he doesn't get it this year, I've already got a deposit down at a safety preschool in the area where I intend to rent a house."

Now it was Chance who felt like he'd received a major blow. Not that he hadn't been warned. He had. "Have you put a deposit down on a home, too?" He kept his attitude casual.

"No." Molly relaxed, as well. "That's the good thing about Dallas. It's so big there are plenty of places that would fit my needs in the short term."

If he couldn't dissuade her, he could sure as hell join her.

"You'll let me know if there is anything I can do to help?"

She smiled at him sweetly. "Of course. But I think I've got everything covered...

Meaning what? Chance wondered.

She didn't need him?

Or didn't want to need him?

How was he going to change that? He wondered, perplexed. Because he sure as hell was beginning to need them.

\* \* \*

"Is there something wrong?" Molly asked Lucille several long, productive days later, when she arrived at the site to find her client upset.

She exchanged puzzled looks with Chance. He seemed as out of the loop as she felt.

"Is there something you don't like, Mom?" he asked in a low tone.

Heaven knew they didn't want Chance's mother to be unhappy with the renovation. This was their first joint project. The reputation of both their contracting firms was at stake.

Lucille glanced around at the finished backsplash, gleaming new appliances, countertops. Although the tile was newly sealed, there were smudges on the windows and stickers on the appliances. The newly finished wood floors bore the occasional dusty footprint. But all that was to be expected.

"We'll get a cleaning crew in here as soon as the touch-up painting is finished. The whole house will sparkle before we bring a speck of furniture in next week."

Lucille waved off the concern. "The renovation looks even better than I imagined. It's the Open House."

Sage walked in. Chance's eldest brother, Garrett, and his wife, Hope—a crisis manager and public relations expert— were at her side. "We got your message," Garrett said, cradling their nine-month-old son, Max, in his arms. The former army doc was now Lockhart Foundation CEO and medical director of West Texas Warrior Assistance.

Hope kissed her mother-in-law's cheek. "I'm not sure we understand the message you left."

Lucille fretted, "You all know I sent out a ton of invitations."

"Because you want to raise as much money as possible for the military vets we're helping," Garrett said.

"Most of the people I invited live in Dallas or Fort Worth. Since it's the holidays, I didn't think we would have that many acceptances."

"Let me guess," Sage said. "You were pleasantly surprised."

Lucille threw up her hands in distress. "We have four *hundred* people coming—so far. I don't know where we're going to put everyone!"

Hope already had her phone out. "It's not a problem. I can get some tents and tables and chairs. Heaters, too, if that cold front continues our way."

"I'll just make a lot more food," Sage said, with a former caterer's aplomb.

Lucille paced. "We're talking five days from now."

"It will work out, Mom." Chance wrapped his arm around Lucille's shoulders.

"The ranch house will not just be done—it will be letter perfect," Molly promised. "It will be decorated beautifully inside and out, too."

Lucille frowned. "What about entertainment? If it was a much smaller gathering, I was just going to have holiday music playing unobtrusively in the house, but now..."

"Some of the military vets have a band," Garrett said, shifting his son a little higher in his arms. "They've played at some of our parties."

"They're really good," Hope put in. She grinned as Max reached over and tangled his fingers in her hair. Pulling her close, he gave his mommy a kiss.

Molly envied the sight of Garrett, Hope and Max. They made such a cute little family. The kind she could have if only she stayed.

"I'll see if I can get the band to play," Garrett offered.

The meeting went on for another twenty minutes. Finally,

everyone left. Molly walked out with Chance to get the lights and garlands that she planned to go ahead and string on the front porch. She sent him a companionable glance. Strange as it was, just now she'd felt a little like family. Maybe because the Lockharts had gone out of their way to include her.

"I've never seen your mom that rattled."

Frowning, Chance carried the stepladder onto the porch. "It's because she hasn't seen a lot of those folks since she left Dallas."

Molly took the lights out of the packaging. "Sage said some of them had turned their backs on Lucille when the scandal regarding the Lockhart Foundation came to light."

The brackets on either side of Chance's mouth deepened. "Actually," he reported grimly, snapping his tool belt around his waist, "it was most of the people Mom knew."

"That must have been hard."

Chance propped the ladder against the roof of the porch and began to climb. "The amazing thing is Mom doesn't blame them. She says if she had been guilty of withholding funds from the nonprofits the foundation claimed it was helping, they'd be right to dismiss her. Anyway, she's all about the fresh start, concentrating on what really matters."

Molly handed him the end of the strand. "And for her, that's helping people."

He secured it to the newly painted facing. "And taking care of her family." Having put up as much as he could reach from that vantage point, he climbed back down the ladder.

Molly tilted her face to his. "What's important to you?"

He grabbed her around the waist, tugging her close. "Right now?" He waggled his brows teasingly. "You."

Before she could stop him, he had delivered a slow, deep kiss that had her knees ready to buckle, her toes tingling.

Molly planted her hands on the center of his chest. "Chance," she reprimanded. "Someone might see."

The pleasure they'd experienced faded. His expression became inscrutable once again. "Right." He nodded, compliant but clearly unhappy, too. "We're still on the down low…"

Molly swallowed. She didn't want to hurt him, but she had to be honest about her needs. "It's just until I get my business efforts in Dallas off the ground," she said.

Chance stepped back, something even more indecipherable in his hazel eyes. "Does that mean I'm uninvited to the preschool program this evening?"

"No. Braden really wants you there. But I think it might be better if we drove separately, and then met up at my house later for a little after-school program gala for Braden." She paused. "Does that sound okay?"

A muscle ticked in his jaw. And for a moment, Molly thought he was going to say, *No, it isn't okay at all.* Then the moment passed. He climbed right back up the ladder again. She handed him the next section of the light strand. "What time should I be there?" Chance asked quietly.

Molly relaxed. "The program starts at seven," she informed him with a relieved smile. "I'll save you a seat." It was going to make Braden so happy, having Chance there. Her, too.

"Chance Lockhart, what are you doing at a preschool program?" Mary Beth Simmons, the local PTA president and resident busybody, demanded.

*Practicing my down low*, Chance thought grumpily, then shrugged and mimed total innocence. "I heard it was an event not to be missed."

Mary Beth squinted. "Who told you that?"

*First rule of hiding something?* Not that he'd had a lot of experience. *Be as honest as possible.* "Braden Griffith," he said and watched Mary Beth's gaze turned speculative. "Molly Griffith and I combined forces on a rush job for my mom, so we've been seeing a lot of each other. I've gotten to know her son. Cute kid."

Mary Beth tilted her head. "There are a lot of cute kids in Laramie, Chance."

*True enough.* He flashed an indulgent smile. "Most of them have a ton of family. Braden doesn't." He leaned toward her in a gossipy manner, meant to satisfy her need to be in the know. "And I think, times like this, the little tyke is beginning to notice the difference between his life, and—" Chance nodded at little Ava Monroe, who had her own fan club of McCabes and Monroes in attendance.

Chastened, Mary Beth straightened. "I see what you mean."

"Anyway, since I was invited, I volunteered to make his lack of extended cheerleaders not so obvious for little Braden."

Mary Beth laid a hand across her heart. "What a giving thing for you to do," she said, impressed.

Chance flashed a humble grin. "'Tis the season…"

"What was that about?" Molly asked, discreetly texting him as soon as he sat down next to her.

Aware she smelled like orchids…which meant she was wearing that perfume he liked. And that this was the closest thing to a date—albeit a clandestine one—that they'd ever had, Chance pulled out his phone and texted her back. I was pretending I was dragged here as a Good Samaritan.

"Oh." Molly formed the words with her soft lips.

He leaned down and whispered in her ear, longing for the day when they would have actual dates. And more. "We both know that's not the case." He hadn't been dragged. He'd been elated to be invited.

Around them, other phones and video cameras were being

readied. He lifted a curious brow. Molly explained. "Everyone's going to record it."

"How about I record, and you just watch? I'll email it to you later. That way you can just enjoy."

"Thank you."

He stifled a smile and kept looking straight ahead at the stage. "My pleasure."

They stopped talking at that point. Nevertheless, they got a lot of curious looks despite their efforts to be casual. Soon the kids marched up onstage, proud as could be, and the program started.

Chance was glad he was focused on recording. Otherwise someone might have seen the tear that came to his eyes as Braden puffed out his little chest, and belted out "We Wish You a Merry Christmas" and a half-dozen other holiday tunes at the top of his little lungs. That was, when Braden wasn't grinning and waving at Molly and him.

When the program came to an end, Chance was on his feet, clapping and whistling and hooting, as proud as any parent there. Everyone else was so caught up in the proud moment that his enthusiasm went unnoticed.

By all but Molly—and Braden.

"Cowboy Chance!" Braden cried, hustling down from the stage. "Hey, everybody!" He turned and waved vigorously at his two frequently mentioned best friends. "Come see— Cowboy Chance!"

Will and Justin got permission from their parents and high-tailed it to Braden's side. "He's got bulls!" Braden declared loudly.

Molly realized her son's vowel sounded more like an *a* than a *u*.

Several horrified adults turned in their direction.

"Black Angus bucking bulls of the national championship variety," Molly explained cheerfully to one and all.

A few parents, apparently not familiar with rodeo terms, looked even more confused.

"And barns!" Braden yelled blithely, as everyone around them chuckled at his earlier mispronunciation.

"And lots of other things, as well," Chance added. "Like bull barns."

"And fences!" Braden shouted.

"And training facilities."

"And *baby* bulls!" Braden repeated his earlier mispronunciation while slinging an index finger in Chance's direction. A gesture that, thanks to the discrepancy in their heights, ended up pointing a foot below Chance's waist.

More chuckles.

A few of the guys sent sympathetic, dad-to-dad glances Chance's way.

Which would have been funny, Chance thought, as the merry double entendres flying right above the toddler's heads increased, if not for Molly's increased embarrassment. Determined to spare them all any more unnecessary attention from the crowd, Chance knelt down so he and the little boy he adored were at eye level. He put his hand on Braden's shoulder. "Proud of you, buddy," he said fiercely, meaning it with all his heart. "That was a *great* job, singing."

Chance expected Braden to grin the way he always did when he was praised. He didn't expect him to look at Chance with equal affection and lift his hands, wordlessly asking to be picked up the way a lot of the other three-year-olds were being picked up for hugs by their dads.

A lump in his throat, Chance complied.

Braden hooked his hands around Chance's neck and hugged him like he never wanted to let go. For the first time in his life, Chance had an inkling, a real inkling of what it would be like to be a father. And not just any father. Braden's daddy. He liked it.

Almost as much as he liked the idea of one day being Molly's husband. Wasn't that a Christmas surprise?

# *Chapter 11*

"There is no doubt Braden is a very bright little boy," Worthington Academy's psychologist, Dr. Mitchard, said when the Skype conference Molly had requested began. "He had no trouble conversing on any subject that interested him. Like bulls."

*Oh, dear.*

"And Cowboy Chance."

Somehow Molly managed to keep a poker face. Even as her heart skipped a beat just hearing Chance's name.

"However, when we attempted to get him to focus on the word or number problems presented to him, he refused to speak," the headmistress told Molly.

"At all?" Molly could hardly believe it. Yes, her son's sentences were rudimentary, but Braden always had something to say. In fact, the hardest thing to do was get him to stop talking.

The psychologist, who had supervised the testing, nodded. "Even when he seemed to know the answer to our inquiries, which I'm sorry to relate, wasn't all that often, he refused to divulge it to us."

"Additionally, he does not have the background of second language, early reading and math, music and art instruction that our accepted students have. Hence, it's our considered opinion that he's not ready for such a rigorous academic pre-K curriculum," Elspeth Pyle said.

"If you know all that," Molly said, feeling hurt and confused, "why did you invite us to come all the way to Dallas for an in-depth admissions interview?" *Why did you have me drop everything to be there on such short notice?*

The two women exchanged glances.

The headmistress said, "Because we are always looking to diversify as much as we can, without lowering our high standards, and we don't currently have anyone in the three-year-old class who has come from a rural environment."

"Actually," Molly said, recognizing an evasion when she heard one, "we live in town."

"Well, he talked like he spent an inordinate time on a bull ranch!" the psychologist said.

"We were confused as to whether he might be living there, instead of the address on the application," Elspeth Pyle reiterated.

Chagrined, Molly admitted, "No. We've never stayed there." *Much as I might have wished.* "Braden's just visited a few times. He loves all animals, though." She spun it as best she could. "And he'd never seen any kind of cattle operation in person. So I guess it made a bigger impression on him than I realized."

"Perhaps so." The two administrators exchanged tense smiles. "Do you have any more questions?" Elspeth asked.

"Just one." Molly asked with a determined smile. "What are my son's chances of getting off the wait list?"

"At this point, not good. Not good at all."

"What you got, Cowboy Chance?" Braden asked several hours later when Chance stopped by just before bedtime, gift bag in hand, and scooped him up in his strong arms.

"A Christmas cowboy?" Braden hoped. He wrapped his arms around Chance's neck, giving him a happy hug. "Just like you?"

"I think we might get a couple more people for the village," Molly said in an effort not to put Chance on the spot. Not that the rugged rancher seemed to mind the request. "They have them at Monroe's Western Wear in town."

Chance set Braden in the middle of the sofa and sat down on one side of him. Molly took the other, watching as Chance opened up the by-now-familiar gift bag. "Let's see." Chance pulled out the first rotund figurine.

"Santa!" Braden clapped his hands.

"And look." He plucked out three Black Angus cattle figures.

"Mommy, daddy and baby bull!" Braden shouted excitedly.

"Hmm." Molly played along with the thoughtful gambit as her son kissed his new figures and hugged them to his chest. "Looks like the toy Santa Claus brought you the toy bull family that you wanted."

"And—" Chance plucked out a small square of Astroturf, surrounded by fence "—a pasture for them to stay in."

Braden turned to her. He seemed to understand in the brief silence that fell that this was a very elaborate consolation prize. So much for the school officials who had deemed him not able to understand enough, Molly thought in vindication.

"Real...want real...for me," Braden said emphatically, looking frustrated they still didn't understand what he was trying to communicate.

Except they did, Molly thought wistfully, withholding a sigh.

Solemnly, Chance interjected, "I talked to Santa on the phone about that."

Oh, boy, they were in dangerous territory now. Territory

they probably should have discussed beforehand. On the other hand, Braden was far more willing to accept what Chance said as gospel than anything his mere mother stated. Probably because Chance cut such a heroic figure. Which was definitely an anomaly around their house...

Braden stared, wide-eyed. "You call Santa?"

Chance shifted Braden onto his lap with the ease of a natural daddy. "He was very upset that he couldn't do this for you, because Santa Claus knows what a very good boy you have been this year, but he said a real bull family would not fit on his sleigh. He only has room to bring you a very special toy present. And you know what I said?"

Braden considered. Finally, he screwed up his little face into a hopeful expression.

"I said, that you know that all the toys that Santa brings are so very special, that you will be happy with whatever Santa brings you."

"Well, do you think we handled it?" Chance asked Molly after they tucked Braden into bed.

A sentimental look on her pretty face, Molly paused to admire the Christmas village they had put together over the course of the last weeks. It had a ranch like Chance's, a bull family, a house that looked like hers, figures that represented her and Braden, and a North Pole with Santa, sleigh and reindeer. The only thing it didn't have was Chance. As Braden had once again noted. The thing that sucked was that Chance wanted to be represented in the panorama that had come to mean so much to Braden, too.

What Molly wanted, however, was a lot more tenuous.

She wanted temporary. He wanted much more. But opinions could change. And he knew how to build on small successes, turn them into more.

"I think so." Molly turned and went into the kitchen, where she was preparing *Lebkuchen*. "I mean, you saw the way his face lit up at the Toy Emporium."

The tantalizing smell of fresh-baked German gingerbread cookies filled the space. Chance settled opposite her, predicting softly, "It'll be a big moment."

Molly bent to pipe white icing on each confection. "It will." She handed him a finished treat to taste. It was, as he had expected, completely delicious. As was everything she made.

Molly eyed him closely. A pulse was suddenly throbbing in her throat. "You know, you were such a big part of it, I think we should invite you. But—" she lifted a wary hand "—only if you want to see him when he first lays eyes on it."

He circled the counter and took her in his arms, aware how frequent moments like these could be if they joined forces and lived not just in the same county but under the same roof. "Is that an invitation to stay the night?"

She relaxed into the curve of his body, looking deep into his eyes. "Ah, no. I'm not doing that until I get married. And who knows if that will ever be."

But she was talking about it. Mulling over the possibility. A month ago she wouldn't have even done that.

He smiled, willing to be patient a little while longer. "Then how will this work?"

She looked up at him, as if in awe how good it felt to simply hang out this way. "Um...well, we could set the time for your arrival on Christmas morning at 5:00 a.m." An affectionate twinkle lit her amber gaze. "If he's not awake yet, we could have *stollen* and coffee while we wait. Then open presents and have a proper man-size breakfast later."

Her excitement was contagious. He kissed her temple. "It's a date."

Smiling, Molly went back to icing cookies.

Chance lounged against the counter. "By the way, how did the Skype meeting with the Worthington Academy staff go this afternoon?" He wanted to hear that Elspeth Pyle, Dr. Mitchard and the others had been as considerate of Molly's feelings as they would have been to any of the wealthy parents they dealt with.

Unfortunately, that did not appear to have been the case. Her expression troubled, Molly briefly related what had been said to her. He couldn't have disagreed more.

"They're wrong about Braden being ready for a more rigorous program," Chance said fiercely. "I've spent time with him. I know he could more than handle whatever they threw at him."

Molly grinned. "Watch it. You're sounding like a proud papa." As soon as the words were out, she blushed. Averting her glance, she amended hastily, "You know what I mean."

Chance curved a comforting hand around her shoulder. "I do," he admitted solemnly. "And you're right. I am very protective of him." *And you, too*, Chance added silently. *Much more than you know.*

Looking as if the Skype meeting had brought out all her worst insecurities, Molly nodded, admitting, "It's hard not to be protective with little kids. They're so vulnerable."

"True." Sensing she needed him more than she would admit, he turned to her and pulled her all the way into his arms. "But there's something very special about Braden." He stroked a gentle hand through her hair and lifted her face to his. "I felt a connection to him the first time we met."

"And he, you," Molly said, her shoulders tense in a way they hadn't been before they'd begun talking about Worthington Academy.

"Did they say anything else?" Chance pressed, wanting to know the whole story.

"No." Her casual, self-effacing tone hinted at the vulnerability she felt inside. "It was more a feeling I had."

He waited. Guilt that she might have found out what he had done to put her in this position, despite the precautions he had taken to prevent just such a revelation, roiled in his gut.

Molly shook her head, moving on to the next tray. "Like…" She struggled to put her intuition into words. "They'd been *forced* to interview him or something."

Maybe because they sort of had been.

He studied her, maintaining a poker face. "They said that?" His temper rose.

"No. It just…" She put more icing into the piping bag. "What they did say about needing to interview him for the diversity in backgrounds of their student body. I didn't buy it."

"How so?" he asked carefully.

"Well… I mean, you saw the children in the classes we observed. Even in identical uniforms, you could see they were all privileged kids from wealthy backgrounds. Their haircuts, their perfect body mass indexes, their posture, their demeanor…" She sighed heavily. "These were all kids who were used to being pampered, revered, adored."

The same could easily be said about her son, except for coming from money. "Braden has confidence, too," he pointed out.

Molly's face took on the fierce, maternal line he knew so well. "Not the confidence that comes from never having to want for or worry about anything."

Money in the bank only went so far. Chance disagreed. "Confidence is confidence."

Molly huffed and went to the sink to rinse the icing off her fingers. "You say that because you come from the other side," she accused him over her shoulder. "The side that had all the advantages. I didn't."

Chance waited until she turned around, then put a hand on either side of her, not touching her but effectively trapping her against the counter just the same. "Do you ever think that's part of what makes you who and what you are?"

His challenging tone had her lifting her chin. "And what am I?" she sassed.

*Plenty.* "Strong, independent, resilient, savvy, talented, gorgeous..." Watching the color come into her cheeks, he teased, "Shall I go on?"

She folded one arm against her waist, not touching him, either, and tapped her finger against her lips. "I like that you put my beauty at the end of the list." She wrinkled her nose playfully. "Such as it is."

Enough of her downgrading herself. He pulled her all the way into his arms, pressing her softness against his hardness. "What it is," he growled, "is amazing. Heart poundingly—" he paused to kiss her deeply "—wonderful."

She shook her head at him in silent remonstration. "You can stop now," she chided, even as her eyes filled with affection. "Compliments are not necessary."

Chance sobered. His heart ached for all that was still missing in her life. That could be so easily corrected. "They're not compliments, darlin'." He stroked his hand down her cheek and bent to kiss her again, tenderly this time. "They are heartfelt observations." And what he felt when he looked at her was all heart.

# Chapter 12

"I can't believe we're doing this," Molly murmured the next afternoon. She stepped out of his shower and wrapped a towel around her.

Chance shut off the spigot, his body still humming from their last incredible bout of lovemaking. Blotting the dampness from his hair and skin, he hung up his towel and joined her at the mirror. Coming up behind her, he aligned his naked body against hers and planted a kiss on the back of her neck. "Taking a long lunch hour?"

Molly turned to give him a mischievous glance that swept over him hungrily from head to toe, then ran a brush through her hair, restoring order to her still-damp curls.

She pivoted to face him. As she pressed against him, he could feel how much she wanted him. If only they had the time…"I can't believe—" she sent him an alluring glance from beneath her lashes, her nipples pearling beneath the towel "—we're taking a long lunch hour in your bed."

"And shower," he teased, following her into the bedroom. "I can." His body humming with resurging need, he watched her bend to pick up her clothes. Not ready to see her leave just yet, he tugged her against him for a sweet, leisurely kiss. "I think that was the best pre-Christmas present I ever had."

"Me, too," Molly murmured, kissing him back even more languidly.

He threaded his hands through her hair, wishing he didn't have to worry about rushing her into the next step. "Besides—" he kissed his way down her throat "—with the Circle H ranch house finished..."

Molly flitted out of his arms with a reluctant sigh, then slipped on her satin burgundy panties and matching bra. Shifting into the business mode he knew so well, she reminded him, "We still have to help decorate the interior for the Open House at the Circle H tomorrow morning. Make sure Sage and her catering staff have everything they need for the evening's festivities."

Noting the pleat of new worry between her brows, he shifted into work gear, too. Pulling on his boxer briefs, then his jeans, he reassured her confidently. "It's all going to go smoothly. We have Garrett's wife, Hope, in charge, remember? There's no crisis my sister-in-law can't handle. So even if there are problems, and I'm not expecting any, Hope will find solutions for them."

"I know." Molly eased a black turtleneck sweater over her head.

Chance's mouth went dry as she shimmied into her jeans. Dressed or undressed, she made him go hard with need. "Garrett and Wyatt have also volunteered to help. In fact, the only family member who won't be around to support Mom's entry back into the fund-raising nonprofit world will be Zane."

Molly sat down on the edge of his bed to tug on her favorite peacock-blue cowgirl boots. She extended one showgirl-quality leg, then the other. "Your mom mentioned Zane was going to try and get home for Christmas this year."

Chance nodded, his worry over his Special Forces brother briefly coming to the fore. "Even if he does make it, and there's no guarantee of that, it would likely be just in the nick of time, not for the Open House."

Molly sobered. "One of the disadvantages of serving in the military, I guess." Her frown deepened.

"I don't think Zane minds. In fact, I'm pretty sure he thrives on all the uncertainty and danger."

Molly nodded, her mood becoming even more distant.

Chance wrapped his hands around her waist and tugged her close. He bent his head to nuzzle the softness of her hair, inhale the sexy fragrance that was uniquely her. "My question is, what's really bugging you today?" Loving the way she felt in his arms, he kissed his way across her temple. She'd been moody all morning. Which was why he'd suggested their noontime rendezvous rather than try to get an actual date with her that evening. "The only time I've had your full attention is when we were making love."

She blushed in a way that made her look prettier, more womanly than ever, then admitted wryly, "Listen, cowboy, it's a little hard to think of anything else when you're…um…"

He chuckled, a deep rumbling low in his throat. "I know." He caressed the slender curve of her hip. "And don't think you're going to distract me asking me to show you what other extraordinary skills I have."

For a second, she looked just as tempted as he felt.

"Seriously." He brushed the pad of his thumb across her lower lip, wanting to help her out if he could. He looked deep into her eyes. "What's bothering you?"

Molly balled her hands into fists and blew out a frustrated breath. "If you must know, I don't have anything appropriate to wear to the Open House."

Chance squinted. "I've seen your closet, Molly. You're a clotheshorse."

She walked out of his bedroom and down the stairs, leaving him to follow. "Yes, but my clothes aren't designer duds. Which is why your lovely sister, Sage, volunteered to act as my stylist for the evening and lent me an absolutely gorgeous cocktail dress and the accessories that went with it."

He caught up with her in the kitchen. "That was nice of her."

Figuring she had to be as hungry as he was, he pulled out the cold cuts and cheeses. Handed her a plate and a loaf of multigrain bread.

With a sigh, she began assembling a sandwich. "Yes, well, we lamented our wardrobe crises together."

He got a plate and did the same. "What has Sage got to worry about?"

Molly looked in his fridge and brought out the mayo, spicy mustard and leaf lettuce. "Promise you won't mention it to her?"

Chance made an X over the center of his chest.

With a commiserating moue, Molly told him, "She had to have the dress she planned to wear to the gala let out at the seams. Apparently she's gained a little weight since coming back to Texas and opening her café bakery."

Chance shook his head in consternation. If he lived to be a hundred he would never understand why women worried about the shift of a few pounds in either direction.

He cut his sandwich in half, then went to find the chips. "Hard to see how, since she's had the stomach flu twice in the past six weeks."

Molly took a seat beside him at the island. "I heard she had been under the weather a couple of times." She picked up a sandwich that was as thin as his was thick. "Anyway, I have to get over there in forty-five minutes to pick up the dress, so as soon as I finish this, I've got to run."

He poured a couple of glasses of iced tea, not about to let her go before he'd nailed down their next time together. "Will I see you tonight?"

If she was free, maybe he could talk her into an official date. Even if they had to go all the way to San Angelo to have it, to avoid her fear of being seen together socially.

"Tomorrow morning. I have to spend the evening completing the pre-enrollment paperwork for Braden's new preschool in Dallas. They need it before Christmas if he's going to start there in January."

Chance was happy Molly had selected a place other than the high-stress Worthington Academy to put her son. Not so happy it was a good 150 miles away. He forced himself to be supportive anyway. "How does he feel about the move?" Chance asked cheerfully.

Molly broke a potato chip in two. "I haven't told him."

Chance narrowed his gaze. Molly was usually very up front with her son about what was going to happen next. And what was expected of him.

Her cheeks turning pink, she explained, "Once I have a rental home picked out to go see and the school set up, we'll take another trip there. I'll explain it all then, when I can show him where we are going to live and so on."

Disappointment knotted his gut. "So you're really doing this?"

She wasn't surprised he didn't want to see her go. However, his feelings did not change her mind. "I really am," she confirmed.

Except, Molly knew, as she left Chance and drove away from Bullhaven, she wasn't nearly as brave as she sounded.

The truth was the closer she got to actually making the big change, the more she did not really want to do it after all.

Yet the more rational part of her knew that she couldn't let last-minute jitters affect putting what had been a years-long plan for her and Braden's future into action.

Her son deserved the very best. She wanted him to have everything he could possibly have. The kind of opportunity and vast choices she had never been afforded.

She wanted the kind of financial security Chance and his siblings had grown up with, so that if, heaven forbid, anything ever happened to her, or Braden, she would have the money and resources to deal with it.

Right now she didn't.

And wouldn't if she stayed in the moderate-income range she currently enjoyed.

So like it or not, she was headed to the big city come January.

And she and Chance would have a casual, long-distance romance, or perhaps just fade out entirely.

Either way, she had to be a grown-up about it. She couldn't do what she did before with Aaron and be ready to base her whole life, all her plans for the future, on a man.

Because if her growing relationship with Chance didn't work out—as the affair with Braden's daddy hadn't—she would be devastated. Professionally and personally. The setbacks and fallout might be impossible to overcome.

She couldn't do that to herself. She couldn't do it to her son. So she would enjoy this Christmas the way she had never enjoyed a holiday before, she reassured herself fiercely, and move on from there.

"Sure you don't want me to pick you up?" Chance asked the following evening. Why was just the sound of his deep, gravelly voice so sexy? Why was his rock-solid presence so comforting and enticing? A lump rose to her throat as unbidden tears sprang to her eyes. Shaking off the unwelcome emotion, Molly finished slipping on the shoes that matched her borrowed dress.

Feeling part imposter, part Cinderella, she cradled the phone to her ear. "No, I have to drop off Braden. He's having a sleepover with Will and Justin tonight, at Justin's house."

"Ah." Chance chuckled softly. "Can we have a sleepover, too?"

*Why not?* Given how precious little time they had left to spend with each other. Plus, if the evening went as well as Lucille had predicted it would go for Molly, she'd likely have a lot to celebrate.

"Possibly," she murmured coyly, moving a small distance away from her son, who was busy playing with his Christmas village. "If you're a good boy and we're discreet."

"Oh, that can certainly be arranged, darlin'," he reassured her playfully. "So." His husky baritone was rife with promises. "My place?"

"Yes." She could leave very early tomorrow morning, before his hired hands arrived to take care of the bulls.

"See you soon then." His enthusiasm engendered her own. "And, Molly?"

Heavens, she was going to miss this man. So much. "Yes?"

"I want you to know." The warmth of his emotions kindled hers. "You and Braden have made this the best yuletide season of my life."

Molly smiled, knowing deep down she could not want for more. "Right back at you, cowboy."

Several hours later, Chance stood at the fringes of the crowd milling through the Open House at the newly renovated Circle H ranch house, making good on his promise not to be seen with Molly. It wasn't easy keeping his distance. She looked gorgeous as hell in a shimmering emerald-green cocktail dress, black velvet evening blazer and stiletto heels.

As previously arranged, his mother had her arm looped through Molly's and was taking her around, introducing her as the hottest up-and-coming interior designer.

From what he could see, a lot of interest was being generated. Which meant Molly would soon be as successful and financially secure as she dreamed of being.

In Dallas...

While he was here. Right where he wanted to be. Or had, until she and her young son had sauntered into his life.

"A million bucks for your thoughts," Chance's younger brother Wyatt gibed, joining him.

They clinked glasses. "Very funny." Chance sipped his Bourbon & Branch.

"Actually, it's appropriate."

Chance lifted a brow at the most cynical of his siblings.

With a knowing smirk, Wyatt informed him, "Mr. X is here, with Babs and Delia, and they're coming for you."

Chance promptly changed the subject to something his horse-ranching brother would *not* want to discuss. "As long as we're talking about affairs that are long over," he said smugly, "I saw Adelaide Smythe." She was Wyatt's very single, very pregnant with twins ex-girlfriend from way back, who Wyatt had never really gotten over.

Wyatt remained unflappable. Which meant, Chance intuited, the two had already crossed swords.

"As the new CFO of Lockhart Foundation, Adelaide would be expected to be here. The piranhas on the lookout for you, however, would not."

*So true*, he admitted reluctantly. "Mom invited them?"

"Apparently, Garrett and Hope found out that Mr. X has

a reputation for supporting nonprofits geared to helping our military and their families, so they suggested to Mom that she invite the very deep-pocketed Mr. X. I don't think they expected him to show up personally. But then, they hadn't heard about how he'd been attempting to buy you out." Wyatt lifted his glass to Chance. He nodded toward the trio emerging from one of the tents. "And here they come…"

Wyatt stepped aside to make room, but he stayed to watch the show. The woman who would have been his mother-in-law closed in. "Last opportunity," Babs told Chance.

Mr. X looked at Chance, too. "I'll even go down to only a forty-nine percent stake in the business, if that will turn the tide in my favor."

Chance shook his head.

Delia rolled her eyes. "Chance is. Just. Not. Interested."

Babs sent an irritated look at her daughter. "Chance doesn't need you to defend him, sweetheart."

Wordlessly, Delia spun away and headed into the crowd. Mr. X followed.

Babs glared at Chance. "I'm going to get Delia to forget you once and for all, if it is the last thing I do, Chance Lockhart!"

Chance was pretty sure that was already the case. He relaxed as Babs stormed off.

"Is Delia still carrying a torch for you?" Wyatt asked curiously.

Chance shook his head. "No."

But Mr. X sure seemed to be intent on pursuing Delia. The slightly geeky billionaire caught up with Babs's daughter at the fringes and put his hand on her waist. Leaning down, he said something into her ear. Delia shrugged free. Took off. Mr. X was right behind her, looking more determined than ever.

Thirty seconds later, Chance got a text from Delia.

* * *

Molly saw Chance winding through the crowd, walking past the bandstand toward the barns. She was about to follow him, hoping to surreptitiously get a moment alone with him, when Babs stepped out in front of her.

For once, the aggressive sales and acquisitions exec was not with her daughter or Mr. X, who, to Molly's surprise, had both also appeared there that evening. "Hello, dear," Babs said cheerfully. "I'd like to speak to you about doing a decorating job for me."

Molly was not at the point she could turn down any business in her new city. Though if she could have, this would have been the job she passed on. Determined to be professional, she plucked her phone from her blazer pocket and brought up her calendar. "Absolutely."

Babs wrote the address on the back of her business card. "The job is here in Laramie County. A house on the lake that I'm considering buying as rental property. Can you be there at 9:00 a.m.? The Realtor is going to open up the house. Then we can talk about what is possible in terms of renovation."

Out of the corner of her eye, Molly saw Mr. X come out from behind the barn. He was alone, and he looked ticked off.

Wondering what that was about, Molly turned her attention back to Babs. "I'll see you then."

Babs pivoted to see what Molly had been looking at, then headed off in the direction of Mr. X. Molly continued threading her way through the dwindling crowds, toward the barn.

As she neared it, she saw Delia standing in the shadows just behind it, arms folded in front of her. Chance was standing opposite his ex. They were talking. Seriously, it seemed. Delia did not seem to like what she was hearing from her ex. She threw up her arms in frustration and walked away, head bowed.

What was going on here? Molly wondered, stalled in her tracks.

Was there still something left between Chance and Delia?

Had Mr. X discovered the two of them together? Or had the three of them been talking in private—about the bucking-bull business yet again?

She had no more chance to ponder because Chance was striding toward her. He stopped just short of her. He waited until they were well out of earshot of other partygoers passing by, then grinned casually and quipped, "Am I allowed to talk to you yet?"

"Yes," Molly said, ready to bolt this fund-raiser once and for all. Right or wrong, she wanted the safety of Chance's arms. "Just not here," she said.

# Chapter 13

As soon as they got back to Bullhaven, Molly filled Chance in on her conversation with Delia's mother. Chance didn't even have to think about what his recommendation would be. "Turn her down," he said.

Molly slipped off her heels. Her lips slid out in the adorable pout he knew so well. And could never stop wanting to kiss. "I can't."

He lit the fire, then went into the kitchen and brought them back a couple of bottles of water. Molly sank onto his big leather sofa and bent over to rub her arches. "Babs is not just one of your mother's longtime friends—"

"I'm not sure I'd call them that exactly," Chance interrupted. "They're more like acquaintances who once frequented the same social scene."

Practically trembling with the exhaustion and adrenaline accumulated after such a long evening, Molly waved off his pointed objection. "Regardless, Babs is very well connected. Doing a job for her, and doing it well, could bring me a lot of future business."

Already wanting her so bad he ached, Chance shifted Molly into the corner of the leather sofa and drew her legs across his lap. Adjusting his posture to ease the pressure building at the front of his slacks, he massaged her left foot gently, from toes to heel. Felt her start to blissfully relax, even as his desire built. "She could also blackball you," he pointed out quietly.

Molly drew her legs away from his lap and swung them back onto the floor. Sitting up, she looked him straight in the eye. Beneath their evening clothes, their thighs touched. "Believe me, I am very well aware of that, too," she snapped. "That's why I'm treading carefully."

*Yes, but you shouldn't have to*, he thought, as a tense silence fell.

They stared at each other.

She sighed and ran her hands through her hair.

Finally, he tried again. "I talked to Delia tonight."

Molly's lips tightened. Briefly she turned her glance away, clearly angry now. "I know. I saw the two of you come out from behind the barn."

That sounded a lot worse than it had been. Knowing how lame it sounded, he explained, "She wanted to talk to me without her mother seeing."

Molly's delicate brow lifted, and the pink in her cheeks deepened. She folded her arms in front of her and glared at him. "Sounds cozy."

She wanted to believe him. He could see that. She just wasn't sure she should.

He tore his eyes from the lush fullness of her lips. "Delia's worried her mother and Mr. X are up to something."

Her expressive brows lowered over her long-lashed eyes. Molly uncapped her water bottle and took a long, thirsty drink. "That's hardly old news." She shrugged. "The two of them have been scheming ways to somehow buy out or take-over your bucking-bull business for weeks now."

"Something besides that," Chance clarified with concern.

"Like what?" Molly asked impatiently.

"Delia doesn't know. But Bab's sudden interest in hiring you indicates you're involved in her devious plans, too."

Molly flinched. He'd never seen her so overwrought or incredibly, passionately beautiful, and he edged closer.

"Babs couldn't just want me on board because I'm talented?"

Chance saw he'd hurt her feelings. But there was too much at stake—most importantly, their relationship—to sugarcoat the situation. "No."

Molly's lips tightened. Slowly but surely the walls around her heart began to go back up. "Thanks a lot."

Wanting to protect her more than ever, he covered her hand with his. "Listen to me, Molly. Mr. X told Delia he's prepared to pull out all the stops to get her to go out with him. And Babs is a manipulative shrew who never forgets a slight."

"So?" Molly shook her head as if that would clear it. "How is any of that our problem?"

"Babs blames me for the fact her only daughter has never married or brought a new influx of major money into their family coffers. She's particularly unhappy about the fact that Delia has been rejecting all of Mr. X's advances thus far. And she's told Delia repeatedly that she would like nothing better than to see me as unhappy as Delia has been. Worse, Babs apparently realized correctly the best way to get her long-awaited revenge on me is through you, Molly." Chance paused to let his words sink in. "I don't want you getting hurt via collateral damage," Chance finished tersely. *I don't want Babs ruining what we have.*

And it was so fragile, Babs just might.

Molly huffed out a breath. "I think you're overreacting."

Chance only wished he was.

Extricating her hand from his, she stood and moved gracefully to the fireplace. She stood with her back to the flames. "Babs doesn't know we're dating. Nor does anyone else. Everyone thinks we've just buried the hatchet long enough to become temporary co-contractors on your mother's renovation and casual friends."

Chance wasn't so sure about that. Molly wore her heart on her sleeve, whether she realized it or not.

He was equally bad at hiding his feelings where she was concerned. Whether she liked it or not, the two of them had been getting a lot of curious looks. People, like his siblings and their crews, were starting to put two and two together. Heck, even three-year-old Braden realized they'd forged a heck of a lot more than a casual connection. And could have a lot more, if Molly would only give them a shot.

Unwilling to see what was right in front of her, Molly continued blithely, defiantly keeping her blinders on. "So there's no reason for Babs to come after me."

*Okay.* So Molly didn't want to believe him. Maybe because she had yet to see the dark side of the world he had grown up in. She'd been raised in Laramie County, where neighbor took care of neighbor, and a man or woman's word was worth more than any gold.

He would have to accept her naive outlook in this matter, and for now, at least, try another tact. "Why risk it, in any case?" he said with a reassuring smile. He rose and joined her at the hearth. "There will be other jobs."

"It doesn't matter if there are, or aren't." Molly angled her chin at him, fury glittering in her amber eyes. "I'm not like you, Chance. I don't have the luxury of turning down work or money!" Her slender body quivered with emotion. "I can't just throw lucrative offers into the shredder without even looking at them."

He returned her pointed look. "You did it once—with Braden's daddy."

"Yes." Sadness turned the corners of her mouth down. "And I've regretted it ever since."

Molly didn't know where the words had come from. She could barely fathom thinking them, never mind saying them aloud. To Chance, of all people.

He clasped her elbow lightly and drew her toward him. "You don't mean that," he said quietly.

The truth hit her with the force of the north wind, chilling her from head to toe. Ignoring the shocked and disillusioned expression on Chance's face, she lifted her face to his and went on with gut-wrenching clarity. "I'm not saying it would have been the right thing to do." She knew, deep down, that morally and ethically it would not have been.

Chance's wish to understand her helped her go on. "Given how Braden's daddy felt about having a child at all, never mind with me, it would have been disastrous to bring Aaron into the equation. Because all Braden would have been to Aaron was a problem to be managed." Her voice cracked a little. "And Braden would have been devastated to realize he wasn't loved or wanted the way he should be."

Chance twined his hands with hers. Squeezed. "I agree."

Molly was determined to let Chance see the differences between them as clearly as she did. She looked him in the eye. "But that doesn't mean I don't wish—on some level, anyway—that I could have figured out a way back then to provide for and protect Braden. Even if it injured my pride."

She paused to let her words sink in.

"Because if I had accepted the money to just go away, then I would be able to afford to put Braden in any elite school I chose without asking for scholarships, and be at least a little more selective about which jobs I took on. I wouldn't have to worry about what might happen to us if I ever got sick or injured or couldn't work."

Chance dropped his grip on her, stepped back. "But you would have been selling your soul had you done that."

"I make compromises all the time."

"Not like that, you don't."

The truth was, Chance thought irritably, Molly had no idea how cold and ruthless some of the truly wealthy could be, and he didn't want her to ever know. Not firsthand, anyway. She'd come close enough to finding out in her dealings with the vaulted Worthington Academy.

"I'm asking you not to be naive," he said again.

Molly angled her thumb at the center of her chest. "And I'm asking you to consider my position." The soft swell of her breasts rose and fell. "To imagine what it is like to not have that fallback of security that comes from family money and connection."

She rushed on, giving him no chance to interrupt, "Because if I did have that, Chance, I wouldn't have to work so hard to build my business."

Her lips pinched together stubbornly. "Or meet Babs tomorrow. Never mind leave everything and everyone I know behind and move to Dallas. But I don't have that luxury, Chance, and odds are, I never will. The most I can do is earn as much money as possible as quickly as possible and provide for my son."

She had a point, he acknowledged silently. For a lot of reasons she wasn't as secure financially as she wanted to be at this point in her life, and given how hard she worked, she should be.

She was also his woman—whether she admitted it yet or not. He was her man. Yes, he had acted on her son's behalf, but he hadn't done nearly enough to protect *her* feelings or keep *her* safe. That would change. Effective immediately. "Let me go with you tomorrow," he said.

She moved away from the mantel. "I don't need your protection."

Except she did. He caught up with her as she retrieved her shoes. Tried again. "Molly…"

She perched on the edge of his sofa and slipped on her heels, then stood. "If you understand nothing else, understand this. I have to move forward and do this the way I always have. On my own."

Molly had plenty of time to regret the abrupt way she'd left Chance's ranch the evening before and returned to her home in town. The truth was she hadn't been nearly as irritated with him as she was with herself.

The womanly side of her kept telling her she was making a mistake in not allowing Chance to stand by her side or run interference for her. Whereas the independent single mom told her it would be a mistake to rely on anyone other than herself, lest she upend the life she had already built for herself and her son.

As for the romantic part of her?

Well, she knew what that required.

A long-term future with Chance.

But was that even realistic, knowing how he felt about everything that mattered to her? The first of which was earning enough money to obtain real financial security.

Molly had no answer. What she did know was the meeting with Babs could be the key to a lot of things. Hence she had to go. Even if it meant disappointing Chance.

So Molly dressed in her most elegant business suit, the one she reserved for premiere networking events, grabbed her briefcase and headed out to Lake Laramie.

Two cars were already in the drive. A sleek white Mercedes

and a minivan with a Realtor sign on the side. She walked up to the fixer-upper, one of many year-round rentals at the lake. It had an artificial wreath on the door and a sparsely decorated small Christmas tree inside. The Realtor, whose daughter attended Braden's preschool, said hello to Molly, then turned back to Babs. "I'll wait to hear from you."

"You'll have an answer on the property by noon," Babs promised.

The Realtor left them to discuss possible renovations. Molly turned to Babs, her attitude professional. "How much were you thinking of doing?"

Babs laid a silk scarf over the worn sofa, then perched on it. "Actually, I'd like to sit and talk first."

Getting better acquainted might help break the ice, but something felt off. Ignoring her growing sense of unease, Molly sat opposite her.

Babs smiled. "I understand you have a son, Braden, and that he was recently wait-listed at Worthington Academy."

Molly's alarm deepened, but she kept her outward cool. "How do you know that?"

"I do background checks on all prospective business associates. As it turns out, Worthington Academy recently did one on you."

Molly had agreed to a credit check as part of the application process. It was standard at most businesses requiring a long-term payment commitment.

She hadn't expected such information to become available to anyone but school officials.

But if Babs had had her investigated, it would have shown up. The same way all the details of her life had shown up when Aaron's family had her life scrutinized by a PI.

Molly felt as punched in the gut now as she had then.

Seeming to realize she'd caught Molly off guard, Babs continued haughtily, "The school wants to know who the parents of their prospective students are. Delia attended WA, and I've maintained my connections there, to help business associates, so I made a few calls to see how the process was going."

*Without my knowledge or consent?* That was unacceptable.

But wary of insulting a person she still hoped to get work from at the end of the day, Molly merely smiled. "I don't understand what my son's education has to do with this job."

"I still have pull at Worthington. I can get him off the wait list before Christmas."

That would be nice. Had it been merit—not connection—based. Doing her best to appear as if this sort of thing happened to her every day, Molly asked calmly, "Why would you want to do that?"

"Oh, honey." Babs shook her head at Molly. "It wouldn't be without quid pro quo. You'd do a favor for me. I want you to help me shake some sense into my daughter once and for all."

Molly's insides twisted with anxiety. Chance had said she had blinders on...

Babs frowned. "She's been mooning after that ne'er-do-well cowboy for years now. Lamenting their breakup to the point she won't date respectable beaux more than once or twice. And then only if forced."

Molly could see why that would not make for a happy situation. For anyone. "Again..." A hint of steel entered her tone. "What does this have to do with me?"

Babs waved a dissolute hand. "Delia, as you know, does not like to chase lost causes. She needs to see that Chance has indisputably moved on. With you. And the most dramatic, lasting impression way for that to happen is for her to catch you with him, in flagrante."

This was getting surreal. Molly felt the room sway. "You're...joking."

Babs opened her handbag. "I assure you I am not. Now,

Chance will be here in about ten minutes. If not sooner, given the message I left for him just shortly before you arrived. Delia will be here ten minutes after that."

Babs fished her keys from her bag. "All you have to do is seduce Chance in plain view, right here in the living room, and you will not only have more work than you can handle in Dallas but your son will be admitted to Worthington Academy, his tuition for the next five years fully paid in advance."

The proposition was so outrageous it took her a moment to recover. "I don't know why you think I would even consider something so preposterous."

"Let's not play games, Molly."

"I'm not," Molly gritted out.

Babs's expression turned ugly. "You had no qualms asking Chance Lockhart to pay for Braden's interview at Worthington Academy."

Sure she hadn't heard right, Molly blinked. "What are you talking about?"

Babs smirked, as if she still held the high card. "You didn't know? How sweet." She leaned closer, telling Molly snidely, "The problem is, as usual, Chance was a little too cheap. It would have taken a much larger donation to secure a spot for Braden at semester. Fortunately, I am prepared to spare no expense, if it means getting my daughter to start taking advantage of her own good fortune with Mr. X." Babs stood and shrugged on her mink coat. "So you see, Molly, you and I have that in common. We're both willing to do whatever it takes to safeguard our children."

Shock reverberated through her. "But I'm nothing like you!" Molly insisted.

Babs flashed a manipulative smile. "Aren't you? We will see. You have approximately six minutes to decide…"

* * *

Chance passed Babs on the road leading to the lake house. She was driving with her usual cool confidence. Which made him wonder what had happened with Molly.

Molly's red SUV was in the driveway.

He walked in. She was on the sofa, her head in her hands. "Molly?"

She looked up, her complexion ashen.

Damning himself for ever letting her make this venture alone, he crossed quickly to her side. He knelt in front of her, consoling her the best he could under the circumstances. "What happened here?"

Molly stared at him, a thousand emotions shimmering in her eyes. Anger, hurt, resentment. Disbelief…

"What in hell did Babs say to you?" Clasping Molly's hands, he pulled her to her feet. She moved woodenly into his embrace.

He wrapped his arms around her. Instead of melting against him the way she usually did, she pulled away.

"Chance, no!" she said in a strangled voice, looking all the more upset and betrayed. "I don't want—" She choked up, shaking her head. "We can't…"

Aware he'd never seen her more devastated, he threaded his hands through her hair and lifted her face to his.

Beneath her confusion, a glimmer of need shone in her eyes. "Molly," he said again as his head lowered to hers. Desperate to comfort her in any way he could, he touched his lips to hers just as the front door opened behind them.

"Really," Delia's low voice rang out in the chilly room. "You don't have to put on a show just for me. I already know what Mother's scheme is."

That was good, Chance thought. Because he sure as hell didn't.

## Chapter 14

Molly could see why Delia was upset. She lifted her hands. "I didn't agree to help your mother with her sleazy machinations."

Delia took off her sunglasses, her demeanor as world-weary as her tone.

"And yet here you are in Chance's arms," the heiress observed, as if she couldn't bear yet another disappointment.

Chance frowned. "I initiated that. Molly wasn't cooperating." Looking irritated to find himself being a third wheel in whatever was going on, he turned his level glance back to Molly. "Is this why?"

Figuring he was going to find out eventually, Molly folded her arms in front of her. Chance had been right. She never should have come here today, no matter how lucrative the job or how coveted the connection. Sometimes a job just wasn't worth it. "Babs offered to get Braden accepted at Worthington Academy, his tuition paid for the next five years, if I would be caught in flagrante with you!"

Chance did a double take. "What the *hell*?"

Delia nodded, her shoulders hunched in defeat. "Mother's

determined to show me that Chance and I are still all wrong for each other. What she refuses to accept is that we've been over for years now."

Molly wanted to believe that. Just as she wanted to believe that the difference between her background and Chance's would not keep them apart. "Babs thinks you still have feelings for him."

Delia scoffed, "Of course I do! I'll always care about you, Chance. Even though things ended badly. We knew each other too long and too well for me *not* to care for you."

Chance exhaled wearily. "Seeing you again has shown me the same thing."

Delia slid her sunglasses on top of her head. She loosened the belt on her black trench and perched on the edge of the sofa. "But coming all the way out here, going through the offer process with you, finding out how you still feel about monetary success, has also shown me that Mother was right to break us up. I never would have been happy living on a ranch named Bullhaven out in the middle of nowhere, with all those big, smelly Black Angus. Never mind going through the hassle of simultaneously building up two relatively small-time businesses from scratch!"

Molly took umbrage with that. "First of all, Chance's bulls don't smell. I've been around them."

Delia waved off the details. "Maybe not to you. To me, everything out on that ranch is yucky and disgusting. I'm a city girl through and through."

That Molly could see.

The question was…was she?

Was Braden—who loved their small town and Chance's ranch so much—a potential city boy?

Or would her son wish for his roots, the way she was beginning to, and they hadn't even left Laramie County yet!

Her expression sober, Delia continued, "Being dragged out here—repeatedly—on what was clearly a lost cause, also made me realize I don't want to work in the family business anymore, even as second in command. I really hate my mother's maneuverings and all the drama."

"What do you want to do?" Chance asked his ex kindly.

Delia gestured haphazardly, her elitist attitude coming to the fore once again. "Honestly? No clue. Thanks to the trust fund my daddy left me, however, I don't have to be in any hurry to find out."

Molly had always wanted to have that particular option. Now, studying Delia's self-indulgent expression, she wasn't so sure that was such a good thing.

"So maybe you should just tell your mother all that," Molly proposed.

"So she'll leave Molly and Braden alone," Chance added protectively.

"And you." Molly turned back to him.

Once again, just like that, they were a team. At least for the moment.

Delia scoffed. "First of all, talking to my mother, telling her what's in your heart never works. She thinks the world revolves around cold hard cash." Delia paused to let her words sink in. "And Mother's right, for people like us, who have grown up with the world as their oyster, it really does. Which is why I've decided to take Mr. X up on his offer to rescue me from all this and fly back to San Francisco with him."

Suddenly Molly realized why Chance was so concerned about Delia. She'd obviously been sheltered to a fault. And hence, she'd remained incredibly naive despite her overall sophistication. "Are you sure you want to do that?" Molly asked gently. *Be used like that? Like I once was? By a rich man who, at the end of the day, only cares about his own happiness?*

Delia paused to look at Chance, who remained stone-faced, then turned back to Molly. "Mr. X and I have been straight with each other. He wants a beautiful woman on his arm, one who's very good at playing hard to get, to enhance the reputation he wants to build as a ladies' man. So he can up his game."

*Game*, Molly thought. *How appropriate.*

"And I need a break from my mother's constant haranguing—which Mr. X has agreed to give—by hinting he wants to marry me. Mother won't do anything to interfere with possible billions coming my way," Delia continued.

They all knew that to be true.

"Anyway," Delia finished with an airy shrug as Chance moved closer to Molly and slipped his arm around her waist. "If you want me to tell Mother you carried through on your end of the bargain and got caught in a passionate clinch with Chance so you'll go ahead and get what you need regarding your son's school, I'm happy to do so."

The knowledge Delia felt Molly could be part of any scheme, never mind one that low-down, rankled. His grasp on her tightening, Chance looked equally ticked off by the intimation.

Her fury rising yet again, Molly reminded Delia, "Except I didn't set you up deliberately." She had been trying to do just the opposite.

"Who cares?" Delia moved gracefully to her feet, suddenly looking very much like her mother. "Mother deserves to get scammed the way she was trying to scam me!"

Molly knew revenge was a dish best *not ever* served. "Thanks," she said tightly. "But Braden and I are fine." In fact, this whole episode gave her second thoughts about trying to enroll her son with other children of the very elite. "I'd just as soon not have your mother's involvement."

Delia sighed. "I hear you. Comes with way too many strings." She said her goodbyes. The door closed behind her.

Chance turned to Molly. "I'm sorry you got dragged into the middle of all this."

Molly thought of all that had gone on behind her back.

All she and Chance still had left to discuss.

She stepped away from his warm, comforting embrace, then said, with a deep soul-wrenching bitterness that surprised even her, "You know what, Chance Lockhart? You really should be."

Chance could tell by the quietly seething way Molly was looking at him that she was accusing him of something. And just when he thought, especially now that Babs and Delia and Mr. X were out of the way, that he and Molly were ready to take that next big step. "Did I do something?"

"Maybe you should tell me." When he said nothing immediately, her brow arched. "Unless there's *more* than one thing?"

There was only one mistake, and he saw now it had been a big one. He swore fiercely to himself, aware he should have leveled with her way before now. "You found out I intervened on Braden's behalf at Worthington Academy to see he at least got an interview."

"Well, you must not have given enough, because he didn't get accepted."

He resisted the urge to haul her into his arms and kiss some sense into her only because he didn't want hot sex being the only thing keeping them together. "Is that what this is about? You wanted me to buy his way in, the way Babs bartered? Instead of just asking that he be tested and interviewed and given a fair shot?" He studied Molly in confusion. "Because I could still do that," he said carefully.

She tossed her head, her silky auburn curls swirling around her pretty face. Edging closer, she glared at him as if it were taking every ounce of self-control she had for her not to slug him on the chin. "No, you moron! It's about the fact that you found it necessary to buy his preadmission interview and consideration at all, never mind behind my back!"

He set his jaw. "How do you think my four siblings and I all got in there? How do you think the academy got such an over-the-top campus and facilities without charging six-figure tuition for each and every student? Parents make *huge* donations to pave the way for their kids and if necessary keep them there. It's just the way things are done at that echelon, Molly."

She inhaled deeply, her luscious breasts lifting beneath the sophisticated evergreen business suit. "I see that now." She raked her teeth across the plumpness of her lower lip. "What I don't see is why you didn't explain all that to me a whole lot earlier."

That part, at least, was easy, Chance thought. He returned her frustrated glare. "Because if I had told you that you needed more than just a letter from Sage, another alumni, to boost consideration chances, that you needed a big fat check of at least five figures just to get an interview there, you wouldn't have allowed me to help. And I knew if you were ever going to understand what you were truly asking, in attempting to move to Dallas so Braden could enroll at Worthington Academy or another place just like it, was if you and he experienced it firsthand."

Hurt shimmered in her pretty amber eyes. "You figured I would think it wasn't for him."

*Another trap.*

"I didn't know how you'd react, frankly. Because, yes, there are a lot of good things about the school, if you subtract the greased wheels and social hierarchy and all that."

"But you didn't think Braden would belong."

Chance stood, legs braced apart, shoulders back, hands on his waist. "He loves bulls, Molly. Loves his cowboy boots. And his hat. And his friends here. Which isn't to say he wouldn't love a uniform, too. But, yeah, I hoped when the decision finally had to be made that you would want to stay in Laramie and leave him in the school he is in right now." Exhaling roughly, he raked a hand through his hair. "Not because it's going to in any way further enhance or detract from his opportunities, academically or any other way, but because he is *happy* there, and if you ask me, *that*'s what school should be about, making a kid feel happy and confident!" Damned if he didn't suddenly sound like a parent. And an incredibly caring and overprotective one at that.

"I agree."

Chance blinked. Almost afraid to think they might be on the same page once again.

Molly shook her head, her mouth taking on a troubled tilt. "I've been reconsidering my education goals for Braden for days now. Ever since I Skyped with the academy administrators and had that uncomfortable meeting about why he didn't get accepted. And then came back here and saw his Christmas program at the preschool."

Chance moved closer. He cupped her shoulders gently. "If you were having second thoughts, why didn't you tell me?" So they could have talked about it. So he could have confessed what he had already done, and why, and had her understand.

She whirled, sending a drift of perfume heading his way. "Because I hadn't made up my mind entirely! And I didn't want to say anything before I had."

He felt like he were facing off with a bear with his paw caught in a trap. "And now?"

"I've decided to stay in Laramie through the rest of the school year."

That didn't have the permanence he yearned for. Yet, wary of pushing her too hard too fast again and ending up pushing her away, he asked quietly, "What about the two jobs you already have set up in Dallas?"

Regret glimmered briefly in her gaze. She seemed to think she had failed on some level.

He wanted to tell her she hadn't.

He didn't think she would want to hear that, either.

So he remained silent.

With a sigh, she pointed out, her dejectedness more chilling than her earlier anger, "As you said, they are small tasks. And if we put our crews together, we could easily get them done in a couple of weeks. I just wouldn't take on any more out of Laramie County for the time being."

"Well, that's great news," he said, beginning to think she was holding out for the same long-term future he was. In fact, the best Christmas present ever. "To have us working together again."

She didn't seem to think so.

She squared her slender shoulders. "But that doesn't eliminate my need to build up a heck of a lot more of a financial safety net." She looked all the more conflicted. "So I'm still going to eventually have to—"

He held up a hand before she could continue. Grasped her hand before she could move even farther away. "I don't want you and Braden to ever have to want for anything, either," he told her huskily, tightening his fingers on hers. He paused to look deep into her eyes. "And you were right, merging our businesses into one would only bring you in another ten or fifteen percent annual revenue. Nothing close to what you're trying to do moving to Dallas and entering that much more lucrative market."

Her eyes were steady, but her lower lip trembled. "I'm glad you understand that," she said quietly.

"I do. And that," he said with a burst of excitement, "brings me to your Christmas gift." Ignoring the skeptical expression on her face, he led her to the sofa. Sure everything was finally going to work out, he sat down next to her. Reaching into his jacket pocket, he pulled out a red envelope with her name on it. Handed it to her with a flourish. "Open it!"

She reacted as if he had given her a time bomb instead of a gift. Lips tightening in distress, she protested, "But…it's not Christmas yet. I haven't even gotten you your gift."

Like he cared what she gave him, if she let him fully into her and her son's life, the way he desperately wanted to be. He regarded her steadily. "I want you to have this now," he told her solemnly, giving her hands another gentle squeeze. "So you'll feel better right away."

Still holding his gaze, Molly drew a deep breath, some of her usual good cheer returning. "Well, now I'm curious…"

She eased open the seal. Unfolded the contract. Read quietly. Blinked once and then again. She stared at him uncomprehendingly. "You're gifting me half ownership of Mistletoe?" She narrowed her eyes as if it couldn't possibly be true.

Heart filling with all he felt for her, he confirmed, "And Braden will get half ownership in Mistletoe Jr." Imagining the little tyke's reaction, Chance grinned. "So he actually will have all his wishes come true and get a Leo and Lizzie train set and a real live bull for Christmas. Which, of course, will be kept at Bullhaven Ranch."

The pages detailing the gift fluttered to her lap. One hand splayed across her heart. "This is crazy," she gasped.

"It's what you and Braden deserve," he said. And so much more!

Molly thrust the papers back at him. Pushing him aside with one arm, she shot to her feet. "Chance, you can't do this on a whim!"

"I'm not." It hurt that she would even think that.

Her delicate brow arched.

"I've been thinking about it for days," he rushed to confess. "Wanting to do it." Just not sure how...

She stared at him, clearly not believing a word he said. "You never share interest in your bulls or co-own them with anybody!"

"Until now," he admitted. "You're right. I haven't."

Expression grim, she snatched up the gift notification and waved it in front of his face. "This is worth—"

"Millions, yes." If that didn't prove his devotion to her and to Braden, what would?

Molly swallowed, tears filling her eyes. "And it's completely one-sided," she said as if he had just plotted to utterly destroy her, heart and soul. Instead of make her feel as safe and secure as she had always wanted to be. "You're giving me a ton of revenue."

Including stud fees and endorsements for the retired Mistletoe? Potential winnings for Mistletoe Jr.? He nodded. "Six figures annually, easy." Enough to make relocating herself and her son completely unnecessary. Starting now.

Molly's chin quivered. "And I'm giving you nothing in return."

Okay, maybe he should have considered how the ultra-independent and self-reliant Molly would feel about any one-sided arrangement.

He could still fix this.

"I wouldn't say that." He attempted a joke to lighten the

mood. "I wouldn't mind, say, a lifetime supply of breakfast *stollen* or homemade German pastries and cookies."

She shook her head. "Chance, this is too much. It's way too much. It's—" Her voice caught on a small sob. She gulped, unable to go on.

Oh, God, he'd hurt her. Which was the last thing he wanted. He pulled her into his arms. Abruptly feeling like his whole life was on the line, he buried his face in the softness of her hair. "The best Christmas gift I could think of to give you."

Her slender body hunched in defeat. "Just like with the Leo and Lizzie train set," she recollected sadly.

He knew he'd gone way overboard there. Maybe here, too. But they had fixed that. And they could fix this, too, if she gave him half a chance. "I care about you and Braden." He let her go long enough to get down on one knee, take both her hands in his. "And if this is what it takes to persuade you to stay in Laramie County, then…" His voice got rusty.

"Wow." Molly shook her head, still looking completely shell-shocked, and something else he couldn't identify. Something really treacherous. Her low voice was taut as a string on a violin. "I don't know what to say." She disengaged their hands.

Trying not to read too much into her stiff posture, he rose. Leaning down, he massaged the tense muscles of her shoulders and whispered in her ear, "How about yes?"

"Braden's daddy wanted to pay us to go away." Her voice rich with irony, she placed both her hands on his chest and shoved him away. "Now you're trying to pay us to stay!"

She shook her head, tears flowing from her eyes. "What's that saying?" she asked as if something inside her had been broken irrevocably. Staring at him, she lifted her chin. "The rich really are different?"

Her words stung. He was not the one here with a cash register for a heart. "You act like I'm trying to insult you," he fired back just as angrily.

Amber eyes narrowed. "Aren't you?"

Gut tightening, he stepped back. Aware that the thought of a life without her and Braden was more than he could bear, he reminded her, "You're the one who's always said what you really want is that big financial safety net so you'll never have to worry." He paused to let the weight of his words, the sheer enormity of his gift, sink in. He spoke slowly and deliberately, so if she thought about it long and hard enough, she would understand this was a gift from the heart, pure and simple. *"I'm giving you that."* He was offering to extend his family and merge it with hers. There was no greater gift.

She nodded, her expression maddeningly inscrutable. "Because, as you've said before, money means nothing to you."

"Well, you can't take it with you." Once again, his attempt to lighten the mood with a joke fell flat. He tried again. "You know money doesn't mean anything to me."

"Except it does mean something to you, Chance, just in a very different way." Her low voice trembled with emotion. "For you, it's the freedom to do what you want, when you want, how you want. Without ever having to worry about it."

He shrugged, not about to argue that. "I agree. It's a means to an end."

"Something that allows you to buy whatever you want and or need? Like, say, me?"

He would never be that coarse and manipulative. And if she thought that…did she really know him at all? Did they know *each other*? His frustration rising, he bit out, "I'm not asking you to be my mistress, Molly."

To his surprise, she looked even more betrayed. "Don't you get it, Chance?" Her voice was as flat and final as the look in her eyes. "I wouldn't accept a gift like this from you even if I were your wife!"

Clearly, Chance noted, that was something not about to happen, either. Unless he miraculously managed to fix things.

He spread his hands wide. Tried again. "You're taking this all wrong—"

This time it was she who cut him off with an imperious lift of her hand.

"No, Chance," she reiterated. "I'm not. In fact, I understand *exactly* what you're trying to do here. And that's fix something that can't be fixed by throwing money at it."

He was getting a little tired of being accused of being mercenary when she was the one all about cold hard cash! He glared right back. "There are worse things than searching for a solution, Molly."

"Not like that, not in my view." She steamrolled past, gorgeous ice princess on parade. Her lips pursed. "Which is why this affair has to end."

Another sucker punch to the gut. What little holiday cheer he had in him evaporated completely.

"You're breaking up with me?" he asked, staring at her in disbelief. "Because you didn't like my gift?"

She grabbed her coat and bag and rushed out the door as if her heart were breaking, pausing only to send him one last glance. "You're damn right I am."

# *Chapter 15*

Early on December 24th, Molly put her personal devastation aside, and set out, as per tradition, to deliver her holiday gifts while Braden played with friends. First stop? The beloved Circle H Ranch.

A warm and welcoming look on her face, Lucille ushered Molly into the bunkhouse where the matriarch planned to continue to live until after the holidays. At which point she'd relocate to the recently renovated main ranch house. She accepted the festive platter of German holiday cookies. "Did you bake all these?"

*With Chance's help.*

But that had been when he'd been at her home almost nightly. Now that seemed unlikely to ever happen again.

A fact Braden was lamenting, too.

Her son hadn't stopped asking for Cowboy Chance.

And Chance was keeping his distance. Going so far as secreting the Leo and Lizzie train set over to Molly's house via his little sister, Sage. So it would be there for her to wrap and Braden to receive "from Santa" Christmas morning, as planned.

Had things turned out otherwise, had Chance not shown her how different they were and always would be, he would have been there, too.

Sharing in the joy. Making the three of them feel like family.

Pushing away the dreams of what might have been, Molly smiled at his mother. "I wanted to say thank you for all you've done for me and for Braden over the last year," she said sincerely.

Lucille responded with a warm hug. "It was my pleasure. And now I have something for you!" She brought something from her desk. "Here is the list of people who've contacted me since the Open House about you doing some work for them."

Molly looked at the printout containing twenty names. She forced a wry smile. "Who says Christmas can't come early?"

Lucille beamed as proudly as if she had been Molly's mother. "Women in my circle like to redecorate yearly, and thanks to the work you did at the ranch house, they all want you."

Molly was pleased with the results. She could not, however, take full credit. "It wasn't just me and my contractors. Chance and his craftsmen put in a lot of effort, too."

Lucille poured Molly a cup of coffee and gestured for her to have a seat at the long plank table. "The two of you make a really good team."

A lump rose in Molly's throat. "We did."

Lucille brought cream and sugar to the table. She sat down. "So it's over?"

*So over.* Yet even as she thought it, it sounded so final. Too final…

Her heart aching, Molly wiped at a tear spilling down her cheek. Had he only understood her. But he hadn't. "He tried to bribe me into staying here in Laramie."

Lucille frowned. "That was wrong. What you do with your future should be your decision. Period."

The irony was Molly had just about decided to stay in Laramie, not just until summer but permanently. Would have, had Chance not shown her what he really thought of her. Although she supposed at least some of that was her fault, since up to now she had based all her life goals on the premise of one day earning more money and securing a very healthy nest egg to fall back on.

"You have to do what is right for you and your son," Lucille continued, patting the back of Molly's hand. She drew back and looked in her eyes, advising gently, "Just don't let your pride stand in the way."

*Pride?* Could that be all it was? Molly hesitated. Ready to partake of the older woman's wisdom, she asked, "What do you mean?"

Lucille ran her hand over the rim of her coffee cup. "When my late husband and I dreamed up the Lockhart Foundation, I am ashamed to admit, it was as much about increasing the stellar reputation of our family as the good works we planned to do with all our accumulated wealth."

Molly paused. "That doesn't sound like you."

Lucille exhaled in regret. "Maybe not now, but I've learned some hard lessons along the way."

Molly guessed Lucille was referring to the financial scandal with the foundation the previous summer that had since been resolved.

Lucille fingered the pearls at her neck. "Although I'd sat on many boards, I'd never actually run a nonprofit."

Molly sipped her coffee. "And that was a problem?"

Grimly, Lucille recollected, "From the very beginning, I realized I was in over my head, but I'd made such a big deal about being the CEO, and I knew it was what Frank had envisioned for my future before he died, so I stayed on the wrong path for much longer than I should have. Because I didn't want to admit I'd made the wrong decision."

Like she was making a mistake now? Molly wondered uneasily.

"Don't let your understandable anger with Chance now rob you of the long-term security that you crave."

Aware Lucille was the closest thing she'd had to a mother in a very long time, Molly fought back the tears clogging her throat. "You think I should stay in Laramie?" *In the community where I grew up, with all my friends? And, like it or not, the man who still turns my heart inside out with just a glance?*

Tenderly, Lucille shook her head. "Only you can intuit what is right for you and Braden, Molly. Just know that if you find yourself headed in the wrong direction, like I once was, that U-turns are not just allowed—they're recommended."

On the morning of Christmas Eve, Chance sat in his kitchen, looking at the set of legal papers he had tried to give Molly before she had shown him the door.

Slowly, he unwrapped the last tiny bit of Christmas *stollen* he'd stored in his fridge and took a bite. Once fragrant, soft and delicious, it was now hard, dry and…still delicious. Like a yuletide biscotti.

He sighed, swallowing the last bite he'd been—up till now—unable to part with. Maybe because he had known in his heart that he and Molly would never work out the way he wanted.

Would it have made a difference if he'd told her how he felt about her and Braden, before he'd shown her the legal papers he had hoped would create their family and cement their future?

He didn't know.

Now, would never know…

Outside, he heard the sound of multiple vehicles. Doors slamming. Footsteps coming across his porch.

Grimacing—because he had an idea who this was—he rose and went to answer the insistent knock on his door.

All four of his siblings stood on the porch. Including Zane, his youngest brother, a Special Ops soldier who was usually deployed to parts unknown.

"What happened to you?" Chance gave Zane a hug. Glad to see he was all in one piece, even if Zane did sport a fading bruise across his jaw, and a thick bandage encompassed his left hand.

"The usual," Zane replied cheerfully, looking happy to be home in time for Christmas—something that had almost never happened since he had enlisted.

"You could tell me, but then you'd have to…" Chance mimed a knockout, finishing the age-old combat joke.

"Sounds like I might need to do that anyway," Zane said, hugging him fiercely, before striding in. "What were you thinking? Giving your woman two live bulls for Christmas!"

"They weren't her only Christmas gift!" Chance retorted. He'd had something even better and more romantic planned for that. Not that he'd ever gotten an opportunity to give that present to her.

Wyatt followed, still in ranch clothes. "Just an enticement?"

Chance threw up his hands. "I was trying to give her a reason to stay here in Laramie County, where she belongs."

Garrett strolled in, too. Now happily married himself, he seemed to be the resident expert on domestic bliss. He prodded, "Just not the right reason?"

Chance exhaled in exasperation. "Molly's never made any secret of the fact she wants real financial security for herself and her son. Big-time connections. She could have had all that with me." Even if social climbing was definitely not his thing.

"Just not what every woman wants most of all," Sage murmured, shutting the door behind them.

"And what is that?" Chance asked in frustration. What was everyone seeing that he was missing?

"If you don't know the answer," she scoffed, "you're more clueless than any of us thought!"

Silence fell all around.

Still on the hot seat, Chance eventually asked Sage, "I'm guessing you organized this?"

His little sister nodded, appearing as ridiculously romantic as ever. "I figured you might not listen to me."

*True*, Chance thought.

"But with all of us here," she insisted stubbornly, "we might have a chance of getting through to you."

He appreciated the sentiment behind their support, if not their actual interference. Chance folded his arms across his chest. "Thanks, but I don't need help with my love life."

Garrett squinted. "The facts say you do."

Wyatt made himself at home. "Look, Chance, we can all see that Molly is the one for you."

Still favoring his injured hand, Zane eased onto a stool, too. "From what I've heard from Mom, the only one."

Glad his Special Forces brother had made it through whatever calamitous event caused his injuries, Chance asked, "Why isn't Mom here, if this is a family meeting?"

"Because," Garrett said triumphantly, "she's at the Circle H, talking to Molly."

Hope rose within Chance. He knew how much Molly loved and respected his mother. If anyone could get his woman—and he admitted he still considered Molly to be his woman—to reconsider their breakup, it was bound to be the matchmaking Lucille.

He studied the faces of his siblings. "Is Mom having any success?"

Shrugs all around. "No clue. You'll have to meet up with Molly to find that out," Wyatt advised.

"The point is," Sage added, "you have an opportunity to make this Christmas the most memorable one you've ever had, Chance, if you can find it in your heart to stop trying to steer the situation to your advantage. Ignore the shield Molly is hiding behind. And give her what she really wants and needs, most of all."

Just after eight o'clock Christmas Eve, Molly kissed her sleeping son and eased from his bedroom. She wasn't surprised they'd only been able to get halfway through "Twas the Night before Christmas." Her son was deliriously excited.

Whereas she knew she still had so much to do to make amends before the holiday ended.

She reached for her phone just as a knock sounded on her front door.

Molly looked through the glass.

*Chance?*

Heart pounding, she opened the door.

He stood on her doorstep in a sport coat, snowy-white shirt, Santa Claus and Rudolph tie, and jeans. He'd recently showered and shaven. His hair had that mussed, sexy look she loved. But it was the hopeful sparkle in his eyes that got to her the most.

She nodded at his tie. "Glad to see you haven't lost your sense of humor."

The crinkles around his eyes deepened. "I thought you might like it."

She liked more than that.

She liked everything about him.

Especially this. The fact that he knew just when she needed him most and showed up.

Because it was the showing up, it was the being there, that was most important of all.

"Seriously." Chance's voice dropped a sexy notch, his gaze devouring her from head to toe. "I hope it's not too late."

Flushing beneath his tender scrutiny, Molly swung the door open wide and motioned him in. "Actually, your timing is perfect," she whispered, ushering him back to the kitchen, where their voices were least likely to carry. "I just got Braden to sleep." Knowing now was the time to give him a gift from the heart, too, she ignored the shaking of her knees and hurried on. "I've been wanting to talk to you. I don't like the ways things ended the last time we—"

He put a finger to her lips. Hazel eyes serious, he interrupted sternly, "If anyone is going to apologize, it's got to be me."

This she hadn't expected.

Shaking his head ruefully, he took her all the way into his arms. Threaded one hand through her hair, wrapped the other reverently around her waist. "I'm sorry, Molly. For trying to maneuver you into making the decisions I wanted regarding your future." He hauled in a rough breath, admitting, "My only responsibility as the man in your life is to do everything I can to support you in whatever you want."

Molly splayed her hands across his chest; the rapid beat of his heart matched hers. Tears of happiness misted her eyes as the relief inside her built. "You mean that?"

"I do." He nodded soberly. Then bent to tenderly kiss her brow. "I don't care where we live, Molly, as long as we're together."

She knew what it took for him to concede that. "But Bullhaven..." Her voice broke.

"Can be run with or without me on the premises every day."

"But there's Mistletoe and all the other bulls, not to mention Mistletoe Jr."

He promised gruffly, "I'll work that out, too."

She saw he meant it. With all his heart and soul. Still... "It's your life work."

He nodded. His eyes held hers. "And only part of what I want," he said thickly.

Her heart pounded like a wild thing in her chest. She moved in closer, taking in all the heat and strength he had to give. "What's the rest?" She let her eyes rove his handsome face. Memorizing this Christmas for all time.

He lifted her hand, kissed the back of it and then held it against his chest. Their gazes still locked, he told her, "I want you. And Braden. And a life together." His voice caught as the tears she'd been holding back spilled over her lashes and flooded her cheeks.

"Which is why you tried to give us part ownership in Mistletoe and Mistletoe Jr. Because they are the most precious gifts you have to offer."

He tightened his grip on her. "So you do understand that I only gifted them to you to secure your financial future, and show you how much I wanted us to be family?"

She nodded. "I know how much you love your prize bulls. And that you giving us half ownership in them was a very big deal."

"Then why did you take it as an insult?"

"Because the enormity of the gift—the long-lasting deeply personal nature of it—scared me, Chance." She tipped her head back to better see into his eyes. "For years now, I've been telling myself I didn't need anyone, so long as I had enough money to keep Braden and I safe. I thought my duty as his parent was to provide all the material things and opportunity denied me as a child. I couldn't see—didn't want to see—that we already had everything we needed, here in Laramie. A great home. A caring community of friends and neighbors."

Chance drew her close. "A school that fits him and his exuberant, engaging personality."

She leaned into him. "I wanted more for him."

He stroked a hand through her hair. "More for you?"

Molly nodded. "All of it, based on the things that I've since realized matter the least." His strength and tenderness gave her the courage to go on. "And then you came into my life. Challenging everything. Showing me whether I wanted to acknowledge it or not that the grass wasn't always greener and the luxe life was no guarantee of happiness."

She wreathed her arms around his broad shoulders. "And while financial security will always be important, it's not nearly as crucial as having someone to love who will love you back." Her voice trembled with emotion as she took the biggest leap of faith of all. "And I do love you, Chance." Letting him see and feel just how much, she kissed him deeply, sweetly.

"Damn, Molly," Chance kissed her back with all the yearning she had ever wished for. "I love you too," he whispered, kissing her again. "So much…"

Chance released her and got down on one knee. He reached into his pocket. "Which is why I got this…"

Inside the box was a diamond engagement ring. He lifted his face to hers, an endless supply of hope and faith shining in his eyes.

Mirrored in her heart.

He clasped her hand tightly, looking as if this were the most important moment in his life. "Marry me, Molly."

The joyful tears overflowed again. She tugged him to his feet and drew him back into her arms. "On one condition," she promised, holding him so close their hearts pounded in unison. "We stay in Laramie."

Surprise warred with the pleasure and relief on his handsome face. "You're not moving to Dallas?"

She shook her head, kissing him again, tenderly and persuasively. "This is where I want to be, for Christmas and forevermore." She gazed into his eyes. "Right here with you."

# *Epilogue*

*One year later...*

"Is it time to go yet?" Braden asked. "Can we give the bulls their Christmas presents?"

Molly looked at Chance. It was still half an hour before the appointed feeding time on Christmas Eve, but if they didn't spring into action soon, their little guy was going to burst with excitement. A fact the love of her life seemed to know very well.

Chance grinned. "I think we can go now, buddy."

The three of them donned their hats, coats and gloves and headed out to the barn, a little red wagon full of specialty grain sacks, emblazoned with each bucking bull's name, behind them. One by one, Braden called out a jubilant "Merry Christmas!" to each and every animal. Then, with Chance and Molly's help, he carefully poured the yuletide gifts into the buckets of regular feed before Chance set them in the stalls.

Finally, they made their way to the barn that held the trio of prize-winning cattle.

Seeing them walk in, Mistletoe let out a low bellow. Jr. and

Momma followed suit. Both bulls came over to the edge of their pens. Chance hoisted Braden in his arms. As had become custom, Braden gently petted their heads under Chance's supervision, while Molly went over to check on the only female of the bunch. Eventually, Chance and Braden came over, too, their twin sets of cowboy boots echoing on the cement barn floor.

Braden peered through the opening in the metal pen rails. "How come Momma Cow is getting so fat?" He frowned at her sagging, barrel-shaped tummy.

Molly had been wondering when Braden would notice the unmistakable weight gain. "She's going to have another baby bull in the spring."

Braden perked up. "I like babies!" he said.

Molly took a deep breath. "That's good." She and Chance had been waiting for the right time. Maybe this was it. "Because Daddy and I like them, too. So we were thinking," she continued as casually as she could, "that the three of us should have a baby, too." Smiling, Chance telegraphed his support and reached over and squeezed her hand. "Then you'd have a little brother or sister."

Braden tipped his cowboy hat back and thought that over. "Is the baby going to be born in the barn?"

Molly and Chance choked back laughter. Soberly, Chance knelt down. "Probably the hospital," he said.

"Okay." Braden happily considered that, then moved on. "Can we put out the treats for Santa?"

It was a little early yet for that.

On the other hand, they had a Lockhart family party to go to in a little bit, so maybe it was good to do as much as possible now. "Sure," Molly and Chance said, as in tune about this as everything else.

They went inside and washed up. Molly poured a small

glass of milk while Braden arranged a selection of treats on a plate, then went to play with his Christmas village and ranch.

As delighted about their expanding family as she, Chance ran his hand possessively over Molly's tummy. Briefly he inclined his head at Braden, murmuring, "That went better than expected."

They hadn't been sure how Braden would take the news. Although they had *hoped*…

The thought of the new life growing inside her filled Molly with warmth. "I think so, too."

She turned to Chance, aware how much had changed in the months since they'd first become involved.

They'd married in July. She'd converted her home in town to an interior design studio and office for their joint general contracting firm. Chance was teaching her and Braden the bucking-bull and ranching business. Best of all, not only was Braden thriving in the school he had always gone to but he was relishing his new "cowboy" life on an actual ranch. And he had the doting daddy she'd always wanted for him, too.

She paused to kiss her ruggedly sexy husband. "Have I told you lately that thanks to you, all my dreams have come true this year?"

All the love she had ever wanted shone in his eyes. "Mine, too," he rasped contentedly.

She hugged him close, aware she had never felt so joyous. "Merry Christmas, cowboy."

Chance stroked a hand through her hair and tenderly kissed the top of her head. "Merry Christmas to you, too, darlin'."

\* \* \* \* \*

# The Rancher's Christmas Promise

*Allison Leigh*

Though her name is frequently on bestseller lists, **Allison Leigh**'s high point as a writer is hearing from readers that they laughed, cried or lost sleep while reading her books. She credits her family with great patience for the time she's parked at her computer, and for blessing her with the kind of love she wants her readers to share with the characters living in the pages of her books. Contact her at allisonleigh.com.

### Books by Allison Leigh

#### *Return to the Double C*

*Show Me a Hero*
*Yuletide Baby Bargain*
*A Child Under His Tree*
*The BFF Bride*
*One Night in Weaver...*
*A Weaver Christmas Gift*
*A Weaver Beginning*
*A Weaver Vow*

#### *The Fortunes of Texas: The Rulebreakers*

*Fortune's Homecoming*

#### *The Fortunes of Texas: The Secret Fortunes*

*Wild West Fortune*

#### *The Fortunes of Texas: All Fortune's Children*

*Fortune's Secret Heir*

Visit the Author Profile page
at millsandboon.com.au for more titles.

Dear Reader,

I've always been a big fan of the Harlequin series books, and Special Edition is a personal favorite. In recognition of this wonderful program, I'll be recommending one Special Edition per month to encourage readers to discover the charm and appeal of these compelling contemporary romances. Many of these books feature Western settings, handsome cowboys, gutsy women and beautiful babies. The heroes and heroines are dynamic and relatable, trying their best to resist their attraction to each other while resolving the conflict that keeps them apart. But the undeniable chemistry that simmers between them cannot be denied. These books will pull you in and take you on an emotional and satisfying journey. Each story ends with a marriage proposal or wedding—delivering the happily-ever-after, because the love and security of family is the ultimate promise of Special Edition.

I'm proud to present the first author in this promotion, *New York Times* and *USA TODAY* bestselling author Allison Leigh. Allison has written more than fifty romances, and has received high praise for her authentic and engaging plots. Her latest release, *The Rancher's Christmas Promise*, is the story of a single rancher, Ryder Wilson, who is suddenly given the responsibility of taking care of a baby from his ex-wife. Although Ryder is unsure of the baby's paternity, he wants the child to have a great home. Greer Templeton steps in to help out when it's obvious Ryder is having a tough time balancing the duties of the ranch and caring for the baby. This memorable holiday tale will surely leave a lasting impression on you.

Please take me up on this invitation to read a Special Edition and indulge in a heartwarming story. I do hope you enjoy the reading experience and will be back next month for another exciting book.

All the best,

Paula Eykel Miller

*For my family.*

# *Prologue*

*"You've got to be kidding me."*

Ryder Wilson stared at the people on his porch. Even before they introduced themselves, he'd known the short, skinny woman was a cop thanks to the Braden Police Department badge she was wearing. But the two men with her? He'd never seen them before.

And after the load of crap they'd just spewed, he'd like to never see them again.

"We're not kidding, Mr. Wilson." That came from the serious-looking bald guy. The one who looked like he was a walking heart attack, considering the way he kept mopping the sweat off his face even though it was freezing outside. March had roared in like a lion this year, bringing with it a major snowstorm. Ryder hadn't lived there that long—it was only his second winter there—but people around town said they hadn't seen anything like it in Braden for more than a decade.

All he knew was that the snow was piled three feet high, making his life these days even more challenging. Making him wonder why he'd ever chosen Wyoming over New Mexico in the first place. Yeah, they got snow in Taos. But not like this.

"We believe that the infant girl who's been under our protection since she was abandoned three months ago is your daughter." The man tried to look past Ryder's shoulder. "Perhaps we could discuss this inside?"

Ryder had no desire to invite them in. But one of them *was* a cop. He hadn't crossed purposes with the law before and he wasn't real anxious to do so now. Didn't mean he had to like it, though.

His aunt hadn't raised him to be slob. She'd be horrified if she ever knew strangers were seeing the house in its current state.

He slapped his leather gloves together. He had chores waiting for him. But he supposed a few minutes wouldn't make much difference. "Don't think there's much to discuss," he warned as he stepped out of the doorway. He folded his arms across his chest, standing pretty much in their way so they had to crowd together in the small space where he dumped his boots. Back home, his aunt Adelaide would call the space a *vestibule*. Here, it wasn't so formal; he'd carved out his home from a converted barn. "I appreciate your concern for an abandoned baby, but whoever's making claims I fathered a child is out of their mind." Once burned, twice shy. Another thing his aunt was fond of saying.

The cop's brown eyes looked pained. "Ryder—may I call you Ryder?" She didn't wait for his permission, but plowed right on, anyway. "I'm sorry we have to be the bearer of bad news, but we believe your wife was the baby's mother, and—"

At the word *wife*, what had been Ryder's already-thin patience went by the wayside. "My *wife* ran out on me a year ago. Whatever she's done since is her prob—"

"Not anymore," the dark-haired guy said.

"What'd you say your name was?" Ryder met the other man's gaze head-on, knowing perfectly well he hadn't said his name. The pretty cop's role there was obviously official. Same with the sweaty bald guy—he had to be from social services. But the third intruder? The guy who was watching him as though he'd already formed an opinion—a bad one?

"Grant Cooper." The man's voice was flat. "Karen's my sister."

"There's your problem," Ryder responded just as flatly. "My so-called *wife's* name was Daisy. Daisy Miranda. You've got the wrong guy." He pointedly reached around them for the door to show them out. "So if you'll excuse me, I've got ice to break so my animals can get at their water."

"This is Karen." Only because she was a little slip of a thing, the cop succeeded in maneuvering between him and the door. She held a wallet-sized photo up in front of his face.

Ryder's nerves tightened even more than when he'd first opened the door to find these people on his front porch.

He didn't want to touch the photograph or examine it. He didn't need to. He recognized his own face just fine. In the picture, he'd been kissing the wedding ring he'd just put on Daisy's finger. The wedding had been a whirlwind sort of thing, like everything else about their relationship. Three months start to finish, from the moment they met outside the bar where she'd just quit her job until the day she'd walked out on him two weeks after their wedding. That's how long it had taken to meet, get hitched and get unhitched.

Though the unhitching part was still a work in progress. Not that he'd been holding on to hope that she'd return. But he'd had other things more important keeping him occupied than getting a formal divorce. Namely the Diamond-L ranch, which he'd purchased only a few months before meeting her. His only regret was that he hadn't kept his attention entirely on the ranch all along. It would have saved him some grief. "Where'd you get that?"

The cop asked her own question. "Can you confirm this is you and your wife in this picture?"

His jaw felt tight. "Yeah." Unfortunately. The Las Vegas wedding chapel had given them a cheap set of pictures. Ryder had tossed all of them in the fireplace, save the one the cop was holding now. He'd mailed that one to Daisy in response to a stupid postcard he'd gotten from her six months after she'd left him. A postcard on which she'd written only the words *I'm sorry.*

He still wasn't sure what she'd meant. Sorry for leaving him without a word or warning? Or sorry she'd ever married him in the first place?

"You wrote this?" The cop had turned the photo over, revealing his handwriting on the back. *So much for vows.*

Ryder was actually a little surprised that it was so legible, considering how drunk he'd been at the time he'd sent the photo. He nodded once.

The cop looked sympathetic. "I'm sorry to say that she died in a car accident over New Year's."

He waited as the words sank in. Expecting to feel something. Was he supposed to feel bad? Maybe he did. He wasn't sure. He'd known Daisy was a handful from the get-go. So when she took a powder the way she had, it shouldn't have been as much of a shock as it had been.

But one thing was certain. Everything that Daisy had told him had been a lie. From start to finish.

He might be an uncomplicated guy, but he understood the bottom line facing him now. "And you want to pawn off her baby on me." He looked the dark-haired guy in the face again. "Or do you just want money?" He lifted his arm, gesturing with the worn leather gloves. "Look around. All I've got is what you see. And it'll be a cold day in hell before I let a couple strangers making claims like yours get one finger on it."

Grant's eyes looked like flint. "As usual, my sister's taste in men was worse than—"

"Gentlemen." The other man mopped his forehead again, giving both Ryder and Grant wary looks even as he took a step between them. "Let's keep our cool. The baby is our focus."

Ryder ignored him. He pointed at Grant. "My wife never even told me she had a brother."

"My sister never told me she had a husband."

"The situation is complicated enough," the cop interrupted, "without the two of you taking potshots at each other." Her expression was troubled, but her voice was calm. And Ryder couldn't miss the way she'd wrapped her hand familiarly around Grant's arm. "Ray is right. What's important here is the baby."

"Yes. The baby under our protection." Ray was obviously hoping to maintain control over the discussion. "There is no local record of the baby's birth. Our only way left to establish who the child's parents are is through you, Mr. Wilson. We've expended every other option."

"You don't even *know* the baby was hers?"

Ray looked pained. Grant looked like he wanted to punch something. Hell, maybe even Ryder. The cop just looked worried.

"The assumption is that your wife was the person to have left the baby at the home her former employer, Jaxon Swift, shared with his brother, Lincoln," she said.

"Now, that *does* sound like Daisy." Ryder knew he sounded bitter. "I only knew her a few months, but it was still long enough to learn she's good at running out on people."

Maybe he did feel a little bad about Daisy. He hadn't gotten around to divorcing his absent wife. Now, if what these people said were true, he wouldn't need to. Instead of being a man with a runaway wife, he was a man with a deceased one. There was probably something wrong with him for not feeling like his world had just been rocked. "But maybe you're wrong. She wasn't pregnant when she left me," he said bluntly. He couldn't let himself believe otherwise.

"Would you agree to a paternity test?"

"The court can compel you, Mr. Wilson," Ray added when Ryder didn't answer right away.

It was the wrong tack for Ray to take. Ryder had been down the whole paternity-accusation path before. He hadn't taken kindly to it then, and he wasn't inclined to now. "Daisy was my wife, loose as that term is in this case. A baby born to her during our marriage makes me the presumed father, whether there's a test or not. But you don't know that the baby was actually hers. You just admitted it. Which tells me the court probably isn't on your side as much as you're implying. Unless I say otherwise, and without you knowing who this baby's mother is, I'm just a guy in a picture."

"We should have brought Greer," Grant said impatiently to the cop. "She's used to guys like him."

But the cop wasn't listening to Grant. She was looking at Ryder with an earnest expression. "You aren't just a guy in a picture. You're our best hope for preventing the child we believe is Grant's niece from being adopted by strangers."

That's when Ryder saw that she'd reached out to clasp Grant's hand, their fingers entwined. So, she had a dog in this race.

He thought about pointing out that he was a stranger to them, too, no matter what sort of guy Grant had deemed Ryder to be. "And if I cooperated and the test confirms I'm *not* this baby's father, you still wouldn't have proof that Daisy is—" *dammit* "—was the baby's mother."

"If the test is positive, then we know she was," Ray said. "Without your cooperation, the proof of Karen's maternity is circumstantial. We admit that. But you were her husband. There's no putative father. If you even suspected she'd become pregnant during your marriage, your very existence is enough to establish legal paternity, DNA proof or not."

The cop looked even more earnest. "And the court can't proceed with an adoption set in motion by Layla's abandonment."

The name startled him. *"Layla!"*

The three stared at him with varying degrees of surprise and expectation.

"Layla was my mother's name." His voice sounded gruff, even to his own ears. Whatever it was that Daisy had done with her child, using that name was a sure way of making sure he'd get involved. After only a few months together, she'd learned enough about him to know that.

He exhaled roughly. Slapped his leather gloves together. Then he stepped out of the way so he wasn't blocking them from the rest of his home. "You'd better come inside and sit." He felt weary all of a sudden. As if everything he'd accomplished in his thirty-four years was for nothing. What was that song? "There Goes My Life."

"I expect this is gonna take a while to work out." He glanced at the disheveled room, with its leather couch and oversize, wall-mounted television. That's what happened when a man spent more time tending cows than he did anything else. He'd even tended some of them in this very room.

Fortunately, his aunt Adelaide would never need to know.

"You'll have to excuse the mess, though."

# *Chapter 1*

*Five months later.*

The August heat was unbearable.

The forecasters kept saying the end of the heat wave was near, but Greer Templeton had lost faith in them. She twisted in her seat, trying to find the right position that allowed her to feel the cold air from the car vents on more than two square inches of her body. It wasn't as if she could pull up her skirt so the air could blow straight up her thighs or pull down her blouse so the air could get at the rest of her.

She'd tried that once, only to find herself the object of interest of a leering truck driver with a clear view down into her car. If she'd never seen or heard from the truck driver again, it wouldn't have been so bad. Instead, she'd had the displeasure of serving as the driver's public defender not two days later when he was charged with littering.

*"I hate August!"* she yelled, utterly frustrated.

Nobody heard.

The other vehicles crawling along the narrow, curving stretch of highway between Weaver—where she'd just come from a frustrating visit with a new client in jail—and Braden all had their windows closed against the oppressive heat, the same way she did.

It was thirty miles, give or take, between Braden and Weaver, and she drove it several times every week. Sometimes more than once in a single day. She knew the highway like the back of her hand. Where the infrequent passing zones were, where the dips filled with ice in the winter and where the shoulder was treacherous. She knew that mile marker 12 had the best view into Braden and mile marker 3 was the spot you were most likely to get a speeding ticket.

The worst, though, was grinding up and down the hills, going around the curves at a crawl because she was stuck behind a too-wide truck hogging the roadway with a too-tall load of hay.

Impatience raged inside her and she pushed her fingers against one of the car vents, feeling the air blast against her palm. It didn't provide much relief, because it was barely cool.

Probably because her car was close to overheating, she realized.

Even as she turned off the AC and rolled down the windows, a cloud billowed from beneath the front hood of her car.

She wanted to scream.

Instead, she coasted onto the weedy shoulder. It was barely wide enough.

The car behind her laid on its horn as it swerved around her.

"I hate August!" she yelled after it while her vehicle burped out steam into the already-miserable air.

*So much for getting to Maddie's surprise baby shower early.*

Ali was never going to forgive Greer. Unlike their sister, Maddie, the soul of patience she was not. Just that morning

Ali had called to remind Greer of her tasks where the shower was concerned. It had been the fifth such call in as many days.

Marrying Grant hadn't softened Ali's annoying side at all.

Greer wasn't going to chance exiting through the driver's side because of the traffic, so she hitched up her skirt enough to climb over the console and out the passenger-side door.

In just the few minutes it took to get out of the car and open up the hood, Greer's silk blouse was glued to her skin by the perspiration sliding down her spine.

The engine had stopped spewing steam. But despite her father's best efforts to teach the triplets the fundamentals of car care when she and her sisters were growing up, what lived beneath the hood of Greer's car was still a mystery.

She knew from experience there was no point in checking her cell phone for a signal. There were about four points on the thirty-mile stretch where a signal reliably reached, and this spot wasn't one of them. If a Good Samaritan didn't happen to stop, she knew the schedules of both the Braden Police Department and the Weaver Sheriff's Department. Even if her disabled vehicle wasn't reported by someone passing by, officers from one or the other agency routinely traveled the roadway even on a hot August Saturday. She didn't expect it would be too long before she had some help.

She popped the trunk a few inches so the heat wouldn't build up any more than it already had and left the windows down. Then she walked along the shoulder until she reached an outcrop of rock that afforded a little shade from the sun and toed off her shoes, not even caring that she was probably ruining her silk blouse by leaning against the jagged stone.

*Sorry, Ali.*

Ryder saw the slender figure in white before he saw the car. It almost made him do a double take, the way sailors did when they spotted a mermaid sunning herself on a rock. A second look reassured him that lack of sleep hadn't caused him to start hallucinating.

Not yet, anyway.

She was on the opposite side of the road, and there was no place for him to pull his rig around to get to her. So he kept on driving until he reached his original destination—the turn-off to the Diamond-L. As soon as he did, he turned around and pulled back out onto the highway to head back to her.

It was only a matter of fifteen minutes.

The disabled foreign car was still sitting there, like a strange out-of-place insect among the pickup trucks rumbling by every few minutes. He parked behind it, but let his engine idle and kept the air-conditioning on. He propped his arm over the steering column and thumbed back his hat as he studied the woman.

She'd noticed him and was picking her way through the rough weeds back toward her car.

He'd recognized her easily enough.

Greer Templeton. One of the identical triplets who'd turned his life upside down. Starting with the cop, Ali, who'd come to his door five months ago.

It wasn't entirely their fault.

They weren't responsible for abandoning Layla. That was his late wife.

Now Layla was going through nannies like there was a revolving door on the nursery. Currently, the role was filled by Tina Lewis. She'd lasted two weeks but was already making dissatisfied noises.

He blew out a breath and checked the road before pushing open his door and getting out of the truck. "Looks like you've got a problem."

"Ryder?"

He spread his hands. "'Fraid so." Any minute she'd ask about the baby and he wasn't real sure what he would say.

For nearly five months—ever since Judge Stokes had officially made Layla his responsibility—the Templeton triplets had tiptoed around him. He'd quickly learned how attached they'd become to the baby, caring for her after Daisy dumped her on a "friend's" porch.

Supposedly, his wife hadn't been sleeping with that friend but Ryder still had his doubts. DNA might have ruled out Jaxon Swift as Layla's father, but the man owned Magic Jax, the bar where Daisy had briefly worked as a cocktail waitress before they'd met. He would never understand why she hadn't just come to *him* if she'd needed help. He had been her husband, for God's sake. Not her onetime boss. Unless she'd been more involved with Jax than they all had admitted.

As for the identity of Layla's real father, everyone had been happy as hell to stop wondering as soon as Ryder gave proof that he and Daisy had been married.

Didn't mean Ryder hadn't wondered, though.

But doing a DNA test at this point wouldn't change anything where he was concerned. It would prove Layla was his by blood. Or it wouldn't.

Either way, he believed she was his wife's child.

Which made Layla his responsibility. Period.

The questions about Daisy, though? Every time he looked at Layla, they bubbled up inside him.

For now, though, he focused on Greer.

It was no particular hardship.

The Templeton triplets scored pretty high in the looks department. He could tell Greer apart from her twins because she always looked a little more sophisticated. Maddie—the social worker who'd been Layla's foster mother—had long hair reaching halfway down her back. Ali—the cop who'd shown up on his doorstep—had blond streaks. And he'd never seen her dressed in anything besides her police uniform.

Greer, though?

Her dark hair barely reached her shoulders and not a single strand was ever out of place. She was a lawyer and dressed the part in skinny skirts with expensive-looking jackets and high heels that looked more big-city than Wyoming dirt. She'd been the one who'd ushered him through all the legalities with the baby. And she was the only one of her sisters who hadn't been openly crying when they'd brought Layla and all of her stuff out to his ranch to turn her over to his care. But there'd been no denying the emotion in her eyes. She just hadn't allowed herself the relief of tears.

For some reason, that had seemed worse.

Ryder had been uncomfortable as hell with so much female emotion. Greer's most of all.

He'd rather have to deal with the general animosity Daisy's brother clearly felt for him. That, at least, was straightforward and simple. Grant's sister was dead. Whether he'd voiced it outright or not, he blamed Ryder.

Since Ryder was already shouldering the blame, it didn't make any difference to him.

Now Greer was shading her eyes with one hand and holding her hair off her neck with the other. Instead of asking about Layla first thing, though, she stopped near the front bumper of her car. "It overheated. I saw steam coming out from the hood and pulled off as soon as I could."

He joined her in front of the car. He knew the basics when it came to engines—enough to keep the machinery on his ranch running without too much outside help—but he was a lot more comfortable with the anatomy of horses and cows. "How long have you been sitting out here?"

"Too long." She plucked the front of her blouse away from

her throat and glanced at the watch circling her narrow wrist. "I thought someone would stop sooner than this. Ali'll think I'm deliberately late."

The only heat from the engine came from the sun glaring down on it. He checked a few of the hoses and looked underneath for signs of leaking coolant, but the ground beneath the car was dry. "Why's that?"

"We're throwing a surprise baby shower for Maddie today. I'm supposed to help set up."

"Didn't know she was pregnant." He straightened. It was impossible to miss the sharpness in Greer's brown eyes.

"Why would you, when you've been avoiding all of us since March?"

"Some law that says I needed to do otherwise?" He hadn't been avoiding them entirely. Just...mostly.

It had been easy, considering he had a ranch to run.

She pursed her bow-shaped lips. "You know my family has a vested interest in Layla. At the very least, you could try accepting an invitation or two when they're extended."

"Maybe I'm too busy to accept invitations." He waited a beat. "I am a single father, you know."

If he wasn't mistaken, her eye actually twitched.

She'd always struck him as the one most tightly wound.

It was too bad that he also couldn't look at her without wondering just what it would take to *un*wind her.

He closed the hood of her car with a firm hand. "You want to try starting her up? See what happens with the temperature gauge?"

He thought she might argue—if only for the sake of it— but she opened the passenger door. Then he had to choke back a laugh when she climbed across and into the driver's seat, where she started the engine. Her focus was clearly on her dashboard and he could tell the gauge was rising just by the frown on her face.

She shut off the engine again and looked through the windshield. "Needle went straight to the red." She climbed back out the passenger side.

"Something wrong with the driver's-side door?"

She was looking down at herself as she got out, tweaking that white skirt hugging her slender hips until it hung smooth and straight. "No, but I don't want it getting hit by a passing vehicle if I open it."

He eyed the distance between the edge of the road and where she'd pulled off on the shoulder. "Real cautious of you."

"I'm a lawyer. I'm always cautious."

"Overly so, I'd say." Not that he hadn't enjoyed the show. She was a little skinny for his taste, but he couldn't deny she was a looker. He pulled off his cowboy hat long enough to swipe his arm across his forehead. "I can drive you into town, or I can send a tow out for you." He didn't have time to do both, because he had to be back at the ranch before the nanny left or his housekeeper, Mrs. Pyle, would have kittens. "What's your choice?"

Greer swallowed her frustration. Considering Ryder Wilson's standoffishness since they'd met, she was a little surprised that he'd stopped to assist at all.

As soon as she'd realized who was driving the enormous pickup truck pulling up behind her car, she'd been torn between anticipation and the desire to cry *what next?*

It was entirely annoying that the brawny, blue-eyed rancher was the first man to make her hormones sit up and take notice in too long a while.

Annoying and impossible to act on, considering the strange nature of their acquaintance.

All she wanted to do was ask Ryder how Layla was doing. But Maddie had been insistent that none of them intrude on him too soon.

They'd all been wrapped around Layla's tiny little finger and none more than Maddie, who'd been caring for her nearly the whole while before Ali discovered Ryder's existence. Yet it was Maddie who'd urged them to give Ryder time. To adjust. To adapt. They knew Ryder was taking decent care of the baby he'd claimed, because Maddie's boss, Raymond Marx, checked up on him for a while at first, so he could report back to the courts. Give Ryder time, Maddie insisted, and eventually he would see the benefit of letting them past his walls.

Didn't mean that it had been easy.

Didn't mean it was easy now, not dashing over to the truck to see Layla.

She didn't know if it was that prospect that made her feel so shaky inside, or if it was because of Layla's brown-haired daddy. She wasn't sure she even liked Ryder all that much.

Yes, he'd been legally named Layla's father and yes, he'd taken responsibility for her. But there was an edge to him that had rubbed Greer wrong from the very first time they met. She just hadn't been able to pinpoint why.

"If you don't mind driving me into town," she managed, "I'd be grateful."

The brim of his hat dipped briefly. "Probably should lock her up." He started for his big truck parked behind the car.

She watched him walk away. He was wearing blue jeans and a checked shirt with the sleeves rolled up to his elbows. Except for when he'd briefly swiped an arm over his forehead, he appeared unaffected by the sweltering day.

"Probably should lock her up," she parroted childishly under her breath. As if she didn't have the sense to know that without being told.

She retrieved her purse and briefcase from the back seat, looping the long straps over her shoulder, then warily lifted the trunk lid higher. The shower cake that she'd nestled carefully between two boxes full of work from the office amazingly didn't look too much the worse for wear. It was a delightful amalgam of block and ball shapes, frosted in white, yellow and blue. How Tabby Clay had balanced them all together like that was a mystery to Greer.

She was just glad to see that the creation hadn't melted into a puddle of goo while she'd waited on the side of the road.

She carefully lifted the white board with the heavy cake on top out of the trunk and gingerly carried it toward Ryder's truck. Her heart was beating so hard, she could hear it inside her head. The last time she'd seen Layla had been at Shop-World in Weaver, when she'd taken a client shopping for an affordable set of clothes to wear for trial, and Ryder had been in the next checkout line over, buying diapers, coffee and whiskey.

Layla had been asleep in the cart. Greer had noticed that her blond curls had gotten a reddish cast, but the stuffed pony she'd clutched was the same one Greer had given her for Valentine's Day.

It had been all she could do not to pluck the baby out of the cart and cuddle her close. Instead, after a stilted exchange with Ryder, she'd hustled her client through the checkout so fast that he'd wondered out loud if she'd slid through without paying for something. *No. That's what* you *like to do*, she'd told him as she'd rushed him out the door.

But now, when she got close enough to Ryder's truck to see inside, her feet dragged to a halt.

There was no car seat.

Definitely no Layla.

The disappointment that swamped her was so searing, it

put the hot afternoon sun to shame. Her eyes stung and she blinked hard, quickening her pace once more only to feel her heel slide on the loose gravel. The heavy cake started tipping one way and she leveled the board, even as her shoulder banged against the side of his truck.

She froze, holding her breath as she held the cake board aloft.

"What the hell are you doing over here?"

She was hot. Sweaty. And brokenhearted that she wasn't getting a chance to see sweet Layla.

"What do you care?" she snapped back. She was still holding the cake straight out from her body, and the weight of it was considerable. "Just open the door, would you please? If I don't deliver this thing in one piece, Ali's going to skin me alive."

He gave her a wide berth as he reached around her to open the door of the truck. "Let me take it." His hands covered hers where she held the board, and she jerked as if he'd prodded her with a live wire.

Her face went hot. "I don't need your help."

He let go and held his hands up in the air. "Whatever." He backed away.

Nobody liked to feel self-conscious. Not even her.

She turned away from him to set the cake board inside the truck, but it was too big to fit on the floor, which meant she'd have to hold it on her lap.

Greer heaved out a breath and looked at Ryder. He wordlessly took the cake long enough for her to dump her briefcase and purse on the floor, and climb up on the high seat.

"All settled now?" His voice was mild.

For some reason, it annoyed her more than if he'd made some snarky comment.

Unfortunately, that's when she realized that she'd left her trunk open and the car unlocked.

She slid off the seat again, mentally cursing ranchers and their too-big trucks as she jumped out onto the ground. Ignoring the amused glint in his dark blue eyes, she strode past him, grinding her teeth when her heel again slid on the loose gravel.

She'd have landed on her butt if not for the quick hand he shot out to steady her.

She shrugged off his touch as if she'd been burned but managed a grudging "thank you." It figured that he could manage to hold on to the heavy cake and still keep her from landing on her butt.

She finally made it to her car without further mishap and secured it. The passenger door of his truck was still open and waiting for her when she returned.

She climbed inside and fastened the safety belt. Then he settled the enormous, heavy cake on her lap, taking an inordinate amount of time before sliding his big, warm hands away.

As soon as he did, she yanked the door closed.

The cool air flowed from the air-conditioning vents.

It was the only bright spot, and gave a suitable reason for the shivers that skipped down her spine.

She wrapped her hands firmly around the edge of the cake board to hold it in place while Ryder circled the front of the truck and got in behind the wheel.

His blue eyes skated over and she shivered again. Despite the heat. Despite the perspiration soaking her blouse.

Annoyance swelled inside her.

"I hope you have someone decent watching Layla."

His expression turned chilly. "I've got plenty of things I needed to be doing besides stopping to help you out. You really want to go there?"

She pressed her lips together. If Maddie ever found out she'd been rude to Ryder, her sister would never forgive her.

"Just drive," she said ungraciously.

He lifted an eyebrow slightly.

*God.* She really hated feeling self-conscious.

"Please," she added.

He waited a beat. "Better." Then he put the truck in gear.

# Chapter 2

"I knew you'd be late."

Greer ignored Ali's greeting as she entered the stately old mansion that Maddie shared with her husband, Lincoln Swift. She kicked the heavy front door closed, blocking out the sound of Ryder's departing truck. Passing the round table in the foyer loaded down with fancifully wrapped gifts and the grand wooden staircase, she headed into the dining room with the cake.

The sight of a cheerfully decorated sheet cake already sitting in the middle of the table shredded her last nerve.

She stared over her shoulder at Ali. Her sister looked uncommonly pretty in a bright yellow sundress. More damningly, Ali was as cool and fresh as the daisy she'd stuck in her messy ponytail. "You have a *backup* cake?"

"Of course I have a backup cake." Ali waved her hands, and the big diamond rock that Grant had put on her ring finger a few months earlier glinted in the sunlight shining through the mullioned windows. "Because I knew you would be late! You're always late, because you're always working for that slave driver over at the dark side."

"Well, I wouldn't have *been* late, if I hadn't broken down on the way back from Weaver! Now would you move that stupid cake so I can put this one down where it belongs?"

"Girls!" Their mother, Meredith, dashed into the dining room, accompanied by the usual tinkle of tiny bells on the ankle bracelet she wore. "This is supposed to be a party." She tsked. "You're thirty years old and you still sound as if you're bickering ten-year-olds." She whisked the offending backup cake off the table. "Ali, put this in the kitchen."

Ali took the sheet cake from their mother and crossed her eyes at Greer behind their mother's back while Greer set Tabby's masterpiece in its place.

"It's just beautiful," Meredith exclaimed, clasping her hands together. Despite her chastisement, her eyes were sparkling. "Maddie's going to love it." As she turned away, the dark hair she'd passed on to her daughters danced in corkscrew curls nearly to the small of her back. "It's just too bad that Tabby wasn't able to come to the party."

"If Gracie weren't running a fever, she'd have brought the cake herself." Greer glanced around. "Obviously Ali didn't have a problem decorating without me. It looks like the baby-shower fairy threw up in here." The raindrop theme was in full force. Silver and white balloons hovered above the table in a cluster of "clouds" from which shimmering crystal raindrops hung down, drifting slightly in the cool room. It was sweet and subtly chic and just like Maddie. Altogether perfect, really.

As usual, Ali hadn't really needed Greer at all.

Meredith squeezed her arm as if she'd read her mind. "Stop sweating the details, Greer. You had a hand in the planning of this, whether you were here to help pull it together this afternoon or not. Now—" she eyed Greer more closely "—what's this about your car breaking down?"

It was a timely reminder that she probably looked as be-draggled as she felt. A glance at her watch told her the guests would be arriving in a matter of minutes. Linc was supposed to be delivering Maddie—hopefully still in the dark about the surprise—shortly after that.

"The car overheated. I left it locked up on the side of the road."

"How'd you get here?"

She felt reluctant to say, knowing the mention of Ryder would only remind them all of how much they missed Layla. "Someone stopped and gave me a ride to town. I'll arrange a tow after the shower." She dashed her hand down the front of her outfit and headed for the stairs. "I need to put on some-thing less wrinkled and sweaty. Hopefully there's more than just maternity clothes in Maddie's closet." She hadn't made it halfway up the staircase before the doorbell rang and she could hear Ali greeting the new arrivals.

She darted up the rest of the stairs.

Even after more than half a year, it was hard to get used to the fact that Maddie lived in this grand old house with Linc. The place had belonged to his and Jax's grandmother Ernes-tine. When the triplets were children, Meredith had cleaned house for Ernestine. Greer and her sisters had often accom-panied her. Now, Jax no longer shared the house with Linc. Maddie did.

She entered the big walk-in closet, mentally sending an apology to her brother-in-law for the intrusion. She knew that Maddie wouldn't mind. Not surprisingly, most of the clothes hanging on the rods were designed for a woman who looked about a hundred months pregnant.

She could hear the doorbell chime again downstairs and quickly flipped through the hangers, finally pulling out a col-orful dress she remembered Maddie wearing for Easter, when she'd had just a small baby bump. The dress had a stretchy waist that was a little loose on Greer, but it would do.

She changed and flipped her hair up into a clip. If there'd been blond streaks in her hair, she'd look just like Ali. Tousled and carefree.

But Greer hadn't felt carefree in what was starting to feel like forever.

She stared at her reflection and plucked at the loose waist of the dress. Maddie was pregnant. Now Ali and Grant were married. Considering how the two couldn't keep their hands off each other, it was only a matter of time before they were starting a family, too.

But Greer?

The last date she'd had that had gotten even remotely physical was more than two years ago, so if she wanted a baby, she was going to need either a serious miracle or big-time artificial intervention. As it was, the little birth control implant she had in her arm was pretty much pointless.

From downstairs, she heard a peal of laughter. Turning away from her reflection, she headed down to join them. She might not feel carefree, but she *was* thrilled about Maddie's coming baby. So she would put on a party face for that reason alone.

And she would try to forget that Ali had gotten a damn backup cake.

Ryder stared at Doreen Pyle. "What do you mean, you're quitting?"

"Just that, Ryder." Mrs. Pyle continued scooping mushy green food into Layla's mouth, even though the little girl kept twisting her head away. "When you hired me, it was to be your housekeeper. Not your nanny."

"That's because I *had* a nanny." His voice was tight. "Look,

I'm sorry that Tina took a hike this afternoon with no warning." At least the others who'd come before her had given him some notice. "I'll start looking again first thing tomorrow."

"It won't matter, Ryder. Nobody wants to live all the way out here." She finally gave up on the green mush and glanced at him. The look in her lined eyes was more sympathetic than her tone had been. "You need to give up the idea of a live-in nanny, Ryder. Or else give up the idea of a housekeeper. You can't afford both."

He could, if he were willing to dip into his savings. But he wasn't willing. Any more than he was willing to take Adelaide's money. She'd made her way on her own, and he was doing the same. On his own. But if he were going to continue growing this small ranch, he couldn't be carting a growing baby around everywhere while he worked. "I'll give you another raise." He'd already given her one. "Stay on and take care of Layla. You're good with her. I'll hire someone to help with the housekeeping."

"I don't want to live out here, either." She pushed off her chair, wincing a little as she straightened. "The only difference between me and Tina is that I won't take off while your back is turned." She grabbed a cloth and started wiping up Layla's face. The baby squirmed, trying to avoid the cloth just like she'd tried to avoid the green muck. But Mrs. Pyle prevailed and then tossed the cloth aside. "You don't need a nanny around the clock, anyway. You're here at night." She lifted the baby out of the high chair. "You can take care of her yourself. Then just get some help during the day. Preferably someone who doesn't have to drive farther than from Braden, or once the winter comes, you're going to have problems all over again." She plopped Layla into his arms and hustled to the sink where she wet another cloth. "But it won't be me. I have my own family I need to look out for, too. My grandson—" She broke off, grimacing. She squeezed out the moisture and waved the rag at him. "I won't apologize for not wanting to be tied down to a baby all over again. Not at my age." She sounded defensive.

"I don't need an apology, Mrs. Pyle. I need someone to take care of Layla!"

The baby lightly slapped his face with her hands and laughed.

Mrs. Pyle's expression softened. She chucked Layla lightly under the chin. "Maybe instead of looking for a nanny, you should start looking for a mama for this little girl."

Ryder grimaced.

"There are plenty of other fish in the sea. All you need to do is cast your line. You're a good-looking cuss when you clean yourself up. Someone'll come biting before you know it."

"I don't think so." One foray into so-called wedded bliss was one disaster enough.

The look in Doreen's eyes got even more sympathetic. "I know what it's like to lose a spouse, hon. Single parents might be all the rage these days, but I'm here to tell you it's easier when two people are committed to their family. You're still young. You don't want to spend the rest of your life alone. I'm sure your poor wife wouldn't have wanted that, either. She'd surely want this little mite to have a proper mama. Someone who won't toss aside caring for Layla on some flighty whim the way Tina just did."

He managed a tight smile. His "poor wife" had been exactly that. A poor wife. But not in the way Doreen Pyle meant. Abandoning Layla had been a helluva way to show off her maternal nature. Tina's quitting out of the blue was a lot more forgivable. "Would you at least stay until I find someone new?" He had to finish getting the hay in before the weather turned. And then he and his closest neighbor to the east were helping each other through roundup. Then he'd be sorting and shipping and—

"I'll stay another week," she said, interrupting the litany of tasks running through his mind. "But that's it, Ryder."

Layla grinned up at him with her six teeth and smacked his face again with her hand.

He looked back at his housekeeper. "A week."

"That's all the time I can give you, Ryder. I'm sorry."

A week was better than nothing.

And it was damn sure more than Tina had given him.

"I don't suppose you could stay and watch Layla for another few hours or so?" As his housekeeper began shaking her head no, he grabbed the refrigerator door and stuck his head inside, so he could pretend he didn't see. "Got a friend—" big overstatement there "—who needs help towing her car back to town. Broke down up near Devil's Crossing." He grabbed the bottle of ketchup that Layla latched onto and stuck it back on the refrigerator shelf. She immediately reached for something else and he quickly shut the door and gave Mrs. Pyle a hopeful look. The same one he'd mastered by the time he was ten and living with Adelaide.

Instead of looking resigned and accepting, though, Mrs. Pyle was giving him an eyebrows-in-the-hairline look. "*Her* car? Is this female friend single?"

Warning alarms went off inside his head. "Yeah."

She lifted Layla out of his arms. "Well, go rescue your lady friend. And give my suggestion about a wife some thought."

He let her remark slide. "Thank you, Mrs. Pyle."

"Not going to change my leaving in a week," she warned as she carried the baby out of the kitchen. "And you might think about washing some of the day off yourself, as well, before you go out playing Dudley Do-Right."

* * *

He hadn't showered, but he *had* washed up and pulled on fresh clothes. And he still felt pretty stupid about it.

It wasn't as if he wanted to impress Greer Templeton. Not with a clean shirt or anything else. And it damn sure wasn't as if he was giving Mrs. Pyle's suggestion any consideration.

Marrying someone just for Layla's sake?

He pushed the idea straight out of his mind and shifted into Park at the top of the hill as he stared out at the worn-looking Victorian house.

The white paint on the fancy trim was peeling and the dove-gray paint on the siding was fading. The shingle roof needed repair, if not replacement, and the brick chimney looked as if it were related to the Leaning Tower of Pisa. But the yard around the house was green and neat.

Not exactly what he would have expected of the lady lawyer. But then again, she worked for the public defender's office, where the pay was reportedly abysmal and most of her clients were supposedly the dregs of society.

He turned off the engine and got out of the truck, walking around to the trailer he'd used to haul Greer's little car. He checked the chains holding it in place and then headed up the front walk to the door.

The street was quiet, and his boots clumped loudly as he went up the steps and crossed the porch to knock on the door. The heavy brass door knocker was shaped like a dragonfly.

If he could ever get Adelaide to come and visit Braden, she'd love the place.

When no one came to the door, he went back down the porch steps. There was an elderly woman across the street making a production of sweeping the sidewalk, though it seemed obvious she was more interested in giving him the once-over.

He tipped the brim of his hat toward her before he started unchaining Greer's car. "Evenin'."

The woman clutched her broom tightly and started across the street. A little black poodle trotted after her. "That's Greer's car," the woman said suspiciously.

He didn't stop what he was doing. "Yes, ma'am."

"What're you doing with it?"

"Unloading it."

She stopped several feet away, still holding the broom handle as if she was prepared to use it on him if need be. "I don't know you."

"No, ma'am." He fit the wheel ramps in place and hopped up onto the trailer. "I assure you that Greer does." He opened the car door and folded himself down inside it.

Maybe Greer—who was probably all of five two or three without those high heels she was always wearing—could fit comfortably into the car, but he couldn't. Not for any length of time, anyway.

He started the car, backed down the ramp and turned into the driveway. Then he shut off the engine, crawled out from behind the wheel and locked it up again before sticking the key back into the magnetic box he'd found tucked inside the wheel well.

The woman was still standing in the middle of the street.

He secured the ramps back up onto the trailer and gave her another nod. "If you see her, tell her she's got a thermostat problem."

"Tell her yourself." The woman pointed her broom handle at an expensive black SUV that had just crested the top of the hill. "Bet that's her now."

He bit back an oath. He still didn't know what had possessed him to haul Greer's car into town for her, particularly without her knowledge. And his chance of a clean escape had just disappeared.

The SUV pulled to a stop in front of Greer's house. The windows were tinted, so he couldn't see who was behind the wheel, but he definitely could see the shapely leg that emerged when the passenger-side door opened.

It belonged to Greer, looking very un-Greer-like in a flowy sort of dress patterned in vibrant swirls of color that could have rivaled one of his aunt's paintings. Half her hair was untidily pulled up and held by a glittery pink clip.

He still knew it was her, though, and not one of her sisters. No question, considering the sharp look she gave him as she closed the SUV door and approached him. "*You* hauled my car here?"

"I suppose there's no point in denying the obvious." He watched the big SUV pull around in the cul-de-sac and head back down the hill. The identity of the driver was none of his business. He wondered, anyway. "Boyfriend?"

She frowned. "Grant. And why did you haul it?"

No wonder the SUV had turned around and left. "You'd rather have it still sitting out on the side of the highway?"

"Of course not, but—" She broke off, looking consternated, and only then seemed to notice that they had an audience. "How are you doing, Mrs. Gunderson?" She leaned down to pet the little round dog. Ryder wasn't enough of a gentleman to look away when the stretchy, ruffled neckline of Greer's dress revealed more than it should have.

"Just fine, dearie. Oh, Mignon, don't jump!"

Mrs. Gunderson's admonishment was too late, though, because the dog had already bounced up and into Greer's arms.

He was actually a little impressed that the fat Mignon could jump.

But he was more impressed by the way Greer caught him and laughed.

He had never heard her laugh before. Not her or her sisters. Her chocolate-colored eyes sparkled and her face practically glowed.

And damned if he didn't feel something warm streak down his spine.

"You probably need a new thermostat," he said abruptly.

The dog was licking the bottom of her chin even though she was trying to avoid his tongue, but she didn't put Mignon down. "How do you know?"

"Because I checked everything else that would cause your overheating before I towed it back here." He stepped around the two women. "And think about keeping your car key in a less obvious hiding spot," he advised as pulled open the door to climb inside his truck.

Greer's jaw dropped a little, which gave Mignon more chin to lick. She set the dog down and trotted after him, wrapping her fingers over the open window. "You're just going to leave now?"

His fingers closed over the key in the ignition, but didn't turn it. "What else do you figure I should do?"

Her lips parted slightly. "Can I pay you for the tow at least?"

He turned the key. "No need."

"Well, I should do something." She didn't step back from the truck, despite the engine leaping to life. "To thank you at least. Surely there's something I can do."

The "something" that leaped to mind wasn't exactly fit for sharing in polite company. Particularly with her elderly neighbor still watching them as though they were prime-time entertainment.

He said the next best option that came to mind. "Next time I need a lawyer, you can owe me one." He even managed a smile to go with the words.

Fortunately, it seemed like enough. She smiled back and

patted the door once. "You'll never collect on that." Her voice was light.

"One thing I've learned in my life is to never say never." He looked away from her ringless ring finger. "Where'd that dog go?"

Greer looked around, giving him a close-up view of the tender skin on the back of her neck. She had a trio of tiny freckles just below the loose strands of hair. Like someone had dashed a few specks of cinnamon across a smooth layer of cream.

He focused on Mrs. Gunderson, who was skirting the back of his trailer, calling the dog's name. "Mignon, get out from under there, right now!"

Greer had joined in, crouching down to look under the vehicle.

He figured if he revved the engine, it might send the fat dog into cardiac arrest. He shut it off again and climbed out. "Where is he?"

"He's lying down right inside the back tire." Mrs. Gunderson looked like she was about to go down on her hands and knees. "Mignon, you naughty little thing. Come out here, right now. Oh, darn it, he seems to have found something he thinks is food."

"Why don't you get one of his usual treats?" Greer suggested.

"Good idea." Mrs. Gunderson set off across the street once more.

If he'd hoped that her departure would spur the dog to follow, he was wrong. He knelt on one knee to look under the trailer. "Come 'ere, pooch."

Mignon paid him no heed at all, except to move even farther beneath the trailer.

Greer crouched next to him. The bottom of her dress puddled around her. "He doesn't like strangers."

Ryder slid his hand out from beneath the soft, colorful fabric that covered it. "He wouldn't like getting flattened by my trailer, either."

"He'll come out for his treats," she assured him.

"Since he looks like he lives on treats, I hope so." It would take the better part of an hour to get home and he'd probably already used up Mrs. Pyle's allotment of patience. If the treat didn't work, he'd have to drag the little bugger out.

"She's actually gotten him to lose a couple pounds."

"He's still wider than he is tall. Reminds me of my aunt's dog, Brutus." He straightened and looked across the street, hoping to see Mrs. Gunderson heading back. Instead, she was just reaching the top of her porch stairs and he could feel the minutes ticking away.

Even though he didn't say anything, Greer could feel the impatience coming off Ryder in waves. She stood, hoping that Mrs. Gunderson moved with more speed than she usually did. It was obvious that he was anxious to be on his way. "Your aunt has an overweight poodle?"

He lifted his hat just long enough to shove his fingers through his thick brown hair. "Overweight pug." His blue gaze slid over her from beneath the hat brim as he pulled it low over her brow. "Adelaide spoils him rotten."

She couldn't help but smile. "A pug named Brutus?"

He shrugged. "She has a particular sense of irony."

"I love your aunt's name," she said. "Adelaide."

A dimple came and went in his lean cheek. "Coming from the woman who lives in that Victorian thing behind us, I'm not real surprised."

She leaned against the side rail of the trailer. "Does she live in New Mexico?" Greer and her sisters didn't know much about Ryder, but had learned that he'd lived in New Mexico before moving to Wyoming.

The brim of his hat dipped slightly. "She has a place near Taos."

"The only place I've ever been in New Mexico was the Albuquerque airport during a layover." She glanced toward her neighbor's house. The front door was still open, but there was no sign of Mrs. Gunderson yet. "Did you grow up there?"

The dimple came again, staying a little longer this time. "In the Albuquerque airport?"

"Ha ha."

His lips actually stretched into a smile. "Yeah. I spent most of my time in Taos."

So she now knew he had an aunt. But she still didn't know if he had parents. Siblings. Other ex-wives. Anybody else at all besides Layla. "What's it like there? It's pretty artsy, isn't it?"

"More so than Braden."

"Does your aunt get to visit you often?"

"She's never been here. She doesn't like to travel much anymore. If I want to see her, I have to go to her." He thumbed up the brim of his hat and squinted at the sky.

"You're anxious to go."

"Yup." He knelt down to look at the dog again. "My housekeeper's gonna be peeved." He gave a coaxing whistle. "Come 'ere, dog."

"Your housekeeper's Doreen Pyle?"

Still down on one knee, he looked up at Greer and something swooped inside her stomach. "Keeping close tabs on me?"

She ignored the strange sensation. "Braden is a small community. And I happen to know her grandson pretty well."

"Dating him, are you?"

She couldn't help the snort of laughter that escaped. "Since he's not legally an adult, hardly. Haven't even had a date in—" She broke off, appalled at herself, embarrassed by the speculative look he was giving her. She pointed, absurdly grateful for Mrs. Gunderson's timely reappearance on her front porch. Her neighbor was holding something in her hand, waving it in the air as she came down the steps. "There's the treat."

And sure enough, before his mistress had even gotten to the street, Mignon was scrabbling out from beneath the trailer, practically rolling over his feet as he bolted.

Ryder straightened and gave her that faint smile again. The one that barely curved his well-shaped lips, but still managed to reveal his dimple. "Never underestimate the power of a good treat."

Then he thumbed the brim of his hat in that way he had of doing. Sort of old-fashioned and, well, *rancherly*. He walked around his truck and climbed inside. A moment later, he'd started the engine and was driving away.

Mrs. Gunderson picked up Mignon, who was happily gnawing on his piece of doggy jerky, and stood next to Greer. "He's a good-looking one, isn't he?"

At least her elderly neighbor could explain away her breathlessness. She'd had to climb her porch stairs to retrieve the dog treats.

Greer, on the other hand, had no such excuse. "He's surprising, anyway." She gave Mignon's head a scratch. "I've got to go call my dad before he drives out to haul my car that no longer needs hauling."

Then she hurried inside, pretending not to hear Mrs. Gunderson's knowing chuckle.

# Chapter 3

"Ryder Wilson towed your truck?"

Greer tucked her office phone against her shoulder. "Hey, Maddie. Hold on." She didn't wait for her sister to reply, but clicked over to the other phone call while she scrolled through the emails on her computer. It was Monday morning. She wished she could say it was unusual coming in to find fifty emails all requiring immediate attention. The fact was, coming in to *only* fifty emails was a good start to a week.

"Mrs. Pyle, as I explained to your son last week, Judge Donnelly has refused another continuance in Anthony's case. He's already granted two, which is unusual. Your grandson's trial is going to be on Thursday and my associate Don Chatham will be handling it. He's our senior attorney, as you know, and handles most of the jury trials." After she had handled all the other steps, including negotiating plea deals. Which the prosecutor's office wasn't offering to Anthony this go-round.

Not surprising. It was an election year.

"I know Judge Donnelly." Doreen Pyle sounded tearful.

"I can't be in court on Thursday. If I just went to him and asked—"

She shook her head, even though Doreen couldn't see. "I advise you not to speak directly to the judge, Mrs. Pyle."

"Then schedule a different date! You know how unreliable my son is. Anthony needs his family there. If his father would have told me last week, I could have made arrangements. But I have to work!"

Doreen Pyle worked for Ryder Wilson.

Greer pressed her fingertips between her eyes to relieve the pain that had suddenly formed there and sighed. The only adult Anthony truly had in his corner was his grandmother. "I'll see what I can do, Mrs. Pyle. I'll call you later this afternoon. All right?"

"Thank you, Greer. Thank you so much."

She highly doubted that Mrs. Pyle would be thanking her later. "Don't get your hopes up too high," she warned before jabbing the blinking button on her phone to switch back to the other call.

"Sorry about that, Maddie." She sent off a two-line response to the email on her computer screen and started composing a new one to the prosecutor's office. She wouldn't present a motion to the court until the prosecutor agreed to another delay. "You all recovered from the baby shower?"

"The only thing that'll help me recover fully from anything these days will be going into labor. About Ryder—"

"Yes, he towed my truck." She switched the phone to her other shoulder and opened the desk drawer where she kept her active files. "I suppose Ali told you?" She'd caught their father before he'd made a needless trip out to Devil's Crossing but she hadn't told him the finer details of who'd taken care of the chore.

She pulled out the file she was seeking and flipped it open

on her desk. Anthony Pyle. Seventeen. Charged with property destruction and defacement. It was his second charge and he was being tried in adult court. Anthony and his grandmother had good cause for worry since he was facing more than six months in jail if convicted.

Greer doubted that his father, Rocky, cared all that much about what happened. He provided for the basic needs of his son, but beyond that, the troubled boy was pretty much on his own. Rocky had told Greer outright that Anthony deserved what he got. Didn't matter to his father at all that the boy had consistently proclaimed his innocence. That the real culprit was his supposed friend—and the son of the man who owned the barn that had nearly burned down.

"Ali? No."

Greer held back a sigh. If Grant had told his wife that he'd seen Ryder with her, there was no way that Ali would have stayed quiet about it. And the fact that Grant hadn't told Ali just meant that he was still conflicted over everything that had happened with his sister.

"You know how news gets around," Maddie said.

In other words, Mrs. Gunderson had told someone she'd seen Ryder towing her car, and that someone had told someone, and so on and so forth.

Greer forestalled her sister's next question, knowing it was coming. "Ryder didn't have Layla with him."

"I heard. Did you know that his latest nanny quit on him?"

Greer's fingers paused on her computer keyboard. Doreen hadn't mentioned *that*. "That's the fourth one."

"Third," Maddie corrected. "Ray has been keeping track."

Greer spotted Keith Gowler in the hallway outside her office and waved to get his attention. He was one of the local private attorneys who took cases on behalf of the public defender's office because they were perpetually overworked and understaffed. "Is Ray concerned?"

"Not that he's said. We have no reason to think Layla's not being properly cared for."

"That's probably why Ryder was anxious to get moving the other evening, then. Doreen must have been watching Layla." And that was why she was upset about not being available for her grandson's trial.

"She's got a lot on her plate, too."

Greer glanced at Anthony's file. Despite the jurisdiction of the case, he was still a minor, which meant the case also involved Maddie's office. "Did you get notice of the trial date?"

"Thursday? Yes. I can't be there, though. Having another ultrasound at the hospital in Weaver and Linc will have kittens if I say I want to reschedule it."

"Everything okay?" she asked, alarm in her voice.

"Everything's fine, except I'm as big as a house and due in two weeks. And don't you start acting as bad as my husband. He's turned into a nervous Nellie these last few weeks. Driving me positively nuts."

"He's concerned. You're having your first baby."

"And I'm already thirty and yada yada. I know."

Keith stuck his head in her doorway. "Got the latest litter?"

She nodded at him and glanced at the round, schoolroom-style clock hanging above the door. It had a loud tick and tended to lose about five minutes every few days, but it had been a gift from one of her favorite law professors what felt like a hundred years ago. "Listen, Maddie, I've got a consult, so I need to go. But I want to know more about the ultrasound. We'll talk—"

"—later," her sister finished and hung up. At least Greer and Maddie were almost always on the same wavelength. It was too bad that Greer couldn't say the same about Ali.

She made a note on her calendar to call her. Maybe if Greer were the one to plan dinner next Monday, she'd get herself back in Ali's good graces. The three of them usually tried to get together for dinner on the first Monday of each month, but their schedules made it difficult. And when it came to canceling, Greer had been the worst offender. The fact that next Monday wasn't the first Monday of the month was immaterial. With Maddie ready to pop with the baby, this might be their only chance for a while.

Keith tossed himself down on the hard chair wedged into Greer's crowded office. "How many assignments this week?"

She closed Anthony's file and plucked a stack from the box on the floor behind her desk. "Too many. Take a look."

"I won't be able to take on as many as usual," he warned as he began flipping through the files. "Lydia and I have set the wedding date next month."

Even though she'd half expected the news, Greer was still surprised. It hadn't been that long since the lawyer was moping around from the supposedly broken heart Ali had caused him when they broke up, before she met Grant. Then he'd met Lydia when he'd taken on the defense case involving her son. "Congratulations. You're really doing it, huh?"

"I'd have married her six months ago, but she wanted to wait until Trevor's case was settled. Now it is and we can get on with our lives." He glanced up for a moment. "How's the Santiago case coming?"

"Pretrial motions after Labor Day. Michael has the investigator working overtime."

"I'll bet he does. Because your boss wants the case dismissed in the worst way."

"We'll see." Stormy Santiago would be the jewel in the prosecutor's reelection crown. She was beautiful. Manipulative. And charged with solicitation of murder. "Don's already prepping to go to trial on it."

"I'll bet he is. He gets her off and he'll be onto bigger pastures, whether he's best buddies with your boss or not. Mark my words."

Greer couldn't imagine Don wanting to leave their department, where he was a big fish in a small pond. "You think?"

Keith shrugged. He slid several folders from the stack toward her. "I can take these."

It was up to her to ensure the assignments were correctly recorded and submitted to the appropriate court clerk. Between municipal, circuit and district courts, it meant even more paperwork for her. "Great. See you in court."

Morning and afternoon sessions were held daily every Monday through Thursday, with Greer running between courtrooms as she handled arraignments and motions and pleadings and the myriad details involved when an individual was charged with a criminal offense. Occasionally, there was a reason for a Friday docket, which was a pain because they all had plenty of non-court details to take care of on Fridays. And increasingly on Saturdays and Sundays, too. Most of those days, Greer was meeting clients—quite often at the various municipal jails scattered around their region.

Such was the life of a public defender. Or in her case, the life of a public defender who got to do all the prep but rarely actually got to *defend*. It was up to Greer to prepare briefs, schedule conferences, take depositions and hunt down reluctant witnesses when she had to. She was the one who negotiated the plea deals that meant Don typically only had to show up in the office on Thursdays, when most of the trials were scheduled. She'd gotten a few bench trials, but thanks to Don and his buddy-buddy relationship with Michael Towers, their boss and the supervising attorney for the region, her experience in front of a jury was limited.

She also photocopied the case files and made the coffee.

But if Don were to ever leave...

She exhaled, pushing the unlikely possibility out of her mind, and sent off her message to the prosecutor. The rest of her email would have to wait. She shoved everything she would likely need into her bulging briefcase, grabbed the blazer that went with her skirt and hurried out of her office.

Michael was sitting behind his desk when she stuck her head in his office. "Any news yet on a new intern?" Their office hadn't had one for three months. Which was one of the reasons Greer had been on coffee and photocopy duty.

He shook his head, looking annoyed. Which for Michael was pretty much the status quo. "I have three other jurisdictions needing interns, too. When there's something you need to know, I'll tell you. Until then, do your job."

She managed not to bare her teeth at him and continued on her way. She didn't stop as she waved at Michael's wife, Bernice, who'd been filling in for the secretary they couldn't afford to hire, even though she hopped up and scurried after her long enough to push a stack of pink message slips into the outer pocket of Greer's briefcase.

"Thanks, Bunny."

Greer left the civic plaza for the short walk to the courthouse. It was handy that the buildings were located within a few blocks of each other. It meant that she could leave her car in the capable hands of her dad for the day. Carter Templeton was retired with too much time on his hands and he'd offered to look at it. He might have spent most of his life in an office as an insurance broker, but there wasn't much that Carter couldn't fix when he wanted to. Which was a good thing for Greer, because she was presently pretty broke.

She was pretty broke almost all of the time.

It was something she'd expected when she'd taken the job with the public defender's office. And money had gotten even tighter when she'd thrown in with her two sisters to buy the fixer-upper Victorian—in which she was the only one still living. She couldn't very well start complaining about it now, though.

The irony was that both Maddie and Ali could now put whatever money they wanted into the house since they'd both married men who could afford to indulge their every little wish.

Now it was just Greer who was holding up the works.

She'd already remodeled her bedroom and bathroom when they'd first moved in. The rest of the house was in a terrible state of disrepair, though. But if she couldn't afford her fair third of the cost, then the work had to wait until she could.

She sidestepped a woman pushing a baby stroller on the sidewalk and jogged up the steps to the courthouse. There were thirty-two of them, in sets of eight. When she'd first started out, running up the steps had left her breathless. Six years later, she barely noticed them.

Inside, she joined the line at security and slid her bare arms into her navy blue blazer. Once through, she jogged up two more full flights of gleaming marble stairs to the third floor.

She slipped into Judge Waters's courtroom with two minutes to spare and was standing at the defendant's table with her files stacked in front of her before the judge entered, wearing his typically dour expression.

He looked over his half glasses. "Oh, goody." His voice was humorless as he took his seat behind the bench. "All of my favorite people are here. Actually on time for once." He poured himself a glass of water and shook out several antacid tablets from the economy-sized bottle sitting beside the water. "All right. As y'all ought to know by now, we'll break at noon and not a minute before. So don't bother asking. If you're not lucky enough to be out of the court's hair by noon, we'll resume at half past one and not one minute after."

He eyed the line of defendants waiting to be arraigned. They sat shoulder to shoulder, crammed into the hardwood bench adjacent to the defendant's table where Greer stood. After this group, there was another waiting, just as large.

Judge Waters shoved the tablets into his mouth. "Let's get started," he said around his crunching.

All in all, it was a pretty normal morning.

Normal ended at exactly twelve fifty-five.

She knew it, because the big clock on the corner of Braden Bank & Trust was right overhead when she spotted Ryder Wilson walking down the street.

He was carrying Layla.

Greer's heart nearly stopped beating. Heedless of traffic, she bolted across Main Street to intercept him.

A fine idea in theory. But she was wearing high heels and a narrow skirt, and had a ten-pound briefcase banging against her hip with every step she took. Speedy, she was not.

He'd reached the corner and would soon be out of sight.

She'd run track in high school, for God's sake.

She hopped around as she pulled off her pumps, and chased after him barefoot.

The cement was hot under her feet as she rounded the corner and spotted him pulling open the door to Braden Drugs halfway down the block.

"Ryder!"

He hesitated, glancing around over his shoulder, then let go of the door and waited for her.

"Hi!" She was more breathless from the sight of Layla

than from the mad dash, and barely looked up at Ryder as she stopped. She knew her smile was too wide but couldn't do a thing about it as she leaned closer to Layla. "Hi, sweetheart. Look at you in your pretty pink sundress. You probably don't even remember me. But I sure remember you."

Layla waved the pink sippy cup by the handle she was clutching and showed off her pearly white teeth as she babbled nonsensically.

Everything inside Greer seized up. She wanted to take the baby in her arms so badly it hurt. She contented herself with stroking the tot's velvety cheek with her shaking fingertip. "I sure have missed you." The words came out sounding husky, and she cleared her throat before looking up at Ryder.

He was looking back at her warily, which she supposed she deserved, after chasing him down the way she had.

"What brings the two of you to town?"

He looked beyond her to the drugstore. "She's got some special vitamin stuff she's supposed to have. Aren't your feet burning?"

She looked down and felt the searing heat that was only slightly less intense than the heat that filled her cheeks. She quickly leaned over, putting her shoes back on. "Probably looks a little silly."

"Yep."

She huffed. "You didn't have to agree. Do you always say what you're thinking?"

"Not necessarily." His eyebrows quirked. It was her only hint that he was amused. "But I generally say what I mean."

Layla babbled and smacked the sippy cup against Greer's arm. "I think I recognize that cup," Greer said to her.

Layla jabbered back. Her bright green eyes latched onto Greer's.

She felt tears coming on. "I can't believe how much you've grown." The huskiness was back in her voice.

"You want to hold her?"

Now, given the opportunity, Greer was suddenly hesitant. "I don't know if she'll remember me. She might not—"

He dumped the baby in her arms.

Layla smiled brightly. She didn't care in the least that Greer's vision was blurred by tears as she looked down at her.

Greer wrapped her arms around the baby and cuddled her. "I thought she'd be heavier." She closed her eyes and rubbed her cheek against Layla's soft hair. "Nothing smells better," she murmured.

Ryder snorted slightly. "Sure, when she's not fillin' her diaper with something out of a horror flick."

Greer smiled. She caught Layla's fist and kissed it. "What's Daddy talking about, huh, baby? You're too perfect for anything like that."

"Excuse me."

They both looked over to see an elderly woman waiting to enter the door they were blocking.

"Sorry." Greer quickly moved out of the way while Ryder opened the door for her.

The woman beamed at him as she shuffled into the drugstore. "Thank you. It's so nice to see young families spend time together these days."

Greer bit the inside of her cheek, stifling the impulse to correct her. It was the same tactic she'd used many times in the courtroom.

Ryder let the door close after the woman. "Proof that appearances are deceiving."

Greer managed a smile. She was suddenly very aware of the time passing, but she didn't want to look at her watch or give up holding Layla a second sooner than she needed to. "What's special about the vitamins?"

He shrugged. "Something her pediatrician has her taking."

"Do you still take her to my uncle?" David Templeton's pediatrics practice in Braden was older than Greer. He'd been the first one to see Layla when Lincoln had discovered her left on the mansion's doorstep last December.

"You mean he hasn't told you?"

She gave him a look. "Wouldn't be very professional for him to talk about his patients to outsiders. And like it or not, that's what we are these days."

Ryder's lips formed a thin line.

Layla suddenly sighed deeply and plopped her head on Greer's shoulder.

Greer rubbed her back and kissed the top of her head. "I've heard about the nanny problems you've had."

"How?"

She stepped out of the way again when the shop door opened and a woman pushing two toddlers in a stroller came out. "Braden is a small town. Word gets around." She turned slightly so that Layla wasn't positioned directly in the sun. "Nannies don't hold to the same principles of confidentiality that a pediatrician's office does."

His lips twisted. "S'pose not." He reached for Layla, his hands brushing against Greer's bare arms as he lifted the tot away from her.

It was insane to feel suddenly shivery on what was such an infernally hot day.

She adjusted the wide bracelet-style watch on her wrist and wanted to curse. She was late getting back to the courthouse. On foot from here, it would take at least twenty minutes. "I still feel I owe you a favor for helping me this weekend with my car."

"Was it the thermostat?"

"I don't know yet. My dad is looking at it. He's pretty good with cars. I told him what you thought, though." She shifted from one foot to the other and smoothed her hand down the front of her blouse, where it was tucked into the waist of her skirt. He'd taken a step toward the drugstore. "Maybe I could help you on the nanny front," she offered quickly.

*"You?"* He sounded incredulous. "Kind of a comedown in the world from lawyering to nannying, isn't it?"

"I don't mean *me* personally." She worked hard to keep from sounding as offended as she felt. She might not have a lot of experience with babies, but Layla wasn't just any baby, either. "I mean with advertising for a nanny. I'm on a lot of loops because of my work. I could post ads if you wanted."

His blue eyes gave away none of his thoughts. "I'll think about it."

She took that as a sign he was willing to negotiate. "I've got a lot of connections," she added. "I'd like to help."

Layla's head had found its way to his wide chest and she was contentedly gnawing the handle of her sippy cup.

"I suppose it wouldn't hurt," he said abruptly.

She'd fully expected him to say no. "Great! That's…that's really great." She cringed a little at her overenthusiasm, not to mention her lack of eloquence. She looked at her watch again and quickly leaned forward to kiss Layla's cheek. Then she started backing down the block. "I'll call you later to get the particulars. Pay range, hours, all that."

He resettled his black cowboy hat on his head, looking resigned. "Are you asking or telling?"

She knew her smile was once again too wide, but so what? She'd finally gotten to see Layla. And even if she earned Judge Waters's wrath for not making it back to court on time, she couldn't bring herself to care.

# Chapter 4

Ryder spotted the little foreign job sitting in front of his house. It looked as out of place there as it had stalled on the side of the road out near Devil's Crossing.

The second thing he noticed was that Doreen Pyle's ancient pickup truck wasn't there.

When he'd set out that morning to get more hay cut, Mrs. Pyle had been sweeping up cereal after Layla overturned her favorite red bowl.

But now, Mrs. Pyle's truck was gone and the lady lawyer's was parked in its place.

It was too much to hope that she'd come all the way out here to tell him she'd found the perfect nanny candidate. She could've done that over the phone, the same way she'd gotten the particulars from him the other day.

He glanced at the cloudless sky. "What fresh new problem are you giving me now?"

As usual, he got no answer. The air remained hot and heavy, filled with the sound of buzzing insects.

He half expected to find Greer in the kitchen with Layla, but the room was empty when he went in.

He flipped on the faucet and sluiced cold water over his head. Then he grabbed the dish towel hanging off the oven door to mop his face as he went in search of them.

There weren't a lot of rooms in the place, so it didn't take him long. He found both females in the living room, sprawled on his leather couch, sound asleep.

Layla wore a pink sleeveless T-shirt and diaper. She was lying on Greer's chest, who was similarly attired in a sleeveless pink shirt and denim cutoffs.

He looked away from her lightly tanned legs and quietly went up the iron-and-oak staircase. At the top, he crossed the catwalk that bisected the upper back half of the barn. All he had to do was look down and he could see his living area and who was occupying it.

Aside from the failed nannies and Mrs. Pyle, the last woman who'd spent any real time under his roof had been Daisy. When he thought about it, Mrs. Pyle had lasted longest.

He entered his bedroom. He'd put up sliding barn doors in the upper rooms after he'd taken custody of Layla. Before then, the only enclosed spaces had been the bathrooms. Two upstairs. One down.

He went into his bathroom now and flipped on the shower. Dust billowed from his clothes when he stepped out of them. He got into the shower before the water even had a chance to get warm.

He still had goose bumps when he stepped out a few minutes later, but at least he wasn't dripping sweat and covered in hay dust anymore.

He stepped over the dirty clothes, pulled on a pair of clean jeans and a white T-shirt from his drawer and went back downstairs.

They were still sleeping. He retrieved a bottle of cold water from the fridge in the kitchen, then wearily sat on the only piece of adult-sized furniture in the living room except for the couch. His aunt had designed the armless, triangular-backed chair during her furniture phase, and he had brought it with him along with the couch more for sentimental reasons than because it was comfortable.

He slouched down in the thing as much as he could and propped his bare feet on the arm of the couch by Greer's feet. Instead of opening the water bottle, he pressed it against his head and closed his eyes. Already the relief from the cold shower was waning and he caught himself having fond memories of the three feet of snow piled up against his house last March.

Not two minutes passed before Greer spoke, her voice barely above a whisper. "Do you think the heat's ever going to end?"

He didn't open his eyes. "I spent a summer near Phoenix once." Adelaide had been doing an exhibition there. "I was fifteen." He kept his voice low, too, because he knew what it was like when Layla didn't get in a decent nap. When he'd been rodeoing, he'd drawn broncs that'd been easier to handle. "It was like living inside a pizza oven."

"Descriptive. But you didn't answer my question."

He ignored that. "Where's Mrs. Pyle?"

"Still not answering my question. Obviously, Mrs. Pyle is at her grandson's trial."

He opened his eyes at that. The baby was still sleeping and Greer watched him over her head, eyes as dark and deep as the blackest night.

"What trial?"

"She didn't tell you?"

He spread his hands. "Obviously not."

"You do recall that Doreen Pyle *has* a grandson?"

He gave her a look.

"Anthony's seventeen. And he's being tried for burning down a barn."

Ryder swallowed an oath and pulled his feet off the couch. "She should have told me." He wasn't an ogre. "So why are *you* here?"

"Because I couldn't get the prosecution to agree to another continuance and Judge Donnelly has a stick up his—" Greer broke off with a grimace. "Anthony has a very competent trial lawyer representing him. Today, it's more important for him to have his grandmother there than me."

"Not because you wanted to spend time with Layla?"

"It's the one thing that made today tolerable. I've been working on Anthony's case since his prelim."

"Did he do it?"

"My client is innocent."

"Spoken like a defense lawyer."

"I am a defense lawyer. Just a poorly paid one, thanks to the great state of Wyoming."

"If he's your client, why is someone else handling the trial?"

Her lips twisted. "That, my friend, is the fifty-dollar question." She rolled carefully to one side so that she could deposit Layla on the couch cushion and then slid off the couch to sit on the floor.

It was almost as interesting as watching a circus contortionist.

Once she was on the floor with her back to the couch, she tugged her shirt down over her flat stomach where it had ridden up and blew out a breath. "This place of yours has a lot going for it, I'll grant you, but you need air-conditioning."

"I have a window rattler upstairs in my bedroom." He wondered why he didn't tell her there was another one in Layla's bedroom, too.

She slanted a look toward him from the corner of her eye. "Meaning?"

He smiled slightly. "Meaning I do have air-conditioning. Just not down here. I wish Mrs. Pyle would have told me."

"She must have her reasons. She's known since Monday."

He sat forward and offered her the unopened water bottle. "Why didn't you say something about the trial when you chased us down the street the other day?"

"Because it was Mrs. Pyle's business to tell you." Her fingers grazed his when she leaned over to take the water.

Adelaide had done her best to give him an appreciation of beauty and the visual arts. She'd always been asking him, *But what do you see?* and he never knew exactly what kind of answer she wanted. But he figured he must have learned something from her after all, given his appreciation of the way Greer tilted her head and tipped the bottle back, taking a prolonged drink. Her neck was long and lovely. Her profile pure. Watching her was almost enough to compensate for her and Mrs. Pyle's keeping him in the dark.

Greer handed him back the half-empty bottle.

Her lips were full and damp.

Even though he didn't need the trouble it would likely bring, he didn't look away from her when he took the bottle from her and finished it.

Her gaze flickered and she looked away as she pushed to her feet. She tugged at the hem of her T-shirt as she paced around the couch. "Did she give you any other reason to be quitting?"

"Maybe you should ask Mrs. Pyle."

She gave him a look and he relented, proving that he needed more willpower to resist the women in his life. "She tells me she's a housekeeper. Not a nanny."

"Because scrubbing floors is so much easier than heating

a bottle?" Her voice rose a little and she pressed her lips together self-consciously.

"Layla doesn't use a bottle anymore. She only uses her cup. The pink cup. And if the pink cup isn't handy, she screams bloody murder until it is. Trust me, Counselor. Cleaning house is easier than childcare." He waved at Layla, who hadn't budged an inch from where she had rolled onto her side against the back couch cushion. She drooled all the time these days, and now was no exception. But the leather had survived him growing up, so he assumed it would survive a while longer.

"Did she say when she's leaving?"

"She gave me a week's notice."

"Even if we haven't found a nanny by then?" Greer propped her hands on her slender hips. "Did she say anything else?"

"Yeah. That I'd be better off finding a wife than a nanny."

Greer's eyebrows rose halfway up her forehead. Then she scrubbed her hands down her face. "I'm sorry."

"For what?"

She dropped her hands. "That she said something so…so insensitive!" She pressed her lips together again and watched Layla warily, as if expecting her to wake because her voice had risen once more.

"Insensitive how?"

A small line formed between her eyebrows. "Your wife passed away less than a year ago," she said huskily. "I'm sure remarrying is the furthest thing from your mind."

"It was until my housekeeper brought it up. But she had a valid point. Layla deserves a mother." At least he'd had Adelaide when his mother had died. He leaned back in the chair again and propped his feet once more on the couch arm. He linked his fingers across his stomach. "You never knew Daisy, did you?"

The line deepened slightly as she shook her head. "I never met her. But Grant has been talking more about Karen these days."

"The man actually talks?"

She gave him a look. "What she did has been hard on him, too. He was Karen's brother, but even then, the court wasn't ready or willing to hand over Layla to him."

He grunted. "She was never Karen to me. She was Daisy Miranda. That was the name she used when we met, the name she used when we got married and the name she used when she left me. She never said she had a brother at all. Either he didn't matter enough for her to mention, or I didn't matter enough. Considering the way things went down, I'll give you a guess which one I'm more inclined to believe."

Greer tucked her hair behind her ears. Her forehead had a dewy sheen. "Regardless of her name, you loved her enough to marry her. You don't just get over that at the drop of a hat."

"You been married to someone who ran out on you? Ever gone through a bunch of tests just to make sure she didn't leave you with something catching to remember her by?"

"No, but—"

"Ever married at all?"

She needlessly retucked her hair. "No. But that doesn't mean I don't have feelings. That I have no appreciation for the pain involved when you lose someone. Hearts don't heal just because we decide they should."

He couldn't help the amusement that hit him.

And she saw it on his face. The line between her brows deepened even more. "What's so funny?"

He schooled his expression. "Nothing."

She let out a disgusted sound and his lips twitched again. Stopping the smile would've taken more willpower than he possessed.

She glared at him even harder and her eye got that little twitch she was prone to.

"Relax, Counselor. You don't have to worry that I'm withering away with grief or anything else because of my beloved wife. You do recall that *she* ran out on me, right?"

"And no matter what you say now, I'm sure that was very painful for you. But you know—" she waved her hands in invitation "—if you feel the need to pretend otherwise so as to maintain some false manly pride, be my guest."

He watched her for a moment. Then he pulled his feet off the couch again and sat forward. "Want a beer?"

She blinked. "What?"

He stood. Layla was still sound asleep. Snoring even, which meant that although he'd showered off the hay dust, she'd still probably gotten a whiff of it and her nose was getting congested. The pediatrician had warned him that Layla seemed to be developing some allergies. "A beer," he repeated, and headed into the kitchen, where he grabbed two cold bottles from the refrigerator.

Greer was standing in the same spot when he returned and handed her one. "It's five o'clock somewhere." He twisted off the cap and set it on the fireplace mantel.

Still looking suspicious, she slowly did the same.

He lightly tapped his bottle against hers and took a drink.

After some hesitation, she took a tiny sip.

"Let's go out back. It might be cooler."

She looked at Layla. "But—"

He scooped up the baby, who didn't even startle, and transferred her to the playpen. Then he picked up the baby monitor and turned it on, showing Greer the screen where the black-and-white image of his living space, including the playpen, was flickering to life. "Happy?"

Beer and monitor in hand, he headed out through the kitchen door, and Greer followed.

It wasn't any cooler outside. But at least there was a slight breeze and the gambrel roof provided shade from the sun. He gestured with his bottle to the picnic table and benches that he'd found stored in the root cellar when he'd bought the place.

"Wouldn't have expected something so fanciful from you," she said as she straddled one of the benches and set her bottle on the cheerfully painted table. "Flowers?"

He took the opposite bench. "Daisies." He set the baby monitor on the center of the weathered table and took a pull on the cold beer. "Twenty-five cents if you can guess who painted them."

"Ah." She nodded and fell silent.

He exhaled and turned so his back was against the table and he could stretch out his legs. The rolling hillside was his for almost as far as he could see. Beyond that was his by lease. His closest neighbor was ten miles away as the crow flew, and just to get to the highway meant driving down his seventeen-mile driveway, three miles of which were actually paved. Until he'd bought the place, he felt like he'd been looking for it his entire life.

But his housekeeper did have a point about his place being remote. "Mrs. Pyle's grandson going to get off?"

"It's a jury trial, so you never know until the verdict comes in. But I believe the facts are on Anthony's side."

"Doesn't it bug you not being there in court?"

"There are a lot of things about my job that bug me."

He took another drink and looked her way.

"Yes. It bugs me. But we've built a solid defense and Don Chatham—much as he annoys me personally—is a fine attorney. I can zealously represent my clients through the fairest plea negotiations to resolve their cases as well as anyone working in the PD's office. But when my client refuses to plea, or when they're truly better served going to trial?" She rolled the bottle between her fingertips. "Anthony *is* in good hands. Better than mine, when it comes down to it, since Don's experience before a jury exceeds mine by about a decade."

"When's the verdict likely to come in?"

"Before six tonight. The judge runs a tight ship and he likes to be home for dinner with his wife every night by seven. If the jury is still deliberating, he'll call a recess and resume tomorrow morning. But he'll be in a bad mood because he doesn't like working on Fridays any more than Don does. Did you move here because of Daisy?"

Her abrupt question was surprising. "No. We didn't meet until after that." He rolled his jaw around. "Not long after," he allowed.

"So why did you buy this place? Did you ranch in New Mexico?"

"I did a lot of ranch work. For other people. Along the way was some rodeoing. A few years in the service. Did you always want to be a lawyer?"

"What branch?"

"Army."

She smiled slightly. "My dad, too. Way before I was born, though." Her smile widened. "And I wanted to be a lawyer from the very first Perry Mason novel I read. My dad has a whole collection of them from when he was a kid and I started reading them one summer when I was grounded. I had romantic visions of defending the rights of the meek and the defenseless. And I also fancied following in Archer's path."

Ryder lifted his eyebrows.

"My older brother. Half brother, to be accurate. On my dad's side. I have a half sister on my mom's side who's also an attorney. But I didn't grow up with Rosalind the way I did with Archer. They're both in private practice."

"Classic yours, mine and ours situation?"

"Sort of. I have another half sister, too, who is a psychologist. Hayley lives in Weaver with her husband, Seth, and their baby. What about you?"

"No sisters. No brothers. Half or otherwise."

"But you have an aunt Adelaide with a pug named Brutus."

"Lawyers and their penchant for details."

"I'd be worried about my memory if I couldn't recall something you mentioned less than a week ago," she said drily. "What about your parents?"

"What about them?"

She waited a beat, and when he said nothing more, she took a sip of her beer. She squinted and her cheeks looked pinched.

Her face was an open book, which for a lawyer was sort of a surprise. Maybe it was a good thing she didn't face juries very often. "Not your cup of tea?"

"It's fine."

He rolled his eyes and took the beer out of her hands. "I suppose you're a teetotaler."

"Not at all. I just… Well, wine is more my thing."

It was his turn to pull a face. "And not mine. Whiskey?"

"If the occasion calls for it."

"We've at least got that in common." He got up and she looked alarmed. "Don't worry. I'm not bringing out a bottle of the good stuff. A cold beer at three on a hot afternoon is one thing. We'll save the whiskey for cold nights and staying warm. I'll get you a soda."

Greer chewed the inside of her cheek, watching Ryder head inside his house.

She thought she'd done pretty well not falling right off the couch when she'd wakened to find him sitting there. He'd obviously showered. His hair was dark and wet, slicked back from his chiseled features. His T-shirt was clinging to his broad shoulders. His feet sticking out from the bottom of his worn jeans had been bare.

And her mind had gone straight down the no-entry road paved with impossibility.

She hadn't expected to doze off along with Layla. But then again, she hadn't expected to be so pooped out after spending six hours taking care of the baby, either.

When she'd arrived out at the house, it had been early enough to relieve Doreen Pyle so she could get into town before court started. But Ryder hadn't been there, even though Greer had spent most of last night sleeplessly preparing herself for the encounter.

Doreen had told her that he'd headed out more than two hours earlier. "Haying," she'd said, as if that explained everything.

Foolishly, Greer had assumed that Doreen would have told her employer that Greer was pinch-hitting that day. And why.

She turned the baby monitor so she could see it better. Layla had turned around in a full circle inside the playpen, but still looked to be sleeping.

She reluctantly set the monitor on the table when Ryder returned. He set a bottle of cola in front of her. "Better?"

She rarely indulged, but it was still better than beer. And it was wonderfully cold. "Thank you."

His lips stretched into a brief smile. Then he sat down again, but this time he straddled his bench the same as her. "Why choose the public defender's office to zealously defend your clients?"

She'd been asked that question ever since she'd passed the bar. She'd always given the same answer. "Because I wanted to help people who really needed it." Her eyes strayed to the baby monitor. She couldn't help it. That grainy little image fascinated her.

"And do you?" His question dragged at her attention. "Help people who really need it?"

She twisted open the soda and took a long drink. The fact that she wasn't really sure what she was accomplishing anymore wasn't something she intended to share. "Everyone deserves a proper and fair defense," she finally said, which she believed right to her very core. "More than eighty percent of criminal defendants in this state end up in the public defender's office. I do my part as well as I can."

"Just not in front of a jury."

She realized she'd picked up the monitor again and made herself put it down. "Not generally. Although, honestly, I stay busier with my cases than Don does. We have a handful of trials a month. Unless it's something really big like the Santiago thing that's been on the news, Don spends most of his weekends fishing while I'm chasing around between courts and jails and—" She broke off. "I've never had a caseload that drops under one hundred clients at any given time."

The slashing dimple in his cheek appeared for a moment. "Do they all say they're innocent?"

She smiled wryly and let that one pass. "We cover a few counties here. But I know some offices with caseloads that are even heavier. We all make use of interns, but getting them can be sort of cutthroat." She shook her head. "The real problem is there's never enough money in the coffers to equip our office with everything and everyone we need."

"Now you sound like a politician."

On the monitor screen, Layla had turned around and was facing the other corner, her little rump up in the air. "Not in this lifetime," Greer responded. "Though I'd probably make more money if I were. Nobody I know has ever gotten rich working as a PD."

"Do you want to be rich?"

She laughed outright at that. "I'm more about being able to pay all the bills on time."

"What about that house of yours? That's gotta be a money pit."

"I'll take the fifth on that. I love my house. It has character."

"Like your car?"

She gave him her best stern look. The one she'd learned from her father. "Don't be dissing my car."

He lifted his hands in surrender.

"It *was* the thermostat, by the way. So thank you for that heads-up."

"Ever considered private practice?"

"Most lawyers do."

"Well, then? It's not like you don't have an in with people in the business."

"Much as I love Archer, I have no desire to actually *work* with him. Rosalind is with *her* father's practice down in Cheyenne and does mostly tax and corporate law. Bo-ho-ring. So—" She took another drink just so she wouldn't pick up the monitor again.

"So...?"

"Why are you so interested?"

"Shouldn't I know more about the woman who's been watching Layla behind my back?"

"For one day. Don't imply it's been a regular occurrence." She nudged the monitor with her fingertip. "We all fell in love with her, you know." She brushed her thumb across Layla's black-and-white image. "Right from the very beginning when Linc called in Maddie because he'd found a baby on his doorstep. The only identifying clue she had on her was the note Daisy left with her."

"'Jaxie, please take care of Layla for me,'" he recited evenly.

"Right. When Daisy cocktailed for Jax at his bar, she routinely called him that. That's the only reason we ever suspected she was Layla's mother in the first place."

Ryder's expression was inscrutable but she could easily imagine what his suspicions were. She'd had them herself. So had Linc. His brother, Jax, had been on one of his not-infrequent jaunts, which was why Linc hadn't immediately turned over the baby when he first discovered her. But whether or not Jax had been involved with Daisy in a more personal way, they'd nevertheless conclusively ruled him out as the baby's biological father last December.

She set the monitor down again. "By the time we knew about Daisy, though, Layla was already under the court's protection. The judge named Maddie as Layla's emergency foster parent while an investigation began." She was reiterating facts that he'd been told months ago.

"Your sister and Linc wanted to adopt her themselves. Before you ever even knew Daisy's brother existed."

She glanced at him. It wasn't a detail they'd shared when he took custody. "Who told you that?"

He swirled the liquid in his bottle and took a drink, making her wonder if he was stalling or if he was simply thirsty.

Then he turned the bottle upside down and poured out the remaining beer onto the grass beneath their feet. "Not cold enough," he said, and she thought he wasn't going to answer her at all.

But he surprised her.

He laid the empty bottle on its side on the table between them and slowly spun it. "As you've pointed out before, Counselor, word gets around in a small town." He stopped the bottle so it pointed her way. "Isn't it true?"

She was a lawyer. Not a liar. And what was the harm if he knew the truth now? Maybe if he really understood, he wouldn't be so standoffish where her family and Layla was concerned. "They would have, but Maddie knew she and Linc would never get her. There were too many people in line ahead of them waiting to adopt a baby."

She clasped her hands on the table in front of her before she could pick up the monitor again. Her fascination with it was vaguely alarming. "The search for Daisy was leading nowhere and it was only a matter of time before Judge Stokes made a permanent ruling about placement. Not even the fact that Ali found Daisy's brother and discovered her real name was Karen Cooper changed that. We couldn't prove Layla was Karen's daughter and Grant's niece through his DNA because both he and Karen were adopted. Siblings by law, but not by genetics. Which meant that not even Grant could stop the legal forces at work. The one established fact the court recognized was that Layla had been abandoned and, as such, would benefit from placement in a suitable home through adoption. A family had even been selected." She sneaked a look at Ryder's face but his expression still told her nothing. She spread her fingers slightly, then pressed the tips of her thumbs together. "And then we discovered that your...that Karen had died in a car accident in Minnesota. Thanks to the photo that Grant and Ali found in her effects, we learned about you. Until then, we had no idea that Daisy Miranda or Karen Cooper had acquired a husband."

"The presumptive father, you mean."

She studied him. He'd had an opportunity to disprove it simply by requesting a paternity test.

But he hadn't.

Instead, he'd admitted—under oath—that he'd known about his absent wife's pregnancy. Combined with all their other information about Karen Cooper, it was enough for Judge Stokes to determine that Layla was legally Ryder's child. She'd been born during their marriage. No further questions asked. Certainly not about why Karen hadn't left their child with Ryder when she'd apparently decided parenthood wasn't for her.

The case may have been closed, but that didn't mean there weren't still questions.

"You didn't have to do it, you know," she said after a moment. "Claim Layla as your child. Not when we'd already failed so spectacularly to prove maternity." She didn't want to know if he'd lied under oath. It was hard enough suspecting that he had.

"It was the right thing to do."

"Even though *we* didn't know for certain that Daisy is… was Layla's mother." She could think of a dozen clients who wouldn't have done what he'd done. He'd told Ali when they'd first notified him that his wife hadn't been pregnant when she'd left him. Yet when he'd appeared before Judge Stokes, he'd attested that Daisy *had* notified him.

"How often do you run into someone named Layla?" He didn't wait for an answer as he spun the bottle again. "It was my mother's name. Daisy knew it. And I know Daisy liked it, because she told me once—in the beginning when I thought we actually had something—that if we ever had a baby girl, she wanted to name her Layla. Daisy *was* Layla's mother." He dropped his hand onto the bottle again, stopping its spinning once more. "It was the right thing to do," he repeated after a moment.

Greer's chest squeezed. He believed Daisy was Layla's

real mother. But did he believe that Layla was his biological daughter?

She reached across the table and covered both his hand and the bottle with hers. "I'm sorry, Ryder. I really am." That he lost his wife. That he'd become a father in such an unconventional way. If she had questions, he surely had many more.

His jaw canted to one side. Then his blue eyes met hers and for some reason, an oil slick of panic formed inside her. She started to pull her hand back, but he turned his palm upward and caught hers.

"Sorry enough to marry me?"

# Chapter 5

*"Marry you?"*

Greer yanked on her hand and nearly fell off the bench when he let go of it. She caught herself, only to knock over the bottle of soda, which gushed out in a stream of bubbly foam, splashing over the front of her T-shirt and shorts. "Now look what you've done!"

It was obvious he was having a hard time not laughing. "Gonna sue me over it? You know, for a woman who looks like she can run the world, you're kind of a klutz. Did you really think I was serious?"

She plucked her wet shirt away from her belly. Now she wasn't just sweaty, she'd be sticky, too. And she'd never been klutzy. Until she was around him. "Of course not," she lied. "You're just full of funny things to say this after—" She broke off when he suddenly stood and went inside the house.

She muttered an oath after his departing backside and swiped her hand down her wet thighs.

He returned a moment later, holding a sleepy-looking Layla and a checkered dish towel that he tossed Greer's way. "She needs a fresh diaper."

"Am I supposed to take out an announcement in the newspaper?" She swiped the towel over her legs. She could feel the damn soda right through to the crotch of her cutoffs.

"You're pretty snarky when you're caught off guard, aren't you?" He went back inside.

Then she realized the baby monitor had gotten doused with soda, too. She snatched it off the table and started drying it with the towel.

The screen had gone black.

She carried it inside. Ryder was bending over Layla on the couch, changing the diaper. "Do you have any dried rice?" She didn't wait for an answer, but started opening cupboard doors. "Ali got her cell phone wet last year and kept it inside a container of rice for a day to dry. I had my doubts, but the thing worked afterward." Greer found plates. Drinking glasses. At least a dozen boxes of dry cereal. Only half of it was suitable for Layla, which gave her quite the insight into his preference for Froot Loops.

She moved on to the lower cabinets and drawers.

"No, I do not have rice."

He spoke from right behind her and she straightened like he'd poked her with an electric prod. "Oh." She slammed the drawer she'd just opened shut. "Well, then I don't know what you'll want to do about this." She set the monitor on the butcher-block counter. "More soda got on it than me."

He lifted an eyebrow as he settled Layla into the high chair and managed to fasten the little belt thing around her wriggling body. "You look pretty soaked."

It was all she could do not to pluck at the hem of her shorts. "Yeah, well, you shouldn't joke like that."

He slid the molded tray onto the high chair and grabbed one of the boxes of cereal. He dumped a healthy helping onto Layla's tray and she dived into it like she hadn't eaten in days.

There was no question that Layla liked her food. Greer had fed her both jars of the food that Doreen had left out, plus a cubed banana and a teething biscuit, right before her nap.

"Yeah, well, maybe I shouldn't be joking. Mrs. Pyle's the one who reminded me Layla'd be better off with a mama than a nanny. Not that I've had any luck keeping either one around," he added darkly.

She felt that slick panic again and opened her mouth to say something, but nothing came. Which was such an unfamiliar occurrence that she felt even more panicky. "You can't judge everyone based on Daisy and a flighty nanny," she finally managed to say.

"Three nannies," he reminded her. "Easier to discount one two-week wife than three nannies. Mrs. Pyle had a point."

She wasn't sure her eyebrows were ever going to come back down to their normal spot over her eyes. "On what planet?"

He slid a look her way. "I know I'm not Wyoming's biggest catch, but you really think I can't find a wife if I set my mind on it? At least this time, I'd be choosing with my head instead of my—"

"Heart?"

His lips twisted. "That wasn't exactly the body part I was thinking about."

She felt her cheeks heat, which was just ridiculous. It wasn't as though she was some innocent virgin. She was well versed in the facts of life, whether or not she'd acted on any of those facts lately.

"Anyway," he went on, "it wouldn't be a one-way deal." He'd pulled a covered bowl from the refrigerator and dumped the contents in a saucepan that he set over a flame on the stove. "I realize that she'd need to get something out of it, too. It'd be a business deal." He bent over, picking up the sippy cup that Layla had pitched to the floor. "Both parties benefit."

Greer nearly choked, looking away from the sight of his very, very fine jean-clad backside.

He set the cup back on the tray. "If you throw it, I'm going to take it away," he warned.

The baby laughed and swept her hands back and forth against the cereal, sending pieces shooting off the tray.

"Yeah, you laugh, you little terror," he muttered. "You know better." He went back to the stove to poke a fork at the concoction he was heating.

It all felt strangely surreal.

"I've always been better in business than relationships. So go with your strengths, right?" He glanced at her again.

"Marriage isn't a business deal."

He snorted. "Better a business deal than the real deal. As they say, Counselor, been there, done that. Not really a fan. You've been a lawyer for a while now. Haven't you seen the value of pragmatism over idealism?"

She wanted to deny it, but couldn't. "I don't think pragmatism is a basis for marriage, either."

"But it's a good basis for good business. At least that's been my experience. So—" he tested the temperature of the contents in his saucepan with his finger and pulled the pan off the flame "—like I said, Mrs. Pyle has a point. Two parents are supposed to be better than one. Didn't have two, myself, so I don't know about that. Maybe if I had—" He broke off, shaking his head and leaving Greer wondering.

He tipped the saucepan over a small bowl and grabbed a child-sized spoon from a drawer before flipping one of the table chairs around to face the high chair. "Every kid deserves a mother. Don't you agree?"

"Yes, but that doesn't mean I agree with this method of acquiring one!"

"People have been marrying for practical reasons a lot longer than they've been marrying for romantic ones. I could advertise for a wife just as easily as I can a nanny."

"You know what this sounds like to me? Like you've put all of five minutes of thought into it."

"And you'd be wrong. What happens to Layla if something happens to me?"

Her lips parted. "You... Well, Grant—"

"Daisy didn't dump Layla on Grant's doorstep. You think that was just an oversight? She didn't want him to have her!"

"You can't blame him for that! She didn't leave Layla with you, either!"

"Yeah, and that's something I get to live with. Daisy still named her after *my* mother. She was as unpredictable as the wind, but that means something to me."

She exhaled, feeling a pang inside. "Ryder. We'll find you a nanny. One who'll stay."

"If you were a kid, would you rather have a mom or a paid babysitter?" He didn't wait for her to answer. "Putting that aside for the moment, I'd rather have another plan in place for Layla if I get stomped out by a pissed-off bull one day."

"I've got to sit down." She grabbed one of the wood chairs from the table and sank down onto it. "I'm a lawyer. I appreciate your wisdom in planning for disasters, but I don't particularly want that vision in my head."

"You've heard worse in court, I'm sure."

She had, but that was different. "You can name anyone you want as a guardian for Layla if something were to happen to you. For heaven's sake, if you want to write up a will right now, I can help you. It doesn't mean you have to have a business-deal wife."

"Fine." He gestured with the spoon. "There's paper in that drawer. Get out a piece."

She slid open the drawer in question and pulled out the

notepad and a short stub of a pencil. "You don't have to do it this very second."

"No time like the present." He scooped food into Layla's mouth.

"Maybe you should give it more thought," she suggested. "Deciding who would best—"

"I, Ryder Wilson, being of sound mind and body, yada yada. I assume you can fill in the blanks."

She exhaled noisily. "I'm not so sure about the soundness," she muttered. "But yes. So who do you want to name as guardian? Your aunt Adelaide?"

"She's already done her time raising me. You."

"Me, what?"

"You. Put your name down."

She dropped the pencil back into the drawer and shut it with a snap. "I don't find this funny."

"I don't find it funny, either, Counselor. There's no denying you've got a strong concern for Layla. But if your concern isn't that strong, no sweat." He scooped up another spoonful of the unidentifiable substance and evaded Layla's grasping hands to shovel it into her greedy mouth.

Something about his actions made Greer's insides feel wobbly. So she focused instead on the goopy little chunks on the spoon. "What *is* that?"

"Sweet potatoes, beets and ground chicken."

"Good grief."

"Don't knock it. I call it CPS."

"What?"

"Cow Pie Surprise."

She grimaced. "You just said it was chicken."

"It is. But doesn't matter what meat I add, it all looks the same. Like Cow Pie Surprise. But Layla loves it and she's sleeping better at night since I started spiking her food with meat." He gave Greer a sideways look. "You're not vegetarian or something, are you?"

She shook her head, keeping silent about her brief stint with the practice during her college years.

"Good." He focused back on Layla, slipping in a couple more bites before she managed to commandeer the spoon and whack it against the side of the tray. She chattered indecipherably, occasionally stopping long enough to focus on drumming her spoon or carefully choosing a round piece of cereal.

He tossed the bowl in the sink and wet a cloth to start wiping up the mess that was all over Layla's face and hands and hair and tray and clothes.

"Don't you have a bib?"

"Couple dozen of 'em. All came in the boxes of stuff your sister sent. Short-Stuff here doesn't like 'em." He freed the baby and set her down on the floor, and she immediately started crawling out of the room. "Decided a while ago that it wasn't worth the battle."

Having spent much of the day keeping up with Layla, Greer was less surprised by the rapid crawl than she was by Ryder's ease with Layla. She'd pictured him as struggling a bit more with the day-to-day needs of a baby.

"Do you have other children?"

His eyes narrowed and Greer knew she'd annoyed him. "D'you see any other kids here?"

She scooped up Layla before the baby could get too far. "Don't be so touchy." She much preferred taking the offensive tack to being on the defensive. "Nanny problems or not, you've obviously settled into the routine."

"Better than you expected."

"Not at all." *Liar, liar, pants on fire.*

"I've got roundup facing me whether this heat breaks soon or not, and it'll mean being gone a couple days. No matter what you think it looks like, I still need help. Nanny, wife or otherwise."

"And I'll remind you yet again that I have an entire family willing to help you out where Layla is concerned."

"Like Maddie? Your sister who is so pregnant she looks like she's about ready to explode?"

"How do you know what she looks like?"

"She was in Josephine's diner the other day."

"She didn't mention seeing you."

"She didn't."

He didn't elaborate, and Greer stomped on her impatience as though she were putting out a fire.

"I've already made some job postings for another nanny. It's only a matter of time before you find the right person. Here." She handed Layla to him. "I have briefs I need to prepare." She'd even brought her case files with her, thinking she might have time to make some notes while Layla napped. But since Greer had napped right along with her, clearly *that* had been a silly notion. And even though she did have work to do, it was the sudden need to escape from Ryder that was driving her now.

"Briefs for a job that's not everything you'd hoped for."

"I didn't say that."

"You didn't have to." His gaze pinned hers and she felt uncomfortably like a witness about to perjure herself before the court.

She dragged her soda-moist shirt down around her soda-moist shorts. "I'll let you know when there are a few candidates—*nanny* candidates—for you to interview." She waved her hand carelessly. "But by all means, don't let that stop you from putting out word that you're wife-hunting if you're actually serious about that."

"Maybe I'll do that."

"If you do, I hope you'll look beyond the pool of cocktail waitresses at Magic Jax." The second she said it, she felt terrible. "I'm sorry. That was in poor taste."

"At least it was honest. You can let me know if you want to toss your name in the pool, after all."

She wasn't falling for that again. She snatched up her purse and her briefcase where she'd stashed them out of Layla's reach and hurried to the front door. "I'll be in touch about your will." She didn't wait for a response as she stepped outside and yanked the door closed.

She stood still for a moment and exhaled shakily. It was that time of day when the sun cast its rays beneath the covered front porch. It shone over her shoes. Her legs.

*Marry Ryder.*

She blinked several times, trying to ignore the words whispering through her mind.

*Marry Ryder.*

Try as she might, the thought would not be ignored.

"Get real," she whispered. He'd been no more serious about that than he had about naming her as Layla's guardian in his will. She stepped off the porch and strode decisively toward the car.

*Marry.*

*Ryder.*

Greer heard the front door open. "In the kitchen," she yelled, where she was putting the final touches on the tray of cold veggies and fruit. The heavens had finally smiled on her and her sisters' calendars, and Monday dinner was actually under way. She picked up the tray and carried it into the living room, where Maddie was struggling to lower herself onto the couch.

"Hold on. I'll help you." She set the tray on the coffee table, but Maddie waved her off.

"It's so hot," she grumbled, pushing her dark hair off her forehead.

"I've got lemonade or iced tea ready."

"Can you throw in some vodka?" Maddie made a face when Greer hesitated. "I'm joking." Even though she'd just sat, she pushed to her feet again and rubbed the small of her back. "Maybe."

The door opened and Ali blew in. "Have you heard Vivian's latest?"

Greer met Maddie's gaze before they both warily looked toward their sister. Where their paternal grandmother was concerned, anything was possible. Vivian Archer Templeton was nothing if not eccentric. And the fact that she was enormously wealthy thanks to Pennsylvania steel and several dead husbands meant she usually had no obstacles standing in the way of exercising those eccentricities.

"No," Maddie said cautiously. "What's she done now?"

"She went out on a *date* with Tom Hook!"

Greer stared. Tom Hook was an attorney. And a rancher. And a good twenty years younger than their eighty-ish grandmother. "Are you sure it was a date?"

Maddie let out a wry laugh. "Better a date than a marriage."

True enough. Their grandmother had already buried four husbands. "Vivian's always saying she has no interest in another husband because she's already had the love of her life in dear Arthur," Greer needlessly reminded them. He'd been the fourth of their grandmother's husbands. The only one who hadn't been rich. And Vivian made no secret of the fact that she would be happy to join him whenever the good Lord saw fit. After a life riddled with mistakes for which she'd been trying to make amends during the last few years, she maintained that Arthur was the one thing she ever did completely right.

"I'm guessing she's not looking for the love of her life," Ali said drily as she dropped her keys on the little table by the stairs. "Maybe she just wants some male companionship." She wiggled her eyebrows, looking devilish.

Greer made a face. "Don't be gross, baby sister."

Instead of getting Ali's goat, the reminder that she was the youngest of the triplets just made her laugh. "I'm a married woman now," she retorted, waggling her wedding rings. "Maybe I *like* thinking that I'll still be interested in that sort of thing when I'm Vivian's age."

"I'm even less eager to hear about your sex life than Vivian's."

Ali's eyes were merry. "Admit it, Greer. You're jealous. You need a date way worse than Vivian."

She rolled her eyes, ignoring the accusation that was too close to the truth. "So we can suspect why Vivian's dating Tom, but what's Tom up to?"

"Greer," Maddie chided. "Vivian's an intelligent, stylish woman."

"She's loaded," Ali said, ever blunt.

"Tom's not seeing her for her money," Maddie argued. "It doesn't jibe with his personality at all. He's a good guy. Tell her I'm right, Greer."

"He's a good attorney," Greer allowed. "I always thought he had a lot of common sense. But to date Vivian? I don't know about that." She was as fond of their eccentric grandmother as her sisters were, but Tom and Vivian dating? "What if he's after her money?"

"You think if he were that she's too feeble to know?" Ali smiled wryly. "Fact is, *he's* the one we should probably be worried about. Vivian's pretty wily."

"It's just a date!" Maddie objected. "It's certainly not the craziest thing that's ever happened around here. And it doesn't have to mean marriage is afoot." She was still rubbing her back as she waddled into the kitchen. "Even for Vivian."

"Watch out for the two loose floorboards," Greer called out to her. What would her sisters say if she told them about Ryder's ridiculous wife idea? "I put a chair over them."

Maddie reappeared in the doorway. She was carrying a second tray and her cheek bulged out like a chipmunk's. "I wondered why it was sitting in the middle of the room," she said around her mouthful of food. She bent her knees enough so that she could slide the tray of cheese and crackers onto the coffee table without spilling the contents, then worked her way back down onto the couch. "When did we start having loose floorboards?"

"When did we not have them?" Ali responded. She sat down in the chair across from Maddie and pulled the trays closer, selecting a cluster of fat red grapes. "Are we having anything hot, or just cold stuff?"

"Just cold." Greer grabbed a fresh strawberry from the tray. "I have cold cuts and rolls, too, if you're interested."

"Much as I love sandwiches, it's too dang hot." Ali propped her sandaled feet on the edge of the couch. "Heard your esteemed colleague got Anthony Pyle off in court last week." She dangled her grapes in the air before plucking one from the stem. "Must feel good to know your department has put another little punk back on the streets."

Greer's nerves tightened. Anthony's verdict hadn't come in until evening on the day that she'd babysat Layla. But instead of being in the courthouse as she should have been, she'd been pacing around her house trying to forget everything that Ryder had said. "It does feel good. Particularly since your department neglected to arrest the right person in the first place."

"Come on," Maddie said tiredly. "No arguments about work, okay?" She winced a little and rubbed her hand over her massive belly.

Greer peered at her. "When are you going to start your maternity leave from Family Services?"

"End of the week. I'm not due until next week, of course, but it's just starting to be too hard to get through—"

"—the doorways?"

Maddie elbowed Ali. "Ha ha. Soon enough you'll be in the same fix." She looked back at Greer. "The days," she finished. "Linc's been on my case to stop working for the past month, and my obstetrician for the past two weeks. Arguing with them both is too much work when—" She winced again and blew out a long breath.

"When you're this close to popping," Ali interjected. She closed her hand over Maddie's and squeezed. "You know you don't have to justify anything to us."

"Ali's right." Greer sat on the arm of the couch next to their pregnant sister. She rubbed Maddie's shoulder, left bare by the loose, sleeveless sundress she wore. "I'm just looking forward to meeting our new niece or nephew."

Maddie's lips stretched into a smile.

"Speaking of nieces and nephews…" Ali looked at Greer over Maddie's head. "Grant wants to know if there's anything we can do legally to ensure access to Layla. Are there visitation rights for uncles or something?"

Maddie made a sound. "Surely that's not necessary."

"It's been nearly six months," Ali said quietly. "Ryder hasn't made any attempts—"

"Has Grant?" Greer asked. She read the answer in Ali's

expression. "Nothing will be accomplished if you and Grant take what Ryder will see as an adversarial angle."

Ali's chin came up. "And you know so much about Ryder's mind-set, do you?"

"I know that unless there's a custodial issue, a parent pretty much has the right to determine who has access to their own child!"

Ali looked annoyed.

"Remember that if it weren't for Ryder, Layla would have been adopted by now and off living in Florida where there would be *no* possibility at all for any of us to have some part in her life."

"That's right." Maddie was nodding. "Everyone just needs time. Things will work out for everyone. I know it will. We just have to have a little more patience. Meanwhile, I know there've been some problems with keeping a nanny, but Ray's last report to the court was positively glowing where Ryder's care of her is concerned."

"That's because Ryder *is* good with her. I've seen it for myself."

Both her sisters looked at her.

"I babysat for him last week. I filled in for Mrs. Pyle so she could be at court with her grandson."

Maddie's mouth formed an O. Ali looked annoyed.

"It was a last-minute decision," she added.

Ali held up her hand. "Thursday, Friday, Saturday." She ticked off on her fingers. "Sunday. Monday." She held up her hand. "Five days, Greer. It took you five days to tell us? What other secrets are you keeping?"

Greer pushed off the couch arm. "I'm not keeping secrets."

"What would you call it then?"

"Okay, fine." Ali had a point. "So I've... I've had a few encounters with Ryder lately."

Maddie's eyebrows rose. "A few?"

"How few?" Ali demanded. "And when?"

"Last week!" Greer hated feeling put on the hot seat, but knew she had only herself to blame for not telling them sooner. "I ran into him and Layla when I was on a break during court on Monday. It was just a coincidence." Though her chasing him right down the street hadn't been.

"So you think there's no reason to mention it?"

"No! I just—" She broke off. "I offered to help him find a nanny."

Maddie had closed her eyes and was breathing evenly. Ali, on the other hand, was watching Greer as though she'd committed a federal offense. "Why?"

"Because I wanted to help! You know that he was the one who got me to Maddie's shower."

"And why *did* he do that? He showed up just like that?" Ali snapped her fingers. "Out of the clear blue sky?"

"For God's sake, Ali. You're always suspicious. Yes, out of the clear blue sky! Maddie's been coaching us since you found Ryder not to push ourselves into his life until he gave some hint he'd welcome it. Well, he gave a hint! I didn't deliberately flag him down when I was stuck out by Devil's Crossing. But he helped and so I offered to help him in return. I'm not going to apologize for it. In fact, I would think you'd be glad for it!"

"Glad that you've been seeing my husband's *niece* without telling us a word about it? You *know* how important that is to Grant! Considering how estranged he'd been from Karen?"

Greer propped her fists on her hips. "I'm telling you now! Look, I know your husband is still dealing with his grief where his sister is concerned. But if he's been so concerned about Layla, why *hasn't he* gone banging on Ryder's door demanding to see her?" She waved at Maddie, who was looking pale. She'd always hated it when Greer and Ali went at it when they were kids, and things hadn't changed much since then. "Don't pretend that a man like your husband will follow *anyone's* advice if he doesn't agree with it! He blames Ryder and we all know it!"

"He *doesn't* blame Ryder! He blames himself!" Ali's raised voice echoed around the room. She was breathing hard. "And judging by Ryder's attitude these past months, he blames Grant, too."

The wind oozed out of Greer's sails. "Of course Grant's not responsible for what his sister did. Any more than Ryder is."

"I know that. And you know that. And my husband knows that, too. In here." Ali touched her forehead. "But in here," she said, tapping her chest, "it's still killing him."

Greer pushed aside the fruit and veggie tray and sat on the coffee table in front of her sisters. She grabbed Ali's hands and squeezed them. "It's not just hot monkey sex, right? The two of you are okay all the way around?"

Ali smiled slightly. She squeezed Greer's hands in return. "All the way around," she said huskily. "Grant is everything to me. I just want to be able to make this better for him."

"You will," Maddie murmured. "Just tell him about the baby."

"The baby," Greer echoed. "You think having another niece or nephew will make him less concerned with Layla?"

"Of course not," Maddie replied.

"She's talking about my baby."

Greer startled, looking at Ali. But Ali was looking at Maddie. "What I'd like to know is how *you* knew? I haven't told anyone yet that I'm pregnant!"

"I could just tell." Maddie blew out another audible breath as she scooted herself forward enough to push off the couch. "Now do me a favor, would you?" She pressed her hands against the small of her back and worked her way around the two of them. "Call *my* husband and tell him it's time."

Alarm slid through Greer's veins. "Time?"

"What d'you mean, *time*?" Ali looked even more alarmed.

"I mean baby time," Maddie exclaimed, thoroughly un-Maddie-like. "Now *move!*"

# Chapter 6

The hands of the clock on the hospital waiting room wall seemed like they had stopped moving.

No matter how urgently Maddie had entered the hospital six hours earlier, time seemed to be crawling now.

Greer's dad was pacing the perimeter of the room, his steps measured and deliberate. Her mom, Meredith, was curled up in one of the chairs, her long hair spread over her updrawn knees. Vivian was sitting next to her, dozing lightly over the *Chronicle of Philanthropy* magazine on her lap. Archer was on his way from Denver, where he'd been consulting on a case, and Hayley and Seth had left only an hour ago, because it was long past time to put baby Keely to bed. Then there were Ali and Grant. Greer's brother-in-law wore the broody sort of expression that never really left his darkly handsome face. But there was still tenderness in his face as he looked down at Ali's tousled head on his shoulder. She was asleep.

"How much longer d'you think it will take?" Carter finally stopped in front of Meredith.

"I left my crystal ball at home." She looked amused. "It's a baby. It'll take as long as it takes."

Her dad made a face. "What if something's gone wrong?"

Meredith smiled gently and took his hand. "Nothing's gone wrong," she assured him.

"You don't know that. Things go wrong all the time."

"Carter." She stood, wrapping her arms around his waist and looking up at him. "It was only a few months ago that Hayley had Keely. That all went perfectly. And things are going to go perfectly with Maddie, too."

He pressed his cheek to the top of her head.

Frankly, Greer sympathized more with her dad. Things did go wrong all the time. Her career proved that on a daily basis.

*What's happens to Layla if something happens to me?*

"I'm going down to the cafeteria," she said, pushing away the thought. "Get myself a coffee. Can I bring back anything?"

Grant raised his hand. "Coffee here. I'll go, though."

Greer waved away his offer. "And wake Sleeping Beauty?" In the commotion of getting everyone to the hospital, Greer couldn't help but wonder if Ali had told him yet that they were expecting. She suspected not.

"Your dad'll take some coffee, too, sweetheart."

"I don't suppose there's a chance for a cocktail here?" Vivian commented, opening her eyes.

Carter grimaced. He didn't have a lot of affection for his mother, but since she'd moved to Wyoming in hopes of making amends with him after years of estrangement, he'd at least gotten to the point where it wasn't always open warfare with her whenever they were in the same room. "It's a hospital, Mother, not a bar."

"You never did have a sense of humor." Vivian looked at Greer with a twinkle in her eye as she patted her handbag sitting on the chair beside her. "I have my own flask with me for emergencies just like this. Just enough to make a cup of the dreadful coffee they have here a little more palatable."

Greer smiled, though it was anyone's guess whether or not Vivian was being serious. Not that it mattered to her if her grandmother wanted to spike her coffee while they waited for the baby to arrive. As far as she was concerned, nearly anything that got them through was fine. "I'll be back in a few."

She left the waiting room and started toward the elevator, but then aimed for the stairs instead to prolong her journey. As she passed the window of the nursery, she slowed to look inside. A dozen transparent bassinets were lined up, four of them holding tiny occupants, wrapped so snugly in white blankets that they looked more like burritos than miniature human beings.

A blonde nurse wearing rubber-ducky-patterned scrubs walked into view and picked up one of the baby burritos, affording Greer a brief view of a scrunched-up red face and a shock of dark hair before the nurse carried the baby out of sight again.

Greer lifted her hand and lightly touched the glass pane with her fingertips as she lingered there.

When Daisy had left Layla on Linc's doorstep, they'd estimated she was about two or three months old.

Looking at the babies inside the nursery, Greer still found it unfathomable how Daisy could have done such a thing. If she had lived, if she'd been charged with child endangerment, if her case had managed to land on Greer's desk like so many others, would she have been able to do her client justice?

The blonde nurse returned to the area with the bassinets. She didn't even glance toward the window, which made Greer wonder if the view was one-way. She plucked another baby from its bassinet, but instead of carrying the infant out of sight, she sat down in one of the rocking chairs situated around the nursery and cradled the baby to her shoulder as she began rocking.

Greer finally turned away, but the hollowness that had opened inside her wouldn't go away.

It was still there when she went down the cement-walled staircase, footsteps echoing loudly on the metal stairs. At the bottom, she pushed through the door, and realized that the staircase hadn't let her out in the lobby like the elevator would have, but in the emergency room.

Since there had been plenty of times when she'd had to visit a new client in Weaver's ER, she knew most of the shortcuts. She headed past the empty waiting area and the registration desk, aiming for the hallway on the other side that would take her back into the main part of the hospital.

"Hey, Greer. Heard that Maddie came in earlier. How's she doing?" the nurse behind the desk asked.

Greer slowed. "Six hours and still at it." She smiled at Courtney Hyde, who'd been an ER nurse since well before Greer had learned that they were cousins a few years ago. "Thought you didn't work nights anymore?"

Courtney tucked her long gold hair behind her ear. "Don't usually. But we're shorthanded at the moment, so." She shrugged. "We're all doing our part." Then she smiled a little impishly. "And it gives Sadie an opportunity to have her daddy all to herself at bedtime. Yesterday when I got home, she'd convinced Mason to build her an 'ice palace'—" she air-quoted the term "—to sleep in, using every pillow and furniture cushion we have in the house. Sadie slept the divine sleep that only a three-year-old can sleep."

"And Mason?"

Courtney grinned. "My big tough husband had me schedule him for a massage just so he could work out the kinks from a night spent on the floor crammed inside an igloo of pillows."

Considering the fact that Mason Hyde was about six and a half feet tall, Greer could well believe it.

"I swear I'll never stop melting inside whenever I see the way he is with her, though," Courtney added, sighing a little. "Just wait. Someday you'll see what I mean."

Greer kept her smile in place, even though the image inside her head wasn't one of Mason Hyde and his little girl. It was of Ryder, scooping Cow Pie Surprise into Layla's greedy mouth.

"You going to be at the picnic?"

"Sorry?"

"Gloria and Squire are hosting a big ol' picnic next week out at the Double C. To celebrate Labor Day. Whole family will be there." Courtney's eyes twinkled. "That includes all of you Templetons now, too."

Greer chuckled wryly. "I kind of need to show my face at the county employee picnic that weekend. My boss's wife organizes it. Besides which, just because the Clay family lines have expanded our way doesn't necessarily mean we're welcome. If *my* grandmother finds out we're consorting with *your* grandfather, who knows how bad the fireworks will be."

"Old wounds," Courtney said dismissively. "Vivian might have shunned Squire's first wife sixty years ago, but she's apologized. It's high time he let it go. At least think about the picnic." She reached out an arm and picked up the phone when it started ringing. "Emergency," she answered. "Think about it," she mouthed silently to Greer.

Nodding, Greer left the other woman to her duties and continued on her way, only to stop short again when the double doors leading to the exam rooms swung open and Ryder appeared. He was holding Layla, wrapped in a blanket.

Alarm exploded inside her.

When he spotted her, his dark brows pulled together

over his bloodshot blue eyes. He stopped several feet away. "What're you doing here?"

"What are *you* doing here?" Without thought, she closed the distance between them and put her hand on Layla's back through the blanket. The toddler's head was resting on his shoulder. Her eyes were closed, her cheeks flushed. "What's wrong?"

"Nothing."

The comment came from Caleb Buchanan, and Greer realized the pediatrician had followed Ryder through the double doors. "However, if she hasn't improved in the next twenty-four hours, give me or her regular pediatrician a call."

"Thanks." Ryder's jaw was dark with stubble and he looked like he hadn't slept in a couple days.

"And don't worry too much," Caleb added. "Kids run fevers. As long as it doesn't get too high, her body's just doing what it's supposed to do."

When Ryder nodded, Caleb transferred his focus to Greer. "Heard Maddie was here. How's everyone doing?" Thanks to the prolificacy of Squire Clay's side of the family, Caleb was also a cousin. His pale blue scrubs did nothing to disguise his Superman-like physique. But Greer knew from experience that the doctor was singularly unconcerned with his looks.

"Fine. Anxious for the baby to get here. We've been waiting hours."

"Want me to check in on them?"

"That'd be great, if you've got the time. Everyone's up in the waiting room. I was just gonna grab some coffees from the cafeteria."

He smiled and patted her shoulder. "I'll see what I can find out." Then he retreated through the double doors.

Greer immediately focused on Ryder again. "How long has she been sick?"

"She didn't eat much of her dinner, but she seemed okay until she woke up crying a couple hours ago." He shifted the baby to his other shoulder. Layla didn't stir. "She threw up all over her crib, then threw up all over me and was hot as a pistol."

Greer couldn't help herself. She rubbed her hand soothingly over the thin blanket and the warm little body beneath. "Poor baby."

"Speaking of. Your sister's having hers?"

She nodded. "Whole family's been here at some point tonight."

"Hope everything goes okay." He took a step toward the sliding glass entrance doors.

"Ryder—"

He hesitated, waiting.

She wasn't sure why her mouth felt dry all of a sudden, but it did. "I... I haven't heard anything on the job postings yet. Have you?"

He shook his head. "Mrs. Pyle said she'd give me the rest of this week, after all." He shifted from one cowboy boot to the other. "Think she's feeling in a good mood after her grandson's acquittal last week."

"But not good enough to stay on indefinitely."

"She's a housekeeper. Not—"

"—a nanny," Greer finished along with him. "Well, I should get back up to the waiting room. They're probably wondering what's keeping me." She chewed the inside of her cheek. "I don't suppose you want to come..."

He was shaking his head even before her words trailed off. "Need to get her back in her own bed." He grimaced a little. "After I've gotten it all restored to rights, at least."

"Of course." She pushed her hands down into the back pockets of her lightweight cotton pants. It was silly of her to even have the notion. "Well." She edged toward the elevator. "Fingers crossed someone nibbles at one of the job posts."

The corner of his mouth lifted slightly and she felt certain he was thinking more about his wife idea than the nanny. "Yeah."

She took two more steps toward the elevator and jabbed her finger against the call button.

"Don't forget the cafeteria."

"What?" Her face warmed. "Oh. Right." The elevator doors slid open but she ignored them.

He smiled faintly. "G'night, Counselor."

She managed a faint smile, too, though it felt unsteady. "Good night, Ryder."

He carried Layla through the sliding door and disappeared into the darkness.

Greer swallowed and moistened her lips, then nearly jumped out of her skin when Courtney walked up and stopped next to her. She was carrying a stack of medical charts. "If I weren't already head over heels for my husband," she whispered conspiratorially, "I'd probably be sighing a little myself over that one."

"I'm not *sighing* over him."

Courtney grinned. "Sure you're not." With a quick wink, she backed her way through the double doors.

Left alone in the tiled room, Greer pressed her palms against her warm cheeks. She shook her head, trying to shake it off.

But it was no use.

And then her cell phone buzzed with a text from Ali. Where are u?! Baby here!

*Forget the coffee.*

She pushed the phone back into her pocket and darted for the elevator.

\* \* \*

"If we're keeping you awake, Ms. Templeton, maybe you should consider another line of work."

Greer stared guiltily up at Judge Manetti as she tried to stop her yawn. It was a futile effort, though.

Just because she'd been at the hospital until three this morning celebrating the birth of her new nephew didn't mean she'd been allowed a respite from her duties at work.

"I'm sorry, Your Honor," she said once she could speak clearly. In the year since Steve Manetti had gone from being a fellow attorney to being a municipal court judge appointed by the mayor, she had almost gotten used to addressing him as such. But it had been hard, considering they'd been in elementary school together.

She glanced down at her copy of the day's docket before slipping the correct case file to the top of her pile. "My client, Mr. Jameson, wishes to enter a plea of not guilty."

Manetti looked resigned. "Of course he does." He looked over his steepled fingers at the skinny man standing hunched beside her. "Is that correct, Mr. Jameson?"

Johnny Jameson nodded jerkily. Every motion since he'd entered the courtroom betrayed the fact that he was high on something. Undoubtedly meth, which was what he was charged with possessing. Again. "Yessir."

Manetti looked at Greer, then down at his court calendar. "First available looks like the second Thursday of December."

She made a note. "Thank you, Your Honor."

Judge Manetti looked at the clock on the wall, then at the bailiff. "We'll break for lunch now."

"All rise," the bailiff intoned, and the small municipal courtroom filled with the rustling sounds of people standing. Manetti disappeared through his door and the courtroom started emptying.

Greer closed her case file and fixed her gaze on her client. "Johnny, the judge just gave you four months. I advise you to clean up your act before trial. Understand me?"

Johnny shrugged and twitched and avoided meeting her eyes. She shifted focus to Johnny's wife behind him. "Katie? Do you want another copy of the list of programs I gave you before?"

"No, ma'am." Katie Jameson was petite and polite and as clean as her husband was not. "Johnny's gonna be just fine by then. I promise you."

Greer dearly wished she could believe it. "All right, then." She pushed her files into her briefcase and shouldered the strap. "You know how to reach me if you need me. Mr. Chatham will be in touch with you to go through your testimony before December."

Johnny grunted a reply and shuffled his way out of the courtroom.

"You're a lot nicer than Mr. Chatham," Katie said, watching her husband go. "I wish you could handle Johnny's trial."

Greer smiled. "Don't worry. You and Johnny will be in good hands."

"Well, thank you for everything you've done so far."

It was a rare day when Greer received thanks for her service. More often than not, she busted her butt negotiating a deal for her client only to have him or her walk away without a single word of appreciation. She shook Katie's hand. "You're welcome, Katie. Take care of yourself, okay? I meant it when I said you can call if you need me."

The young woman nodded, ducking her chin a little, then hurried after her husband.

Greer stifled another yawn as she walked out of the courtroom. She had two hours before her next appearance. If she'd had more than a few dollars left in her bank account after spending most of her paycheck on bills, she would have gone down to Josephine's for a sandwich. Instead, she walked back to her office, where she closed the door and kicked off her pumps. Then she sat down at her desk, and with a good old peanut-butter-and-jelly sandwich in one hand and a pencil in the other, she started in on the messages she hadn't been able to respond to before morning court.

She'd been at it for barely an hour when her office door opened and her boss tossed another stack of papers on her desk. "We're not getting an intern this round. There were only two available and the other offices needed them more." He pointed at the papers he'd left. "Plead all those out."

She swallowed the bite of sandwich that had momentarily stuck to the roof of her mouth and thumbed the latest pile. "What if they don't all want to plead?" She knew the futility of the question, but asked out of habit.

"Talk them into it," he said, and then left as unceremoniously as he'd entered. He always said that. Even though he knew some cases and some defendants never would plead.

Or should.

She glanced at the clock above the door. She started to lift her sandwich to her mouth, but her phone rang and she answered it. "Public defender's office."

There was a faint hesitation before a female spoke. "I'm calling about the job posting? The one for a nanny?"

Greer sat up straighter.

"This is the right number, isn't it?" The woman had a faint accent that Greer couldn't place. "You said public defender's office?"

"Yes, yes, it's the right number." She set her sandwich down on the plastic wrap. "I'm Greer Templeton. I represent—" She cringed, realizing how that might sound. "I'm *assisting* a friend with his search for a nanny."

"He's not in trouble with the law?"

"No, not at all."

"That's a relief," the woman said with a little laugh. "The last thing I desire is another job that leaves me wanting. I prefer something that will be steady. And lasting. Your post said you're—he, your friend—is looking for a live-in? Is that written in stone?"

"It's probably negotiable. Why don't you give me your contact information and you can discuss it with him directly."

"Very good. My name is Eliane Dupre."

"Would you mind spelling—"

The caller laughed lightly. "Like Elaine but reverse the *i* and *a*. It's French."

Greer immediately imagined a beautiful, chic Parisian singing French lullabies to Layla while Ryder looked on. She cleared her throat, and her head of the image. "Is that where you're from? France?"

"Switzerland, actually. I moved to the States a few years ago with my husband. Alas, that didn't work out, but here I am. I'm a citizen," she said quickly, "in case that is a concern."

Her right to work should have been more of a concern to Greer, but her imagination was still going bananas. Swiss? Had Maria in *The Sound of Music* been Swiss? She sure got her man. No, that was Austria.

Still, the loving governess had captured the heart of the children and their father.

She shook her head at her own nonsense, making notes as Eliane provided her phone number and an address in Weaver in her musical, accented voice.

"You understand that the location where you'd be working is fairly remote?"

"Yes. Quite to my liking."

"How long have you lived in Weaver?"

"I've only been here a few weeks. I'm staying with an acquaintance while I look for employment. Shall I expect a call from your friend, then?"

There was no reason to hesitate, but Greer still felt like she had to push her way through the conversation. "Yes, I'll get your information to him as soon as I can."

"Thank you so much. Have a lovely day."

"You, too," Greer said faintly. But she said it to the dial tone, because Eliane had already ended the call.

She dropped the receiver back on the cradle and stared blindly at her notes. Then she snatched up the phone again and punched out Ryder's phone number.

Neither Mrs. Pyle, Ryder nor the machine picked up.

Was Layla still sick? Maybe Ryder had caught whatever bug she'd had. Or maybe her fever had gotten worse.

Greer rubbed at the pain between her eyebrows. "Stop imagining things," she muttered, "and be logical here."

She pulled up the information she had on record for Anthony Pyle. But when she called that number, there was no answer.

She hung up and looked at the time. She couldn't very well drive Eliane's information out to the Diamond-L and check on Ryder and Layla herself. Not when she was supposed to be back in court in less than an hour.

She looked at the docket she'd printed that morning. Hearing conferences and motions.

She reached for the phone again and dialed. This time, she received an answer. "Keith? It's Greer. Can you pinch-hit for me this afternoon? I know it's short notice, but I have a personal matter that's come up."

"Personal matter!" He sounded surprised. "You're joking, right?"

She made a face at the wall. "Does it sound like I'm joking?"

He chuckled. "I'm just yanking your chain. Nice to know that you're human like the rest of us. So, yeah. Sure. Just for today?"

"Just for today. I'll leave my files at the front desk with Bunny. Court's back in session at two."

"I'll be there," he promised. "Everything all right? I heard Maddie had the baby last night—"

"They're all fine," she assured him. It never failed to surprise her how quickly news spread in this town. "It's nothing to do with that. I really appreciate the favor. I'll owe you one."

"And I plan on collecting," he said with a laugh before hanging up.

Now that she'd made the decision, she tossed the rest of her sandwich in the trash. The bread was already getting stale, anyway. She bundled up everything that Keith might need for the afternoon and left it with Bunny Towers. Then she went back to retrieve her shoes and purse and left the office.

Not even Michael noticed, which had her wondering why she'd never tried taking off an afternoon before. No matter what she did, her boss seemed to remain unimpressed.

It took nearly an hour to get to Ryder's place. There were no vehicles parked on the gravel outside the house. Even though she'd seen it more than once now, the sight of the converted barn was still arresting. The only barn conversions she'd ever seen before were in magazines and on home decorating shows.

No doubt, Eliane-of-the-beautiful-accent would only add another layer of interest to the surroundings.

"Get your brain out of high school," she muttered, and snatched up her purse before marching to the front door. There was no answer when she knocked, but the door was unlocked when she tried it. She cautiously pushed it open. "Hello? Mrs. Pyle?" She stepped inside. "Ryder?"

The last time she'd been there, the house had been as tidy as a pin.

Now it looked like a tornado had hit.

Layla's toys were everywhere. Laundry was piled on the armless chair, overflowing onto the floor. The couch was nearly hidden beneath a plastic bin that she felt certain contained the baby gear that Maddie and Linc had given Ryder when they'd turned Layla over to him.

She dropped her purse on top of it and walked into the kitchen. Cereal crunched under her shoes. The sink was filled halfway to the top with dirty dishes.

She crunched her way to the back door and looked out at the picnic table with its painted daisies. It hadn't even been a week since she'd been there, but the grass was already overgrown.

Weren't Swiss people notoriously tidy? Maybe Eliane would take one look and run for the hills.

The thought should have been worrying.

The fact that it was not was an entirely different cause for concern.

She left the door open slightly to allow for some fresh air— hot as it was—and went upstairs.

Layla's nursery was empty. The mattress had been stripped of bedding. It was probably sitting in the pile of laundry downstairs.

The air was stuffy here, too. One window held a boxy air conditioner. It wasn't running, and Greer left it off. She went to the second window and opened it; the hot breeze fluttered at the simple white curtains.

She left Layla's room, intending to go back downstairs, but she hesitated, looking down the hall toward the other open door. She could see the foot of a bed where a navy blue quilt was piled half on and half off the mattress. A pair of cowboy boots were lying haphazardly on the wood floor.

Unquestionably, the room was Ryder's.

When she'd babysat Layla, the sliding door to the room had been closed.

She knew the house was empty.

Still, Greer's heart beat a little faster as she stepped closer to the room. She peered around the edge of the doorway. The dresser was wide, with six drawers. One framed picture sat on top, but otherwise it was bare.

His bed was big with an iron-railed headboard. Three white pillows were bunched messily at the head of the mattress. Instead of a nightstand next to the bed, there was a saddletree complete with a fancy-looking tooled leather saddle. An industrial sort of lamp was attached directly to the wall. There was an enormous unadorned window next to the bed, and before she knew it, she'd walked across the room to look out.

Directly below was the picnic table.

She wondered how often he looked out and thought about his late wife.

She wondered if he'd look out and still think about her when he had a delectable Swiss confection under his roof tending to his child.

Disgusted with herself, she turned away from the window. She bent down slightly to look at the framed photograph on his dresser. It was an old-fashioned black-and-white wedding photo. Maybe his parents? Or the aunt named Adelaide? Then she heard a faint sound and her nervousness ratcheted up.

She darted out of the bedroom and was heading to the staircase when Ryder—looking entirely incongruous in cowboy hat and boots with a pink-patterned baby carrier strapped across his chest—appeared.

Even before he saw her, his eyes were narrowed. "What're you doing here?"

# Chapter 7

*What're you doing here?*

Ryder's question seemed to echo around her.

He looked hot and sweaty, as did Layla in the carrier, and Greer's mouth went dry.

Not only from nearly being caught out snooping in his bedroom, but from the strange swooping feeling in her stomach caused by the sight of him.

"Greer?"

She felt like her brains were scrambled and gestured vaguely toward Layla's bedroom. "I was…ah—"

"Never mind." In a move that she knew from personal experience was more difficult than he made it look, he unfastened Layla from the carrier and handed her to Greer. "Take her for a few minutes while I clean up."

Layla's green eyes were bright and merry as she looked at Greer. She was wearing a yellow T-shirt that felt damp and a pair of yellow shorts with a ruffle across her butt. Her reddish-blond curls were spiked with perspiration. "Is she still running a fever?"

"Nah. Even on a cold day the carrier gets hot." He pulled

off his hat as he brushed past Greer, smelling like sunshine
and fresh hay. He continued along the hallway, pulling off
not only the carrier, but his T-shirt, as well. "She popped out
two more teeth this morning, though. I don't care what that
doc said last night about teething not causing a fever. Soon
as those teeth showed up, she was right as rain, just like my
aunt Adelaide predicted." He stepped inside his bedroom and
looked at Greer. "Be down in a few." Then he pulled on the
rustic metal handle and slid the door closed.

She closed her eyes. But the image of his bare chest remained.

Heaven help her.

She opened them again to find Layla smiling brightly at
her, displaying the new additions to her bottom row of teeth.
She jabbered and patted Greer's face.

Greer caught the baby's hand and kissed it. "Hello to you,
too, sweetheart."

She heard a couple thuds from behind Ryder's bedroom
door. It was much too easy imagining him sitting on the foot
of that messy, wide bed, pulling off his boots and tossing
them aside.

After the boots would come the jeans—

"Let's go downstairs," she whispered quickly to Layla, who
laughed as if Greer had said something wonderfully funny.

"At least *you* think it's funny." Greer hurried to the staircase. "You have a lot in common with your aunt Ali, that's
for sure."

Once downstairs, she settled Layla into her high chair. It
was much cleaner than the kitchen counters were, so she had
to give Ryder points for that.

She opened the back door wider so there was more air
flowing, then found a clean cloth in a drawer. She wet it down
with cool water and worked it over Layla's face and head.

Layla took it as a game, of course, and slyly evaded most of Greer's swipes before gaining control of the cloth, which she proceeded to shove into her mouth.

Chewing on a wet washcloth wasn't the worst thing Greer could think of, so she let the baby have it and turned her attention to the dishes in the sink. They weren't quite as dirty as she'd first thought. At least they'd been rinsed.

Loading the dishwasher didn't take much time. She found the soap and started it. But the sound of the dishwasher wasn't enough to block the sound of water running overhead, and Greer's imagination ran amok again.

To combat it, she found another cloth and furiously began wiping down the counters. When she was done with that, she found the broom and swept up the scattered cereal crumbs. And when she was done with *that*, she grabbed an armful of clothes from the pile on the chair and blindly shoved it into the washing machine located in a sunny room right off the kitchen.

The cheeriness of the room was almost enough to make up for the laundry drudgery, and she wondered if he'd made it that way for Daisy.

With the washing machine now running, too, she went back into the kitchen, lifted Layla out of the high chair and took her outside.

"You like this soft grass as much as I do?" Greer unfastened the narrow straps around her ankles and kicked off her high-heeled shoes, curling her toes in the tall grass. She bent over Layla, holding her hands as the baby pushed up and down on her bent knees, chortling.

"Wait until next year. You're going to be running all over the grass on your own." They slowly aimed toward the picnic table. But they made it only partway before Layla plopped down on her diaper-padded, ruffle-covered butt. She grabbed at the grass undulating around her and yanked, then looked surprised when the soft blades tore free.

Greer tugged her skirt above her knees so she could sit in the grass with her. She mimicked Layla's grass grab and then held open her hands so the pieces of green blew away on the breeze.

Layla opened her palms and her grass blew away, too. Instead of laughing, though, her brows pulled together and her face scrunched.

Greer laughed. "Silly girl." She tore off another handful of grass and let it go again. "See it blow away?" She leaned over and nuzzled her nose against Layla's palms. "Smells so good." Then she rubbed her nose against Layla's and plucked a single blade of grass and tickled her cheek with the end of it. "Smells kind of like your daddy, doesn't it?"

"Mama mamamama!" Layla laughed and grabbed the grass, but missed and rolled onto her side. She immediately popped up and crawled over to Greer, clambering onto her lap.

Knowing Layla hadn't really said *mama* didn't stop Greer's heart from lurching. She wrapped her arm around Layla's warm body and kissed the top of her head.

Then they both yanked hunks of grass free and tossed them into the air.

He had a perfect view of them from his bedroom window.

Ryder dragged the towel over his head and down his chest. The water in the shower hadn't been much above tepid to begin with, but it had turned altogether cold after only a few minutes.

Probably a good thing.

Below, Layla had crawled onto Greer's lap. As he watched, Greer rolled onto her back, heedless of her silk blouse and her hair that today had been pulled back into a smooth knot behind her head. She pushed Layla up into the air above her, and even through his closed window, he could hear her peals of laughter.

He'd been cursing Mrs. Pyle's absence after she'd promised him another week of work. With no alternative, it had meant hauling a baby around with him on a tractor for half the day. Which meant he still wasn't finished haying. He was falling behind on everything.

But right now, looking down at Greer and the baby, he almost didn't care.

Almost.

As if she sensed him watching, Greer suddenly looked up at his window. It was too far for him to see her exact expression, but he had no trouble imagining her dark brown eyes.

They were mesmerizing, those eyes of hers. They kept entering his thoughts at all hours of the day.

And the night.

The air-conditioner kicked on, blowing cold air over him and drowning out the sound of Layla's high-pitched squeals.

He took a step back and blew out a long breath, not even aware that he'd been holding it.

"You're losing it, man," he muttered to himself, roughly dragging the towel over his head once more before tossing it aside. It knocked over his grandparents' picture and he automatically set it to rights while he pulled out the last clean shirt he possessed, plus a pair of jeans that weren't so clean. He quickly got dressed and went downstairs.

As soon as he walked through the kitchen, he understood why his shower water had been cold. Both the washing machine and the dishwasher were going.

It wasn't Mrs. Pyle's doing, that was for certain.

The mug tree sitting on one corner of the butcher-block island had three clean mugs still hanging from the metal branches. He took two, filled them with water and pushed open the wooden screen door.

When it slammed shut behind him, Greer froze and looked his way. Her face was as flushed as Layla's and dark strands of hair had worked loose to cling to her neck.

The ivory blouse she wore had come partially free from the waist of her light gray skirt. As if she were following the progression of his gaze, she suddenly pushed the hem of her skirt down her thighs and swept her legs to one side as she set Layla down on the grass. "It's still crazy hot," she commented, not exactly looking his way. "What happened to Mrs. Pyle?"

"Her grandson." He was as barefoot as the two females, and the earth beneath his feet felt cooler than anything else as he walked toward them. It was no wonder Greer had chosen to sit in the grass rather than at the picnic table. He extended one of the mugs to her. "It's just water."

She smiled a little as she took it from him. "Thank you." Before she could get the cup to her mouth, though, Layla launched herself at it, and Greer wasn't quite quick enough to avoid her. Half the water sloshed out of the cup and onto her blouse, rendering several inches of silky fabric nearly transparent.

Ryder was polite enough not to comment, but too male to look away. He could see the scrolling lacework of blue thread beneath the wet patch and had no trouble at all imagining the soft flesh beneath that.

Greer plucked at the fabric, though as far as he could tell, she only succeeded in pulling the rest of the blouse loose from the skirt. She took a sip of what was left of the water, then held it to Layla's mouth. "What's going on with Anthony? He was just acquitted last week."

"And he turned around and got picked up on drunk driving last night."

She jerked, giving him a sharp look that was echoed some-what by the sharp look that Layla gave *her*. "What? Where? I haven't heard about it."

"I don't know where." He sat on the grass, leaning his back against the picnic table. "I just know she dropped everything and immediately took off to rescue him." Mrs. Pyle had given him the courtesy of a rushed phone call, but that was it.

Greer frowned, then focused once more on Layla, who'd started fussing for the mug of water. "I'm sorry, sweetheart. It's empty now. See?" She turned the mug upside down and glanced back at Ryder. "You make that sound like a bad thing."

"I don't have a lot of sympathy for people who drink and drive."

"Because of what happened to Layla's mother."

"Because of what happened to my mother." The second the words were out, he regretted them. "Here." He leaned for-ward and poured half his water into her mug, then sat back again. "You obviously didn't come out here because Mrs. Pyle asked you to sub for her." He repeated what he'd asked when he walked into his house and found her there. "So what *are* you doing here?"

"Someone called me about the nanny position."

"You must be pretty excited about the prospect to drive out here to tell me. I do have a phone, you know."

"Which nobody answered when I called. And then after last night... Layla's fever and all." She lifted one shoulder, watching Layla, who'd lost interest in the mug and had started crawling toward the far side of the picnic table. "I was con-cerned. So I drove out."

"And found the place looking like a bomb had hit."

"You want me to say it wasn't that bad?"

"I have a feeling you're not much for lies, even the polite ones."

She got on her hands and knees and crawled after Layla. "I did watch her for the better part of a day," she reminded him. "I can appreciate that she's kind of a force of nature." She looked over her shoulder at him for a moment. "Toss in last night's trip to the hospital, and a messy house doesn't seem so strange."

The afternoon was admittedly hot. But that wasn't the cause for the furnace suddenly cranking up inside him. He looked away from the shapely butt closely outlined by pale gray fabric. "What did she sound like?"

"Who? Oh, right." Greer pushed herself up to sit on the bench. "Her name's Eliane. Eliane Dupre."

"French."

She gave him a surprised look.

"I knew an Eliane once."

Surprise slid into something else. Something on the verge of pinched and suspicious. "Oh?"

"She was a model for Adelaide during her nudes phase."

"Excuse me?"

"My aunt's an artist." And Eliane had been an incredible tutor for a horny seventeen-year-old. He didn't share that part, though, much as he was coming to enjoy the game of keeping the lady lawyer a little off-balance. It was his one way of feeling like things were sort of even between them. "What else did you learn besides her name?"

Greer was still giving him a measuring look.

Or maybe she was just trying to keep her eye from twitching.

"She's currently staying in Weaver. She did ask if the live-in part was negotiable. So when you talk with her, be prepared."

"What else?"

"She's from Switzerland. Divorced, it sounds like. And looking for a steady job. I have her phone number in my purse."

He pushed to his feet. "Let's do it, then."

Greer's expression didn't change as she lifted Layla and stood. But he still had the sense that he'd surprised her. And not necessarily in a good way.

They went inside and she handed him a slip of paper from her purse. Then she carried Layla back outside.

To give him privacy? Or because she wasn't interested in the conversation in the first place?

Even wondering was stupid. Pointless.

Maybe he needed more sleep.

He snatched the phone off the hook and looked at the paper. Greer's handwriting was slightly slanted and neat. *Spare*, as Adelaide would say. There were no curlicues. No extra tails or circles. While he dialed the number, his mind's eye imagined her hand quickly recording the information on the paper.

Daisy's handwriting had been all over the place. All loopy letters and heart-dotted *i*'s.

He pushed away the thought. He definitely needed more sleep.

The phone rang four times before it went to voice mail. He wasn't sure if he was disappointed or not. He left his name and number and hung up, then went back outside. It was hotter outside than in, but at least the air was moving.

This time Greer was sitting at the table bouncing Layla on her lap.

"No answer. I left a message."

"I'm sure she'll call you back. She sounded pretty interested to me."

The wet patch on her blouse had dried. No more intriguing glimpses of white lace with blue threads. But there was a smudge of green on her thigh. "You have grass stains."

Her eyebrows rose, then she quickly looked down at herself. She swiped her hand at the mark. "Dry cleaners will get it out. Hopefully." Her shoulders rose and fell as she took a deep breath. "I should be going."

"Back to the office, I suppose."

She glanced at the narrow watch on her wrist. "Court should be finished for the day, but yes, I probably should go back. Start reviewing everything for tomorrow's docket."

"Probably." He waited a beat, but she didn't move an inch. "Or—"

Her gaze slid toward him.

"Or I could pull out a couple steaks." He jerked his thumb toward the covered grill. "Throw 'em on the grill after I give Short-Stuff a badly needed bath."

Greer's lips parted slightly. The top one was a little fuller than the bottom, he realized.

"Or you could give her a bath," he said casually. "If you wanted."

Her lips twitched. "I do like steak. Medium rare."

"I wouldn't do well-done even if you asked."

She ran her fingers over Layla's curls. "You feed her *after* her bath?"

"Counselor, sometimes I'm feeding her ten times a day. I learned real quick there's no point in sweating about the order of things when it comes to her."

"My mother would love you," she murmured. She stood with Layla. "And I'm clearly not above a bribe, whether there's dinner payment or not." She marched past him into the house.

He scrubbed his hand down his face and followed her inside. She was fastening Layla into the high chair.

"Have any of your cow pie stuff?"

"Not today." He took the last banana from the holder and started peeling it. "Personally, I hate bananas, but she loves 'em." He tossed the browning peel in the trash, then cut the fruit into small chunks and dropped them into a shallow plastic bowl that he set in front of Layla.

She was already starting to look heavy-lidded, but she dived into the bowl with both hands. "Greedy girl." He plucked a mushy piece of banana from her cheek and fed it to her.

Greer was watching him when he turned away. "What?"

She just shook her head slightly and cleared her throat. "What else besides overripe banana? Does she still have a bottle?"

"Formula, but she wants it in her cup." He looked in the sink.

"I loaded everything in the dishwasher."

He pulled it open and steam spewed out. He plucked out the cup and lid, then closed the door and started it up again. He rinsed both pieces under cold water, then filled it with pre-mixed formula. "There's a container in the fridge with some cooked vegetables. She didn't eat 'em last night."

Greer went to the refrigerator and opened it.

He glanced over. "Top shelf. Red lid."

She pulled out the glass container and peeled off the lid. "Yum. Carrots and peas."

"Don't knock it." He gave Layla her sippy cup, then took the container from Greer, dumped the vegetables in a pan and set it on the stove.

"Wouldn't the microwave be faster?"

"Yep." He made a face as he lit the flame under the pan. "Adelaide'll lecture me for a week about the dangers."

"There are dangers?"

"Probably not as many as my aunt can name." He jabbed

a spoon at the vegetables. "It's one of those lose-the-battle-win-the-war things, I think."

"You're in a war with the microwave?"

He chuckled. "More like a war with my aunt over the microwave. You might say she's a little—" He broke off when the phone rang. "Eccentric," he finished. "Watch these, would you?"

"An eccentric aunt who paints nudes and names her dog Brutus. She sounds like quite a woman. You mention her a lot." Greer's fingers brushed his as she took over the spoon. "Afraid I'm not much of a cook."

"She photographs nudes," he corrected. "Among other things. And I'm afraid I'm not much of a cook, either. But I like to eat, so—" He picked up the ringing phone. "Diamond-L."

"Is this Mr. Wilson?" The voice was female. Accented. "I'm Eliane Dupre."

"Eliane," he repeated, watching Greer turn toward the stove so that her slender back was to him.

Her shoulders were noticeably tight beneath the thin, silky blouse.

*Interesting.*

The conversation was brief.

Greer's back was still to him when he hung up. She was stirring the vegetables so diligently, he figured they'd end up mushier than the banana. He moved next to her and turned off the heat beneath the pan.

"I'm meeting her tomorrow over lunch at Josephine's," he said.

She gave him an overbright smile. "Great." She brushed her hands down the sides of her skirt. "You know, I just remembered I *do* have to go back to the office before tomorrow morning. So I'm going to have to pass on the bribery, after all." As she spoke, she was backing out of the kitchen, stopping only long enough to lean over and kiss Layla's head as she passed.

"You sure?" He tested the vegetables. Definitely mushy. But at least not too hot. He dumped some into Layla's now-empty banana bowl.

Greer's head bobbed. "I'm sure. Let me know how it, uh, how it goes tomorrow." She grabbed her purse that was sitting on the couch and clutched it to her waist with both hands.

"Will do."

"Great." Her head bobbed a few more times. "Well, good... good luck." She quickly turned on her bare feet and hurried to the front door.

"By the way, what did she have?"

She'd made it to the vestibule and she gave him a startled look. "Excuse me?"

"Your sister."

She looked even more deer-in-the-headlights. "Maddie! She had a boy. Seven pounds, thirteen ounces. Twenty-one inches long. They named him Liam Gustav after Linc's grandfather. Mommy and son are doing well." She smiled quickly and yanked open the front door. "Daddy is, reportedly, a basket case." She lifted her hand in a quick wave and darted out the door, closing it behind her.

He waited.

But she didn't come back.

Even though her feet were bare, since her high-heeled pumps were still out back, lying in the grass.

He looked at Layla.

She was plucking a pea out of the carrots with one hand and clutching her pink cup with the other.

"Interesting, indeed," he told her.

She smacked her cup against the high chair tray and gave him a beatific smile. "Bye bye bye bye!"

"You got that right, Short-Stuff. She sure did go bye-bye." He chucked her lightly under the chin. "But I'm betting she'll be back."

# Chapter 8

"What the hell did you do to your feet?"

Greer looked up to see Ali standing in the doorway to her office and yanked her feet down from where they were propped on the corner of her desk. "Nothing." She tugged her black skirt down around her knees.

"You have bandage strips all over the soles of your feet."

"I know you're in uniform, but you can stop the interrogation. Bandage strips aren't a criminal offense." Greer slid her feet into the shoes under her desk. She was still embarrassed over the way she'd raced out of Ryder's place the evening before. She didn't particularly want to explain why to her sister. "What brings you to the dark side?"

"Glad you're finally ready to admit the truth about your work." Ali grinned and threw herself down on the chair inside the doorway. She leaned back and propped her heavy department-issue boots on the corner of the desk.

"Hey!" Greer shoved at them. "Just because I did, doesn't mean you can. Have a little respect, please."

"For the dark side? Never." She put her feet on the floor, still smiling.

"You're in an awfully good mood," Greer complained. "If you've come to brag about the latest night or morning or afternoon of hot sex you've had with your new husband, spare me."

Ali looked at her fingernails. "Well, it is pretty brag-worthy," she drawled.

"Save me."

"You don't need saving. You need sexing."

"Ali, for God's sake."

Her sister laughed silently. "Your chain is so easy to yank these days."

"And if you weren't pregnant, I'd yank yours but good. Speaking of." She pinned her sister with her fiercest lawyer look. "Have you told Grant?"

"Yes."

"And?"

"Between looking like he wanted to pass out and suddenly treating me like I'm made of Dresden Porcelain, I think he's pretty much okay with it." Her expression sobered. "He still needs to create some kind of relationship with Layla, though. He's not going to let it go, Greer. He can't."

"Nor should he even think he has to." She dropped her head onto her hands, pressing her fingertips into her scalp. She exhaled and lifted her head. "Ryder's coming along, Ali." She hoped. "Is that what you came here to find out?"

"Actually, I came here to invite you to lunch. Josephine's. On me."

"Oh, that's right. You're not living only on a public servant's salary anymore. You have a bestselling thriller writer as a husband now."

"Poke as much as you want. Do you care for a free lunch or don't you?"

"I do." She glanced at her watch. "It'll have to be quick,

though. I have less than an hour before I need to be over at the courthouse."

"Yeah, yeah." Ali pushed to her feet. "I know the drill. Josephine's pretty much makes a living off the police department and the courthouse. It's always quick." She waited while Greer collected her purse and they left her office. "Seriously." Ali gave her a sidelong look. "What is going on with your feet? You're limping. You didn't actually fall through one of the floorboards in the kitchen, did you?"

"Of course not. I just, uh, just broke a glass."

Ali pushed through the entrance door first. "You never could lie for squat." She stopped short. "Hello, Mr. Towers. Out enjoying the weather?" She smiled the same sweet smile she'd used all her life when she didn't particularly like someone. "I've heard you like things hot."

Michael looked right through Ali to focus on Greer. "I learned that you didn't take the plea on Dilley."

"The client refused."

Her boss looked particularly annoyed. "I told you to plead them all."

"I cannot force a client to accept a deal! Particularly one that isn't even a good deal. Come on, Michael. We're better than that, aren't we?"

His jaw flexed. His gaze slid to Ali, then back to Greer. "We'll talk about it later," he said brusquely and pushed past them, going inside.

"How do you stand working for him?" Her sister made no effort to lower her voice.

Greer closed her hand around Ali's arm, squeezing as she pulled her farther away from the office. "Michael has a lot on his plate."

"Yeah, Stormy Santiago, from what I hear."

"It's a big case."

"Considering he's sleeping with her, yeah."

Greer dropped her hand from her sister's arm. "What?"

Ali gave her an incredulous look. "Don't tell me you haven't heard the rumors."

"Michael Towers is not sleeping with Stormy Santiago," Greer said under her breath. "He could get disbarred!"

"And maybe he should." Ali's voice was flat. Disregarding the fact that she was jaywalking, Ali set off across the street, leaving Greer to catch up.

"He's also happily married," Greer said when they reached the sidewalk on the other side.

Ali just shook her head. "And I thought Maddie was the naive one. Maybe you're just so busy with your clients that you can't notice what's going on right in your own office." She pulled open the door to Josephine's and gestured. "Age before beauty, dear sister."

Greer went inside, only to stop short at the sight of Ryder sitting in a booth across from a very attractive blonde.

Ali practically bumped into her. But she couldn't fail to notice, either. "*Who* is that?"

"Eliane Dupre," she said in a low voice, steering her sister toward an empty booth on the opposite side of the nearly full restaurant.

"And who is Eliane Dupre?" Ali asked with an exaggerated accent once they were seated. She looked over her shoulder in Ryder's direction.

*Maybe the next Mrs. Ryder Wilson.*

Greer kept the thought to herself. "Don't stare. They might notice you."

Ali looked back at her and spread her hands. "So?"

"Eliane is interested in the nanny position. She responded to one of the notices I placed for Ryder."

"Ah."

"Mrs. Pyle must be back. Otherwise he'd have Layla with him."

"Too bad. *I* would've loved a chance to see her."

Greer snatched one of the laminated menus out from where they were tucked against the sugar shaker and the bottles of ketchup and hot sauce. It didn't matter that she knew the contents by heart. She still made a point of reading it. Or pretending to read it.

"How's that new baby doing?" Josephine herself said, stopping at the table and without asking, setting glasses of water in front of them before flipping over both of their mugs to slosh steaming coffee into them.

"Liam's perfect," Ali said. Her gaze slid over Greer. "Went over to see them at the hospital yesterday evening. Maddie's supposed to be released today sometime."

"Give her and Linc my best when you see them. You two know what you'd like today?"

"French dip," Ali said immediately. It was pretty much what she always ordered.

"Chef's salad." It was pretty much what Greer always ordered, too. She slid the menu back where it belonged.

"Coming up." Josephine headed back toward the kitchen.

"I suppose that was a dig about me not going to the hospital last night."

"It wasn't a dig. More like a...curiosity. I was there for a few hours. Mom and Dad came by. Vivian. Squire and Gloria Clay. Fortunately, Vivian had already left before they got there. We all sort of just assumed you'd show up after court was through for the day."

Greer grimaced. "I wasn't in court yesterday afternoon. Keith Gowler stepped in for me. Did I tell you that he and Lydia Oakes are getting married?"

Ali wasn't sidetracked. "You took off work? That's the second time this month. You never do that."

"Well, I did. I'll go see Maddie and the baby tonight when they're home." From across the busy diner, she heard a laugh and looked over toward Ryder's booth. His back was to her. But that only meant she had a perfect view of the fair Eliane.

Despite Greer's ripe imagination where the nanny applicant had been concerned, she'd nevertheless pictured someone older. Someone old enough to have left her own country for another. Someone old enough to have a failed marriage under her belt.

But Eliane—with her long, shiny, corn silk–colored hair and perfectly proportioned features—looked no older than Greer.

Younger, even.

"Because of Ryder?"

She belatedly tuned back into Ali. "What?"

Ali turned sideways in the booth. A move clearly designed so that she could look at the man in question without craning her head around.

Greer's lagging brain caught up. "I took off work because of *Layla*," she corrected.

Ali unrolled her knife and fork from the paper napkin. "Sure you did."

"Ali—" She broke off when another musical laugh filtered through the general noisiness of the diner. She exhaled and rubbed her fingertips against her scalp again.

"Having headaches a lot these days?"

"No," she lied.

Ali just watched her.

Greer dropped her hands. The sight of Ryder's booth in her peripheral vision was maddening. "Change seats with me."

Ali's brows disappeared beneath her bangs. But she slid

out of the booth and they traded places. Greer pushed Ali's coffee mug over to her and wrapped her fingers around her own. She swallowed. "What if I told you I might have the solution to all of our problems where Layla is concerned?"

Ali mirrored her position: arms resting on the Formica tabletop, hands cupped around her mug. Her voice was just as low as Greer's. "The only problem we have with Layla is Ryder refusing all the offers of help he's gotten from us these past months. The fact that he's still keeping us all at a distance."

"Particularly your husband."

"He *is* her uncle. So what's the solution? Did you find some legal loophole?"

"It's something legal," Greer allowed. "But not a loophole." And she was insane to even be mentioning it to Ali. Much less to think that somewhere along the line, she'd even been giving it the slightest consideration.

"Just cut the mystery, Greer. What?"

Greer exhaled. "Ryder mentioned finding a wife instead of a nanny. You know. For Layla's sake." She took a quick, nervous sip of coffee.

Ali immediately looked toward his booth. "Are you kid—" She broke off when Josephine appeared, carrying their lunch plates.

She started to set down the meals, but stopped. "You switched places. I remember when you used to do that when you were girls, trying to pass for one another."

Ali flicked her streaky hair. "Don't think we'd have much luck on that anymore," she said lightly. "Don't s'pose you have any of that chocolate cream pie left, do you? I thought I'd take a slice home to Grant."

"I'll package one up for you," Josephine promised, and headed off.

"He's buried himself in a new manuscript he started," Ali confided.

"I thought he never intended to write another T. C. Grant book."

"I don't know if it will be another CCT Rules military thriller or not." Ali picked up half of her sandwich. "For all I know, it might be a children's book. I'm just thrilled that he's feeling an urge to write again. As for Ryder—" She broke off, glancing around and lowering her voice. "You think he's going to marry the nanny?"

Greer pressed the tip of her tongue against the back of her teeth for a moment. "Or…someone else," she said huskily. "Me, for instance."

The sandwich dropped right out of Ali's hand, landing on the little cup of au jus and sending it splashing across the table toward Greer.

Greer barely noticed until Ali slapped a napkin over the spill before it dripped onto Greer's lap.

Then her sister sat back on her side of the booth and stared at her with wide eyes. "How long have you two been…" She trailed off and waved her hand.

"We haven't been." Greer mimicked the wave. She didn't mention the fact that she'd thought about it often enough.

Ali leaned closer. "Yet he *proposed* to you."

"N-not really." He'd been joking. Hadn't he? "But the subject has come up. It would just be a business arrangement," she clarified. "Not a romantic one."

Ali sat back again. She picked up a french fry and pointed it at Greer. "Are you crazy?" She shoved the fry in her mouth.

"Nobody thought the idea was more insane than me." Greer forced herself to pick up her fork and at least look like she was eating. "At first."

"When did all this come up?" Ali waved another fry.

"Last week."

Ali suddenly dropped her french fry and assumed an overly casual smile.

And the back of Greer's neck prickled.

A second later, Ryder was passing their table. He was following Eliane, his hand lightly touching her arm as they progressed through the busy diner. They made a striking couple. Both tall. Both perfect specimens of their gender.

His blue eyes moved over Greer's face and he gave a faint nod.

*Heaven help me.*

Then he was reaching around Eliane to open the door for her, and they were gone.

Greer's breath leaked out of her. She actually felt shaky.

"Here." Ali pushed a water glass into Greer's hand. "Drink. You look like you're going to pass out."

"I've never passed out and I'm not going to start now." Still, she sucked down half the contents. Then she picked up her fork and jabbed it into her salad, even though the thought of food was vaguely nauseating.

She was well aware of Ali's concern, which was the only reason she was able to swallow the chunk of ham and lettuce. But as soon as had, she set her fork down again. "Layla deserves a mother," she said huskily.

Ali's eyes immediately glistened. "You can't marry someone just because you love a little girl," she said softly.

"Want to bet?" Greer cleared her throat, but it still felt tight. "I also love my sisters. And if I did this, Layla *would* be part of our family. For real. For good. You know I would be able to make certain of it."

"And you? What about you?"

"What about me? I'd be getting the best part of the deal. Layla."

"You know that's not what I mean."

Greer swallowed. "You know I've never thought about the whole marriage thing. My career's been everything."

"Are you sure this isn't *about* your career?" Ali pushed aside her plate of food and leaned her arms on the table again. "Six months ago you told me you were thinking about quitting. Remember that?"

"Trust you to throw a moment of weakness in my face."

But Ali didn't bite. She just sat there, watching Greer, eyes more knowing than Greer wanted them to be.

"It's not about my career," she finally said. "At least I don't think it is. Entirely, anyway."

"Gotta say, Greer. I'm feeling a little freaked out at this indecisive version of you."

"Yeah, well, I'm a little freaked out by the settled-and-married-gonna-have-a-baby version of you. Maddie was one thing. She's had *mama* written all over her since she was playing with dolls. You used to cut off the heads of your dolls and shoot them out of your slingshot."

Ali snorted softly. "I did not."

"Just about. You were both the ultimate tomboy and the ultimate flirt. Everything you want to try your hand at, you succeed at. I'm sure you'll be the same way with motherhood."

"So says Madame Lawyer," Ali said drily. "Maybe I had to try so hard because you've always been the brilliant one. Well. Until now." She spread her palms. "You cannot marry a man you don't love, Greer. Not even for Layla."

"Even if it means solving this problem between Grant and Ryder? I'm at a crossroads here. All I have to do is turn the right way! Maddie's a mom. You're going to be a mom. Well, maybe I want to be one, too!" So what if he'd been joking? He'd been serious enough about the will. She could do a business deal just as well as *Eliane*.

"What happens if you meet someone you really *do* love?"

"I'm thirty years old. It hasn't happened yet."

"You're already talking yourself into it. I can tell."

Maybe she was.

"If you do this, what're you going to tell Mom and Dad? The truth? Or are you going to try making up some story about a sudden romance between the two of you? Because we all know what a rotten liar you are. They'll see right through it. And Mom'll be brokenhearted at the thought of you locked in a loveless marriage."

Greer exhaled. "It wouldn't be like her history with Rosalind's dad."

"She stayed married to Martin Pastore for years because of Rosalind. How's it different?"

"Well, for one thing, Ryder isn't like Martin!" Her encounters with their mother's first husband were mercifully few and far between. "He's not cold and controlling."

"Could've fooled me by the way he's acted for the last six months."

"You don't know him. He's…warm and…and loyal."

"Sounds like a lapdog."

Greer glared.

"Oh, come on. You left yourself wide open for that one."

"You're impossible."

"Admittedly, he's an awful good-looking lapdog. We've grown up around guys in boots and cowboy hats. He does the whole rancher look better than most."

"He does the entire *male* look better than most." She dropped her head into her hands again and massaged her temples. Then she raised her head again and looked at her watch. "I have to get to court."

"You didn't eat anything."

"Trust me. Judge Waters isn't going to care about that."

She slid out of the booth. "I appreciate the thought, though." She headed for the door.

Ali followed her, calling out to Josephine that she'd be right back. Then she pursued Greer right out onto the sidewalk. "Promise me you'll think about this a little longer."

A gust of hot wind buffeted the striped awning over the door and she glanced up, absently noticing the clouds gathering overhead. Maybe the weatherman was finally going to get a prediction right.

"All I've been doing is thinking. Maybe it's time I stopped and just—" She broke off. Shook her head.

"Tossed a coin?"

She managed a faint smile. "Maybe."

Ali grabbed her hands and squeezed them. "Greer, I know what marriage is really supposed to be. I want that for you."

Her throat tightened. "Baby sister, I'll never forgive you if you make me cry now."

Ali made a face.

Greer kissed her cheek and pulled away, checked the street for traffic, and started across.

Ali's voice followed her. "What *did* you do to your feet?"

Greer waved her arm without answering and quickened her pace, trying harder to ignore the tiny cuts she'd gotten from the gravel outside Ryder's house.

She was breathless when she rushed past Bunny Towers sitting at the reception desk and headed straight for her office.

"Oh, Greer. You have some—"

Greer nearly skidded to a halt at the sight of Ryder leaning against her desk. His arms were crossed over his wide chest. He'd set his cowboy hat on the desk beside him.

She swiped her palms down the sides of her black skirt and briskly entered her office, moving around to the opposite side of her desk. "I have to be in court in a few minutes." She started shoving files into her briefcase, heedless of whether or not they were the right ones. "The interview with Eliane went well?"

"She's ready to start tomorrow if I say the word. Didn't even ask about the live-in part. She also agreed to sign an agreement that she'd stay at least six months."

Greer felt a pang in her chest. Who was it that said timing was everything? "I see. Did you tell her about your other idea?"

His eyes narrowed slightly. "You haven't tossed your name in the pool. Does it matter to you?"

She pulled out the will she'd drafted for him and handed it to him. "Not as long as you sign that." Not as long as he didn't decide the lovely Eliane would make a lovely mama and there was no need to plan for disasters.

He tossed the document down onto her desk. "No. I didn't tell her. Yet."

She shoved in a few more files, then hefted the strap over her shoulder. "A live-in nanny's a lot easier to manage than a wife." She edged out from behind her desk again and scooted past him to the door. "I'll cancel the job postings when I finish with court today. Thanks for coming by to tell me."

"I came to bring those, too." He nodded toward the chair sitting inside her doorway and she felt her cheeks turn hot.

Her high-heeled shoes were sitting there.

The same pale gray high-heeled shoes that she'd left in the grass at his place the night before when she'd run out on him like the devil was at her heels.

"Right," she said in a clipped tone. "Thank you. I'm sorry if that took you out of your way."

"Not out of my way. I was in town, anyway."

The clock on the wall above her head seemed to be ticking more loudly than usual. "Did Eliane, uh, remind you of your aunt's model?"

His lips twitched slightly and she wished the floor would open up and swallow her.

"Hey. Didn't expect to catch you."

She whirled to see Ali striding up the hall carrying two plastic bags containing takeout.

"Figured you might as well have your uneaten lunch for—" Ali obviously noticed Ryder then. "Dinner, instead," she finished more slowly. "I'll just stash it in the break room fridge for you. Leave you two to…talk…or whatever."

"No need." Ryder straightened away from the desk and slid his hat in place with a smooth motion. "I was just dropping off those." He pointed at the shoes. "Your sister left 'em behind last night."

Greer cringed even as she saw her sister's gaze drop to the chair.

Ryder's chin dipped a fraction as he thumbed the brim of his hat and turned sideways to go past Greer through the doorway. His arm still managed to brush against hers and she felt hotter inside than ever.

*Tick.*

*Tick.*

The clock above Greer sounded louder and louder as Ali slowly looked from the shoes back to Greer.

Her mouth felt dry, which was ridiculous. Ali was her sister. Together with Maddie, they were triplets, for God's sake. "It's not what you're thinking."

*Tick.*

"Sure," Ali finally said. "Circumstantial evidence, right?"

"Exactly!"

"I think I'm worrying about the wrong thing."

"You don't have to worry about anything, period."

Ali pointed. "You can tell yourself this is about Layla. And you can tell yourself this is about your job. About being at a crossroads. And I get that it's all true. But if you think you're considering marrying Ryder only because of all that, you're dreaming, big sister. So what happens if you end up actually going through with this, only to realize you're not on the business track at all, but *he* is?"

"That's not going to happen," Greer said flatly. "And it's all semantics, anyway. He's set to offer the job to Eliane."

"The job of wife?"

"Nanny!"

"Are you sure about that?"

*Tick.*

# Chapter 9

"Templeton! Get your rear end in here."

Greer's shoulders slumped at the command.

She dumped her overstuffed briefcase on her desk and backtracked to Michael Towers's office. *You bellowed?* "Yes?"

"Shut the door."

After her encounters with Ryder and Ali, she'd had a crappy afternoon in court. She'd been late getting to two different arraignments. One of her clients already facing a misdemeanor drug charge got popped with a second offense, meaning she'd lost all the ground she'd made on negotiating a fair plea deal. And she'd gotten into an entirely uncharacteristic argument with Steve Manetti about Anthony Pyle's DUI charge, nearly earning herself a contempt charge.

She closed the door uneasily.

"Sit."

Michael's office was twice the size of hers. Which still meant that there was only room for two chairs. She nudged the one on the right slightly and sat. "If this is about Manetti, I can expl—"

"I warned you to plead out Dilley."

Her lips parted. She swallowed what she'd been going to say about Judge Manetti.

"I tried," she said. "Mr. Dilley refused. He's insistent on having his day in court."

"You have more clients going to trial than any other attorney in my jurisdictions." He was drumming the end of his pencil against his ink blotter. "I think you'd be more effective in Hale's office."

"Hale!" She popped to her feet and the chair wobbled behind her. "He's eighty-five miles away!"

"He's getting ready to retire. You'd be the senior attorney on staff. You could take as many cases as you want to trial."

"Sure. In municipal court." It was the only one located in Lillyette, Wyoming. "Which is in session maybe three times a week. On a busy week. You're punishing me for something. What?"

"I'm not punishing you. I'm trying to promote you."

"By sending me to Lillyette." Braden was a booming metropolis in comparison to the tiny town. "What if I turn down this…kind…promotion?"

Michael stared back at her, unmoving.

Her jaw was so tight it ached. "I see." She aligned the chair neatly where it belonged. She felt blindsided. She'd never lost a job in her life. But she knew that if she didn't accept the reassignment, that was what would happen. "When do you need my decision?"

"End of the week."

She supposed it was better than at the end of this little tête-à-tête. Unable to get out a polite response, she nodded and left his office.

She returned to her own. It was a closet of a space. But whether she'd been feeling frustrated there or not, it had been hers.

Her eyes suddenly burned. Blinking hard, she emptied her briefcase of files and loaded it up for the following day. She scrolled through her email and sent a few brief replies.

Then she shut down the computer, shouldered her briefcase once more and looked up at the clock above the door. As usual, it was a few minutes behind.

She set down her briefcase and moved the chair so she could stand on it to reach the clock. She pulled it off the wall and adjusted the time.

She started to hang it back in place but hesitated. It would just continue to tick along, losing time along the way.

She inhaled deeply and held the clock against her chest as she exhaled.

*Tick. Tick.*

She climbed off the chair. Moved it back against the wall. Then she tucked the clock inside her briefcase and left.

Ryder barely heard the knock on his front door above the sound of thunder. The clouds had been building all afternoon. But it hadn't helped with the heat. And aside from the noise, there hadn't been any rain.

The knock sounded again. He closed the logbook he kept on his livestock and went to the door.

Greer stood on his front step.

Her windblown hair gleamed in the porch light. She was still wearing the closely fitted white blouse and black skirt from this afternoon. But she'd unbuttoned a couple of the buttons and rolled up the sleeves. She had bright orange flip-flops on her feet.

And a bottle of whiskey in her hand.

She held it up for his inspection. He looked from the familiar label to her face. It wasn't the finest whiskey on the planet. But in his experience, it did the job pretty well. "Does the occasion call for it?"

"You tell me. I think I quit my job today."

Without asking, she stepped inside, brushing past him.

Another low rumble of thunder rolled through the night. Greer's car, parked on the gravel, was little more than a shadow.

Layla had been asleep for the last few hours. Hopefully she would sleep all the way through to morning, though with the thunder he wasn't going to hold his breath.

He closed the door.

Greer had sat down on one side of his leather couch and propped her feet on the coffee table. The fluorescent orange flip-flops looked more like they belonged on a teenager. But the slender ankles and long calves belonged to a grown woman.

He sat down on the other side of the couch—one full cushion between them—and took the bottle from her. He, too, propped a bare foot on the coffee table. He peeled off the seal on the bottle and pulled out the cork. "Ladies first."

Her dark eyes slid over him as she took the bottle. She lifted it to her lips and took a sip.

He expected a cough. A sputter. Something.

She merely squinted a little, obviously savoring the taste as she swallowed.

When he'd ridden rodeo, the girls had tended toward beer. Daisy had liked a strawberry daiquiri, sweet as hell and topped with hefty swirls of whipped cream. Eliane—the model, not the nanny—had given him his first taste of red wine before Adelaide caught them. Instead of firing Eliane, his aunt had sat down and poured herself a glass, too. Then made him finish the bottle.

To this day, he couldn't drink wine without thinking about that.

It occurred to him now that there was something a little

dangerous about being turned on by the way Greer drank a shot of whiskey straight from the bottle.

She handed it to him.

Their fingers brushed. Him, taking. Her, not yet releasing.

"When Daisy first left, I spent a fair amount of time in Jax's company."

Her fingers slid away from his. Away from the bottle. "You must have loved her very much."

"I thought I did. Enough to give her a wedding ring." Just not *the* ring. His grandmother's ring. The one his aunt had kept in safekeeping for him since he'd been a kid. Since she'd taken him in when there was no one else to do so.

He took a drink, squinting a little at the familiar burn and savoring the warmth as it slid down his throat. "Adelaide says I've got a hero complex. That marrying Daisy was more about trying to save her than loving her."

"What do you think?"

He thought about his mother, who'd been just as troubled as his erstwhile bride. He took another drink and handed Greer the bottle.

She cradled it, running her thumb slowly over the black label. Her nails were short. Neat. No-nonsense. "I've never loved anyone like that," she murmured. "I think it might not be in my makeup."

"Just don't tell me you're a virgin," he muttered.

If he'd thought he would set her off guard, he was mistaken. She made a dismissive sound. "Sex and love don't have to be the same thing."

"Adelaide would agree."

"I think I'd like your aunt. You talk about her, but you don't talk about anyone else in your family."

"There wasn't anyone else."

Greer studied him for a moment, then looked away. She

took another sip. A longer one this time. She tilted her head back a little and her eyelids drifted closed.

He got up and opened the kitchen door. The breeze was finally cooler. He stood in the doorway for a long minute and felt the base of his spine prickle when she came up to stand beside him in her silly orange flip-flops.

"D'you think it'll actually rain?" Her voice was little more than a whisper.

"Finished haying this morning. It can rain for a week straight, as far as I'm concerned."

She pressed her fingertips against the wooden frame of the simple screen door. "Layla?"

"Asleep."

She pushed open the screen door and went outside, taking the whiskey bottle with her. Ryder hadn't turned on the back porch light. Her blouse showed white in the light coming from the kitchen, but the rest of her melted into the darkness.

He caught the door before it could snap shut and followed her out, holding the screen until it sighed silently closed.

He sat on the end of the picnic table, watching the gleam of her blouse moving around as she swished her feet through the grass. Her restlessness was as palpable as the weight of thunder overhead.

"How old are you, Ryder?" Her voice sounded farther away than she appeared.

"Thirty-four." He cupped his hands around the edge of the table. The wood felt rough. It would be full of splinters if he didn't sand it down sometime soon. While he was at it, he could slop a coat of barn-red paint over the whole thing. Cover up all the flowery stuff.

"I'm thirty."

"Are we trading statistics? Want to know my boot size?" He listened to the grass swishing and wasn't sure if it was from her feet or from the breeze. But the gleam of her blouse was getting closer and then she stopped a few feet away from him. "Thirteen."

"Did you give Eliane the word?"

"No."

She took another sip from the bottle, then stepped close enough to set it next to his hip. "Why?"

He moved it down to the bench seat. "Why do you think you quit your job today?"

She started to move again, but he reached out and caught her hands and she went still. Her palms were small. Her long fingers curled down over his. He could see the faint sheen of moisture on her lips.

"Because I don't want to drive eighty-five miles to work every day. Or move eighty-five miles away from my home. Because." She took a step closer. She exhaled a shaky-sounding sigh. "Because."

He let go of her hands and slid his palm behind her neck. Her skin was warm. Silkier even than his imagination had promised. But that was as far as he went. He didn't pull her forward. Didn't make another single move.

It was one of the hardest attempts at self-control he'd ever made.

"Were you really joking the other day?"

He didn't have to ask what she meant. He didn't have to think about the answer. "No. Are you tossing your name in the pool?"

After a moment she took another step forward and stopped against the edge of the table, between his thighs. When she drew breath, he could feel the press of her breasts against his chest.

"If we do this—" his voice felt like it was coming from

somewhere way down inside "—I know what I get out of it. What do you get out of it?"

"Are we talking about marriage?" Her fingertips drifted over his knees, slowly grazing their way higher up his thighs, leaving heat in their wake even through his denim jeans. "Or this?"

He pressed his hands over hers, flattening them. Stilling their progress. "Counselor, I know what you'll get out of *this*."

She leaned closer, bringing with her the seductive scents of warmth and whiskey and woman. The breeze blew over them, and her hair danced against his neck. Her lips brushed against his jaw, slid delicately across his chin. Then she found his mouth for a moment that was strangely endless but much too brief. Her fingers pressed into his thighs. "I get the assurance that Layla will be part of our lives. Permanently. If you want to marry to give her a mother, then I want to *be* her mother. Legally."

He caught her behind the neck again, pulling back so he could see her face. But it was too dark. The sky too black with clouds. Her cheekbones were a faint highlight. Her lips a dark invitation. And her thickly lashed, deep brown eyes… they were the most mysterious abyss of all. "You want to adopt Layla."

"Is that so strange?"

He wasn't sure what it was, except that it made something inside his chest feel strange. "I'll consider it. What else?"

"Our wills. Anything happens to us both, then Layla goes to Grant and Ali. Those are my terms."

"What about starting your own legal firm?"

"Maybe someday when I've won the lottery and can afford it, I'll have one."

He moved his hand along her neck and over her shoulder.

The gleam of white fabric looked crisp but did a poor job of hiding the heat radiating from her. "I could stake you."

"It's not just money. An office. Equipment. All that sort of thing. It's time. Time I won't have much of, if I'm out here taking care of Layla."

"You're a lawyer. Your greatest equipment is your brain. And you can turn that fancy-ass Victorian house you're supposedly renovating into an office."

Her hands slid out from beneath his as she stepped back from him. Cool air seemed to flow between them. "You're full of ideas all of a sudden."

"I've given it a thought or two."

"Why does it matter to you? I've already said that Layla is what's important."

"Because I'm never going to be the cause of a woman giving up her dream." He reached for the bottle of whiskey and cradled it in his hand.

She was silent for a moment while the thunder rumbled. "Is this about Daisy?"

"The only dream that Daisy claimed to have was being married to me." He scratched at the edge of the bottle label with his fingernail. "Whatever her real dreams were, she obviously never shared them with me." He figured it was progress that he could make the observation without feeling much of anything.

"What's your dream?"

He spread his arms. "This place."

"The Diamond-L."

"Named for my mother. The original Layla. You want me to talk about her?" He felt the label tear. "She was born here. In Wyoming."

He felt her surprise.

"Her dad—my grandfather—was a minister. Moving his

family from one small town to another every few years. They died before I was born. But my mom dreamed of adventure. Of seeing more of the world than a string of tiny towns needing a preacher. Finding the end of the rainbow. And she gave it all up because she got pregnant with a baby she wasn't at all equipped to handle." He took a last burning sip of whiskey before tossing the bottle away into the dark, even though it meant a waste of perfectly good liquor. "She was an alcoholic. One night, she got behind the wheel of a car, drunk, and killed herself as well as two other people."

"Oh, Ryder." Greer's sigh was louder than her words. "How old were you?"

"Eight."

"Your father?"

"She never said who he was."

"And your aunt?"

"Adelaide didn't know who he was, either. She was the only one left to take me in. She's not my real aunt. She was my grandmother's best friend. She was there when my mother lost her mother. And she was there when I lost mine. Adelaide gave me a home." He felt a raindrop on his hand. "I asked her why once. She said it was the right thing to do."

Greer stepped close again and slid her arms around his shoulders. "The Victorian would make a good office," she whispered. "I'll consider it. Put your arms around me."

He didn't need to be told, though it was a novel enough occurrence that it appealed to him. Her waist was so slender, his fingers could span it. But as he slowly ran his hands down over the flare of her hips, he discarded the notion that he'd ever considered her too skinny for his tastes.

"If we do this, it doesn't change anything." She arched slightly when his hands drifted down over her rear. "Layla will have two parents. We'll raise her together. But the deal between us stays—"

"—business." He'd discovered the zipper on the back of her skirt and slowly drew it down. The skirt came loose and slid down her thighs. All she wore beneath was a scrap of lace.

"That's right." She angled her head and brushed her lips against his ear. "Business," she breathed.

He slid his fingers along her slender neck. Felt the pulse throbbing at the base. The way she swallowed when his fingers curled beneath her chin. He nudged at it slightly, lifting it. "You saying this is a one-and-done, Counselor?"

"I'm saying let's not call this marriage something it's not. It'll be a marriage of convenience. Pure and simple."

He lowered his head and slowly rubbed his lips across hers. Felt the softening. The parting. The invitation.

He lifted his head again. Eased his fingers behind the nape of her neck once more. "I'm not thinking too many pure thoughts at the moment."

Her breasts rose and fell, pressing against him. Retreating. "Neither am I. As long as we don't confuse this with something it's not, I don't see the problem. Just because marrying would be convenient doesn't mean it has to be sterile. It'd be a different matter if we weren't attracted to each other. But we are." Her lips were close to his, her whisper soft yet clear. "So we might as well be realistic from the start."

"Realistic. Works for me."

She took a deep breath again. Her breasts pressed against his chest and stayed there. "And…and if…*when* it stops working, when Layla's older, we'll end the deal. No fuss. No muss." She waited a beat. "As long as I'm just as much her legal parent as you. My family—*all* of my family—becomes her family. That means Grant, too."

He felt another plop of warm rain. This time on his arm.

"If I agree to you adopting her, you have to agree about your own practice."

"Negotiation?"

"You told me you were good at it."

"Okay. Agreed."

The second she said the words, he closed his hands around her hips again, pulling her in tighter. She was warm. Soft. "It's going to rain."

"As far as I'm concerned, it can rain for a week." He felt her words against his lips.

He smiled slightly and pushed her away. Only a few inches. "Take off your shirt, Counselor."

She made a soft sound. He sensed more than saw her dark eyes on him. "I'd rather you take it off me."

There were invitations to ignore.

There were ones he couldn't.

His fingers brushed against her skin as he found the tiny buttons on her shirt. Impatience raged inside him, but he took his time. One button. Two. All the way down, until it took only a nudge of his fingers and the shirt fell away, too. The bra and panties she wore were as white as the shirt had been. But lacy. Stretchy. No protection at all when he tugged them off.

And then she took a full step backward, giving him enough room to push off the table and pull his shirt over his head. He unfastened his belt and jeans and shoved them down his legs.

Then she crowded close again, slipping her hand under his boxer briefs. She inhaled audibly when she closed her fingers around him. "Perfect," she breathed.

He looked up at the sky, dragging in an audible breath of his own. Another raindrop hit him square on the face. His shoulder. His back. "I should take you inside."

"I'm not sugar." She dragged his briefs down, bending her knees, going down with them, setting them aside when he stepped out of them. But she didn't stand back up. "I'm not the Wicked Witch. I won't melt from some water." Her hair brushed his knee. His thigh. And her lips…

"Maybe not," he said. Her mouth closed over him and he exhaled roughly. He slid his fingers through her hair. He couldn't help himself. She had a lot of hair. The strands were silky. Slippery. He wanted to wrap his fingers in it and hold her. His hands were actually shaking from resisting the urge. "But what you're doing feels damn—" another oath slid through his teeth "—wicked."

The air suddenly felt electric and thunder cracked. She made a sound. Sexy. Greedy. And took him even deeper.

He let her go. Let her do as she pleased. And oh, how it pleased. For as long as he could hold out. Then a flash of soft light flickered in the distance, giving shape to the canopy of clouds. Giving shape to the woman kneeling before him.

"Enough." It was a rough order. A rough plea. He pulled away. Pulled her up. Maybe it wasn't going to be one-and-done. Maybe they'd manage a year. Two. Before convenience didn't matter to her so much and she'd want more out of life than a business deal of a marriage.

But he wanted more this time—this first time—than just *this*.

Another fat raindrop splashed on his shoulder as he drew her up to him and found her mouth with his. Found her breasts with his hands. And she was right there with him. Pressing herself against him, her nipples tight points against his palms. Her tongue mingling with his, her hands dragging up and down his spine before closing over his head.

He could feel her heart pounding as hard as his own as he lifted her against him. Her legs slid along his thighs and wrapped around his hips. And then she cried out when he slid inside her, and he froze. Because she was so tight. So small in comparison to him, and he was suddenly afraid of hurting her.

Thunder cracked overhead and the clouds finally opened up, drenching them in seconds.

Holding her ought to have been impossible. Water rained down on them, making her flesh slick. But she simply twined herself around him, holding him tightly gloved within. "Don't stop now." She sounded exultant as she dragged his mouth back to hers.

And then everything that was perfect overrode his fear.

Wet inside.

Wet outside.

And she wanted him as much as he wanted her. He backed up until he felt the table. There'd be time for bed later. Time for every other thing he could possibly imagine. He ignored the rough, splintering wood as he leaned against it and took her slight weight in his hands and thrust.

"Yes." She arched in perfect counterpoint.

Again. And again. And again. He wanted to go on and on and on, but he knew he wouldn't last. Not with the way he could feel her quickening. Tightening. Shuddering.

Lightning flashed.

Her head dropped back but she clung to him. "Yes!"

The rain fell and the world shrank down to this one woman in his arms.

And he let himself go.

"Yessssss."

# Chapter 10

"Yes. I do."

Judge Stokes smiled at Ryder and turned to Greer to repeat the vow. "And will you, Greer Templeton, take this man, Ryder Wilson, to be your lawfully wedded husband? To have and to hold, in sickness and in health, for richer or for poorer? Forsaking all others and keeping only to him?"

It was vaguely surreal, standing there in Judge Stokes's chambers.

But there was nothing surreal about Greer's answer. Since she'd made the decision to marry Ryder, she hadn't suffered any second thoughts. "Yes," she said just as clearly as he had. "I do."

The judge smiled benevolently at them. With his white hair and beard, and his tendency toward wearing red shirts, he looked a bit like Santa Claus. Even though it was only the end of August. "Then—" he closed his small black book "—by the authority vested in me by the State of Wyoming, and with a great deal of personal delight I might add, I declare you to be husband and wife." He spread his hands. "Congratulations. You may kiss your bride."

Ryder, looking uncommonly urbane in a dark gray suit with a lighter gray striped tie knotted around his neck, turned to her. He took her hands and his thumb brushed over the narrow platinum band he'd given her. His thick hair was brushed back from his face. There was no hatband mark in evidence. His jaw was clean-shaven and his blue eyes were brilliant. When he leaned down, instead of his usual scent of hay or grass or fresh open air, he smelled faintly woodsy. Exotic.

He was entirely *un*-rancherly.

And for the first time in thirty-six hours—since the night she'd gone to his house and she'd thrown herself, mind and body, into his marriage plan—she felt a wrinkle of unease.

How well did she really know this man to whom she'd just promised herself? This rancher who had a beautiful gray suit that looked as if it had been custom tailored just sitting around in his closet?

Was it a leftover from his Vegas wedding to Daisy?

It was just a suit, she reminded herself. She'd pulled her dress from her closet, too.

Then his eyes met hers, and it felt as though he knew exactly how she was feeling.

"We can do this," he murmured. Low. For her ears only.

She gave a tiny nod.

The faint lines beside his eyes crinkled slightly and his dimple appeared. Then his lips brushed slowly, lightly across hers.

It was barely a kiss. Yet it was still enough to make her feel warm way down inside.

But there was no time to dwell on it, because the judge's wife and his usual clerk, Sue, who were acting as their witnesses, had started clapping. Layla, dressed in a ruffled yellow jumper, jabbered and clapped her hands, too. Sue had insisted on holding her during the ceremony.

"Just lovely," Mrs. Stokes said. "So romantic."

Greer bit back a spurt of amusement that she knew Ryder felt, as well, and relaxed even more.

They were of one mind when it came to that particular element of marriage. They could rock each other's socks off in the bedroom while Layla slept. Or on a picnic table in the rain. Or in his shower that ought to have been too cramped, but wasn't. All of which they'd done in the span of a mere day.

But this legal union of theirs wasn't about romance. It was because of Layla, and for no other reason.

"If I could get your signatures here?" Sue pointed to the marriage license they'd obtained just that morning from the county clerk's office. She evaded Layla's grab for the pen and handed it to Ryder.

He signed the document and handed the pen to Greer before lifting Layla out of Sue's arms. "Thanks."

"My pleasure. It's just so exciting to see a happy ending for all of you."

Greer finished signing her name next to Ryder's and she capped the pen before handing it back. "Thanks, Sue."

"I still can't believe you did this without your family, though. They're going to be so surprised."

"We didn't want anything or anyone—not even family—delaying it," Greer explained smoothly.

"That's how it is, isn't it?" Sue's eyes sparkled. "When you know you absolutely can't spend one more minute without committing to the person you love?"

"It was like that for us, wasn't it, Horvald?" Mrs. Stokes commented as she signed the witness line.

It was easier to let them think that than to tell them the truth. That Greer hadn't wanted to give her family a chance to talk her out of it. Which they would surely have done, no matter how much they, too, loved Layla.

Ryder had disagreed with her. Said they should wait, at least long enough to tell her family. It wasn't about seeking approval or blessings. It was about respecting them enough to give them the truth.

Greer had prevailed, though. They'd made the decision. If they'd waited, they'd have had to wait through Labor Day holiday weekend to be married. Meaning she'd also have to wait four more days to file the petition to adopt Layla.

Sue took up the pen and signed after Mrs. Stokes. Then the court clerk set the document on the judge's desk. "Congratulations again." Sue linked her arm through Mrs. Stokes's and the two of them left the judge's chambers.

"All right." The judge signed the license with a flourish after they'd gone. "I guess I can trust you to turn that in to the recorder's office." He slid the paperwork into its envelope and handed it to Greer. "And now for your next item of business."

He moved another document to the center of his desk. "I've reviewed your petition for Layla's adoption and everything is in order." As he spoke, he signed his name and then he flipped open an enormous date book in which, Greer knew, he kept all of his case schedules. It didn't matter that Sue managed his official calendar by more efficient—namely computerized—methods. Horvald Stokes still liked his old-fashioned calendar. And it was legend how he'd never once made a scheduling mistake.

He flipped through it, studying and muttering to himself under his breath. Then he went back a few pages. Then forward again. And finally he stopped. "Hearing will be November 19." He made the notation in his book and then on the petition. "That's before Thanksgiving."

For the first time that day, Greer's smile felt shaky. Becoming Layla's mother was the crux of the matter, the reason they were there at all. When they were done, Layla would have a father and a mother. The hearing in November would be little more than a formality before Judge Stokes could sign the final decree. "Sounds perfect to me, Your Honor."

"It really is my genuine pleasure." He stood and pulled one of the black robes off the coat stand behind his desk and slipped his arms into the voluminous sleeves. "Layla had a rocky start through no fault of her own. I'm more than pleased that things have resolved themselves in this manner."

A manner that Greer never would have imagined six months ago.

Her throat felt tight. "Thank you again for fitting us into your schedule today."

He winked. "Fifteen minutes for a good cause."

Sue returned then and gathered up both the thick, stapled document that he'd signed and his oversize date book. "Both parties for your next case are present, Judge Stokes, whenever you're ready."

He nodded and she went through the doorway that Greer knew led directly from his chambers into his courtroom. The fact that he zipped up his robe before he headed toward the door meant he was prepared to get straight to business. "Will we be seeing you at the county picnic this weekend?"

Greer moistened her lips and adjusted the band of black velvet fabric around her waist. By itself, her knee-length ivory cotton sundress had seemed a little too casual to wear to her own wedding. Marriage of convenience or not. After seeing Ryder's suit, she was glad she'd made her outfit a bit more formal by adding the wide black belt. The black touches were repeated in the jet clip she'd pinned into her chignon and her black suede pumps.

"I'm afraid not. I've left the public defender's office." She'd turned in her notice to Michael the day before. He'd been livid and told her she needn't serve out the two weeks. Considering the choice he'd given her, she felt like she was the one who had a right to be livid. "I'm cleaning out my desk when we're finished here, actually."

The judge was clearly surprised. "You're not leaving the practice of law, I hope. You're an incredibly valuable part of the legal community, Greer."

The praise was as unexpected as it was touching and she didn't know quite what to say.

"She's opening her own firm," Ryder said.

Greer understood why it was so important to Ryder, even though, in her own mind, it was a much hazier proposition.

The judge's expression cleared. "Good for you! I look forward to you really spreading your wings." His smile broadened. "And one day, Mrs. Wilson," he said, winking, "I'll expect to see you on the bench." He pulled open the door and went into his courtroom.

Which left Greer alone with Ryder.

Her husband.

They'd married so quickly she hadn't even thought whether she was going to take his name. Mrs. Wilson...

Layla was yanking on his tie, jabbering away in her sweet little-girl babble, and Greer pushed away the thought.

"That went smoothly," she said. "Don't you think?"

"It was smooth enough." He tugged at his tie, but Layla looked ready to do battle over it. "I should have said before— you look real pretty."

She dashed her hand quickly down the skirt of her dress, suddenly feeling self-conscious. "I guess the dress did the job. It's ancient. Back from law school days. You...you look very nice, too." She snatched up the small black clutch she'd brought with her, along with the entirely unexpected nosegay of fresh lavender stalks wrapped in gray ribbon that he'd given her. "I guess you must subscribe to the theory that every man should have a decent suit in his closet."

His dimple appeared. "I was afraid it would be a little tight. Last time I put it on was at least five years ago." He looked at Layla, chuckling. "Gonna need a new tie now, though."

So. *Not* the suit from his Vegas wedding.

She lifted the bouquet and inhaled the soothing fragrance. "Looks like it fits you just fine," she managed, and led the way out of the judge's office.

As she clutched the lavender, she noticed how foreign the shining ring felt on her wedding finger. It was a little too loose.

She honestly wasn't sure what had surprised her more.

The flowers or the ring.

He'd chosen both. She couldn't imagine when he'd had the time.

She reminded herself that the ring would simply take some getting used to. As would chasing after Layla instead of chasing clients right here among these courtrooms every day.

Simple enough.

They'd reached the wide central staircase. Her high heels clicked on the marble as she started down. It was only ten in the morning. But it was a Friday, which meant that most of the courtrooms weren't in use and the building was pretty empty.

The recorder's office on the first floor was open every weekday, though, and they stopped there to turn in their signed wedding license.

"Don't forget this." The girl working behind the counter was new. She didn't know Greer. She was holding out the certificate portion of the wedding license. Though it was nothing more than a souvenir, the reality suddenly sank in.

Greer's head swam. She took the certificate, feeling embarrassed by the way her fingers visibly trembled. "Thank you."

She went to tuck the folded paper in her clutch, but the thick parchment slid out of her grasp. She knelt down to grab it.

When she rose, she swayed.

Ryder's hand closed over her elbow, steadying her. "When's the last time you ate?"

"Yesterday evening." She'd spent the night before at home, wrapping up the details of her resignation. Contacting her former clients and letting them know that she wasn't abandoning them, even though it felt like it. That someone else from her office would be taking good care of them.

She'd fallen asleep in the middle of making case file notes for the attorney who would come after her.

When she'd woken up, she had a crease in her cheek from the folders and a stiff neck from sleeping with her head on her desk. She still felt a little stiff now.

"Let's get you fed, then," he said, caressing her neck, his fingertips somehow magically discerning the tight spots.

"After I clean out my office."

His hand closed around her shoulders. "Your office can wait." Holding her in one arm and Layla in the other, he headed toward the courthouse exit.

"But—"

He didn't slow his long, measured strides. "What's left that matters, Greer? You told me about the clock."

"I don't know," she admitted. "I have stuff there still."

"Paper clips?" They'd reached the courthouse doors and he let go of her to hold one open. "Face it, Counselor. If anything else had truly mattered, you'd have taken it the same time you took the clock."

She hated to admit he was right. "I need to at least drop off the box of files I still have."

"Fine." When they stepped outside, they were greeted by

clear blue skies. The heat had broken a little. "*After* you've eaten."

"Is this what being married to you is going to be like? You telling me what's what?" She stopped on the courthouse steps, tucking her clutch beneath her arm and pointing her lavender bouquet at him. Layla was playing with his ear and yanking on his tie as though it was a rein.

"It is when I know I'm right." He tried to smooth his tie; the attempt seemed futile. He took Greer's hand in his and they began to descend the courthouse steps.

That's when she saw them.

Her parents. Vivian. Her brother and sisters. Their husbands. All of them were there. Even Rosalind, who hadn't visited Braden in years.

Greer yanked her hand from Ryder's. "What did you do?"

"You want Layla to be part of your family. So." He took her hand again, firmly, and nodded toward the not-so-small crowd assembled at the bottom of the stairs. "I called them. Last time I got married it was supposedly for the right reasons. We eloped. Never told a soul until after the fact. And you know how that turned out. So I'm doing things differently this time. I'm not going to pretend we're living in a vacuum. We can't shut out the people who care about us the most." He looked into her eyes, his expression intense. "They're gonna say we didn't marry for the right reasons but I don't care. Our reasons are our own. As long as you and I are on the same page, we're good." He squeezed her hand. "We are good," he repeated. "*Showing* them is the only way they'll get on board."

She moistened her lips. "I'm not so sure I like it when you're right."

He smiled faintly. "You'll get used to it in time."

A fine idea in theory. So why did it make her feel increasingly disconcerted?

*Adjustments, Greer.*

She tugged his tie away from Layla and smoothed it down the front of his hard chest. Her fingers wanted to linger. Her common sense insisted otherwise. "I guess now I don't have to keep running scenarios in my mind about how to tell my parents."

His dimple appeared. "There you go."

"Have you told Adelaide?"

He smiled slightly. "Who do you think reminded me that a bride should have flowers on her wedding day?"

And just like that, her chest felt tight all over again. "You called my family, but will she come, too?"

He shook his head. "She doesn't travel anymore, remember?"

"Has she met Layla?"

"I had sort of figured I'd visit for Christmas. A few days. Can't spare a lot of time away from the ranch." He was silent for a moment. "We could go. You know. As a family."

"That sounds nice." She lifted her small bouquet and inhaled the lovely, calming scent, though it wasn't quite enough to soothe away the disconcerting butterflies flitting around inside her. "Did she tell you to choose fresh lavender, too?"

"Didn't need to. They were the only flowers that seemed fitting for a woman who lives in a house like yours."

"Lived," she corrected, and looked down at her family. "Well. We can't stand here forever, I suppose. At least they're smiling."

"Yep." He muttered an oath when Layla yanked his tie again. "You're gonna strangle me with it, aren't you, Short-Stuff?"

"I'll take her." Greer handed him her clutch and bouquet, lifted Layla out of his arms and propped her on her hip. Then she took back her bouquet.

He gave her clutch a wry look, then slid it into his pocket. "Ready?"

She nodded.

And they continued down the stairs.

They'd barely made it to the bottom before a collective command came for them to stop where they were. Out came a half dozen cell phones to take their pictures. But then, clearly too excited to wait a second longer, Meredith darted up to greet them, throwing her arms around Greer and Layla, engulfing them in her familiar, uniquely Meredith fragrance.

"Oh, my darlings," she cried, and somehow Greer managed to lose Layla to Meredith in the embrace. But then her mom always had been sly that way. She kissed the baby's face. "You've grown so much! And you!" Meredith dragged Ryder's head down and gave him a smacking kiss on the cheek before he had a hope in heaven of avoiding it. He gave Greer a vaguely startled look. "I knew you were a special man," Meredith was saying, "and when you called us last night, I—"

"Last night!" Greer gave him a look.

"You were home doing your thing. I was doing mine."

Meredith laced her free arm through Ryder's and pulled him the rest of the way down the steps. Since his hand was locked onto Greer's, that meant she went, too, and they didn't stop until they came up against her father's stalwart body. Carter's service in the military might have ended decades earlier, before Greer, Ali and Maddie were even an idea, but he still carried himself as though he wore a uniform and a chest full of medals.

He and Ryder were about the same height. But Ryder's brawny build, hidden so spectacularly beneath his tailored suit, made him seem even larger than her dad.

The men were eyeing each other. Taking measure.

Predictably, her dad went on the offensive. "Guess you

didn't figure you needed to call and get permission to marry my daughter before you just did it."

"Dad! I don't need—" Greer broke off when he lifted his hand. She looked to her mother. "Mom."

Meredith just gave her an amused look. She was as unconventional as her husband was conventional, and yet together, they were the perfect couple.

"If I'd done that, and Greer had found out, I'm pretty sure she wouldn't be standing here this morning with my ring on her finger," Ryder replied easily.

"Darn right," Greer started, only to break off again when her dad gave her the same silencing look he'd given all of them growing up.

"The fact that you didn't call for permission makes me feel you know my girl pretty well. The fact that you let us know so we could be here this morning makes me think you've got a few good brain cells."

"Dad!"

"But the fact that my girl chose you, well, that says a lot, too." He looked over at Greer's sisters. "I didn't raise any of my daughters to choose badly. So." He stuck out his hand. "Welcome to the family, son."

It was ridiculous, but Greer's eyes stung a little as her father shook Ryder's hand.

After that, it was pretty much a free-for-all. She wasn't sure if they would have made it from the courthouse steps to Josephine's diner if Ryder hadn't taken charge and made it happen. There was a general jostling for seats and the usual chaos of menus and ordering for such a large party, but the diner was half-empty and nobody else there seemed to mind.

Greer now had stiff competition for Layla's attention. Between Ali and Maddie and her mother fawning, Layla was wholly and delightedly occupied. Linc, with tiny Liam sleeping against his shoulder, was holding his own in a debate about politics with Vivian and Hayley's husband, Seth, who had tiny Keely sleeping against his shoulder. Hayley was trying in vain to change the subject before Carter blew a gasket and jumped into the lively exchange. At the other end of the tables, Rosalind and Archer were giving each other the same fulminating glares they'd always exchanged growing up. Which left Grant. Sitting on the other side of Ryder.

Greer considered offering to switch seats with Ryder, but decided not to. Instead, she just stood up from her own chair and crouched a little, wedging herself in the narrow space between them. A human buffer between her new husband and his former brother-in-law.

The looks she earned from both of them were nearly identical.

She wanted to point that out but knew better. Among her relatives, there was already the likely explosion over politics before too long. She didn't want to chance adding more combustible material because of Ryder's and Grant's mutual grudges.

The fact that Grant had accompanied Ali was promising as far as Greer was concerned, and she gave him a bright smile. "Ali tells me you're working on something new. I think that's great. How's it coming?"

"Fair."

She looked from him to Ryder. Grant's hair was blacker than Ryder's, his blue eyes lighter. Grant had a swimmer's build. Ryder, a linebacker's. Grant was an author who'd already made a fortune several times over with his military thrillers. Ryder was a rancher, whose resources were considerably more modest. They couldn't be more different.

Their only common ground was Layla and the mother who'd abandoned her.

"Ryder was in the army," she said brightly. She rested her hand on his shoulder. "How long were you in?"

He knew what she was trying to do. She could tell. "Four years. Right outta high school."

"And you, Grant?" She glanced at Ryder again. "He served in the air force. That's how he started writing the CCT Rules series. From his experiences there." She looked from Ryder's face to Grant's. "You put in a fair amount of time, didn't—"

*"Yoohoo!"* The loud greeting came from across the diner and Greer automatically glanced over. Ryder, on the other hand, shoved back his seat with an exclamation and strode toward the tall, gangly woman who'd entered the restaurant.

She had hair dyed black, and turquoise dripping from her ears and her neck and surrounding nearly every finger. A designer dog carrier hung from one skinny shoulder and Greer could hear the yapping of a dog.

There was no question in Greer's mind who the woman was when Ryder swung her right off her feet in a boisterous hug.

No matter what he'd said, Adelaide had still come.

Across the table, Vivian suddenly stood. She was staring at the woman, too. "Oh, my word! That's Adelaide Arians."

"Who the hell's Adelaide Arians?" Grant asked.

"She raised Ryder." Greer had to push the words through the ache in her throat. Across the restaurant, Ryder had set Adelaide back on her feet and she'd handed him something. As Greer watched, he shook his head as if refusing, but then he looked her way and seemed to still.

"She's only considered one of the seminal artists of our age," Vivian was saying as if it were a fact any person should know. "Her work hangs in the Museum of Modern Art! Wyoming and *culture* are simply two different universes," she huffed. "Sometimes I wonder why I bothered coming here."

She tugged at the sleeves of her Chanel suit, and the diamonds on her fingers winked.

"Spoken like the snob you are," Carter observed acidly.

"Dad," Hayley started to caution. She was always trying to be the peacemaker between their father and his mother.

"The apple doesn't fall far from the tree, son." Vivian spoke right over her. "You just save your judgment for *me.*"

"You are *impossible!*" At the other end of the table, Rosalind had risen from her seat and was glaring at Archer. In turn, he wore the goading expression he always had around her. "Just crawl back under your rock!" Rosalind was practically shrieking.

Liam and Keely were no longer sleeping like little angels against their daddies' shoulders. They both were crying. Which had their mamas jostling to get out of their chairs to resolve the situation.

Layla was banging her sippy cup against the table and joyfully knocking down the towers of plastic creamer containers that Meredith built for her.

And there was Ryder, drawing his aunt up to their table, which had suddenly lost its collective mind. Whatever his aunt had given him was no longer in evidence.

"And this must be her." Adelaide had an unexpectedly booming voice that carried over the bedlam. She gave Greer an appraising look, but there was a glint of humor in her heavily made-up eyes and a smile on her deeply red lips that helped calm the sudden butterflies inside Greer's stomach. "I've got to say, Ryder my boy, your taste has sure improved since that last one."

Grant shoved his chair back and stood. He tossed down his napkin and walked out of the restaurant.

"Oh, dear." Adelaide's voice could have filled an auditorium without need for a microphone. She set the dog carrier on the chair he'd abandoned. "Did I say something wrong?"

Ryder looked at Greer.

She exhaled. "So. Not everything can go as smoothly as it did with the judge."

He frowned. But the lines beside his eyes crinkled slightly and his dimple came out of hiding.

Greer held out her hand toward his aunt. "I'm very pleased to meet you, Ms. Arians. I'm Greer."

"Call me Adelaide," she boomed, and jerked Greer into a nearly bone-crushing hug. "Oh, yes, indeed, the next few months are going to be *great fun*!"

She let go of Greer so suddenly, she had to catch her balance. "You're going to stay for a while, then?"

"Right through Christmas, sugar pie." Adelaide adjusted the eye-popping tie-dyed scarf she wore around her wrinkled neck. "Now where's the little peanut at the center of all these goings-on? Oh, there you are." She strode around the table. "Cute little thing!"

Layla's eyes went round as saucers as she stared warily up at the tall, loud Adelaide. She banged her cup a few times, but without her usual emphatic enthusiasm. Then she opened her mouth and wailed.

Adelaide whipped one of her chunky rings off a finger and waved it in front of Layla. The distraction worked enough to have Layla grabbing the bauble, but not enough to silence her plaintive howling. Adelaide laughed delightedly. "Little thing already knows what she likes and doesn't like!"

"She's gonna put that ring in her mouth," Ryder warned.

"And why not? You used to do that when you were a little mite, too. Stone's the size of a golf ball. She's not gonna choke on it!" She stood there, hands on her skinny hips, and grinned down at Layla.

Greer's arm brushed Ryder's. She was curious about what Adelaide had given him, but figured if he wanted to mention it, he would. Meanwhile, the cacophony around them was only increasing, made worse by the dog's shrill yipping from inside the carrier. She had to raise her voice. "Still think the one-big-family thing is going to be all it's cracked up to be?"

He dropped his arm around her shoulder. "Time'll tell, Counselor. Time'll tell."

## Chapter 11

"...Happy birthday, dear Layla, happy birthday to you!"

While their party guests finished singing, Greer set the cake she'd gotten from Tabby Clay in front of Layla. It was shaped like an enormous white cupcake with huge swirls of pink frosting on top, and had a single oversize white candle.

"No, no, no," Layla chanted as she looked at the confection facing her. It had become her favorite word of late. Along with "Dadda" and "bye-bye" and "sus-suh," which Greer had figured out was her version of "Short-Stuff." She even had a name for Brutus and Adelaide.

But there had been no more instances of "mama," inadvertent or otherwise.

"Yes, yes, yes," Greer told her, and shooed Brutus away so she could scoot Layla's chair with its booster seat closer to the table. "It's the prettiest cake for the prettiest girl."

"You guys need to sit next to her," Maddie ordered, gesturing at Ryder. "I want a picture of the three of you together." She had Liam strapped to her chest in a fabric carrier and a camera in her hand.

It was October 27.

And though they'd planned to have Layla's first birthday party outdoors, an early snow had put paid to the notion. Which was why the family was instead crowding around the dinner table inside.

"So we don't really know for sure this is her birthday?" Even after two months with them, Adelaide's voice could still reach the back row of an auditorium.

Greer, sitting down on one side of Layla, looked over at Ryder, who'd pulled out the chair on the other side.

He returned her wry look. "No, we don't know for sure," he told his aunt, not for the first time, "but since we could never find out exactly where or when she was born, it's as close as we can determine. So this is what we've chosen."

"You know it was your grandmother's birthday, too!" Adelaide now had her camera out. But since she was just as likely to take a photo of a dust mote that caught her interest as she was to capture Layla's expression when she smashed her hands into the cake, Greer was glad Maddie was there with the fancy digital camera that Linc had gotten after Liam's birth.

Ryder caught Greer's eye above Layla and winked. He hadn't shaved in the last few days, and Greer hadn't quite decided whether she liked the stubbled look or not. "I know it was, Adelaide," he said patiently.

"Don't you think it'll be confusing if you ever find out where and when she really *was* born?"

"It won't really matter," Meredith answered before they could. She slipped closer to the table, snapping off pictures with her cell phone while skillfully managing not to trip over Brutus. "Layla's going to have a brand-new birth certificate once the adoption's final."

Ryder's hand went to the back of Layla's chair, and his fingers came close to touching Greer's.

But didn't.

"You going to let my niece demolish that cake, or what?" That came from Grant, who was leaning against the couch with Ali beside him.

It might have been two months since he'd walked out on Greer and Ryder's wedding breakfast, but there had been little sign of softening between Ryder and him. The two men were grudgingly polite whenever there was a family event, like today, but that was as far as it went.

Frankly, it made Greer want to smack their two stubborn heads together. But generally, she didn't have time to worry about it too much. Not with taking care of Layla, who was walking now and getting into everything. It was almost impossible to take the toddler with her to the Victorian, where she was trying to supervise the work of the two-man crew Ryder had found. Luckily, Meredith had come to the rescue. She never missed an opportunity to babysit. She'd started on the day of the wedding, insisting that Ryder and Greer should have a proper wedding night.

What Ryder and Greer had had was an awkward wedding night spent sleeping on opposite sides of his wide bed. As if their marathon of lovemaking the night of the rainstorm had never occurred.

She'd never believed that night would be a one-and-done, as he put it. Yet it basically was. Sure, they'd indulged themselves several times that night. So was it a one-and-done or three-and-done? What was the difference?

There had been no repeat performance.

"Of course she's going to demolish her cake," she assured Grant, blocking the memories as she drew it a little closer to Layla. "This is all yours, sweetie." She pulled one of Layla's fingers through the icing and caught it in her mouth, sucking it off noisily. It was more whipped cream than frosting. "Yum yum."

"Num!" Layla lovingly patted Greer's face. Her green eyes were full of devotion. "Nummy."

Feeling like her heart would burst, Greer pressed a kiss to their toddler's palm. She couldn't keep herself from looking up at Ryder.

He was grinning; he looked dark and piratical with his short, stubbly beard. "Nummy, indeed."

She tried to ignore the heat shimmering through her, but it was futile.

Instead, she turned her focus back to Layla. Camera shutters clicked all around them as she suddenly launched herself toward her cake, squealing with pure, excited delight, sending Brutus into a frenzy of yipping.

It was, Greer decided, a very perfect first birthday for their little girl.

Eventually, though, it was time to clean up the mess.

Not surprisingly, at that exact moment, everyone conveniently found something else to do.

Vivian and Meredith took off in Vivian's ostentatious Rolls-Royce; heaven only knew where or for what purpose. Her grandmother was a terrible driver, but as long as Vivian didn't run her car over something or someone, Greer wasn't going to worry about it. Maddie and Ali were upstairs, giving Layla and Liam a bath. And all of the men, along with Adelaide and the dog, were out checking the cows Ryder had gathered in the big pasture over the last few weeks.

With the dishwasher already full, Greer set herself to the enormous stack of dishes still waiting on the counter and in the sink. She moved them aside, fit the stopper in the drain, squirted dish soap under the running water and got to work.

Overhead, she could hear laughter from the bath and she smiled to herself.

It hadn't been a bad two months since she and Ryder signed their name on that marriage certificate. Moments like this— even elbow-deep in dish water and dirty dishes—were pretty sweet. Ryder had been able to catch up on his nonstop chores and Greer hadn't even missed the PD's office too badly. Particularly once the scandal broke that Michael Towers really was sleeping with their most notorious client, Stormy Santiago. From what Greer had been hearing, nobody from the office was escaping entirely unscathed. There were rumors that a new supervising attorney was going to be brought in from Cheyenne.

Most important of all, though, Layla was thriving.

Greer let out a long breath and turned on the tap to rinse the stockpot she'd just washed.

"That's a big sigh."

She startled, looking over to see Grant closing the kitchen door. "Decide one cow looks pretty much like the next?" she asked.

A smile touched his aquamarine-colored eyes. "Something like that."

She hesitated, wanting to say something, but not knowing what. Instead, she turned back to the stockpot and tipped it upside down on the towel she'd spread on the counter for the clean dishes. "Ali's upstairs. I'm sure Layla and Liam have both had plenty of time in the tub by now."

He didn't head upstairs to retrieve his wife, though. He stopped next to Greer, picked up one of the towels from the pile she'd pulled from the drawer and lifted the stockpot.

"Thanks."

"That was good chili you made. Reminded me of my mom's cooking."

She shoved her hands back into the water. The suds were all but gone. "Thank Adelaide. She supervised. On top of all the other stuff she's done, she wrote a cookbook more than twenty years ago. There are a few used copies still out there. Selling for a ridiculous amount of money online."

"She's something, that aunt of his." He didn't look at her as he ran the towel over the pot. "Whatever comes into her head seems to go right out her mouth."

"At broadcast decibels," Greer added wryly. "I thought at first that maybe she was hard of hearing, but she's not. I think she could hear a pin drop from a mile away. It's just her way."

"Ali says you must be pretty cozy here, all three of you. There are only two bedrooms?"

"Yeah." She rinsed the last pot and handed it to him, then let out the water so she could start with fresh. She had all of the glassware yet to wash. "We've got Layla's crib in with us." More often than not, the toddler ended up in bed with them, usually sprawled sideways and somehow taking up the lion's share of the mattress. Fortunately, Ryder had drawn the line at Brutus coming into the room. Adelaide's rotund pug seemed to think he owned the place now and he'd have been up with them for sure.

"I'm surprised Adelaide didn't take up Vivian's offer to stay with her in Weaver. She's got a lot more space."

"Ryder would sleep on the floor before he'd let Adelaide stay somewhere else. I know she's a bit of a character, but she means a great deal to him. Her coming here at all is major. She doesn't travel." She chanced a quick glance at Grant's profile as she stoppered the sink again and waited for it to fill once more. She knew he'd had a troubled early childhood until he'd been adopted as an adolescent by the same family who'd adopted his sister. "He lost his mother when he was young, too."

"Ali told me."

She turned off the faucet and set a few glasses in the water. "Oh, stuff it," she said under her breath, and angled sideways to look straight at him. "He blames himself, too, Grant. For what happened. Daisy, Karen, whatever name she went by, she was his *wife*. She didn't turn to him any more than she turned to you when she chose to leave her baby with someone else."

He cleared his throat. His jaw looked tight. "I was her big brother a lot longer than she was his wife," he said in a low voice.

"So that means his self-blame is misdemeanor level but yours is felony grade?" She shook her head. "It doesn't work that way, Grant. You must know that. Time is not the measure. You've been married less than a year to my sister. If— God forbid—something happened to her, would your loss be less devastating than mine or Maddie's? We shared our mother's womb."

Heedless of the water still on her hands, she closed her fingers over his arm. "You and Ryder knew your sister in different ways. She didn't tell you everything. She certainly didn't tell him everything. She married him entirely under false pretenses. Whatever your childhoods were like, as an adult, Daisy did some things that were terribly wrong. I get that she was troubled. I do. But she abandoned her child when she had other options she could have taken! Maybe she regretted it but didn't know how to make it right before it was too late. I know that's what Ali says you believe. And maybe she didn't regret what she'd done at all. Regardless, what she did was what *she* did. What she did not do, *she* did not do. Neither you nor Ryder was her keeper. And you're both losing out, because out of all the people Layla has in her life, the two of you were the ones closest to her real mother!"

Greer's eyes were suddenly burning. "I'm adopting your niece. I don't see how I can possibly love her more than I already do. We can give her an official birthday and a new birth certificate. But one day Layla is going to want to know about her biological mother. Who else is going to be able to give her the answers she needs besides you and Ryder? Seems to me that would be a lot easier if the two of you would stop acting like adversaries and start acting like what you are! Two men who cared deeply for the same woman who deeply hurt you both!"

She huffed out a breath and turned to plunge her hands back in the suds. "I'm sorry." The glasses clinked as she grabbed one and started scrubbing it with her dishrag. "I'm sure Ali won't appreciate me sticking my nose into your business."

"As you've just eloquently put it, Karen wasn't only my business." He gently pulled the glass away from her furious scrubbing. "That's quite a closing argument you give." His hand lingered on the glistening glass after he'd rinsed it and turned it upside down onto the cloth. "I just wish things had been different," he said after a moment.

"I'm sure you do." Her eyes were still burning. She couldn't bring herself to say that she wished things had been different, too.

Because if they were different, she believed Ryder would still be with Daisy. Because that was the kind of man he was.

The kind of man who did what was right.

Her stomach suddenly churning, she pulled her hands from the water and hastily dried them. "I'm just going to run up and see what's going on with bath time. The babies must be prunes by now." She hurried out of the kitchen, but instead of heading up the stairs, she bolted for the bathroom behind them and slammed the door shut. She barely made it to the commode in time to lose all of the dinner she'd eaten.

Afterward, feeling breathless and weak, she just sat there on the wood-tiled floor, her head resting against the wall.

It had been two months since she and Ryder had stood in front of Judge Stokes and repeated those simple vows.

It had also been two months since she'd had a period. And this was the fourth time in as many days that she'd lost her cookies after supper.

That little implant in her arm had proven itself to truly be pointless.

She hadn't taken a test. But she knew the truth, anyway.

She was pregnant.

The house had been quiet for hours since the party when Ryder quietly stepped into the dark bedroom and slid the heavy door shut.

He didn't need a light to see. The moonlight shining through the windows gave him plenty.

He expected to see Layla's crib empty. But there was a bump in one corner: her diapered fanny sticking up in the air.

There was also a bump visible on the far edge of the bed. The sheet and blanket were pulled up high, only leaving visible Greer's gleaming brown hair spread out against the stark white pillow.

He turned away from the sight and exchanged his flannel shirt and jeans for the ragged sweatpants that he'd taken to wearing to bed ever since he'd gotten himself a wife.

The irony wasn't lost on him.

He could say he'd gotten into the habit because his aunt was right there under their roof, snoring away in the second bedroom. He could say it was because they had a toddler in the room.

He could say it.

Couldn't make himself believe it.

He went into the bathroom and quietly closed the door before turning on the light. He brushed his teeth and when he was finished, rubbed his hand down his unshaven jaw. The beard was part laziness, part convenience. It helped keep his face warmer when he was out on horseback gathering cows and the wind was cold and whipping over him.

Mostly, though, it was just his way of being able to face himself in the mirror every morning.

He tossed the soft, plush hand towel over the hook next to the sink. Somewhere along the way since he'd married Greer, things like threadbare towels and wrinkled bedding had been replaced by thick terry cloth and smooth, crisp sheets. There were clean clothes in his drawers and sprigs of fresh flowers stuck inside glass jars on the dinner table. And though Greer claimed not to be much of a cook, Layla had learned there were good things to eat besides Cow Pie Surprise. Greer hadn't just kept to the inside of the house, either. The picnic table he'd intended to sand and repaint had gotten sanded, all right. Just not by him. And the daisies he'd thought to cover with red paint, she'd sealed with shellac instead.

Greer's mark was everywhere. Even when it meant preserving something he hadn't really cared to preserve.

He went back into the bedroom and lowered himself to his edge of the bed.

It had been two months of nights lying on his side, one pillow jammed under his neck. Watching her in the moonlight as she slept on the other edge.

As always, she wore striped pajamas. The kind with the buttoned top and the pull-on pants. She had them in yellow. And blue. And red and purple and pink.

The few months that Daisy had been there, she'd worn slippery satiny lace things or nothing at all. The bed he'd had then had been smaller. There hadn't been so much space between them.

He'd gotten rid of the bed.

Gotten rid of the slippery satiny lace things, along with every other item she'd left behind, except the picnic table. And he'd only kept that because it was practical.

He'd never figured striped two-piece pajamas were a particularly sexy thing to wear to bed.

Until he'd spent two months of nights thinking about reaching across the great divide to unbutton that buttoned top. To slide those pull-on pants off.

Thoughts like that tended to make a long night even longer. So he'd started earlier in the morning with chores. Gone later at night before finishing.

Every square foot of his ranch was benefiting from the extra hours of attention.

Except for the 150 square feet right here in his own bedroom.

He could have made things easier on himself. Could have refrained from insisting Adelaide stay with them even though she'd clearly been interested in taking Vivian up on her offer to stay at her place. The two women couldn't be more different; the one thing they had in common was that they both were uniquely eccentric. Yet they'd hit it off. Ryder knew that big house Vivian had built on the edge of Weaver had more than enough space for a half dozen Adelaides and their pain-in-the-butt pugs.

Yeah, Ryder could have let Adelaide accept Vivian's invitation. If he had, Layla's crib wouldn't be blocking half his dresser drawers. He wouldn't be waking up six nights out of seven to her toddler feet kicking him as she rolled around in her sleep, unfettered in the space between Ryder's edge of the bed and Greer's because she wasn't even sleeping in her crib.

It was his own fault.

The night of their courtroom wedding, he should have pulled Greer across the mattress. Should have met her halfway.

He should have started as he meant to continue. Should have given her his grandmother's wedding ring that Adelaide had produced when she'd shown up so unexpectedly on their wedding day. Should have made love with her on their wedding night.

But he hadn't. And he was damned if he knew why.

The ring was sitting in its box inside the dresser half-blocked by Layla's crib.

And here they were.

As far apart as humanly possible on a king-size bed.

He lifted his head, rebunched the pillow and turned to face the saddle propped on the saddletree. If he moved the damn thing to the tack room where it belonged, there'd be room for the crib there instead.

But he was proud of that saddle. He'd won it at the National Finals the last year he'd competed. The same year he'd won the money that he'd kept so carefully in savings because ranching was never a sure thing and he'd wanted to be certain he had enough to carry him when times were lean.

The money that he was dipping into now just to make sure his wife from the other edge of the bed had a place to hang her legal shingle that didn't have rotting floorboards and dicey electrical wiring.

Two minutes later, cursing inside his head, he turned over again to stare at his sleeping wife's back.

Only she'd turned, too.

And she wasn't asleep.

And so there they lay. Facing each other across the great divide. Her eyes were dark pools of mystery.

Finally, she whispered, "What are you thinking?"

He cast around for something to say. "It was a nice party."

"Mm." She shifted a little. "Even after Brutus jumped on the counter to eat the leftover cake." She tucked her hands beneath her cheek in the same manner as Adelaide's angels from her ceramic phase. "Can I ask you a question?"

She was still whispering. Probably didn't need to. At least not for Layla's sake. Lately, the baby had been able to sleep through anything. Not even Adelaide's booming voice disturbed her anymore.

"What?"

"Why didn't you want to do the paternity test?"

Of all the things she might have asked, that was the last thing he expected.

She shifted again, and for half a moment, he thought maybe she was shifting closer. An inch. Even two.

But no. Nearly an entire mattress still lay between them.

"What purpose would it have served? Soon as I learned her name, I knew I was going to take her."

"But don't you want to *know*?"

"Have it confirmed that on top of everything, she cheated on me?"

"It might confirm that she didn't."

"And which is worse?"

Greer didn't respond to that. She turned her head slightly and he knew she was looking toward the crib. At Layla inside it. "Are you afraid it will change how you feel about her?"

"No."

"Are you lying?"

He thought about not answering. But there was enough distance between them just from the gulf of mattress. "Maybe." He wasn't proud of it. "She's mine. *Ours*," he corrected before she could. The adoption wasn't yet final, but it might as well have been. "I don't want what the DNA test says to matter, and that is more about Layla's mother than it is about Layla."

Greer was silent for so long, he thought maybe she was simply going to turn over once more. Turn her back to him. But she didn't. "Do you still love her?" she finally asked in her hushed voice.

"No. And you don't have to ask if I'm lying. The answer's no." On that his head was clear. He wished it were as clear when it came to the woman lying across from him.

"There might come a day when Layla wants to know."

He knew she meant about the DNA. "That's another matter." He'd given it some thought. "I already have a DNA profile. If it ever comes time to use it, it'll be waiting."

She pushed up onto her elbow, obviously surprised. Her hair had grown since they'd said "I do." It curled around her shoulders now. Softer. Lusher. It was almost as unfamiliar as his beard. "You do?"

"That last year I was bronc bustin'." He pushed up onto his elbow, too, and nodded his head toward the saddle behind him. "When I won that. I was served with a paternity suit. The girl was looking for a piece of my winnings. She thought I'd just let her take it. But I knew it was bull. I'd slept with her, but that baby wasn't mine. Test proved it."

"But Layla's different?"

"Layla had no one else. She was my wife's child."

She lowered herself back down off her elbow with her hands tucked beneath her chin. "So it was the right thing to do," she whispered.

He lay back down, too. Bunched the pillow beneath his neck. There was no need to answer, but he did. "Yes."

She exhaled softly. Leaving him wondering what she was thinking.

All he had to do was ask.

All he had to do was stretch his arm toward her. Offer his hand.

It wasn't too late to break the habit of two months of long nights. The great divide could be breached. Could be destroyed.

All it would take was a step.

He shifted and in the moonlight he could see the way she tensed.

He lifted his head, rebunched his pillow and closed his eyes.

# Chapter 12

"Happy Thanksgiving!"

Greer smiled at her mom as she walked into the house where she'd grown up. Layla was walking at her side. Her steps were the sweet, plopping sort of steps that all toddlers took at first. She had one hand clasped in Greer's, the other in Ryder's. "Happy Thanksgiving. Smells great in here."

Despite the bare, frozen ground outside, the house was warm. Greer noticed Meredith's feet were typically bare as she hurried out of the kitchen and across the foyer to give them a hug. The tiny bells around her ankle jingled and Layla immediately crouched down, trying to catch them. "Bell," she said clearly.

"That's right, darling. Grandma's bells." Meredith scooped up the baby and nuzzled her nose. Layla's rosy-gold hair would probably never be as thick as Greer's mom's, but it might turn out to be just as curly. "Did you get it?"

Greer held up the envelope she was carrying. "It's official. I picked up our copy of the final adoption decree yesterday just before the recorder's office closed for the holiday." She pulled out the document and handed to her mother.

"Well." Meredith was teary as she paged through it before setting it on the entryway table. Her gaze shifted from Ryder to Greer. "Congratulations, Mommy."

*If they only knew.*

Greer blinked back the moisture in her own eyes. She glanced at Ryder and quickly looked away. She still hadn't told him that she was pregnant. She hadn't told anyone, except her doctor.

"It's a fabulous day," Adelaide practically shouted in greeting, coming inside behind them. She was carrying Brutus inside his expensive leather transport. "Meredith, I've decided I need to photograph you."

Her mom's eyebrows flew up. "Whatever for, Adelaide?"

"Just be glad she's out of her nude phase," Ryder commented drily.

He was still wearing the closely cut beard he'd started before Layla's birthday. Now the stubble was full-on beard. Still short. Still groomed. But his dimple was hidden.

"She'd still be a fine-looking nude," Carter said as he walked past. He was carrying two bottles of beer and handed one to Ryder.

"Dad!"

Meredith was smiling, though, and the look that passed between her parents was almost too intimate to bear.

"Pardon me while I go throw up," she muttered for effect as she walked around them and headed into the kitchen. Her mother's laughter followed her.

Fortunately, Greer's after-dinner morning sickness had faded. Unfortunately, she knew she was going to have to fess up sooner rather than later to everyone—her husband most particularly. So far, she hadn't even let her belt out a notch; her stomach was as flat as ever. The obstetrician she'd sneaked over to Weaver to see had needlessly reminded her it wasn't going to be long, though. When Maddie was carrying Liam, she'd been visibly pregnant at four months. Same with Ali, who was now six months along.

Greer could either admit the truth in the next few weeks, or she'd be showing it, if her sisters were anything to go by.

But that didn't mean she was going to worry about the fallout today.

Not when it was Thanksgiving. Not when she felt positively ravenous and there was a veritable feast for the taking.

Every inch of kitchen counter was covered with trays of food. She grazed along, plucking olives and candied pecans with equal enthusiasm. Within minutes, she could hear more people arriving. More family members. More friends. Even Vivian, despite the ongoing animosity between her and Greer's dad and uncle. And soon the house was bulging at the seams.

There was laughter and squabbling and it was all dear and familiar. And despite the secret she harbored, Greer felt herself relax. Even when she and Ryder were sitting so close to each other at the crowded table that the length of his strong thigh burned against hers, and they couldn't lift their forks without brushing against each other.

After the glorious feast, it was football. The options were to watch it on television or play it on the winter-dead front yard, where Archer was warming up, tossing the football around with their cousins and their brothers-in-law.

Ali intercepted the ball and looked toward her sisters and their cousins. "Guys against the girls? Cousins against cousins? What'd we do last year?"

"Cousins," Maddie reminded her with a laugh. "And it was a slaughter."

"Only because Seth turned out to be a ringer." Quinn was

the eldest of their cousins and, like Archer, had only sisters. "I say Templetons against the spouses!"

His wife, Penny, rubbed her hands together and laughed. "I'm game for that. Means I've got nearly all the guys on my side!"

Ali looked toward Greer where she stood on the sidelines.

"Count me out," Greer said hastily. She had her hands tucked into her armpits and was stomping her feet to keep them warm. The snow in October had been a onetime occurrence and melted away, but the temperatures had hovered around freezing ever since. "It's too cold!"

"What a wuss you've become," Ali chided with a laugh. "Go find Maddie, then. And Ryder. It's his first Thanksgiving game, same as Grant and Linc." Her smile was devilish. "Gotta initiate these men of ours into the family just right." She tossed the ball from one bare hand to her other. "Rules are same as always. No tackle. Just touch."

"Think you've been touched enough," Archer called to her. "Don't know what's bigger, that football or your belly."

Ali preened, tucking the ball under her arm as she framed her bulging bump against the Green Bay sweatshirt she wore in honor of their father's favorite team.

Then Grant, the guy responsible for her baby bump, came up behind her, poked the ball free, and the game was on in earnest even though the teams weren't entirely present and accounted for.

But that was always how it went.

The most basic rule of Templeton Family Football was for everyone to have fun. The second basic rule was for everyone to stay out of the hospital.

Greer was smiling as she went back inside. She found Maddie in the study, nursing Liam while she ate another piece of pumpkin pie with her fingers. Greer let her be and went to find Ryder. He wasn't in the family room, where her dad and uncle were sprawled out in front of the large-screen television. Nor in the kitchen, where her mom and aunt were still cleaning up the dishes.

"Have you seen Ryder?"

Meredith pointed toward the screened sunporch off the kitchen. Beyond that, Greer could see him and Adelaide sitting outside on the park-style bench in the middle of the flower garden. Right now, the only flowers in view were the brightly painted metal ones that were planted in the ground on long metal spikes. Layla was chasing after Brutus as he ran around the yard sniffing every blade of dead grass.

Greer smiled at the picture they all made and opened the kitchen door, going out to the sunporch. She peeled back a corner of the thick clear plastic that her dad hung up in the screened openings so that Meredith could enjoy the space whether it was cold or not. "Ry—"

"Why haven't you?" From all the way across the yard, Adelaide's voice wasn't quite megaphone-ish, but it was still audible.

Something about the tone made Greer swallow the rest of her husband's name.

"It's my decision, Adelaide." Ryder's voice was much quieter. Underlaid with steel.

Disquiet slithered down her spine. One part of her urged retreat. The other part refused. Morbid curiosity kept her pinned to the spot, prepared to witness disaster.

"If I wanted to give her the ring, I would have."

"It's a mistake, Ryder."

Oblivious to their audience, Ryder shoved off the filigreed bench. "Consider it one more mistake I've made when it comes to marriage." He whistled sharply. "Brutus. No." The dog had started digging near the base of a tree. His words had no effect on the little dog. "Adelaide—"

"Brutus, come." At least the pug sometimes listened to his mistress. The dog retreated and hopped up onto Adelaide's lap.

Ryder swung Layla up high and she laughed merrily, sinking her hands into his hair when he put her on his shoulders as he headed in Greer's direction.

Closer. Closer.

She exhaled, finally managing to drag her mired feet free as she hurried back into the house before he could see her.

She caught the glance her mother gave her as she scurried through the kitchen. "Cold out there," she said a little too loudly.

"Your dad's got a fire going—"

Greer waved her hand in acknowledgment as she fairly skidded around the corner and escaped into the hallway by the front door.

She sucked in a breath, pressing her palm against her belly, knowing she had to keep it together even though inside she felt like she was unraveling.

Ryder never said what he didn't mean.

No matter what he'd said the day they got married, he obviously considered the business of *their* marriage as one more mistake.

"There you are." The man in her thoughts rounded the corner of the hallway and she froze. Layla was no longer on his shoulders. "Adelaide's getting pretty tired. I thought I'd run her back to the ranch."

"I can do it," she heard herself offer. "Layla's going to need her bath and bed soon, anyway. Your...your presence is wanted on the football field."

Even as she said the words, the front door flew open and

Grant rushed in. His hair was windblown, his cheeks ruddy. "Tell me you played football."

Ryder's eyes narrowed slightly. "Running back, but not since high school. Helluva while ago."

Grant beckoned. "Better'n nothing." He looked at Greer. "I'm pretty sure we've been sandbagged. Archer—"

Any other day, Greer would have enjoyed the moment. "All-state quarterback."

"And my wife? What was she? All-state sneak?"

"Track. All three of us." She spread her hands, managing a smile even though it felt as brittle as her insides. "We grew up on football. Dad didn't care whether we were girls and more interested in horses and ballet or not."

"Should've known." Grant turned to Ryder. "We spouses lose this game and you know it's gonna follow us the rest of our married lives." He clapped his hand over Ryder's shoulder. "It's a matter of pride."

Ryder looked her way.

"It's a matter of pride," she parroted. "Vivian'll give you a ride home. I'm sure she'd be happy to detour to the ranch on her way back to Weaver."

"She'd be happy, but I've seen her drive." Still, he was smiling a little as he went out the door with Grant.

As if all was right.

As if it mattered to him that losing this first game might seal his fate for all their Thanksgiving football games to come.

She looked out at the two of them jogging out to join the scrimmage. She called after them. "Just remember, no tackling!" If her voice sounded thick, it didn't matter.

She was the only one who noticed.

She closed the door.

The adoption decree was sitting on the table against the

opposite wall. She picked it up and slid it carefully back into its envelope.

Then she went to retrieve her daughter and Adelaide and her yapping dog, and they went home.

She was glad that all of her passengers fell asleep on the way.

It meant that they never saw the tears sliding silently down her cheeks.

"Here." Ali handed Greer a hanger. "Try that one."

Greer slid the red tunic off the hanger and pulled it over her head. It hung past her hips over her long black palazzo pants She turned sideways to view herself in the full-length mirror.

The small bulge of her abdomen was disguised among the ridges of the cable knit.

She exhaled. "Okay. This one'll work." She dashed her fingers through her hair. She hadn't had it cut in months. Not since she'd left the PD's office. With the help of her prenatal vitamins, it was growing even faster than usual. It was already down to her shoulder blades.

Unfortunately, her good hair days weren't making up for all that was wrong.

Ali just shook her head, looking decidedly Buddha-like as she sat cross-legged on the counter in Greer's bathroom at the Victorian. "You should've told him by now, Greer."

"I will." She lifted her chin as she peered into the mirror and applied some blush so that her face wouldn't look quite so washed out against the brilliant vermilion tunic. "Adelaide is leaving the day after Christmas. I'll tell him about the baby after she's gone. That's only four days from now."

Ali folded her hands atop her round belly. While Greer was hiding the changes in her body, her sister was delighting in showing off hers. At that moment, she wore a clingy white sweater and burgundy leggings that outlined every lush curve she'd developed.

And why not?

Ali and Grant were besotted with each other. She had no reason whatsoever to want to hide what that love had produced.

It was Greer's bad luck that she'd somehow fallen in love with her own husband. She knew when he learned about the baby, she wouldn't be just another mark in his column of marital mistakes. She—and their baby—would become his next "right thing to do."

And it was almost more than she could bear.

She didn't want to be his responsibility. And she didn't want to be his business partner in this sterile marriage.

"I still can't believe Ryder hasn't noticed," Ali was saying. "Maybe you can hide that bump under thick sweaters and shapeless pajamas, but your boobs are another story. Is the guy blind?"

Greer tossed the blush in the vanity drawer and pulled out the mascara. They'd met at the Victorian—which was still undergoing renovations—to finish wrapping the Christmas gifts they'd been stashing away there, before heading over to Maddie and Linc's place. They were hosting a party for his employees at Swift Oil.

Grant was waiting downstairs in what was originally the living room, but was now a framework for a reception area and two offices.

Ryder hadn't come at all. He'd been moving the bulls to their new pasture that day and the task was taking longer than he'd planned.

Greer suspected he was just as relieved as she was that he had a valid reason to miss the party.

"He doesn't have to be blind when he doesn't look to begin with." Her voice was flat.

"I don't know." Her sister was unconvinced. "You guys still share a bed."

Greer cursed softly when she smudged her mascara. "A bed where he stays on his side and I stay on mine. And never the twain shall meet."

"Seems to me you could twain your way over to him if you wanted to. You did it before. That's how you got yourself in the family way."

Greer ignored that as she snatched a tissue from the box next to Ali's knee and dabbed away the mess she'd made.

It was too bad she couldn't dab away the mess of her marriage with a simple swipe.

"I should have never confided in you in the first place," she told her. Not about the rainstorm. Definitely not about the great divide that existed between her side of the bed and his.

"I think you needed to tell somebody," Ali said quietly. Her eyes were sympathetic. Ali was always easier to take when she was full of sass and vinegar than when she wasn't.

Greer cleared her throat as she balled up the tissue and tossed it in the trash. "You just happened to catch me in a bad moment."

"Sure. Sitting on the side of the road near Devil's Crossing bawling your eyes out. A little more than a bad moment in my view, but if that's what you want to call it."

She'd been on her way back from an appointment with her obstetrician in Weaver. She'd started blubbering near the spot where Ryder had rescued her that day in August, which now felt so long ago. She had pulled off the road before she ran off it. Ali, in her patrol car, had spotted her. And the entire story had come pouring out of Greer, along with her hiccupping sobs.

"Hormones." Finished with the mascara, Greer capped the tube and tossed it next to the blush, then shut the drawer with a slap. "I'm ready." She tugged her pants hem from beneath her high heel where it had caught.

"More like a broken heart," her sister was muttering under her breath as she unfolded her legs and slid off the counter. "I warned you that something like this would happen." She followed Greer through the bedroom and downstairs.

While Greer didn't appreciate the "I told you so," she did appreciate Ali's return to form.

"Finally," Grant said when he spotted them. "Sooner we get to this deal, sooner we can leave. We're already going to be late."

"Party animal," Ali joked. She lifted her hair when he helped her on with her coat.

Grant's smile was slanted. "I'll party your socks off when we get home."

"Well, now, that *is* a good reason to get moving along."

Greer grabbed her coat and headed out the door. She didn't begrudge her sister's happiness. Truly, she didn't. But her hormones were at work again, and she really didn't want to have to go back upstairs and redo her mascara again.

She paused on the front porch as she pulled on her coat. Every house down the hill from the Victorian was outlined in bright Christmas lights. There still hadn't been any snow since October, but it was pretty all the same.

At the ranch, Ryder had put up the Christmas tree he'd cut down himself. He'd left the decorating of it to Greer and Adelaide, though. The results had been interesting, to say the least. Adelaide's unusual eye might be highly regarded at MoMA, but Greer was probably a little too traditional to fully appreciate the strange paper clip–shaped objects juxtaposed with the popcorn garland she was used to.

She stifled a sigh, climbed behind the wheel of her car and pulled away from the curb. Ali and Grant were in their SUV behind her. She'd become accustomed to using Ryder's truck, because Layla's car seat fit so much better into it. But Layla was back at the ranch with Adelaide. Ryder's aunt had declined the invitation, saying that two parties within just a few days of each other were more than she was used to. And Vivian's annual fete was the night after next on Christmas Eve.

Greer wondered if Ryder would find an excuse to miss that party, too. If he did, it was going to be a little harder for her to explain away his absence. Her brother-in-law's company party was one thing. Vivian's, quite another.

As Grant had predicted, the party was in full swing when they arrived at the Swift mansion.

Greer left her coat in the foyer with the teenager who'd been hired to handle them and aimed straight for the bar. She longed for a cocktail, but made do with cranberry juice and lime. Then she filled a small plate with brownies that she knew Maddie had made from scratch and a half dozen other little morsels.

If anyone did notice her bump, they'd just figure it was from gorging herself.

Christmas music was playing in the background, loud enough to cover awkward silences as employees settled in but not so loud that it was annoying. If Vivian held true to form for *her* party, she'd have a live quartet. When it came to her grandmother, expense was no object. She imported the musicians from wherever she needed to.

Greer wandered through the house, smiling and greeting those she knew as if she wouldn't want to be anywhere else. There wasn't a corner or a banister that hadn't been decked with garland and holly, and the tree that stood in the curve of the staircase was covered in pretty red-and-gold ornaments. She stood admiring it, sipping her juice.

"Looks a little more like a normal tree than ours."

Greer jerked, splashing cranberry juice against her sweater. She blotted the spot with her cocktail napkin and stared at Ryder. "I thought you weren't coming." He was wearing an off-white henley with his jeans, and it just wasn't fair that he should look so good when she felt so bad.

"I thought I wasn't." He shrugged. "But I got the bulls settled finally and decided to come." His blue eyes roved over her face, but they didn't give a clue to what he was thinking. They might be married, but she felt like she knew him no better than she had when they'd first met.

He took the napkin from her, folded it over and pressed it against her sweater. "Would you have preferred I hadn't?"

Her heart felt like it was beating unevenly and she hoped he couldn't feel it, too. "Of course not," she managed smoothly. "You just surprised me, that's all." She tugged the napkin away from him and crumpled it. "There's a bar and an entire spread." She gestured with the hand holding her plate of food. "You should go help yourself. Maddie's brownies will go fast."

His gaze seemed to rest on her face again for a moment too long before he headed off.

She blamed the impression on her guilty conscience.

No matter how strained things were between them, she knew she needed to tell him about the baby.

This time, there'd be no room for him to doubt the paternity. It was the only positive note that she could think of in what felt like an intolerable situation.

"That you, Greer?"

She looked away from watching Ryder to see a familiar face. "Judge Manetti!"

He smiled. "It used to be Steve, remember? We're not in

my courtroom now." He leaned over and kissed her cheek. "When I saw you at first, I thought you were Maddie." He waved his fingers. "The hair's longer. You're looking good. Heard you got married. It must suit you."

She kept her smile in place. It took an effort, but she'd had a lot of practice. "I didn't know you were part of Swift Oil."

"My wife started there a few months ago." He looked around the room. "Always wondered what it was like inside this old mansion. Pretty impressive."

It was a little easier to smile at that. "I think so, too. How're things over at civic plaza?"

"Crazy. You know about—" He broke off and nodded. "Of course you know about it. Heard they've got a short list for the top spot in your old office."

From the corner of her eye, she saw Ryder returning. "Oh? Someone from Cheyenne, I suppose."

He shook his head. "You really don't know?"

"I really don't—ah. Keith Gowler? He's got the trial experience. I think he's pretty happy being in private practice, though. Means he can take cases for PD when he chooses."

"Not Keith. You."

She blinked, then shook her head. "No. Not possible. There're too many other attorneys in line ahead of me. And I quit, remember?"

Ryder stopped next to her and set his hand against the small of her back. She nearly spilled her drink again. "Friend of yours?"

She turned and set the cranberry juice on the edge of a stair tread at the level of her head, along with her still-full plate. "This is Judge Steve Manetti," she introduced. "Steve, my...my—"

"Ryder Wilson." He stuck out his hand. In comparison to Steve's, his was large. Square. A working man's hand.

She moistened her lips, reminding herself to keep a friendly smile in place. "Steve and I have known each other since elementary school."

"I was just telling your wife that she's on the short list for replacing Towers."

Ryder's brow furrowed. "She's opening her own practice."

"No kidding!" Steve gave her a surprised look. "I hadn't heard that. Not that you wouldn't be great at it, but I always thought you had the public defender's office running in your veins."

"Guess not," Ryder answered before she could. His fingers curled against her spine. "If you'll excuse us, there's someone we need to see."

The judge smiled as Ryder ushered her away, but Greer recognized the speculation in his gaze. As soon as they were out of earshot, though, she jerked away from Ryder. "I didn't know caveman was your style. What was that all about?"

"You're not going to work for the PD office again."

She felt her eyebrows shoot up her forehead. "First of all, I haven't heard this short-list rumor. And second of all, even if I had, I would think that's my decision, wouldn't you?"

"Working in that office ran you ragged. And that's when you were an expendable peon."

She stiffened. "Good to know you had such respect for the work I did there!"

His lips tightened. "That's not what I meant and you know it."

She propped her hands on her hips and angled her head, looking up at him. "No, I don't know it. Why don't you explain it to me?"

"You really want to run that place? What about Layla? Months ago, you told me she was what was important and I believed you. Who's going to take care of *our daughter* when you're spending eighty hours a week defending drunk drivers and shoplifters?"

She gaped. "If that's the way you feel, why on earth did you ever insist on my opening my own practice? And don't go on about it being my *dream*! You think I'd be able to grow a practice from scratch with Layla on my hip 24/7?"

"You'd be calling your own shots," he said through his teeth. "Controlling your own schedule. You'd still have time to be a mother. Or now that you've finally got that right legally, has it lost the luster? You want to dump her off on someone else while you go off to do your own thing?"

She could barely form words for the fury building in her. She was literally seeing red. "You can regret marrying me." Her fingers curled into fists as she pushed past him. "But don't you *ever* compare me to Daisy."

He caught her arm. "Where are you going?"

She yanked free. "Away from you."

The foyer had become a traffic jam of people arriving at the party. Greer veered away and started up the staircase instead.

"Dammit, Greer." He was on her heel. As unconcerned as she was that they'd begun drawing attention. He closed his hand over her shoulder and she lost it.

Quite. Simply. Lost it.

She whirled on him. *"Don't touch me!"*

He swore and started to reach for her again.

That he kept doing so now infuriated her, when he hadn't reached for her at all in the way that mattered most ever since they'd been married. She swatted his hands away, taking another step. But her heel caught again in the long hem of her pants and she stumbled. She steadied herself, though, grabbing the banister, and blindly took another step.

Right into the plate that she'd set on one of the treads. Her shoe slid through brownies and ranch dressing and she felt herself falling backward, arms flailing. Some part of her mind heard someone gasp. Another part saw Ryder's blue eyes as he tried to catch her.

And then she landed on her back and bounced against the banister so hard the Christmas tree next to the staircase rocked.

And then she saw no more.

# *Chapter 13*

"How is she?"

From the hard plastic chair he'd been camped in, Ryder lifted his head and looked from Meredith and Carter to Greer. She was lying asleep in the hospital bed. The white bandage on her forehead was partially hidden by her hair. The rest of the damage from her fall was harder to see. Harder to predict.

Which was why she was still lying in the hospital bed at all thirty-six hours later.

His jaw ached. "She hasn't lost the baby." *Yet.* He didn't say that part. But it felt like the word echoed around the small curtained-off area all the same.

He still was trying to resolve the fact that he'd learned she was carrying his child at the same time he'd learned she was very much in danger of losing it.

Now his wife was being carefully sedated while they waited.

Meredith's hand shook as she pressed it to her mouth.

"She's going to be all right," Carter told her, kissing her forehead. His arm was around her shoulder. "Nothing is going to happen to our girl on Christmas Eve."

Ryder wished he were so convinced.

Meredith finally lowered her hand. "Where's Layla?"

"Ali picked her up this morning." Much as he loved Adelaide, she wasn't up to the task of keeping up with an active one-year-old for more than a few hours at a time.

"That's good." Meredith nodded. She scooted past Ryder's legs until she reached the head of the bed, and then dropped a tender kiss on her daughter's forehead.

Ryder looked away, pinching the bridge of his nose.

"Have you gotten any sleep?" That was from Carter.

He shook his head. How could he sleep? Every time he closed his eyes, he saw Greer tumbling backward down those stairs.

"Maybe you should."

He shook his head.

"At least take a break."

He shook his head.

Carter stopped making suggestions. He sighed and squeezed Ryder's shoulder. "She's going to be all right, son. If the baby—" He broke off and cleared his throat. "I know you don't want to hear it. But there can be other babies."

But Ryder knew otherwise. This baby was their only chance. Greer was never going to forgive him no matter what happened. He was never going to forgive himself.

He propped his elbows on his knees again and stared at the floor.

Eventually, Meredith and Carter left with promises to return later. They'd bring him something to eat. They'd bring him something to drink.

It didn't really matter to him.

The only thing that did was lying in a hospital bed.

Inevitably, more family members visited. Hayley. Archer. Cousins he knew. Cousins he didn't.

Nobody stayed long. There wasn't space for more than the one chair Ryder was occupying. And he was too selfish to give up his spot by Greer's bed, even to all the other people who loved her, too. Finally, he must have dozed off. But he jerked awake when he heard a baby cry.

But when he opened his eyes, there was no baby. Only his wife. Eyes still closed. Breath so faint that he had to stare hard at the pale blue–dotted gown covering her chest to be certain that it was moving.

"How is she?"

How many times had he heard the question? A dozen? Two? He focused on the petite woman standing inside the curtain. "Vivian? What're you doing here?"

"Checking on my granddaughter, of course." She slipped past him to peer closely at Greer. "You're a Templeton," she told her. "We're many things, but we're not weak." She kissed Greer's forehead, much like Meredith had, and straightened.

Her face seemed more lined. Wearier. He offered her the chair.

She took it and held her pocketbook on her lap with both hands. "I've spent so many days in my life at a hospital." She shook her head slightly and reached out to squeeze his hand. "It's Christmas Eve. Nothing's going to happen to our girl on Christmas Eve."

"That's what Carter said."

Her lips curved in a smile. Bittersweet. "He's like his father," she murmured.

Then it occurred to him. "Your party is tonight."

"It's on hold."

"Greer said you invited a hundred people."

She waved her fingers dismissively. "And they'll likely come when I reschedule. When you and Greer can both be there."

"I don't know if that's gonna happen," he admitted in a low voice.

She smiled gently. "I do." Then she pushed to her feet. "I've picked up Adelaide. She wanted me to see Greer first, but she's in the waiting room."

"That was nice of you, Vivian. Thank you."

"Don't get too sentimental on me. I have a selfish motivation, as well. She and Brutus will be coming home to stay with me. I convinced her to stay awhile." She reached up and patted his cheek. "And that's final, dear boy." Then she tugged on the hem of her nubby-looking pink suit and left.

Ryder moved back next to the bed. Greer's hand was cool when he picked it up. He pressed it to his mouth, warming it. He was still like that when he heard the curtain swish again.

Adelaide stood there.

He exhaled and lowered Greer's hand to the bed. Then he stood and let his aunt wrap her skinny, surprisingly strong arms around him. "You love her," she said in a whisper. He hadn't ever heard her speak so softly. "You need to tell her."

"How do you know I haven't?"

She pulled back and gave him a look out of those crazy made-up eyes of hers. "I've been living in the same house as the two of you for four months. How do you think I know?" Then she set a familiar-looking ring box in his hand.

He slid his jaw to one side. Then the other. "How'd you find it?"

Now she just looked droll. "You've always hidden your treasures in your sock drawer. Not very imaginative if I must say, and it was quite the nuisance getting past Layla's crib to get the drawer all the way open."

There was nothing to be amused about. Yet he still felt a faint smile lift his lips. Then he looked back at his wife. Lying in that bed.

And he closed his eyes.

"Ryder," Adelaide whispered. "Have faith."

"Faith hasn't gotten me very far before, Adelaide. You know that."

"You just weren't looking." She gestured toward the bed with her turquoise-laden hand. "What do you see when you look at her?"

*My life*.

"Tell her you love her. Give her your granny's ring. I know you said before that you were afraid to. Afraid she wouldn't want it. Wouldn't understand the treasure you were trying to give. This last thing that remains from your family." She squeezed his hand around the ring box. "And I'm telling you that she will." She went from squeezing his fingers to squeezing his jaw. "What do you *see* when you look at her, Ryder?"

His eyes burned. "My life."

She gave a great sigh and smiled. She pulled on his jaw until he lowered his head and she kissed his forehead, like she'd done about a million times before.

Then she, too, went back outside the curtain.

Ryder pushed open the ring box. The box alone was ancient. The filigreed diamond ring inside was from the 1920s. He slid it free from the fading blue velvet. It was so small it didn't fit over the tip of his finger.

He sat down beside the bed again. Slowly picked up Greer's hand. It was still cool. Too cool.

When they'd brought her to the hospital, they'd taken her jewelry. Her wedding band. Her earrings. Placed them in a plastic bag that they'd given to him. He wasn't sure where he'd even put it.

He slowly slid his grandmother's ring over Greer's wedding finger. He didn't expect it to fit. But it did. "With this ring," he whispered huskily.

"I thee wed." Her words were faint, her touch lighter than a whisper as she curled her fingers down over his.

His heart charged into his throat and he looked up at her face. Her eyes were barely open but a tear slid from the corner of her eye. "The baby…" Her lashes closed.

He leaned close and smoothed away that tear. "The baby's okay." His voice was rough. "You're okay. All you have to do is rest."

Her lashes lifted again. A little more this time. Her hand slowly rose. The back of her knuckles grazed his cheek. "You're crying. Just tell me the truth. The baby—"

"Is going to be okay."

Her eyes drifted closed again. "I should've told you." Another tear slid from her eye. "I'm so sorry I didn't tell you the truth."

"I should've seen." He cupped her head in his hand. "I should have seen all along. And you are the truth." He pressed his mouth against hers. "You're my truth. I just didn't let myself see it. You're my wife, Greer. For all the right reasons, you're my wife." He pulled in a shaky breath. "So just get better and come home with me and Layla. You can work any damn job you want. Just…don't give up on me. Don't give up on our family."

Her eyes opened again and she stared up at him. "I thought you gave up on me," she whispered.

"Not in this lifetime," he promised thickly. He pressed another shaking kiss to her lips, and her hand lifted, closing around his neck.

"Don't leave me."

He shook his head, but her eyes had closed again. He lowered the rail on the side of the bed. Carefully, gingerly, with the same caution he'd felt when he'd first taken Layla all those months ago, he moved her an inch. Two. Just enough that he could slide onto the edge of the hospital bed with her. It was crowded. He had to curl one arm awkwardly above her just to be sure that he wouldn't jostle her. Jostle their baby. But he managed.

"I love you, Greer."

She exhaled. Turned her head toward him. "Love...you..." Her fingers brushed his cheek. "No more great...divide."

A soft sound escaped him. "No more great divide," he promised. "Never again."

And then he closed his eyes, cradling his life against him. And they both slept.

# *Epilogue*

"Welcome home, Mrs. Wilson."

Greer smiled up at Ryder as he carried her across the threshold of their house. It was an interesting experience. He carried her. She carried Layla. "We could've walked, you know. The doctors said the baby was okay. So long as I don't try running a marathon, we're all good."

"I know." He shouldered the door closed behind him. "But then I wouldn't have this opportunity to impress my ladies with my manliness as we made the trek through the deep, freezing snow."

Greer pressed her cheek against his chest and looked at their daughter. "Daddy's very silly today. Two snowflakes. That's what we trekked through."

Layla's green eyes were bright. "Dadda!"

Ryder's dimple appeared. "Daddy's very happy today," he corrected. He carried the two of them right through the house and deposited them carefully on the couch. He peeled off his coat and pitched it aside, then sat down beside them, his fingers twining through Greer's. "It's Christmas Day and I've got the very best presents. Because Mommy's home."

"Mama!"

Greer went still. "Did she just—"

"She did. Who's Mama, Short-Stuff?"

"Mama." Layla patted Greer's cheek and pressed a wet kiss on it. Then she patted Ryder's face, kissing his clean-shaven jaw. "Dadda."

She clambered off Greer's lap and ran over to the oddly decorated Christmas tree. She started tearing into the wrapped presents beneath it. "Sus-suhs," she chanted.

"She's gonna demolish them all," Ryder commented.

"Probably." Greer slid her fingers through his and pulled his hand over the baby nestled inside her. "I wouldn't be too concerned. Most of them are hers, anyway. Between you and me and Adelaide, we might have gone a little overboard with the gifts."

"It's our first Christmas together. Overboard is expected."

"Now you sound like Vivian."

He grinned. "She rescheduled that party of hers for tomorrow night, you know. Just like that." He snapped his fingers.

"The advantages of outrageous wealth."

"Mama." Layla toddled back to the couch, her fists filled with the shreds of Christmas wrapping paper. She dropped it on Greer's lap.

"For me?"

Bright-eyed, Layla returned to the tree and started back in on the presents.

"We could go over to your parents', you know. Everyone's there. Hoping to see you."

She shook her head and wrapped her arms around his neck. "Maybe later. Right now...right now, everything I never even knew I wanted is right here."

His eyes smiled into hers. "Merry Christmas, Layla's mommy."

She smiled back. He thought he'd gotten the best gift. But she knew better. They'd all gotten the best gift. And she was going to treasure it for now and for always.

"Merry Christmas, Layla's daddy."

\* \* \* \* \*

Keep reading for an excerpt of
*What Happens At Christmas...*
by Yvonne Lindsay.
Find it in the
*Christmas Blockbuster 2024* anthology,
out now!

# CHAPTER ONE

"MOM, I'M SORRY. I won't be able to make it tonight. I have too much work on my plate."

Kristin eyed the Christmas decorations that festooned her office, with a baleful eye. She wasn't lying, exactly. She did have a ton of work to get through, but she wasn't in the mood for yet another happy family gathering where everyone except her was paired up with a significant other. Normally, it didn't bother her, but lately she'd been more unsettled than usual.

"Kristin, I won't take no for an answer. I'm done with your excuses. Tonight is important to me and I expect you to be here at seven sharp."

Kristin's mom, Nancy, abruptly ended the call, leaving her daughter staring at the phone on her office desk with a mixture of frustration and curiosity. Kristin rolled her chair from her desk, pushed her hands through her long hair and massaged her scalp with her fingertips. It didn't ease the perpetual headache she'd had for the past several months.

Her identical twin brothers, Keaton and Logan, had been putting pressure on her to cut her workload, citing their father's massive fatal stroke almost a year ago as a fine example of why you shouldn't burn the candle at both ends. She was doing the work of two people at the moment since she hadn't yet been able to bring herself to replace the man she'd trusted as her right hand here at work, and as her lover in the bedroom.

And all along Isaac had been a spy working for their biggest rival, Warren Everard. While everyone involved in the corporate espionage was now facing charges, it still galled her, even all these months later, that she'd never suspected—not even for a moment—that he was capable of such subterfuge. And it made her doubly wary of replacing him—in the office, or at home. Business was hard enough right now, without worrying about having to second-guess everyone around you. It had been the easier option to simply assimilate Isaac's workload into her own. After all, it wasn't as if she had any reason to rush home.

Isaac's betrayal was doubly cruel because she hadn't shared with her family how intimate she and Isaac had become. They'd kept their relationship under wraps. Not a single person in the office had ever suspected that they were more than boss and employee. She'd technically been in a position of power over him. Forming a relationship would have been frowned upon, so when he'd suggested they initially keep things quiet, she'd been in full agreement. But all along his plan had been to abuse her trust, which was, in her book, far more damaging. And she'd borne the pain of that betrayal and her broken heart alone.

Kristin rose from her seat and turned to face the darkening sky outside her office window. The Richmond Tower commanded exceptional views of the Seattle cityscape, but she rarely took the time to appreciate it. Christmas was only a little over three weeks away but her gaze remained oblivious to the glittering outlook spread before her like a pirate's jewel casket.

Instead, her thoughts turned inward. So much had changed in the past year. Courtesy of the double life her father had successfully lived, right up until the moment he'd dropped dead in his office, she'd gained not just one brother—Logan had been kidnapped as a child and was now reunited with the family—but two half brothers, and a half sister to boot.

And while it had been a joy to watch her full brothers both find love with amazing women whom she respected and adored, seeing her brothers' happiness only made Isaac's duplicity all the more painful.

Was it too much to expect to be able to build a relationship founded on mutual attraction, affection and trust? Kristin shook her head. Apparently, for her, it was. And now she had to present a cheerful face at another family dinner. Ah, well, she thought as she returned to her computer and backed up her work, at least she could depend on a better meal than the microwave instant dinner option in her apartment's freezer. She chuckled ruefully. She sounded like a total loser.

Kristin checked that the backup was complete, grabbed her bag and coat and locked her office door behind her. She fingered her car keys, wondering if she should drive to her mom's place in Bellevue. No, she decided. She'd order a driver and leave her car in its secure parking space below the building. The way she was feeling right now, she might indulge in a glass or two of wine tonight.

Half an hour later, Kristin let herself into the large two-story mansion that had been her parents' home for as long as she could remember and shrugged off her coat. She loved coming here. There was a sense of stability about the place that she desperately craved now. The clipped sound of heels on the parquet floor alerted her to the arrival of the family housekeeper, Martha.

"Ah, Kristin. It's good to see you. Your mom and the others are in the main salon having drinks before dinner. Here, let me take your coat."

"The main salon? I thought this was a casual thing," Kristin commented as she passed her coat to the older woman.

Martha had been in her parents' employ since Kristin had

been a baby and, since Kristin's father's death last year, had become more of a companion to her mom.

"Mrs. Richmond asked that I send you through when you arrived," the housekeeper continued smoothly without actually answering Kristin's question.

A sense of unease filled her. Her mom only used the main sitting room for formal occasions. What was going on? Realizing it would be useless to press Martha, who was already walking away to hang up her coat, Kristin made her way across the foyer to the double wooden doors that led to the rest of her family. A murmur of voices came through the door and she hesitated—reluctant, for some reason, to join them. A burst of laughter from inside the room motivated her to reach for the handle and join her family.

She scanned the room as she entered, noting the beautifully decorated Christmas tree her mom had erected immediately after Thanksgiving, and relaxed as she identified her brothers and their partners, her mom and Hector Ramirez. Hector was the family's attorney and had been an absolute rock of support for her mom since Douglas Richmond's sudden death. So much so, the two of them had vacationed together in Palm Springs a few months ago.

As Kristin entered the room, her mom rose from Hector's side and crossed toward her daughter to welcome her.

"I made it," Kristin said with a smile as her mom enveloped her in a loving embrace.

"Thank you, my darling girl. It's always so good to see you."

"You know, if you came back to the office we'd see each other every day."

Nancy had worked side by side with her husband until his death nearly a year ago and had been heavily involved in the family's charitable foundation. But now she rarely entered the building where he'd died and had established a base here at home to manage the Richmond Foundation remotely.

"What can I get you to drink?" Nancy asked, ignoring Kristin's not-so-subtle comment.

"My usual white wine would be great, thanks."

Kristin turned to say hi to her brothers and their partners. Logan and Honor had married in the summer and, last week at Thanksgiving, announced they were expecting a baby. While Honor wasn't showing yet, there was a glow about her that inspired a prick of envy in Kristin's heart. And the way Logan looked at Honor these days? Well, his love for her and their child was tangible. More than anything Kristin ached to have that level of commitment with someone else.

Keaton and Tami were equally tightly knit. They'd originally started as an office romance at Richmond Developments, but Tami now worked as a project manager and liaison between the Richmond Foundation and other charities on special ventures. Tami rose from her seat and hugged Kristin in greeting.

"I was hoping you would make it," Tami said with a welcoming smile. "We hardly get to see you outside of work these days."

"Do you know what this is all about?" Kristin whispered to her.

"Not a clue. It doesn't quite feel like Nancy's regular family dinner vibe, does it?"

"True," Kristin conceded. She couldn't quite shake the apprehension that niggled at the back of her mind.

Her mom returned with Kristin's glass of wine and then turned and faced the room. Some silent communication must have passed between her and Hector, because he rose and stood next to her, one arm casually draped around Nancy's waist.

"If I could have all your attention, please," Nancy started, sounding a little nervous.

That niggle in the back of Kristin's mind grew stronger.

"Hector and I have an announcement to make. As you know, we've been friends for many years and he's been an incredible support to me since Douglas passed away. In fact, he's become so important to me that I can't see my future without him...

and I'm very proud to tell you that he has consented to be my husband."

There was a sudden murmur in the room and Kristin felt her stomach twist in a knot.

"You asked Hector to marry you?" she blurted.

"He was too much of a gentleman to do it so soon after your father's death. But if Douglas's passing taught me anything, it was to grab hold of what's important and keep it close to you. I didn't want to waste any more time following other people's expectations or beating around the bush." Nancy turned and faced Hector and beamed at him, her love for him radiating from her. "I love him and that's why I asked him to marry me. He said yes and I couldn't be happier."

The others rose from their seats, offering their congratulations and hugging Nancy and shaking Hector's hand, but Kristin stood on the periphery. Nancy extricated herself from the rest of the family and came over to Kristin.

"Kristin? Aren't you happy for us?" she asked, a worried frown pulling at her brows.

"Isn't it a bit soon, Mom? Dad hasn't even been dead a year. I mean, I have nothing against Hector and I know how much he's come to mean to you, but don't you think you're rushing things?"

Nancy laughed and patted Kristin's arm. "Oh, my darling. We're both nearing sixty. We want to spend the rest of our lives together, properly, as husband and wife. It's important to us both and I trust Hector. He would never let me down the way your father did. Seriously, Kristin, you wouldn't stand in the way of our happiness, would you?"

Kristin hesitated. Of course she wanted her mom to be happy.

Hector joined them. "Everything okay, ladies?" he asked.

"Everything is fine," Nancy assured him and gave Kristin a look that brooked no argument. "Isn't it, Kristin?"

"Yes, absolutely," Kristin said, forcing a smile to her face. She still couldn't put a finger on why she felt uncomfortable.

Sour grapes because everyone around her was paired up and living their happily-ever-afters and she wasn't? She raised her glass. "Congratulations to you both. May you be exceptionally happy together."

"Thank you, Kristin," Hector said, his eyes glistening with moisture. "It means a great deal to us to hear you say that. We understand how close you were to your father and how much you miss him. He was my best friend but I can't deny that I've loved Nancy for many years and I feel privileged to be able to plan the rest of our lives as one."

His words struck Kristin to her core. There was no doubt Hector's feelings for Nancy were genuine.

"And what about your work for us, Hector? Will you remain our family attorney?" she asked.

"I'm glad you asked." He smiled. "It leads us to our second announcement for this evening. I've decided to take early retirement—I sold my practice to a longtime friend and colleague. To facilitate a smooth takeover, I will remain on in an advisory capacity for the next six months."

"A longtime friend? Who?" Kristin pressed. "Have we met him before?"

"I don't believe so," Hector replied.

"Then how can we be sure he'll be a good fit for us? How can we trust him?"

She spoke the words without thinking. Hector was saved from answering by the echoing tones of the front doorbell.

"Well, it sounds as if he's arrived to join us, so you can find out the answers to those questions yourself," Hector said with a confident smile.

Kristin helped herself to a generous swig of her wine. While the fine vintage was like a kiss of velvet on her tongue, it burned all the way to her stomach, reminding her she hadn't eaten much today. She didn't like the sound of any of this. What if the new person wasn't good enough? Their family had been through hell and back these past several months, first with Logan popping out of the woodwork thirty-four years after his abduction as a baby, then her dad dying, then the discovery that he had a another family and business mirroring theirs on the other side of the country. After that there'd been the corporate espionage, of which Isaac had been an integral part.

How could they be expected to trust a stranger?

"Darling, don't worry so much. Hector's friend has an exceptional reputation," her mom murmured in her ear.

"He'd better have," Kristin muttered before taking another sip of her wine.

She turned to face the sitting room doors as they swung open. Martha announced the new arrival.

"Mr. Jones has arrived," she said before ushering him through.

Logan and Keaton had moved forward and obstructed her immediate line of sight to the newcomer.

"Good evening, everyone. I hope I'm not late?"

The man's voice was deep and resonant and there was something disturbingly familiar about it. The niggle in Kristin's mind morphed into a full-blown sense of misgiving.

"No, not at all," Hector hastened to assure him. "Everyone, please welcome my good friend Jackson Jones."

And there he stood. All six feet three inches of him clad in bespoke Armani and, according to her accelerated heart rate, looking even more fiercely attractive than she remembered. His dark blue eyes focused on her with laser precision. His nostrils flared ever so slightly on a sharply indrawn breath.

Jackson Jones.

The first man she'd ever loved.

The first man she'd ever slept with.

The man who'd walked out on her without a single word or a backward glance.

The man she'd sworn to hate for eternity.

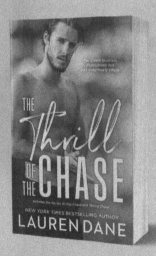 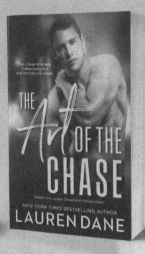

# Subscribe and fall in love with a Mills & Boon series today!

You'll be among the first to read stories delivered to your door monthly and enjoy great savings.

WE SIMPLY LOVE ROMANCE